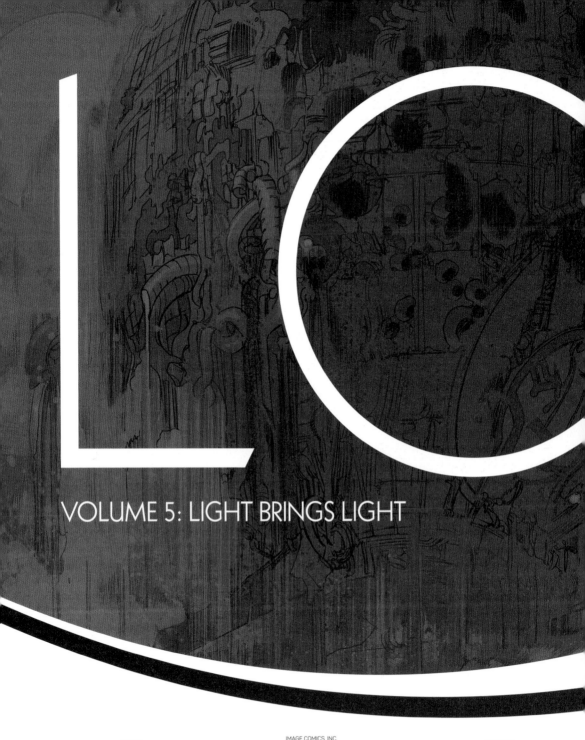

VOLUME 5: LIGHT BRINGS LIGHT

IMAGE COMICS, INC.

Todd McFarlane: President / Jim Valentino: Vice President / Marc Silvestri: Chief Executive Officer / Erik Larsen: Chief Financial Officer / Robert Kirkman: Chief Operating Officer / Eric Stephenson: Publisher / Chief Creative Officer / Nicole Lapalme: Controller / Leanna Caunter: Accounting Analyst / Sue Korpela: Accounting & HR Manager / Marla Eizik: Talent Liaison / Jeff Boison: Director of Sales & Publishing Planning / Dirk Wood: Director of International Sales & Licensing / Alex Cox: Director of Direct Market Sales / Chloe Ramos: Book Market & Library Sales Manager / Emilio Bautista: Digital Sales Coordinator / Jon Schlaffman: Specialty Sales Coordinator / Kat Salazar: Director of PR & Marketing / Drew Fitzgerald: Marketing Content Associate / Heather Doornink: Production Director / Drew Gill: Art Director / Hilary DiLoreto: Print Manager / Tricia Ramos: Traffic Manager / Melissa Gifford: Content Manager / Erika Schnatz: Senior Production Artist / Ryan Brewer: Production Artist / Deanna Phelps: Production Artist
IMAGECOMICS.COM

GIANT
GENERATOR

ERIKA SCHNATZ
Collection Design

ISBN 978-1-5343-0504-5

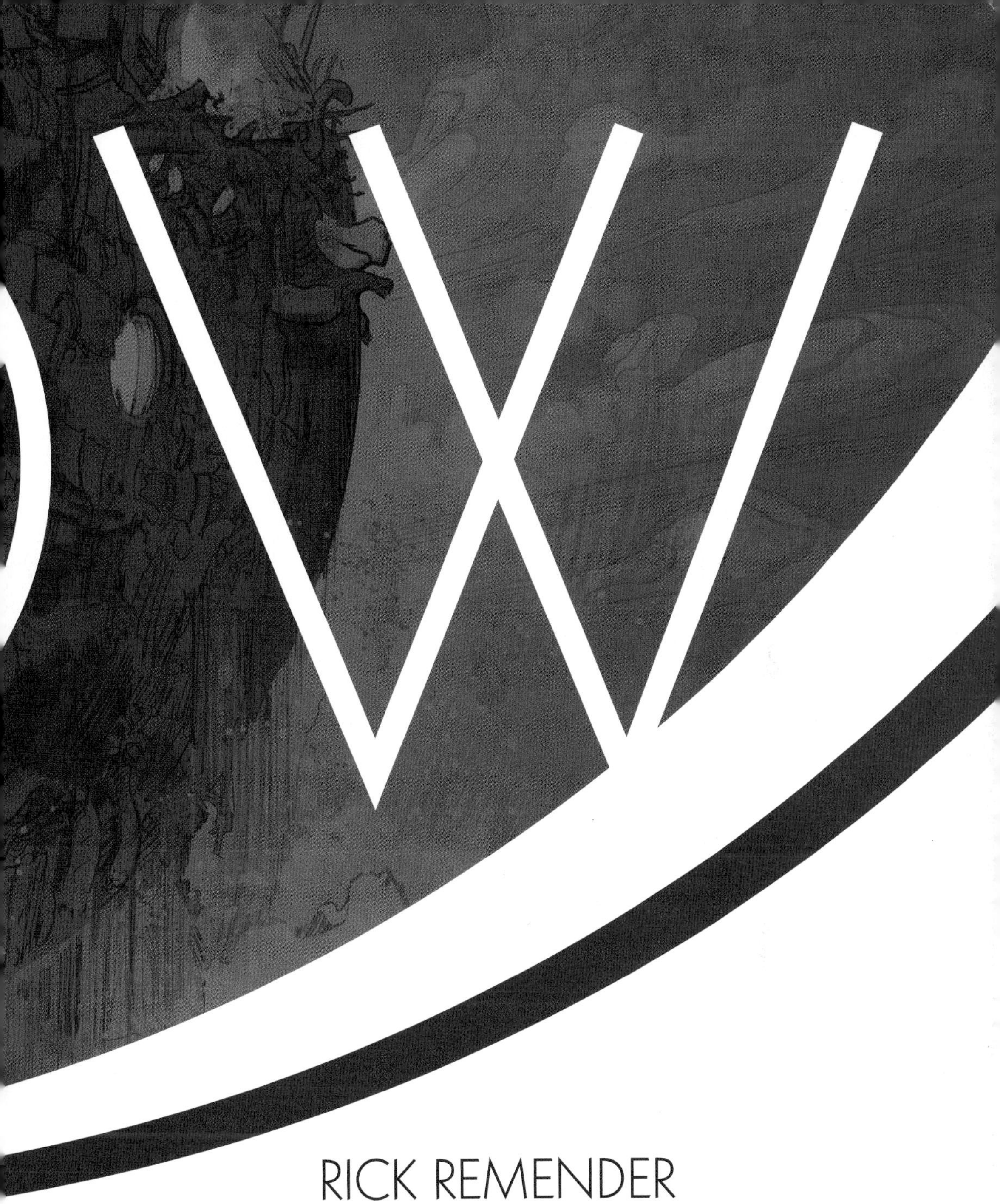

RICK REMENDER
writer

GREG TOCCHINI
artist

DAVE McCAIG
colors

RUS WOOTON
letterer

SEBASTIAN GIRNER BRIAH SKELLY WILL DENNIS
editors

TYLER JENNES
asst. editor

Created by Rick Remender & Greg Tocchini

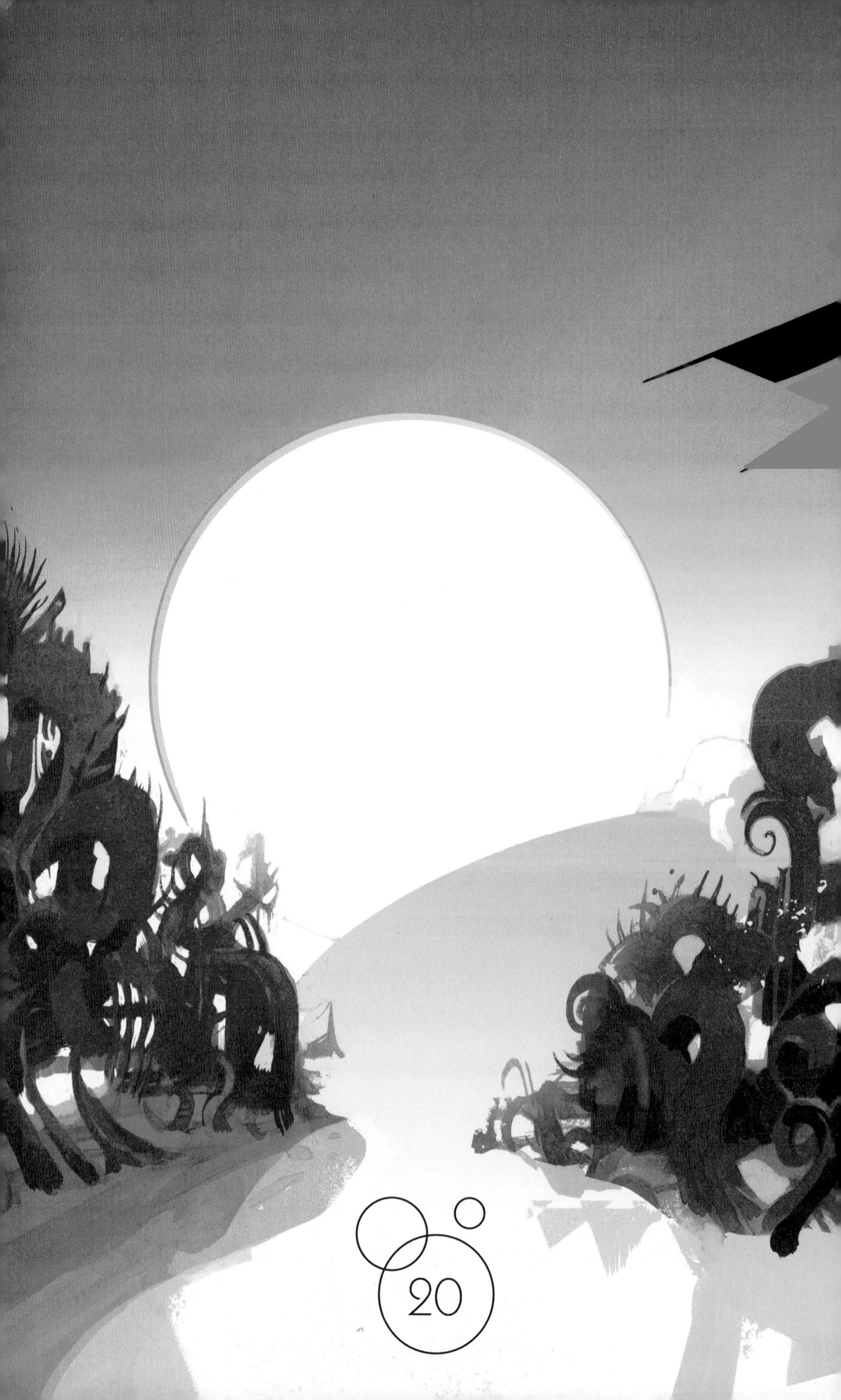
20

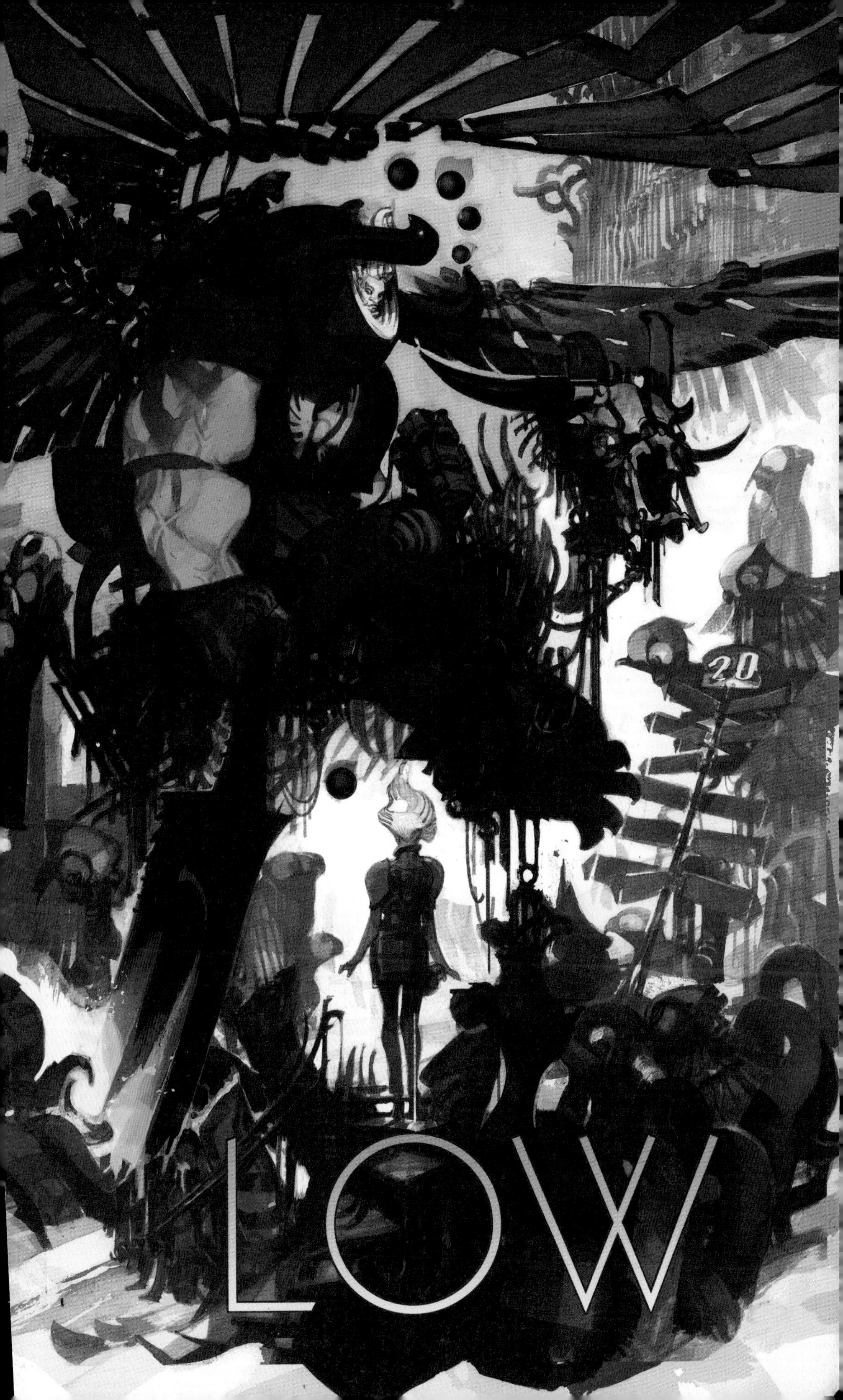
20
LOW

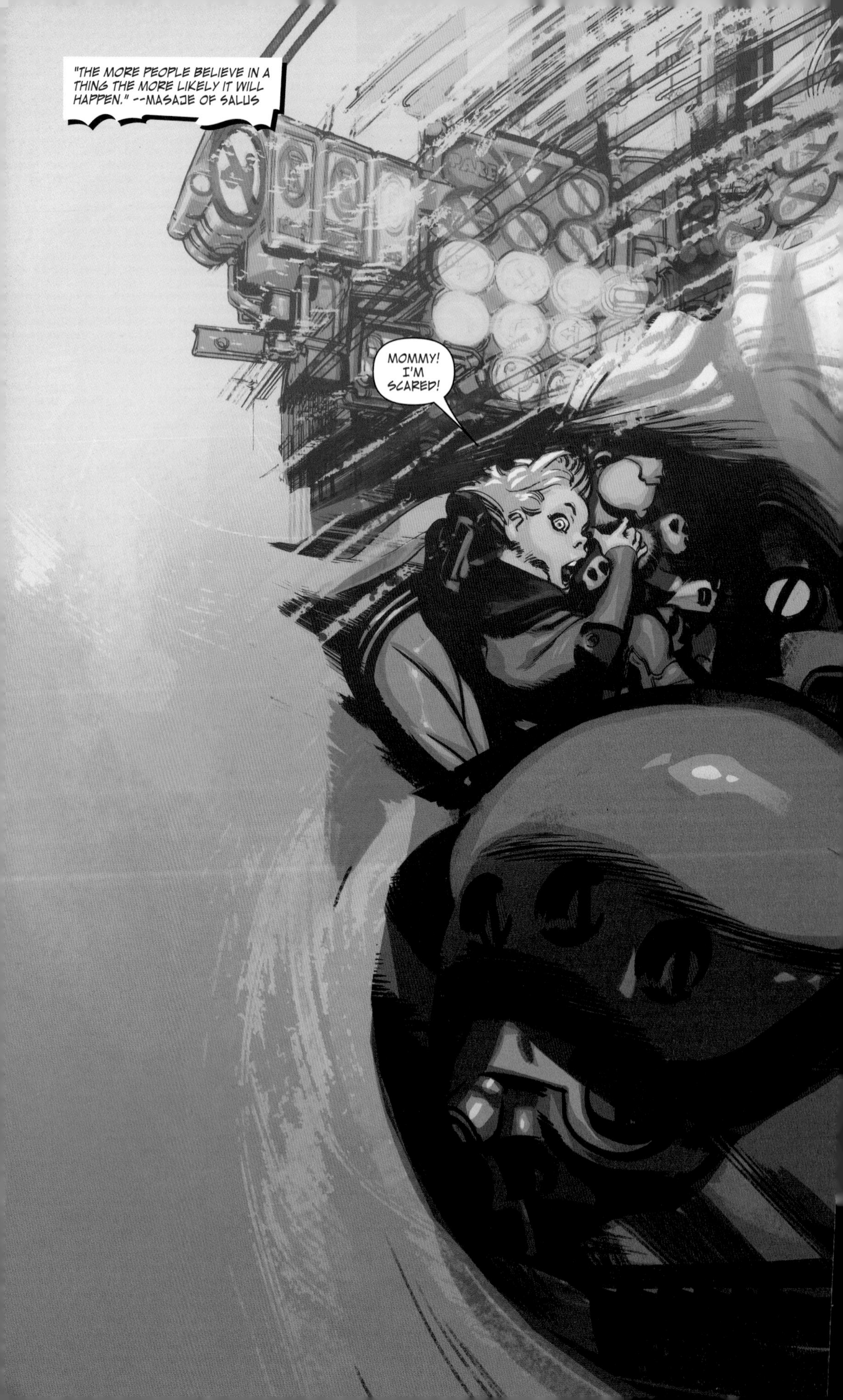
"THE MORE PEOPLE BELIEVE IN A THING THE MORE LIKELY IT WILL HAPPEN." --MASAJE OF SALUS
MOMMY! I'M SCARED!

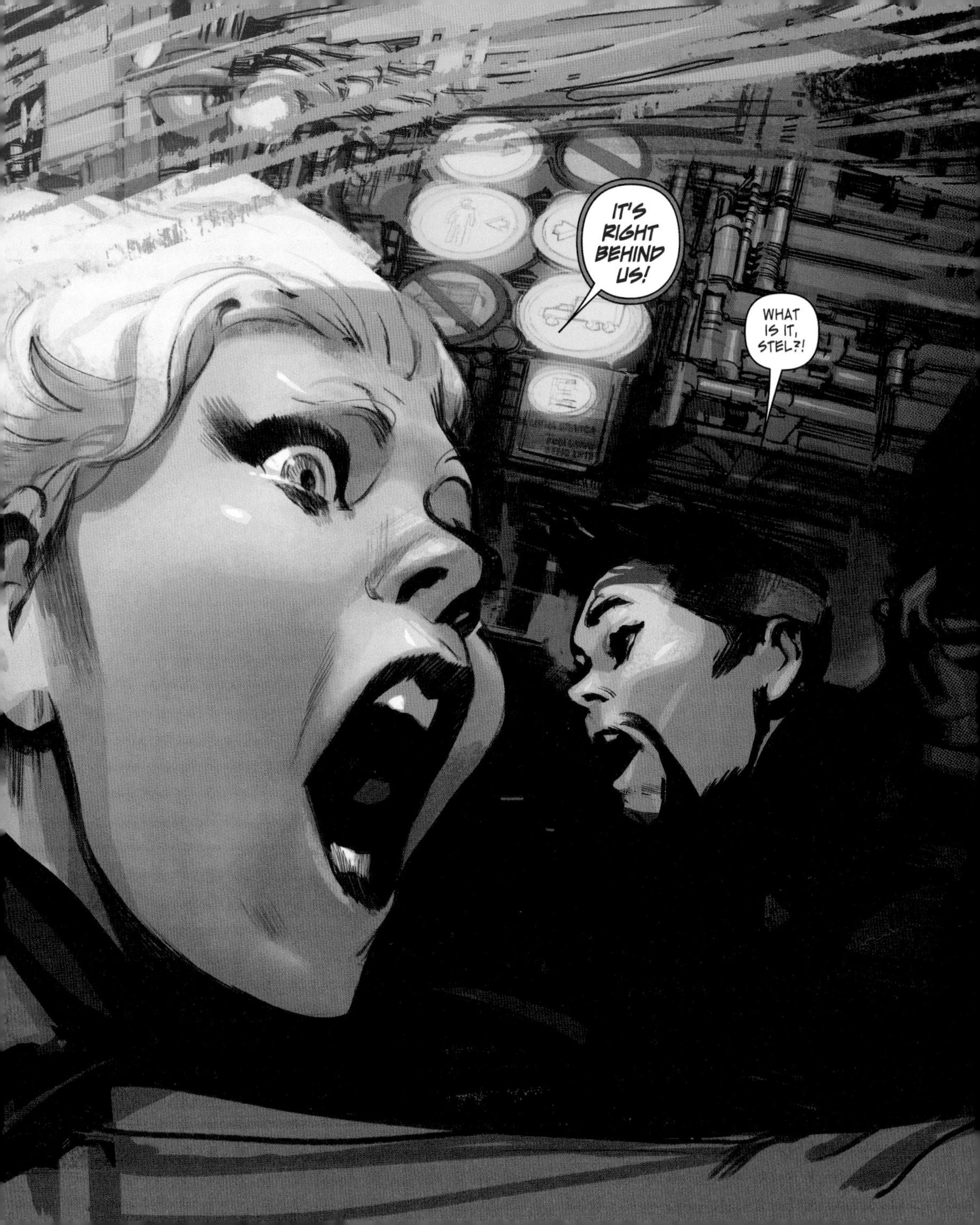
IT'S RIGHT BEHIND US!
WHAT IS IT, STEL?!

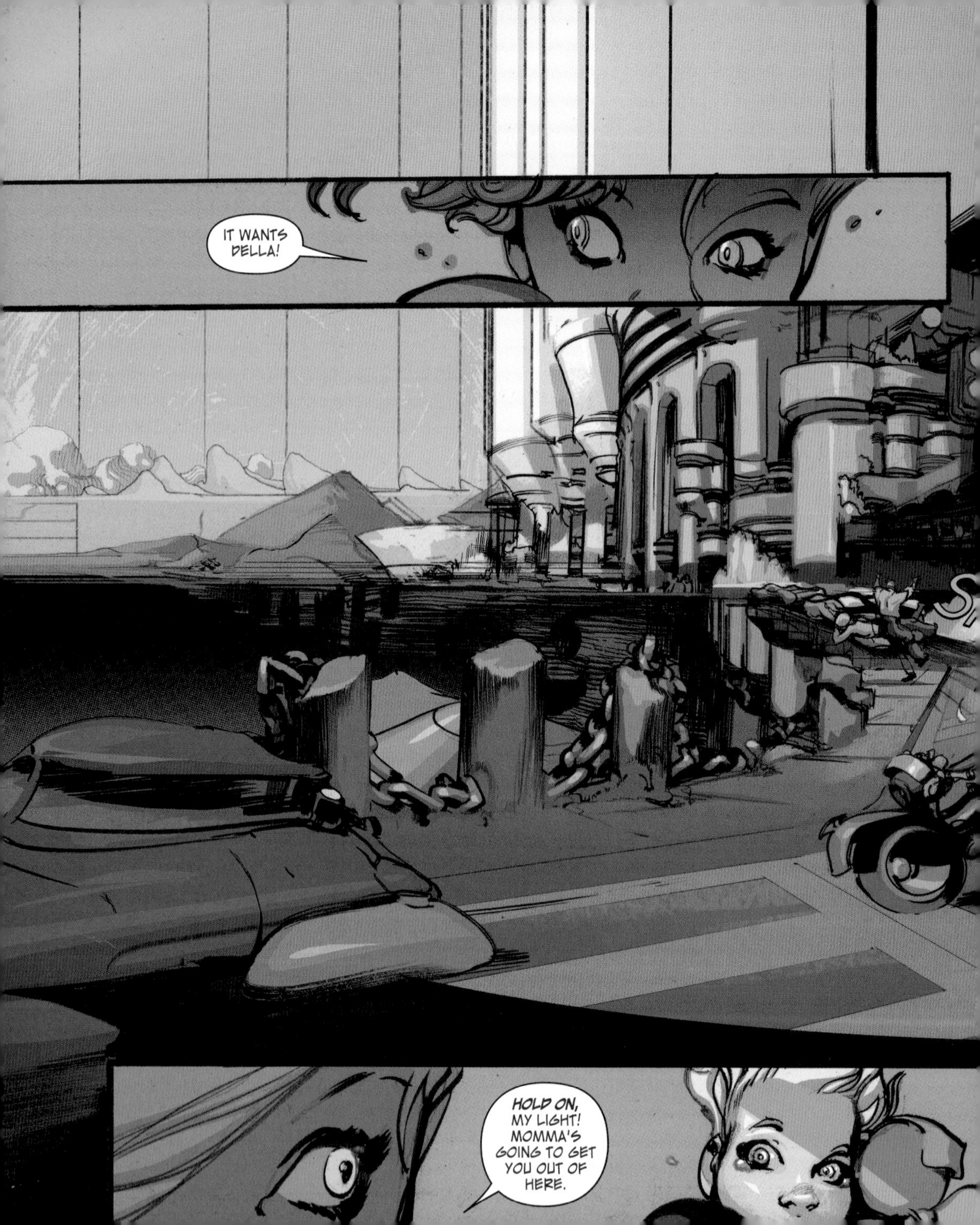
IT WANTS DELLA!
HOLD ON, MY LIGHT! MOMMA'S GOING TO GET YOU OUT OF HERE.

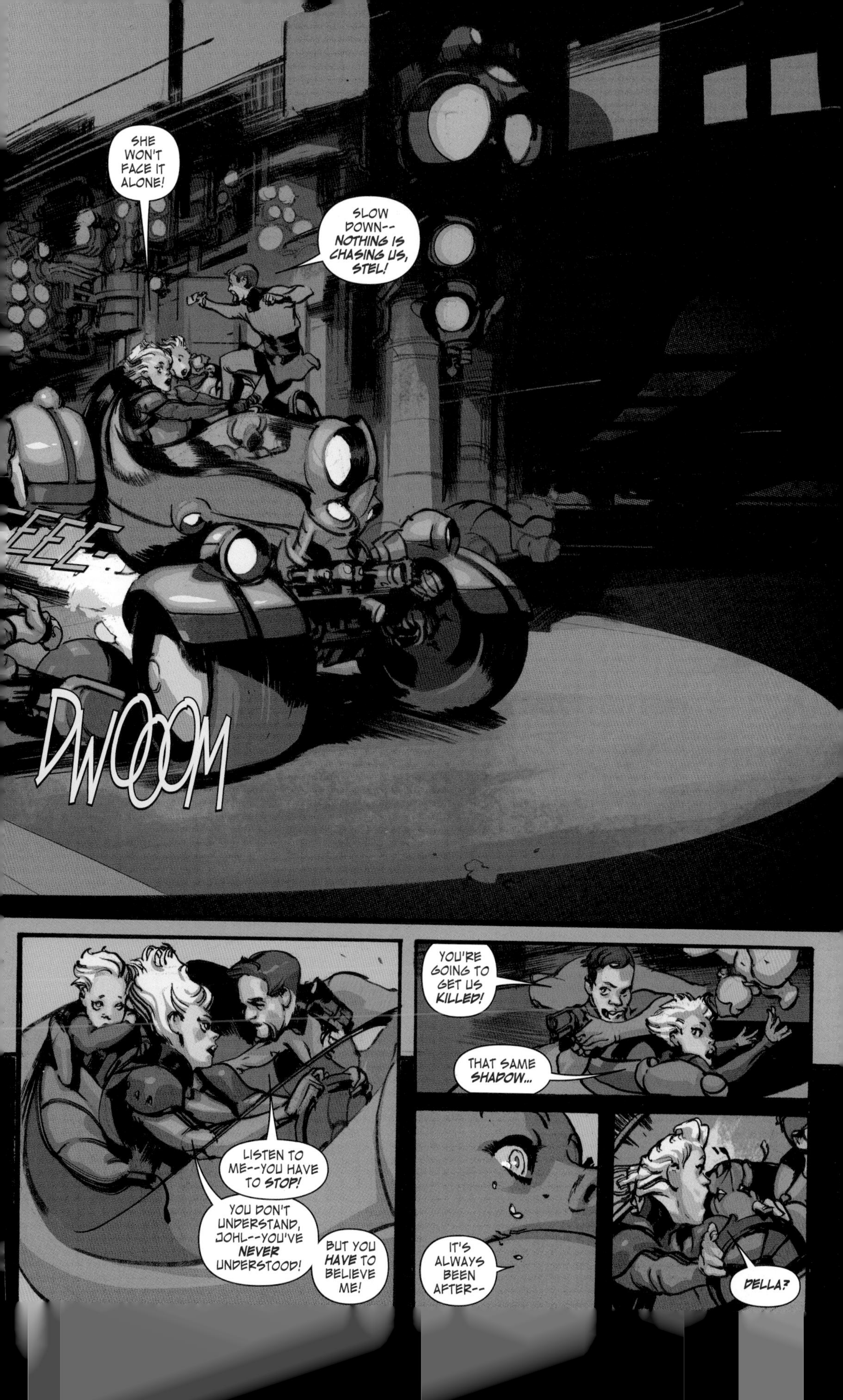
SHE WON'T FACE IT ALONE!
SLOW DOWN-- NOTHING IS CHASING US, STEL!
EEEE!
DWOOOM
LISTEN TO ME--YOU HAVE TO STOP!
YOU DON'T UNDERSTAND, JOHL--YOU'VE NEVER UNDERSTOOD!
BUT YOU HAVE TO BELIEVE ME!
YOU'RE GOING TO GET US KILLED!
THAT SAME SHADOW...
IT'S ALWAYS BEEN AFTER--
DELLA?

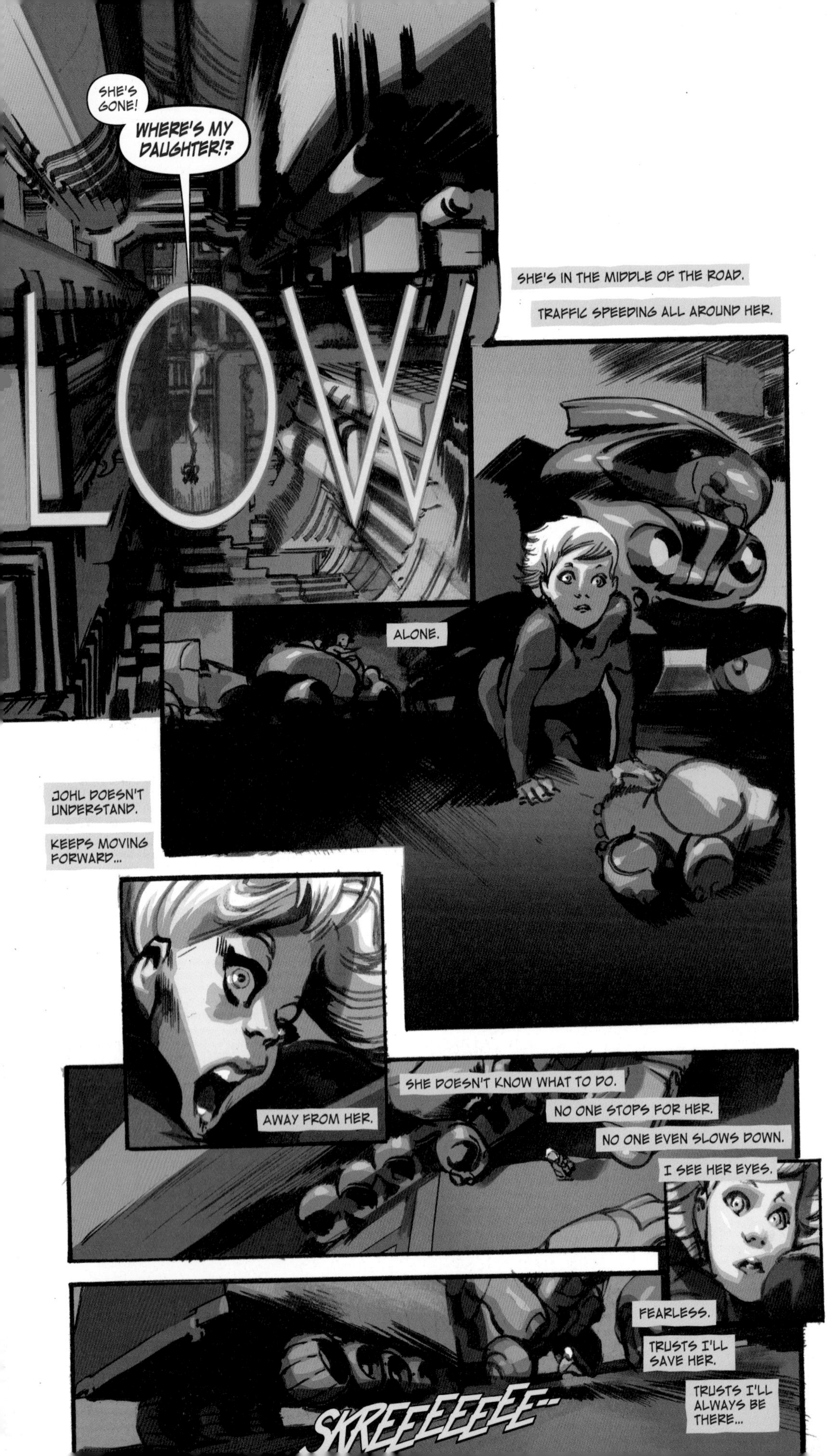

SHE'S GONE!
WHERE'S MY DAUGHTER!?
LOW
SHE'S IN THE MIDDLE OF THE ROAD.
TRAFFIC SPEEDING ALL AROUND HER.
ALONE.
JOHL DOESN'T UNDERSTAND.
KEEPS MOVING FORWARD...
AWAY FROM HER.
SHE DOESN'T KNOW WHAT TO DO.
NO ONE STOPS FOR HER.
NO ONE EVEN SLOWS DOWN.
I SEE HER EYES.
FEARLESS.
TRUSTS I'LL SAVE HER.
TRUSTS I'LL ALWAYS BE THERE...
SKREEEEEEEE--

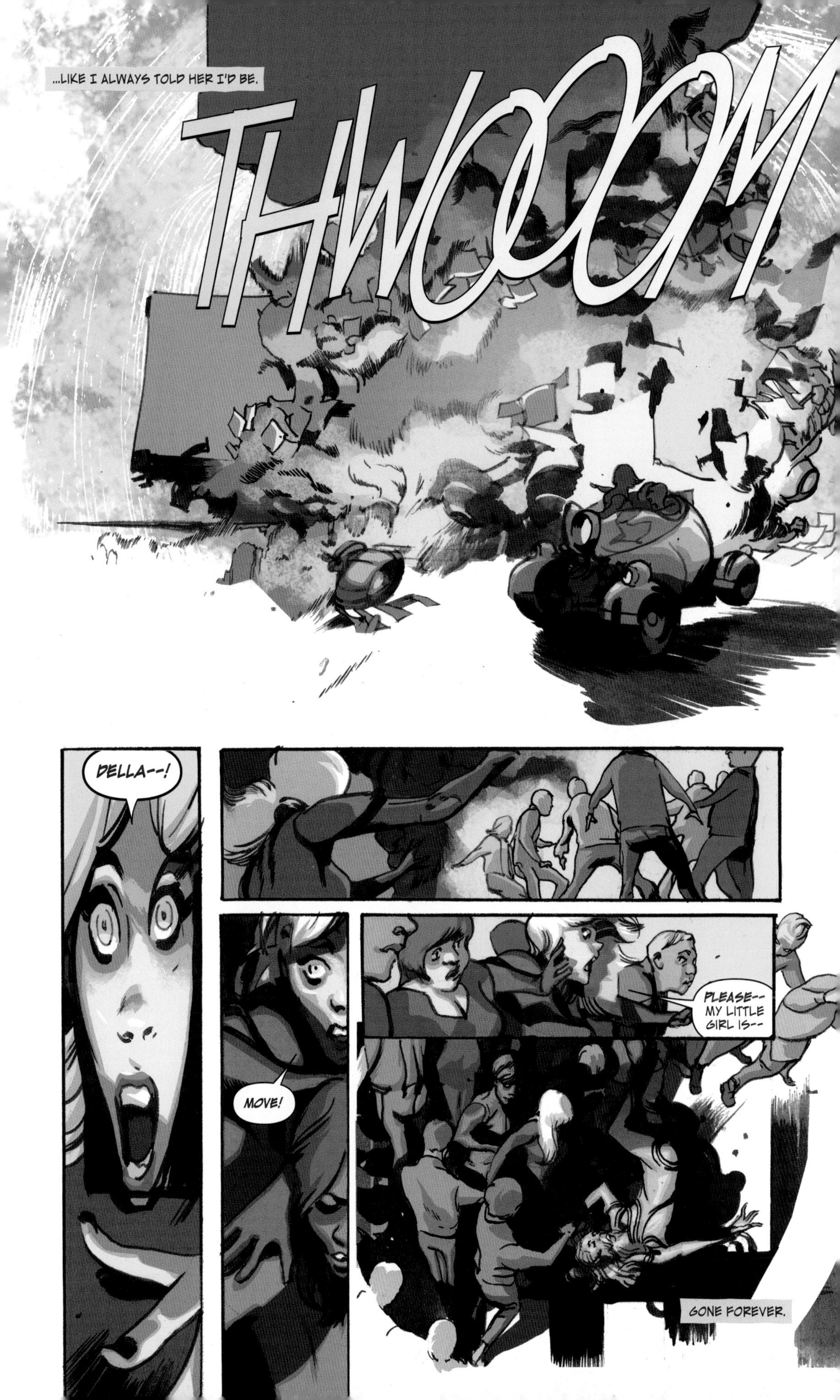

...LIKE I ALWAYS TOLD HER I'D BE.
THWOOOM
DELLA--!
PLEASE-- MY LITTLE GIRL IS--
MOVE!
GONE FOREVER.

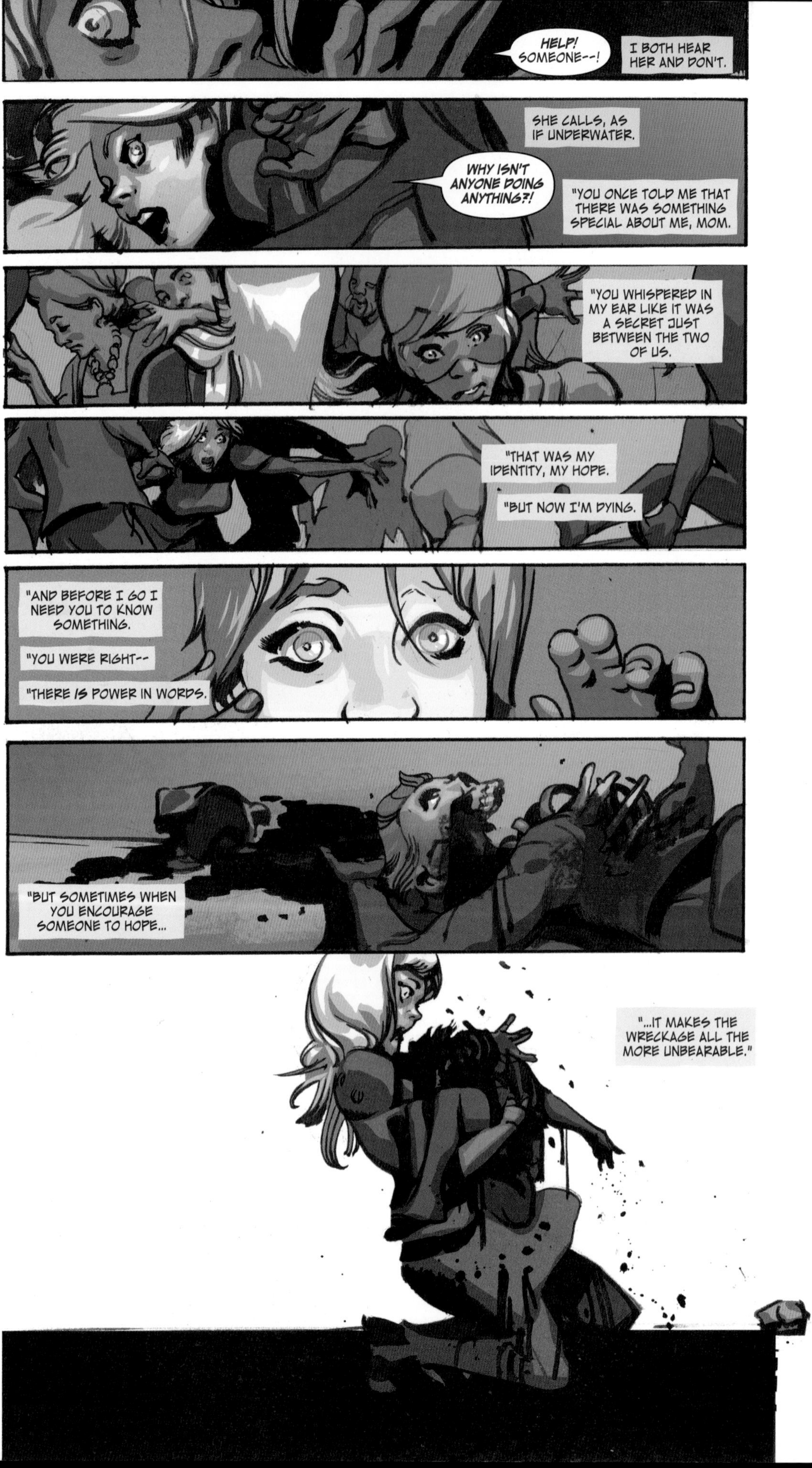
HELP! SOMEONE--!
I BOTH HEAR HER AND DON'T.
SHE CALLS, AS IF UNDERWATER.
WHY ISN'T ANYONE DOING ANYTHING?!
"YOU ONCE TOLD ME THAT THERE WAS SOMETHING SPECIAL ABOUT ME, MOM.
"YOU WHISPERED IN MY EAR LIKE IT WAS A SECRET JUST BETWEEN THE TWO OF US.
"THAT WAS MY IDENTITY, MY HOPE.
"BUT NOW I'M DYING.
"AND BEFORE I GO I NEED YOU TO KNOW SOMETHING.
"YOU WERE RIGHT--
"THERE IS POWER IN WORDS.
"BUT SOMETIMES WHEN YOU ENCOURAGE SOMEONE TO HOPE...
"...IT MAKES THE WRECKAGE ALL THE MORE UNBEARABLE."

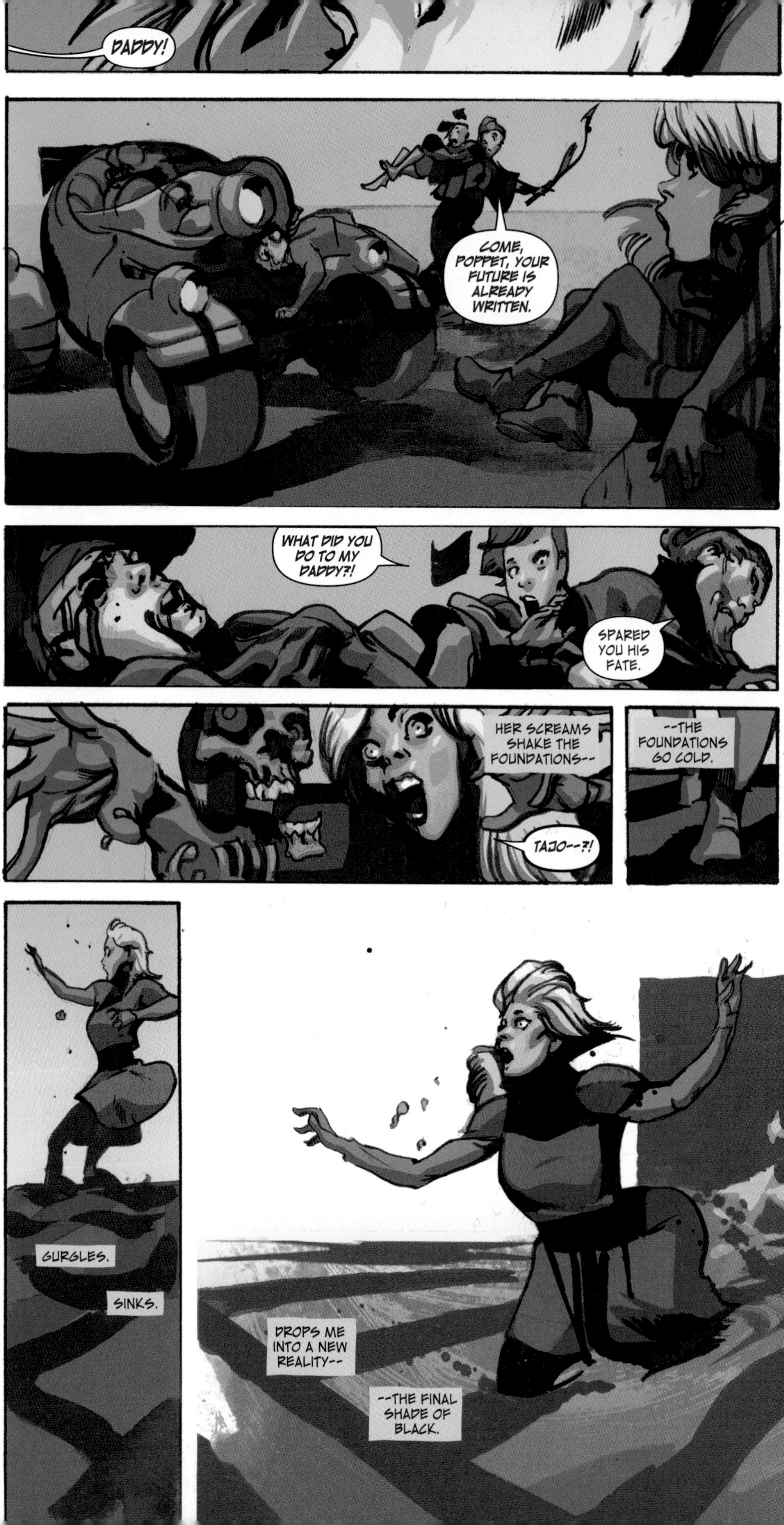
DADDY!
COME, POPPET, YOUR FUTURE IS ALREADY WRITTEN.
WHAT DID YOU DO TO MY DADDY?!
SPARED YOU HIS FATE.
HER SCREAMS SHAKE THE FOUNDATIONS--
TAJO--?!
--THE FOUNDATIONS GO COLD.
GURGLES.
SINKS.
DROPS ME INTO A NEW REALITY--
--THE FINAL SHADE OF BLACK.

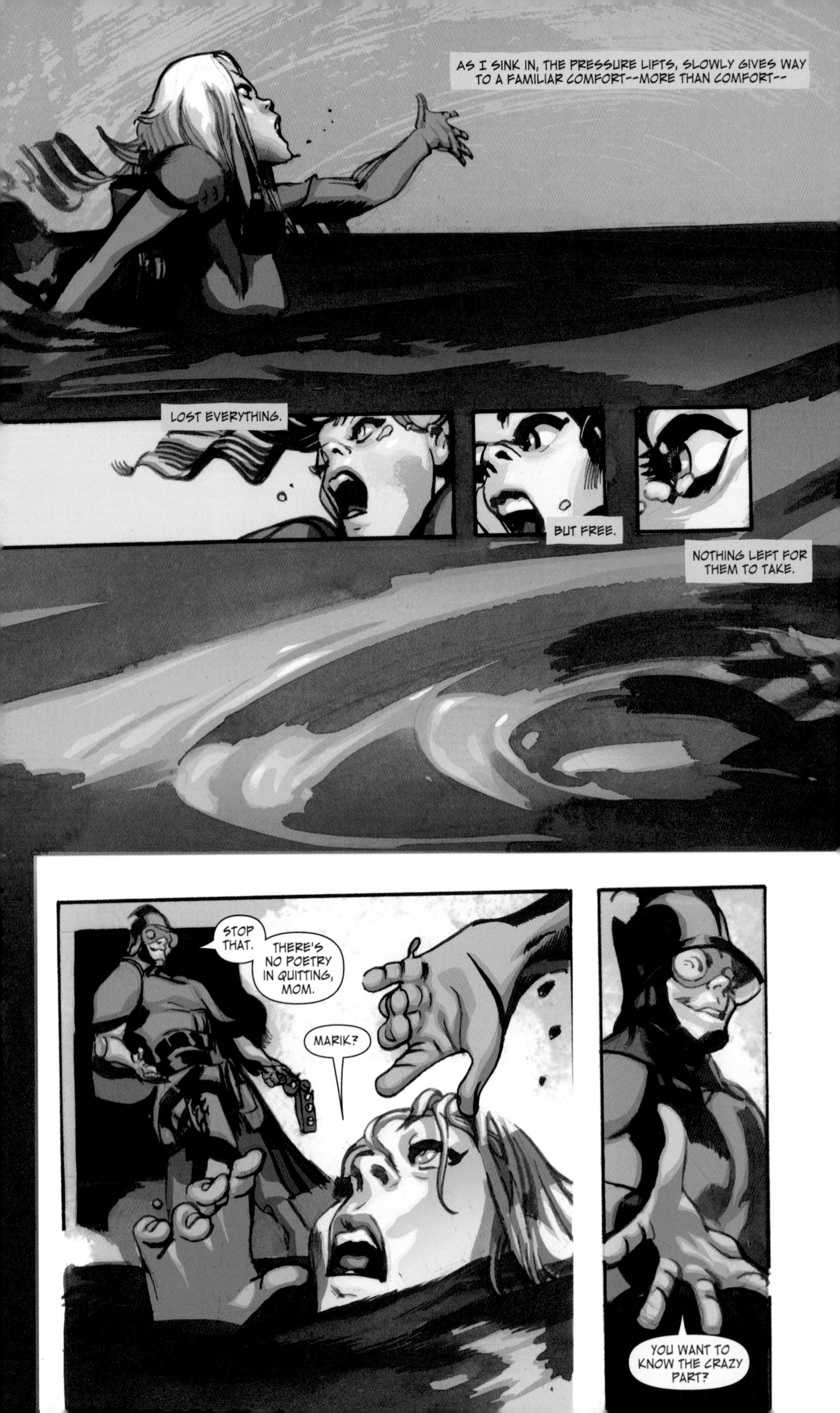
AS I SINK IN, THE PRESSURE LIFTS, SLOWLY GIVES WAY TO A FAMILIAR COMFORT--MORE THAN COMFORT--
LOST EVERYTHING.
BUT FREE.
NOTHING LEFT FOR THEM TO TAKE.
STOP THAT.
THERE'S NO POETRY IN QUITTING, MOM.
MARIK?
YOU WANT TO KNOW THE CRAZY PART?

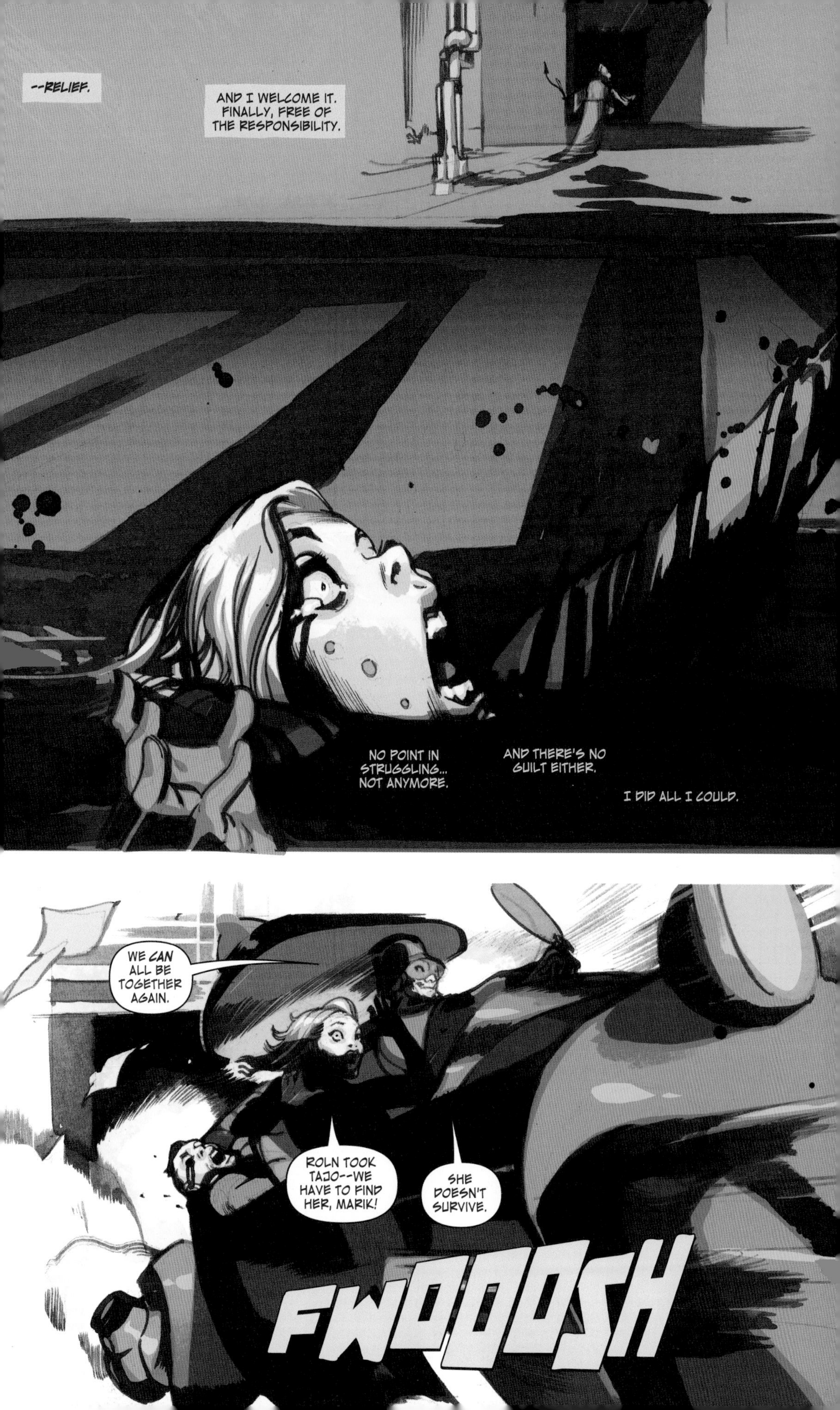
--RELIEF.
AND I WELCOME IT. FINALLY, FREE OF THE RESPONSIBILITY.
NO POINT IN STRUGGLING... NOT ANYMORE.
AND THERE'S NO GUILT EITHER.
I DID ALL I COULD.
WE CAN ALL BE TOGETHER AGAIN.
ROLN TOOK TAJO--WE HAVE TO FIND HER, MARIK!
SHE DOESN'T SURVIVE.
FWOOOSH

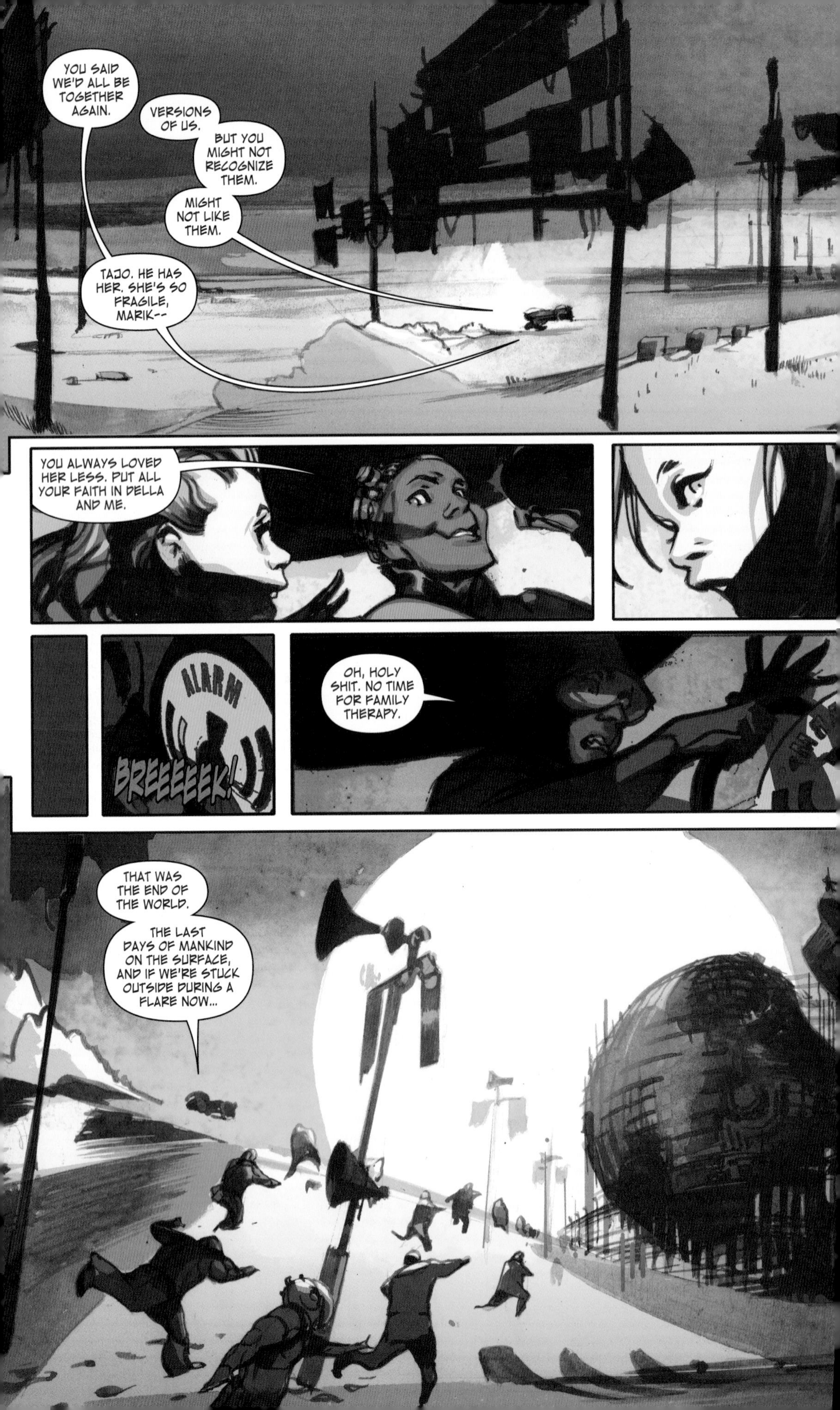
YOU SAID WE'D ALL BE TOGETHER AGAIN.
VERSIONS OF US.
BUT YOU MIGHT NOT RECOGNIZE THEM.
MIGHT NOT LIKE THEM.
TAJO. HE HAS HER. SHE'S SO FRAGILE, MARIK--
YOU ALWAYS LOVED HER LESS. PUT ALL YOUR FAITH IN DELLA AND ME.
ALARM
BREEEEEK!
OH, HOLY SHIT. NO TIME FOR FAMILY THERAPY.
THAT WAS THE END OF THE WORLD.
THE LAST DAYS OF MANKIND ON THE SURFACE, AND IF WE'RE STUCK OUTSIDE DURING A FLARE NOW...

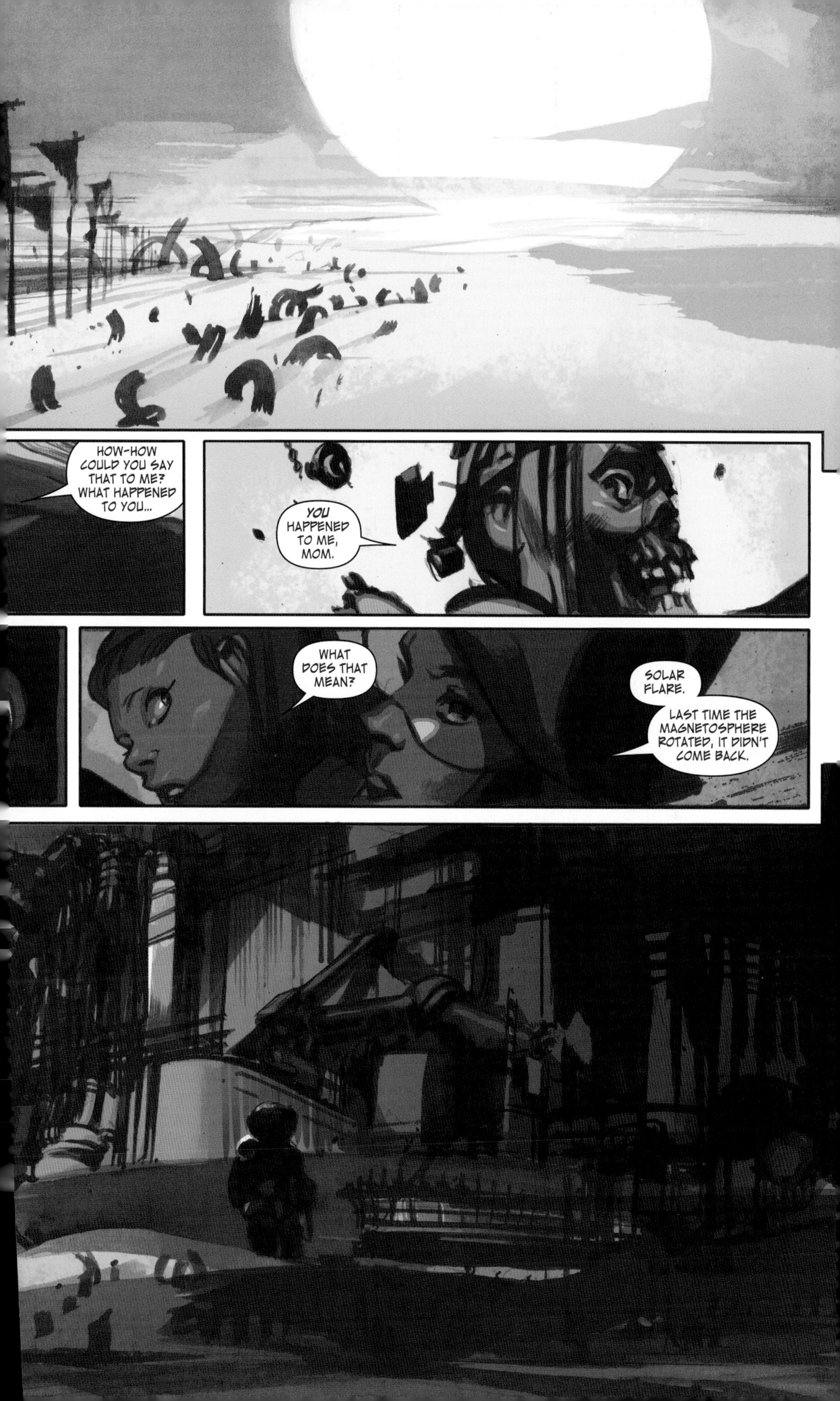
HOW-HOW COULD YOU SAY THAT TO ME? WHAT HAPPENED TO YOU...
YOU HAPPENED TO ME, MOM.
WHAT DOES THAT MEAN?
SOLAR FLARE.
LAST TIME THE MAGNETOSPHERE ROTATED, IT DIDN'T COME BACK.

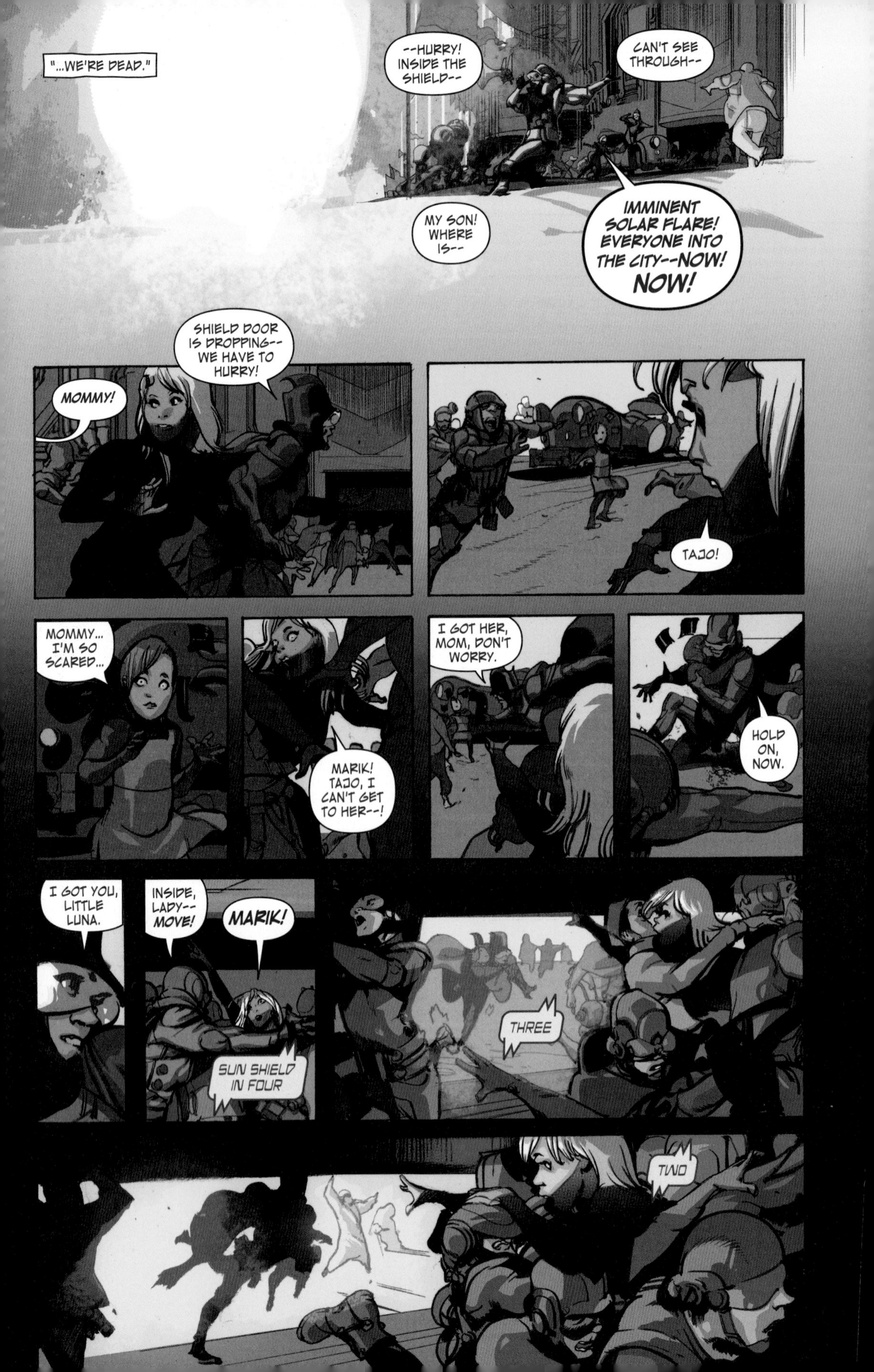
"...WE'RE DEAD."
--HURRY! INSIDE THE SHIELD--
CAN'T SEE THROUGH--
MY SON! WHERE IS--
IMMINENT SOLAR FLARE! EVERYONE INTO THE CITY--NOW! NOW!
SHIELD DOOR IS DROPPING-- WE HAVE TO HURRY!
MOMMY!
TAJO!
MOMMY... I'M SO SCARED...
MARIK! TAJO, I CAN'T GET TO HER--!
I GOT HER, MOM, DON'T WORRY.
HOLD ON, NOW.
I GOT YOU, LITTLE LUNA.
INSIDE, LADY-- MOVE!
MARIK!
SUN SHIELD IN FOUR
THREE
TWO

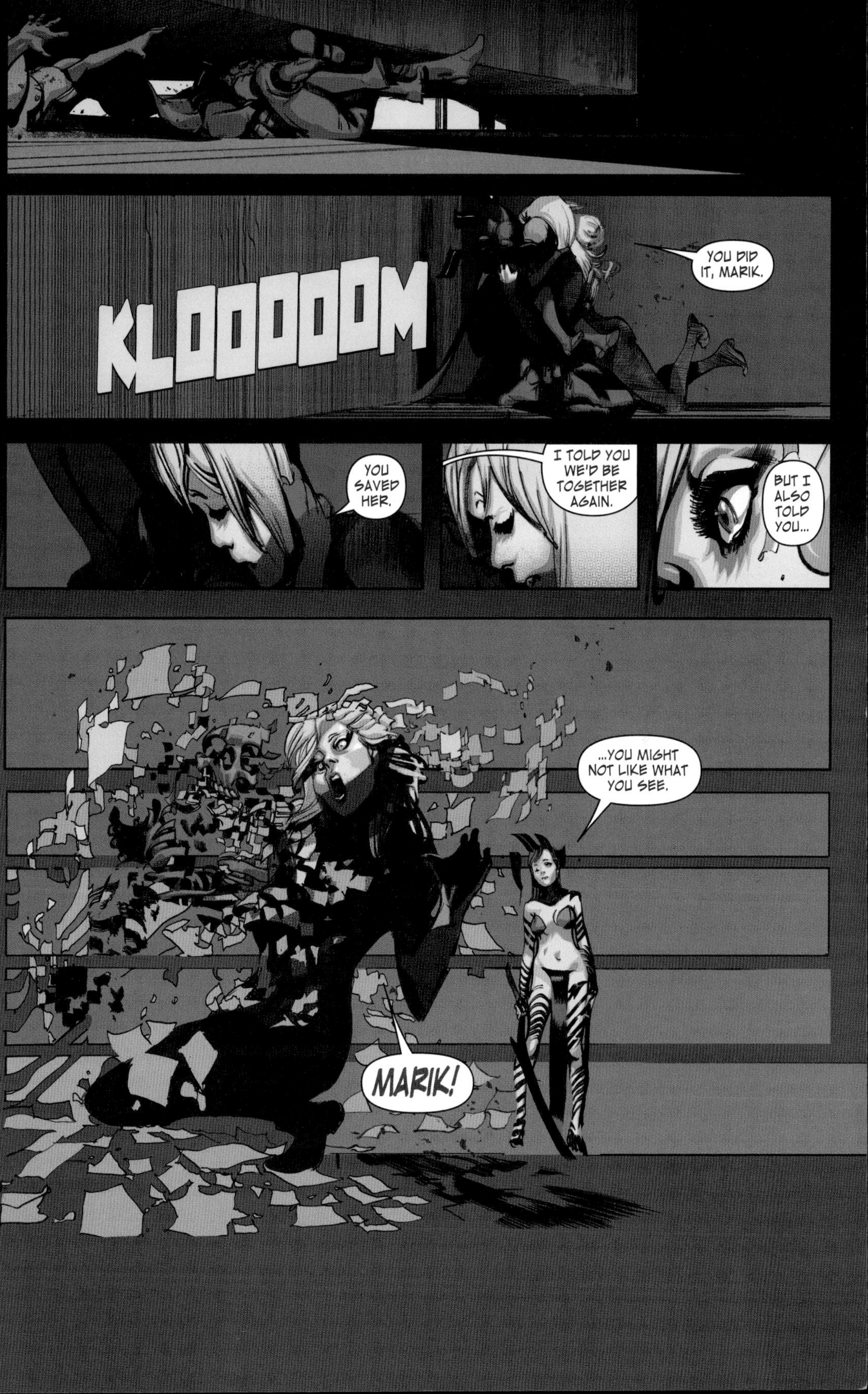
KLOOOOOM
YOU DID IT, MARIK.
YOU SAVED HER.
I TOLD YOU WE'D BE TOGETHER AGAIN.
BUT I ALSO TOLD YOU...
...YOU MIGHT NOT LIKE WHAT YOU SEE.
MARIK!

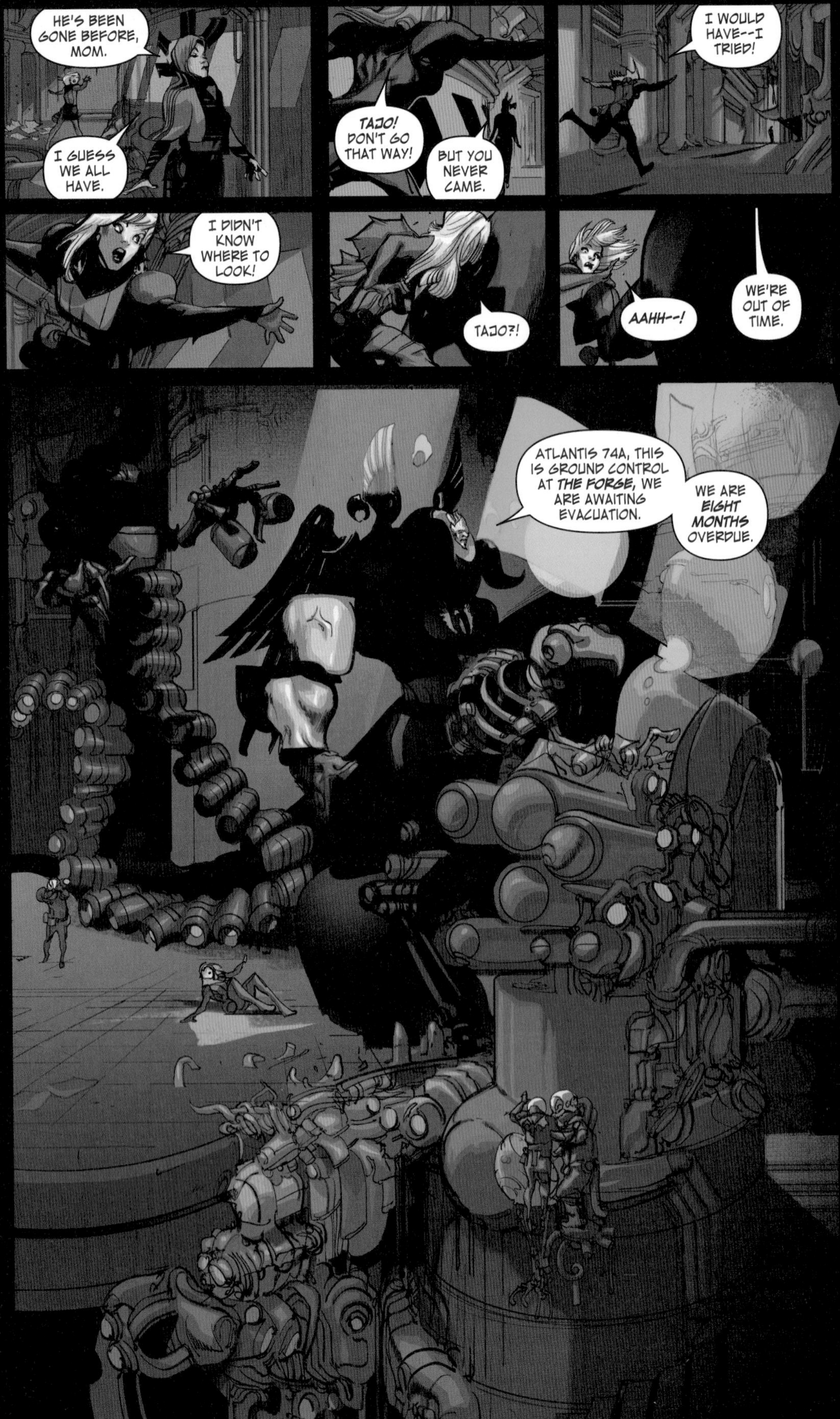

HE'S BEEN GONE BEFORE, MOM.
I GUESS WE ALL HAVE.
TAJO! DON'T GO THAT WAY!
BUT YOU NEVER CAME.
I WOULD HAVE--I TRIED!
I DIDN'T KNOW WHERE TO LOOK!
TAJO?!
AAHH--!
WE'RE OUT OF TIME.
ATLANTIS 74A, THIS IS GROUND CONTROL AT THE FORGE, WE ARE AWAITING EVACUATION.
WE ARE EIGHT MONTHS OVERDUE.

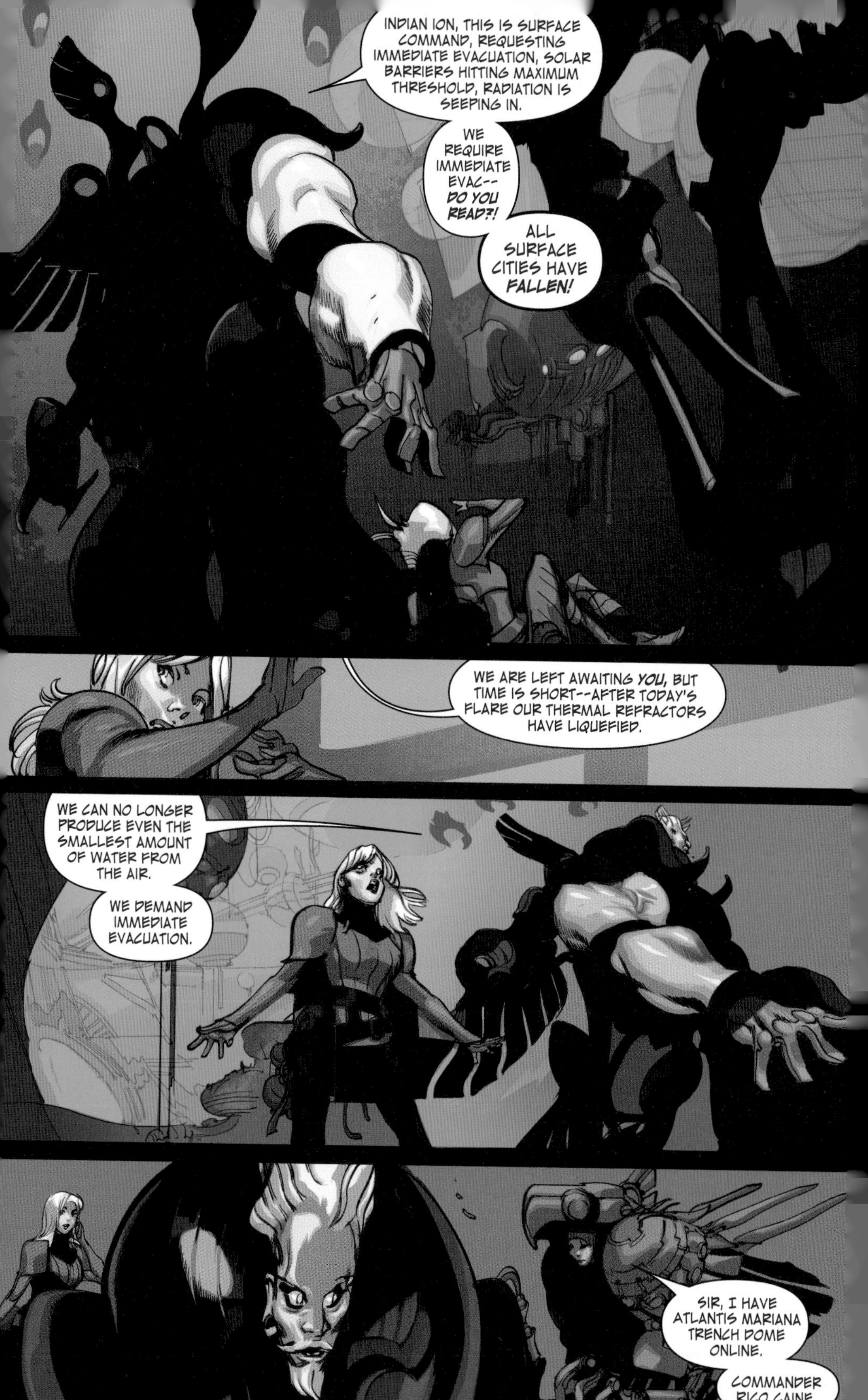
INDIAN ION, THIS IS SURFACE COMMAND, REQUESTING IMMEDIATE EVACUATION, SOLAR BARRIERS HITTING MAXIMUM THRESHOLD, RADIATION IS SEEPING IN.
WE REQUIRE IMMEDIATE EVAC-- DO YOU READ?!
ALL SURFACE CITIES HAVE FALLEN!
WE ARE LEFT AWAITING YOU, BUT TIME IS SHORT--AFTER TODAY'S FLARE OUR THERMAL REFRACTORS HAVE LIQUEFIED.
WE CAN NO LONGER PRODUCE EVEN THE SMALLEST AMOUNT OF WATER FROM THE AIR.
WE DEMAND IMMEDIATE EVACUATION.
SIR, I HAVE ATLANTIS MARIANA TRENCH DOME ONLINE.
COMMANDER RICO CAINE.

HELMSMAN CAINE, I APPRECIATE YOU TAKING MY CALL, IT SEEMS EVERYONE WOULD RATHER FORGET WE'RE STILL UP HERE.

WE STAYED TO COMPLETE THE CALIUL DOME. BY THE TIME WE LOWERED IT, WE'D MISSED THE WINDOW.

EVERY DOME WE LOWERED HAS REFUSED TO RESPOND TO US-- LEAVING US STRANDED UP HERE.

I APPRECIATE YOUR POSITION, HELMSMAN ZOSKE. THE FLARES ARE DISRUPTING ALL COMMUNICATION RELAY IN SALUS.

WEREN'T YOU SUPPOSED TO BE EVACUATED BY THE ALEUTIAN TRENCH DOME?

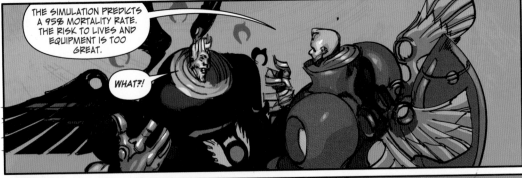

WE'RE GOING ON MONTHS NOW, HELMSMAN CAINE.

WE REQUIRE A FLEET OF SUB-X IMMEDIATELY.

HELMSMAN ZOSKE, I CAN OFFER ONLY AN HONEST TRUTH...

THERE ARE NO PILOTS WILLING TO RISK THIS MISSION.

THE SIMULATION PREDICTS A 95% MORTALITY RATE. THE RISK TO LIVES AND EQUIPMENT IS TOO GREAT.

WHAT?!

WITHOUT US, *NONE* OF YOU WOULD EVEN BE DOWN THERE!

WE HAVE HELD UP OUR END OF THE BARGAIN.

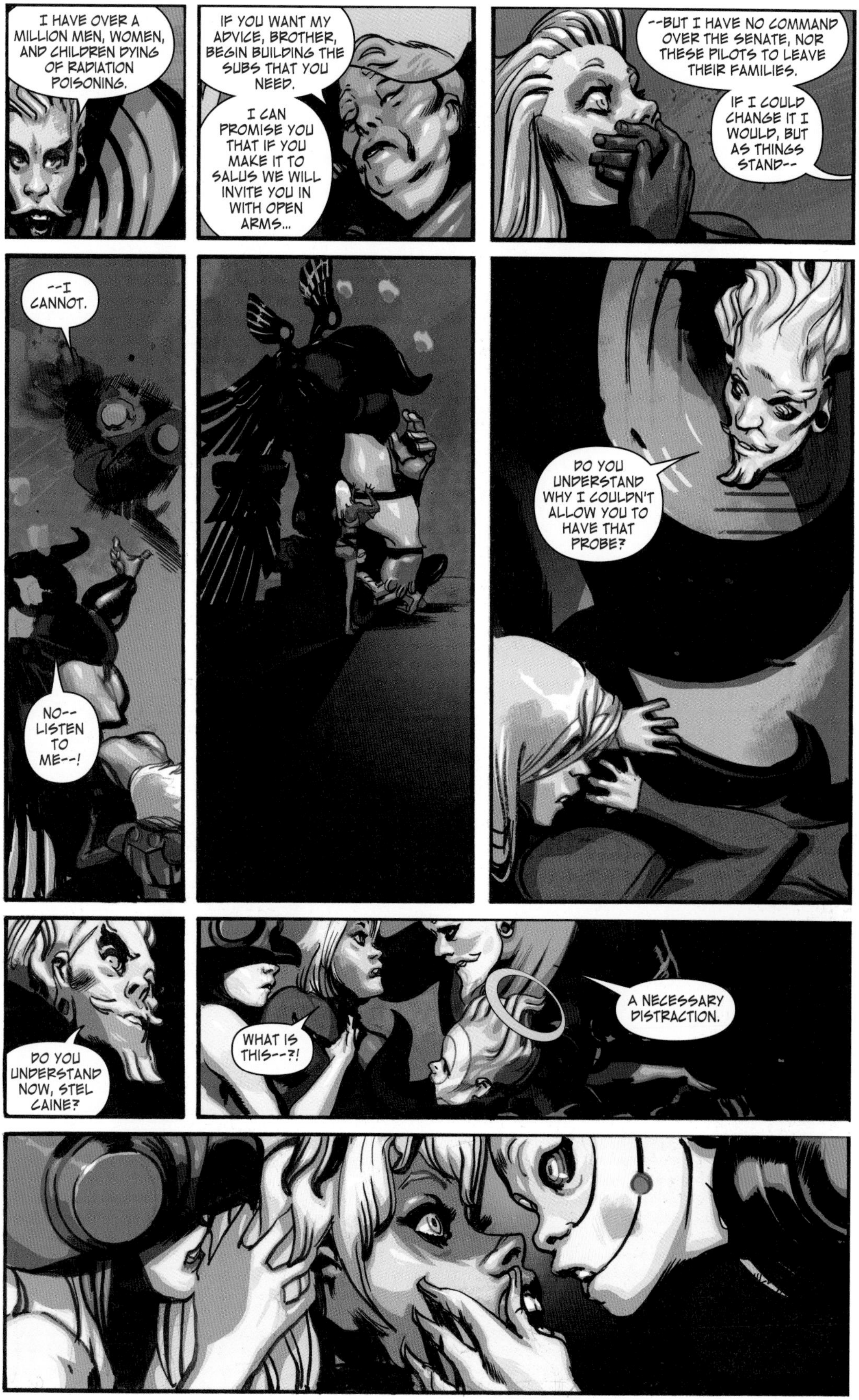
I HAVE OVER A MILLION MEN, WOMEN, AND CHILDREN DYING OF RADIATION POISONING.
IF YOU WANT MY ADVICE, BROTHER, BEGIN BUILDING THE SUBS THAT YOU NEED.
I CAN PROMISE YOU THAT IF YOU MAKE IT TO SALUS WE WILL INVITE YOU IN WITH OPEN ARMS...
--BUT I HAVE NO COMMAND OVER THE SENATE, NOR THESE PILOTS TO LEAVE THEIR FAMILIES.
IF I COULD CHANGE IT I WOULD, BUT AS THINGS STAND--
--I CANNOT.
NO-- LISTEN TO ME--!
DO YOU UNDERSTAND WHY I COULDN'T ALLOW YOU TO HAVE THAT PROBE?
DO YOU UNDERSTAND NOW, STEL CAINE?
WHAT IS THIS--?!
A NECESSARY DISTRACTION.

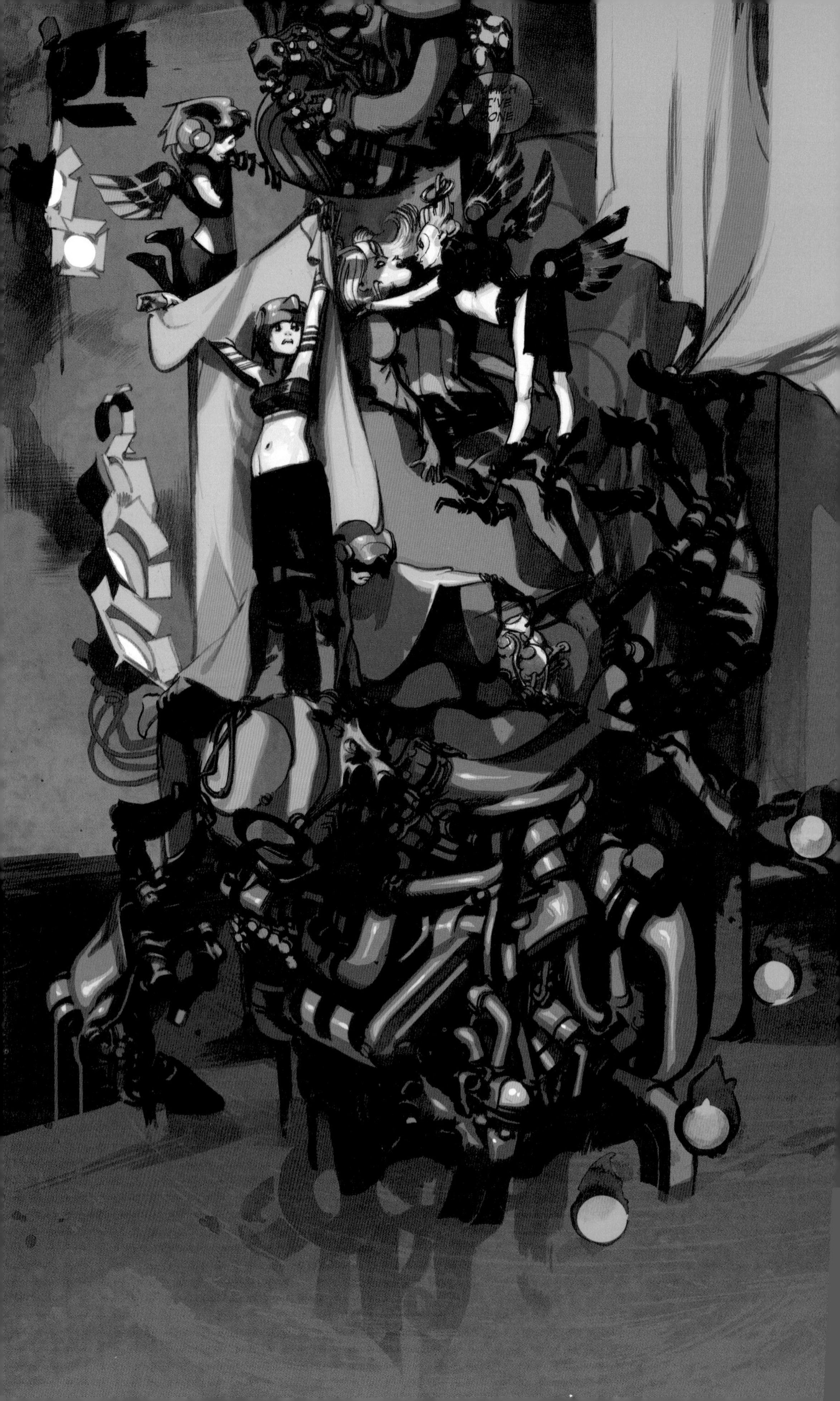

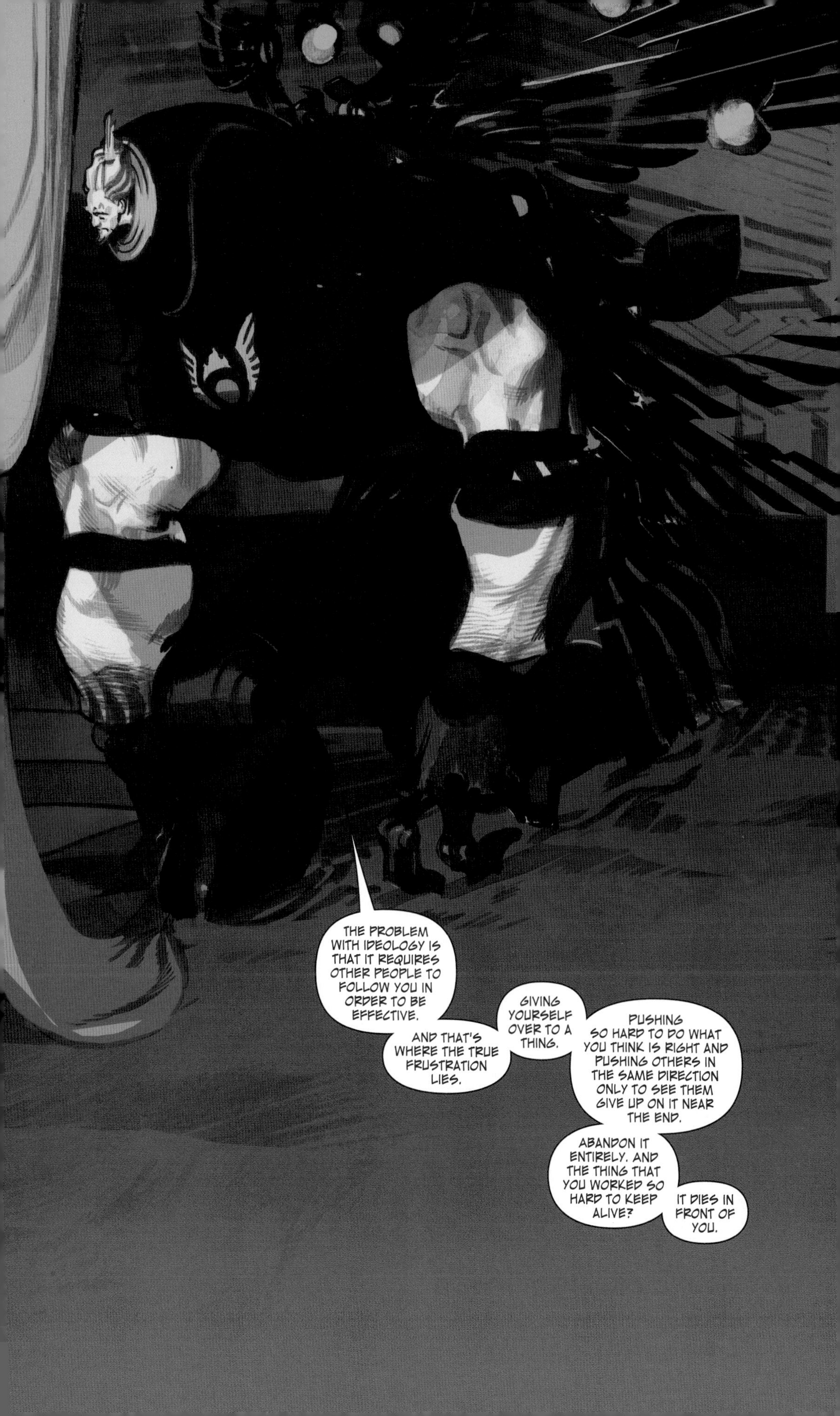
THE PROBLEM WITH IDEOLOGY IS THAT IT REQUIRES OTHER PEOPLE TO FOLLOW YOU IN ORDER TO BE EFFECTIVE.
AND THAT'S WHERE THE TRUE FRUSTRATION LIES.
GIVING YOURSELF OVER TO A THING.
PUSHING SO HARD TO DO WHAT YOU THINK IS RIGHT AND PUSHING OTHERS IN THE SAME DIRECTION ONLY TO SEE THEM GIVE UP ON IT NEAR THE END.
ABANDON IT ENTIRELY. AND THE THING THAT YOU WORKED SO HARD TO KEEP ALIVE?
IT DIES IN FRONT OF YOU.

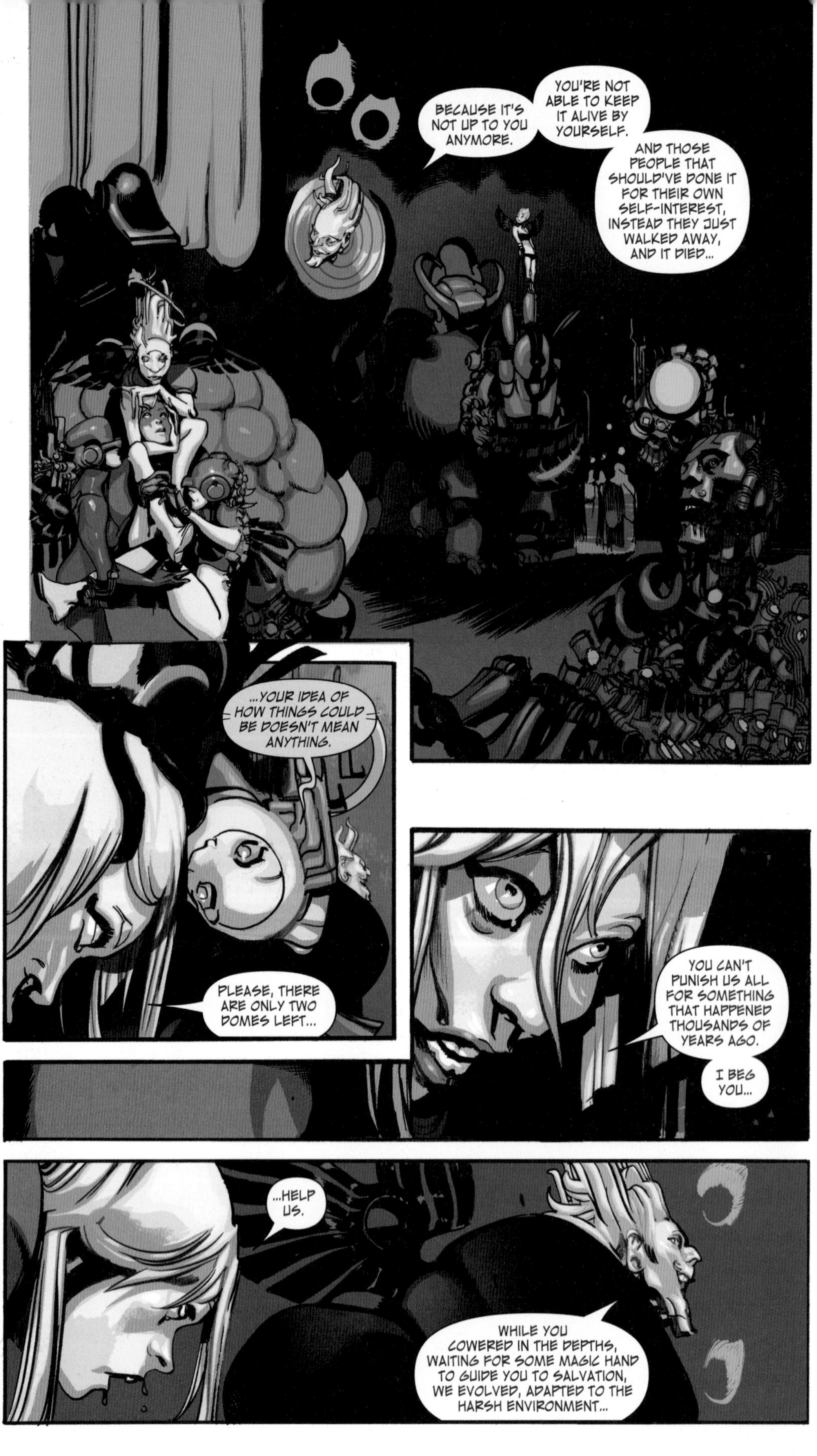
BECAUSE IT'S NOT UP TO YOU ANYMORE.
YOU'RE NOT ABLE TO KEEP IT ALIVE BY YOURSELF.
AND THOSE PEOPLE THAT SHOULD'VE DONE IT FOR THEIR OWN SELF-INTEREST, INSTEAD THEY JUST WALKED AWAY, AND IT DIED...
...YOUR IDEA OF HOW THINGS COULD BE DOESN'T MEAN ANYTHING.
PLEASE, THERE ARE ONLY TWO DOMES LEFT...
YOU CAN'T PUNISH US ALL FOR SOMETHING THAT HAPPENED THOUSANDS OF YEARS AGO.
I BEG YOU...
...HELP US.
WHILE YOU COWERED IN THE DEPTHS, WAITING FOR SOME MAGIC HAND TO GUIDE YOU TO SALVATION, WE EVOLVED, ADAPTED TO THE HARSH ENVIRONMENT...

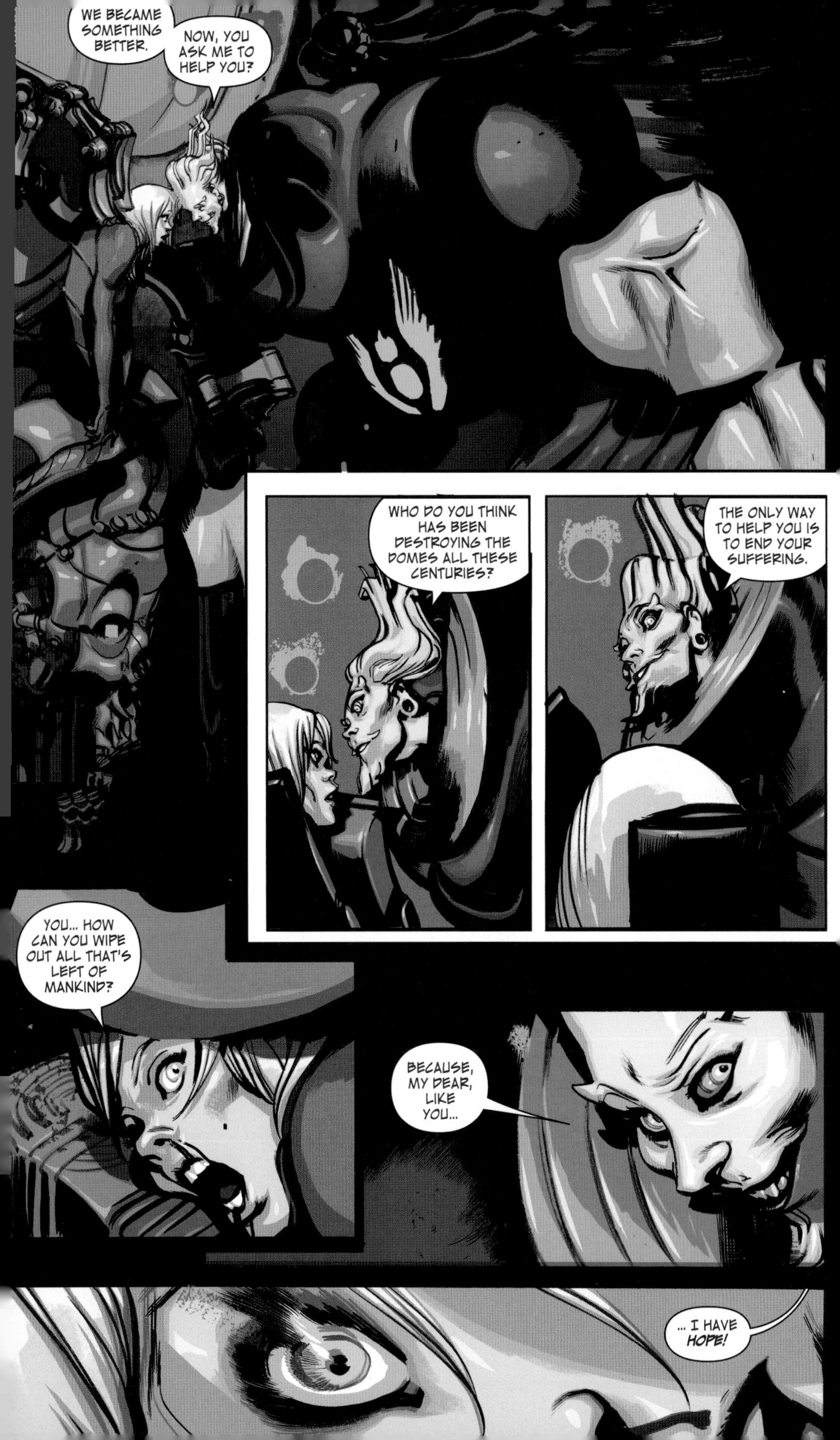
WE BECAME SOMETHING BETTER.
NOW, YOU ASK ME TO HELP YOU?
WHO DO YOU THINK HAS BEEN DESTROYING THE DOMES ALL THESE CENTURIES?
THE ONLY WAY TO HELP YOU IS TO END YOUR SUFFERING.
YOU... HOW CAN YOU WIPE OUT ALL THAT'S LEFT OF MANKIND?
BECAUSE, MY DEAR, LIKE YOU...
... I HAVE *HOPE!*

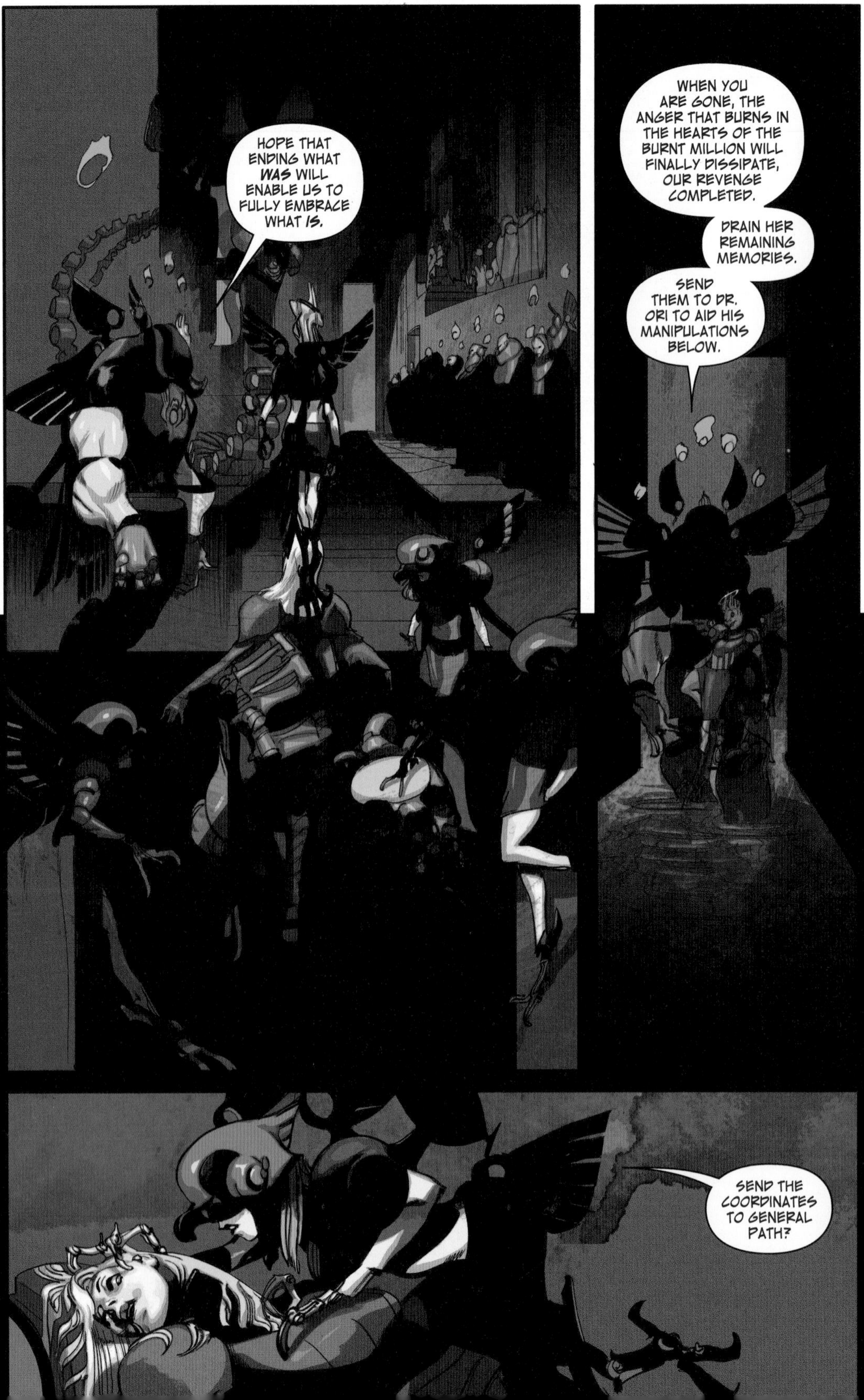
HOPE THAT ENDING WHAT WAS WILL ENABLE US TO FULLY EMBRACE WHAT IS.
WHEN YOU ARE GONE, THE ANGER THAT BURNS IN THE HEARTS OF THE BURNT MILLION WILL FINALLY DISSIPATE, OUR REVENGE COMPLETED.
DRAIN HER REMAINING MEMORIES.
SEND THEM TO DR. ORI TO AID HIS MANIPULATIONS BELOW.
SEND THE COORDINATES TO GENERAL PATH?

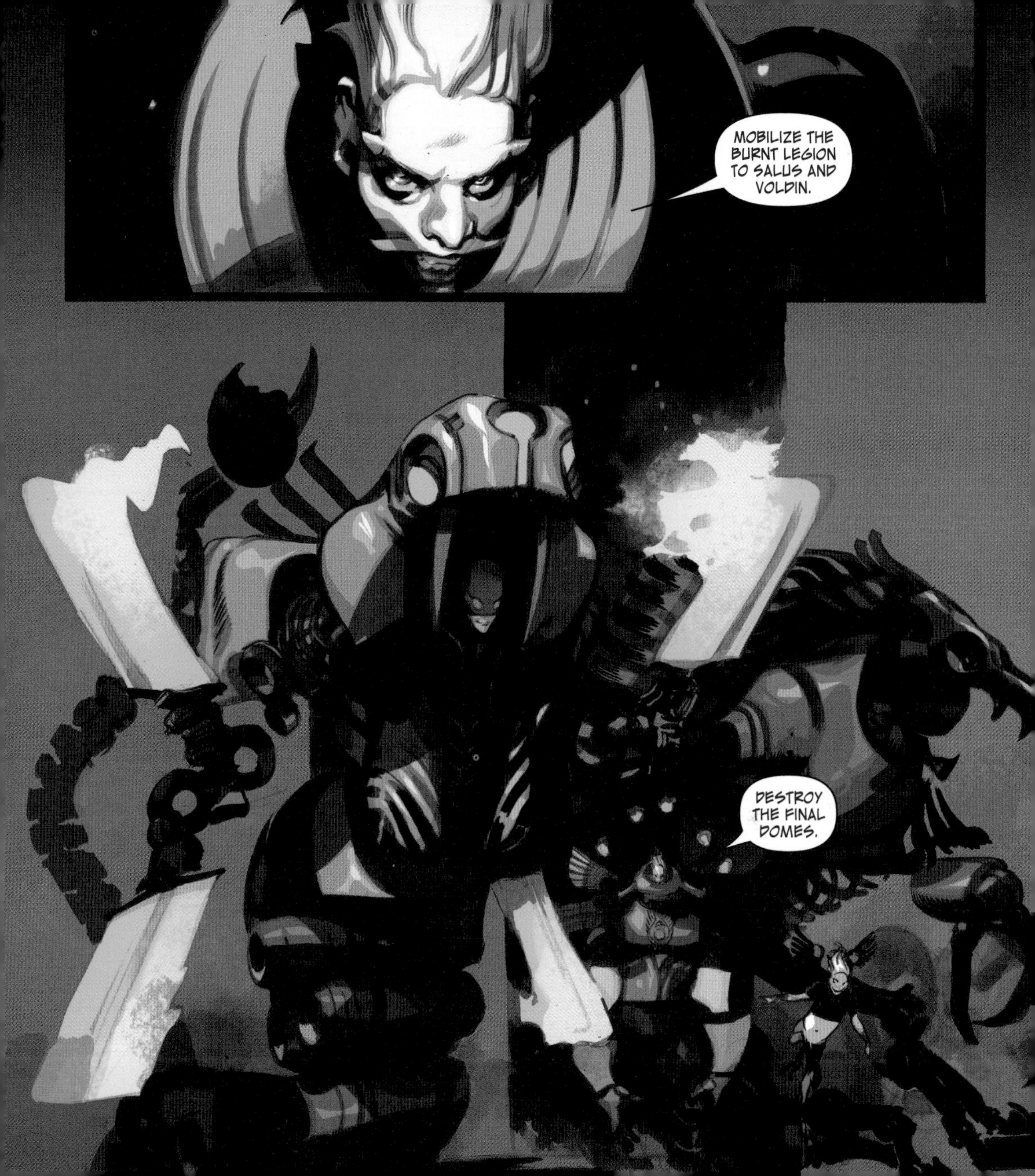
MOBILIZE THE BURNT LEGION TO SALUS AND VOLDIN.
DESTROY THE FINAL DOMES.

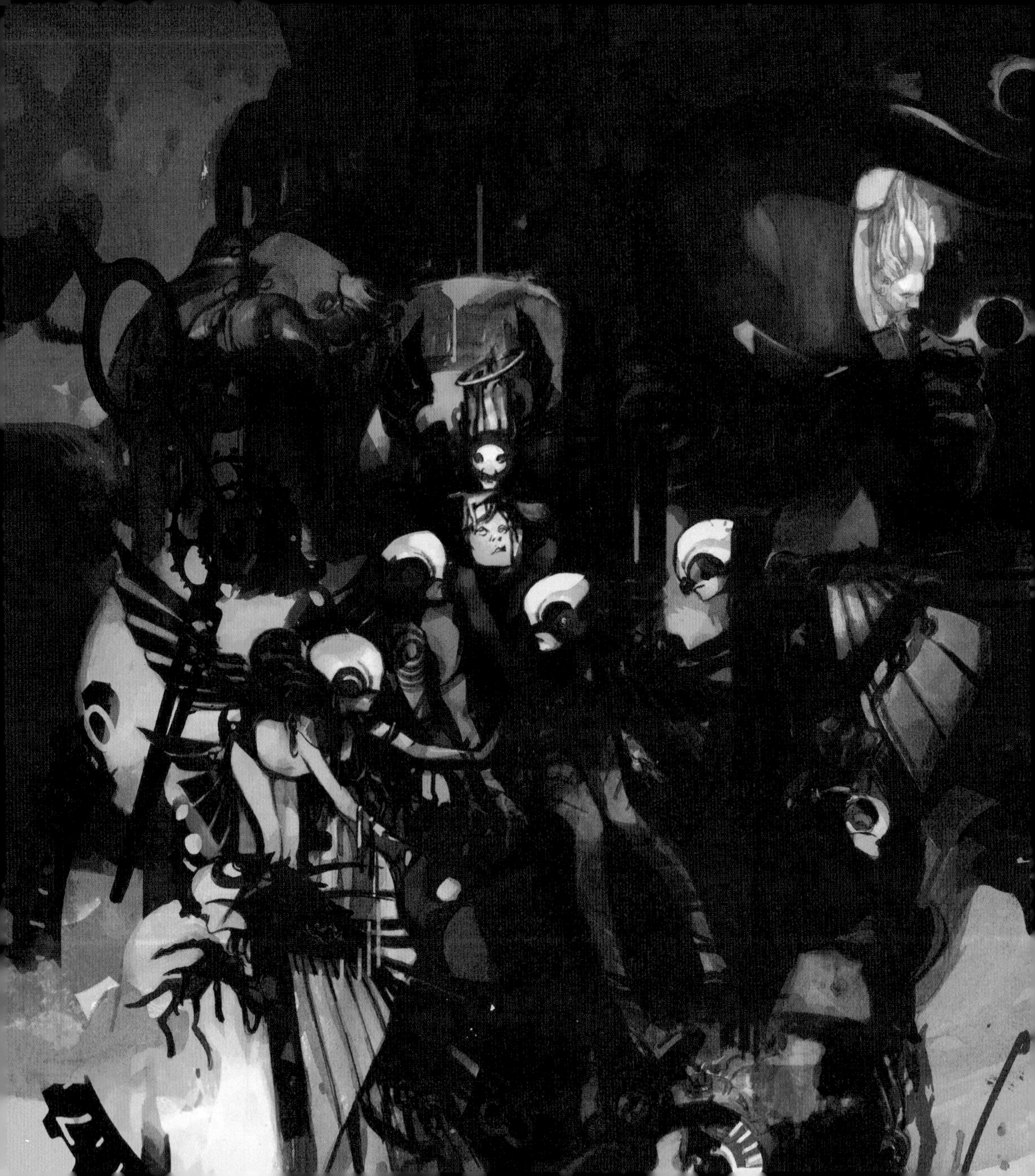

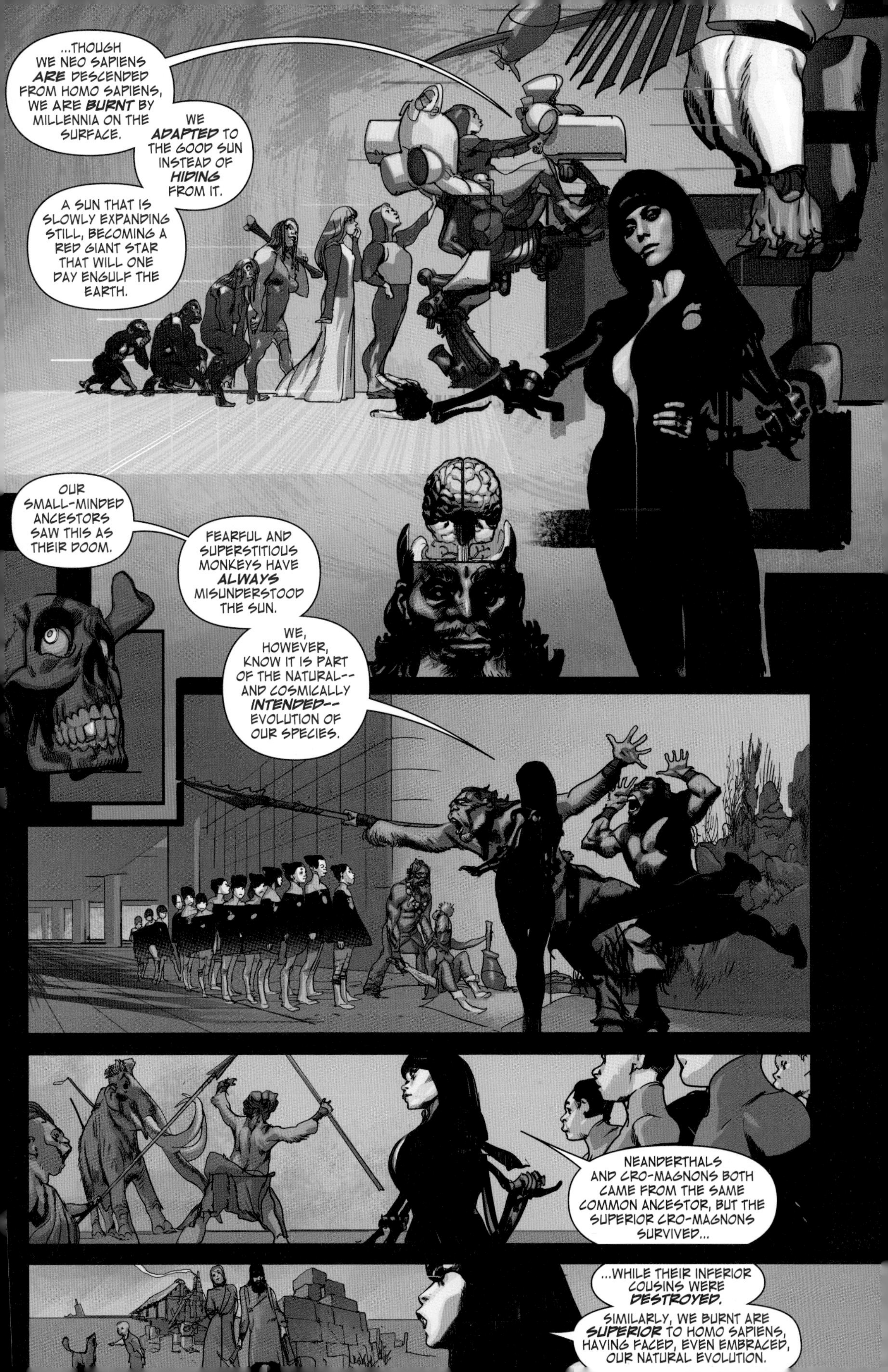

...THOUGH WE NEO SAPIENS ARE DESCENDED FROM HOMO SAPIENS, WE ARE BURNT BY MILLENNIA ON THE SURFACE.
WE ADAPTED TO THE GOOD SUN INSTEAD OF HIDING FROM IT.
A SUN THAT IS SLOWLY EXPANDING STILL, BECOMING A RED GIANT STAR THAT WILL ONE DAY ENGULF THE EARTH.
OUR SMALL-MINDED ANCESTORS SAW THIS AS THEIR DOOM.
FEARFUL AND SUPERSTITIOUS MONKEYS HAVE ALWAYS MISUNDERSTOOD THE SUN.
WE, HOWEVER, KNOW IT IS PART OF THE NATURAL-- AND COSMICALLY INTENDED-- EVOLUTION OF OUR SPECIES.
NEANDERTHALS AND CRO-MAGNONS BOTH CAME FROM THE SAME COMMON ANCESTOR, BUT THE SUPERIOR CRO-MAGNONS SURVIVED...
...WHILE THEIR INFERIOR COUSINS WERE DESTROYED.
SIMILARLY, WE BURNT ARE SUPERIOR TO HOMO SAPIENS, HAVING FACED, EVEN EMBRACED, OUR NATURAL EVOLUTION.

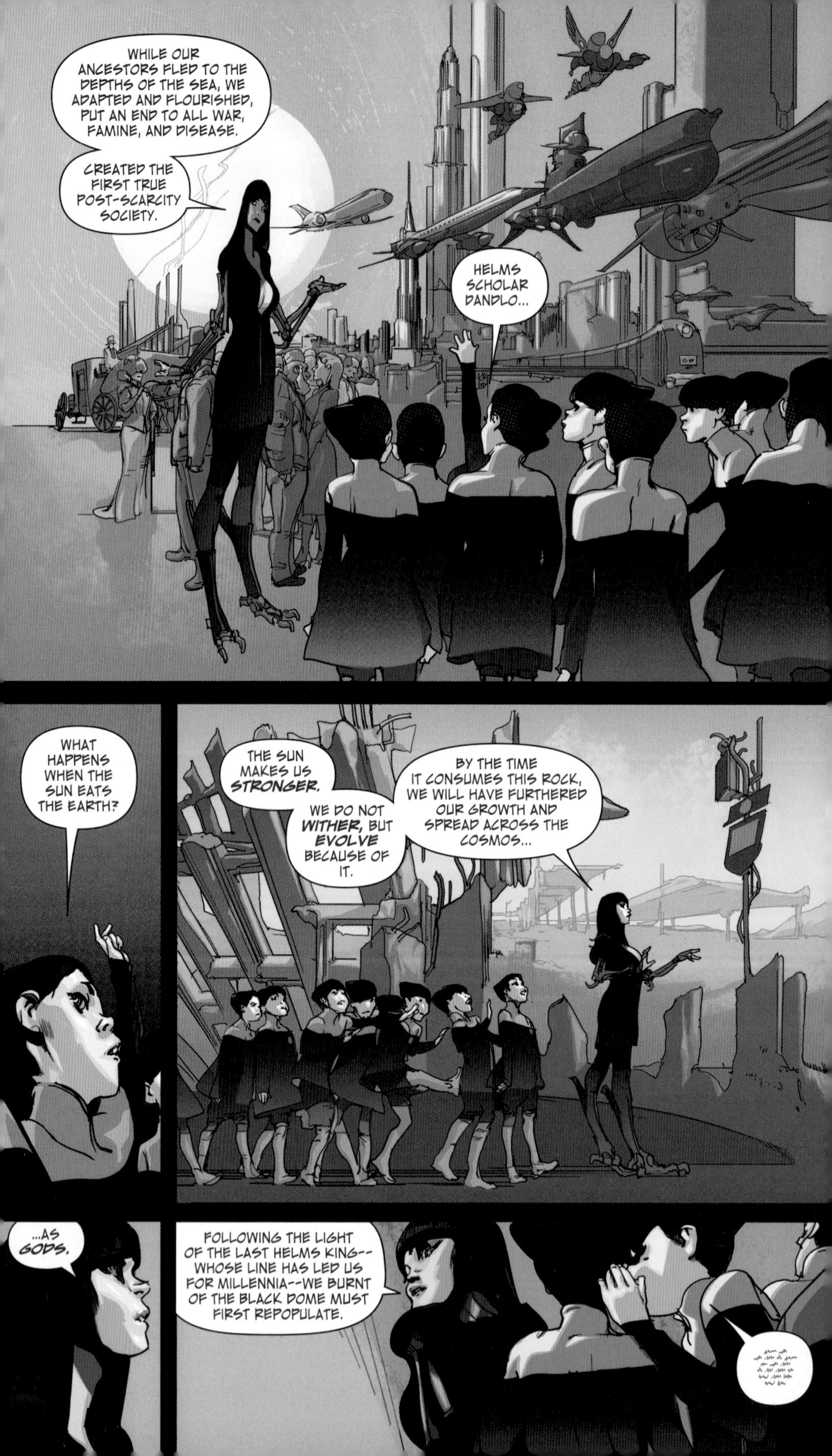
WHILE OUR ANCESTORS FLED TO THE DEPTHS OF THE SEA, WE ADAPTED AND FLOURISHED, PUT AN END TO ALL WAR, FAMINE, AND DISEASE.
CREATED THE FIRST TRUE POST-SCARCITY SOCIETY.
HELMS SCHOLAR DANDLO...
WHAT HAPPENS WHEN THE SUN EATS THE EARTH?
THE SUN MAKES US STRONGER.
WE DO NOT WITHER, BUT EVOLVE BECAUSE OF IT.
BY THE TIME IT CONSUMES THIS ROCK, WE WILL HAVE FURTHERED OUR GROWTH AND SPREAD ACROSS THE COSMOS...
...AS GODS.
FOLLOWING THE LIGHT OF THE LAST HELMS KING--WHOSE LINE HAS LED US FOR MILLENNIA--WE BURNT OF THE BLACK DOME MUST FIRST REPOPULATE.

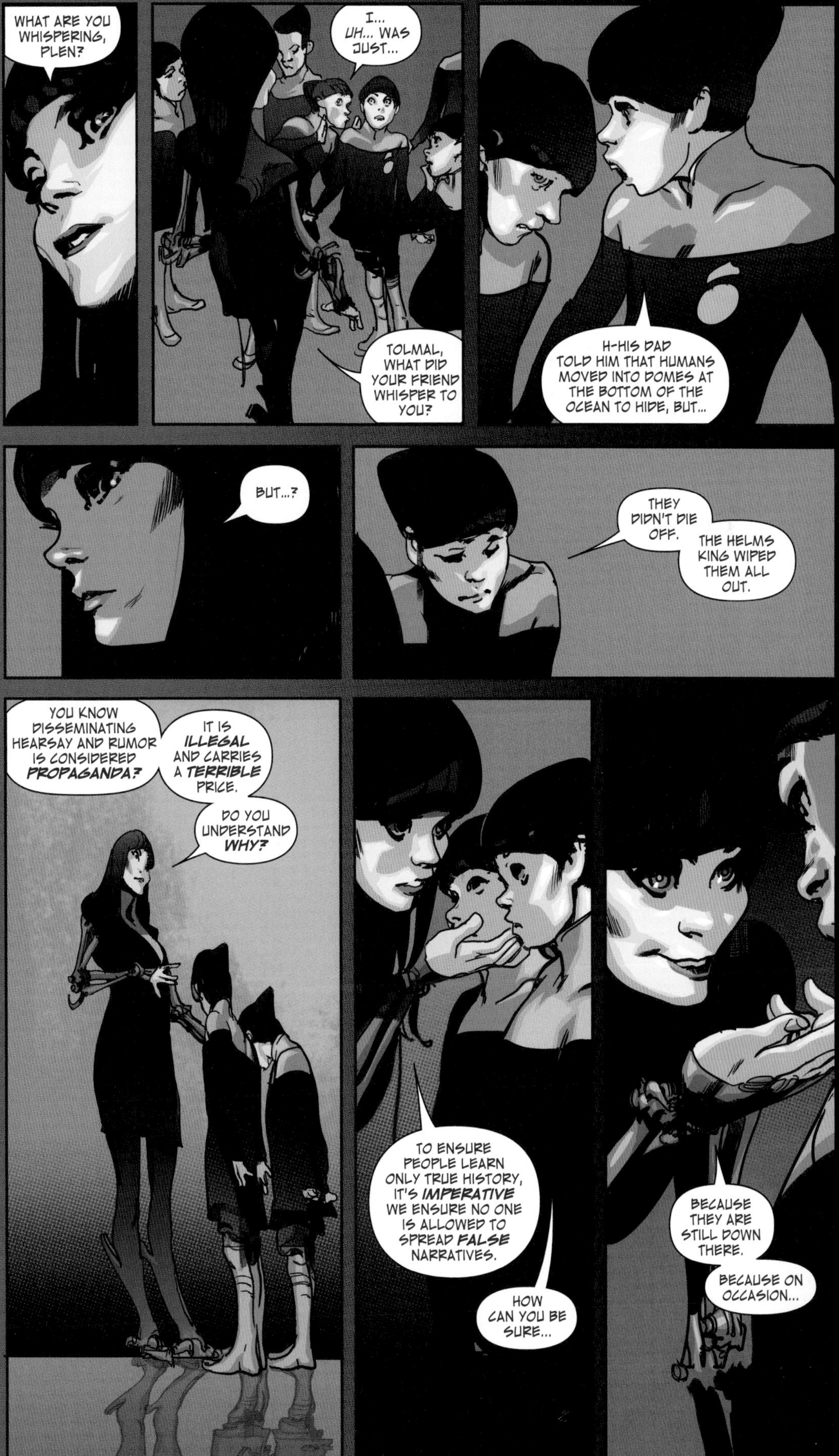
WHAT ARE YOU WHISPERING, PLEN?
I... UH... WAS JUST...
TOLMAL, WHAT DID YOUR FRIEND WHISPER TO YOU?
H-HIS DAD TOLD HIM THAT HUMANS MOVED INTO DOMES AT THE BOTTOM OF THE OCEAN TO HIDE, BUT...
BUT...?
THEY DIDN'T DIE OFF.
THE HELMS KING WIPED THEM ALL OUT.
YOU KNOW DISSEMINATING HEARSAY AND RUMOR IS CONSIDERED PROPAGANDA?
IT IS ILLEGAL AND CARRIES A TERRIBLE PRICE.
DO YOU UNDERSTAND WHY?
TO ENSURE PEOPLE LEARN ONLY TRUE HISTORY, IT'S IMPERATIVE WE ENSURE NO ONE IS ALLOWED TO SPREAD FALSE NARRATIVES.
HOW CAN YOU BE SURE...
BECAUSE THEY ARE STILL DOWN THERE.
BECAUSE ON OCCASION...

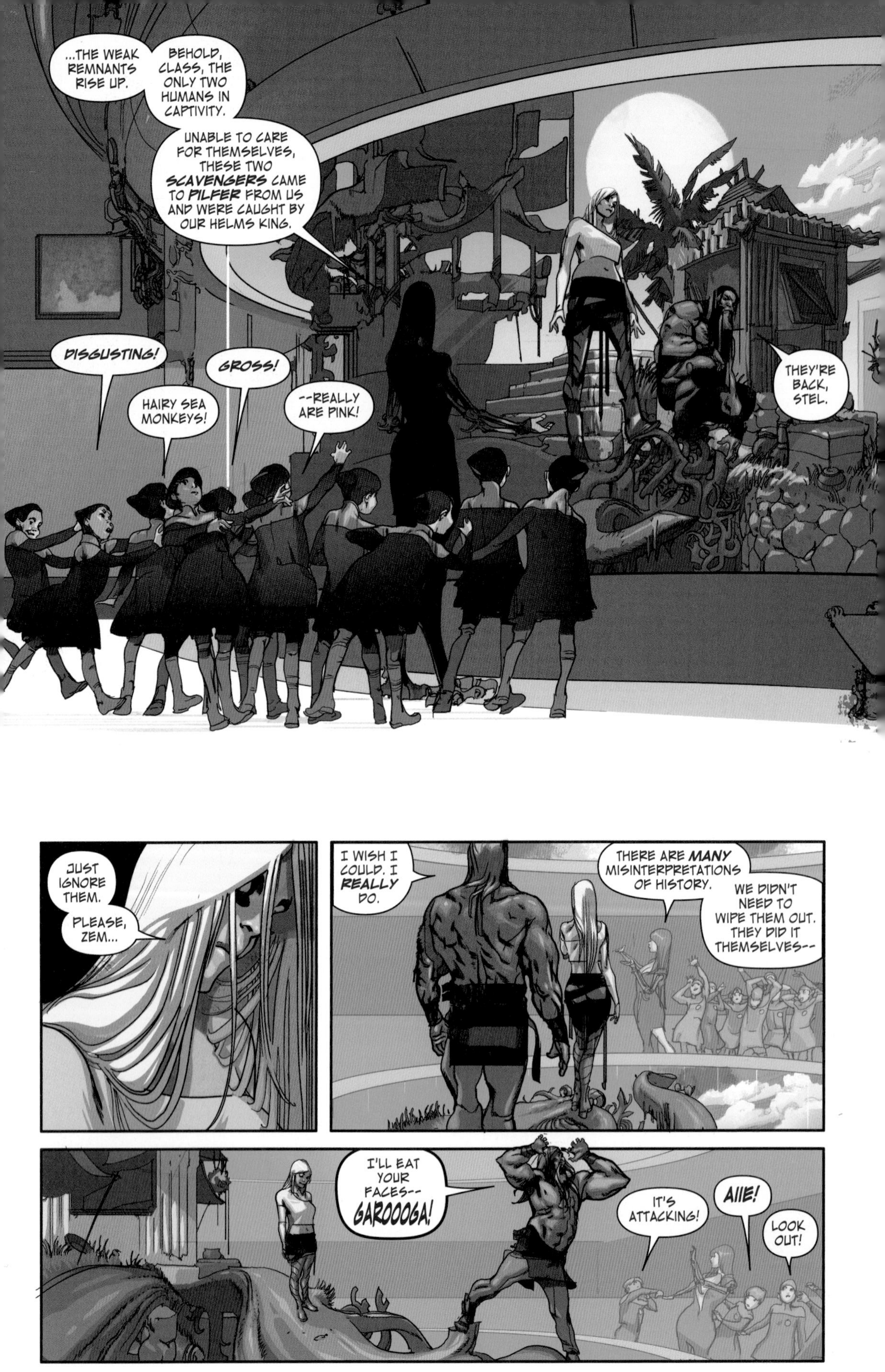
...THE WEAK REMNANTS RISE UP.
BEHOLD, CLASS, THE ONLY TWO HUMANS IN CAPTIVITY.
UNABLE TO CARE FOR THEMSELVES, THESE TWO SCAVENGERS CAME TO PILFER FROM US AND WERE CAUGHT BY OUR HELMS KING.
DISGUSTING!
HAIRY SEA MONKEYS!
GROSS!
--REALLY ARE PINK!
THEY'RE BACK, STEL.
JUST IGNORE THEM.
PLEASE, ZEM...
I WISH I COULD. I REALLY DO.
THERE ARE MANY MISINTERPRETATIONS OF HISTORY.
WE DIDN'T NEED TO WIPE THEM OUT. THEY DID IT THEMSELVES--
I'LL EAT YOUR FACES-- GAROOOGA!
IT'S ATTACKING!
AIIE!
LOOK OUT!

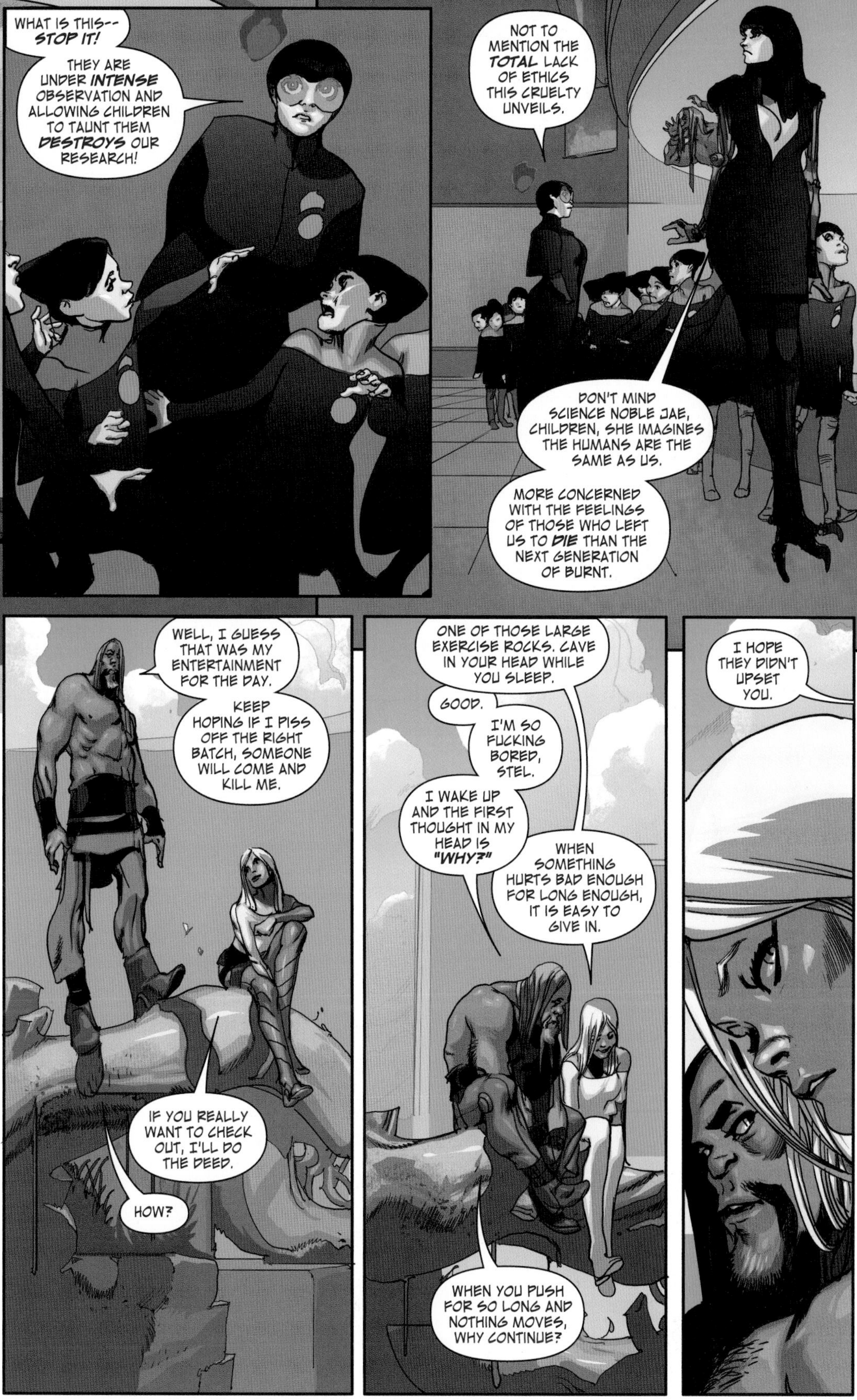
WHAT IS THIS-- STOP IT!
THEY ARE UNDER INTENSE OBSERVATION AND ALLOWING CHILDREN TO TAUNT THEM DESTROYS OUR RESEARCH!
NOT TO MENTION THE TOTAL LACK OF ETHICS THIS CRUELTY UNVEILS.
DON'T MIND SCIENCE NOBLE JAE, CHILDREN, SHE IMAGINES THE HUMANS ARE THE SAME AS US.
MORE CONCERNED WITH THE FEELINGS OF THOSE WHO LEFT US TO DIE THAN THE NEXT GENERATION OF BURNT.
WELL, I GUESS THAT WAS MY ENTERTAINMENT FOR THE DAY.
KEEP HOPING IF I PISS OFF THE RIGHT BATCH, SOMEONE WILL COME AND KILL ME.
IF YOU REALLY WANT TO CHECK OUT, I'LL DO THE DEED.
HOW?
ONE OF THOSE LARGE EXERCISE ROCKS. CAVE IN YOUR HEAD WHILE YOU SLEEP.
GOOD.
I'M SO FUCKING BORED, STEL.
I WAKE UP AND THE FIRST THOUGHT IN MY HEAD IS "WHY?"
WHEN SOMETHING HURTS BAD ENOUGH FOR LONG ENOUGH, IT IS EASY TO GIVE IN.
WHEN YOU PUSH FOR SO LONG AND NOTHING MOVES, WHY CONTINUE?
I HOPE THEY DIDN'T UPSET YOU.

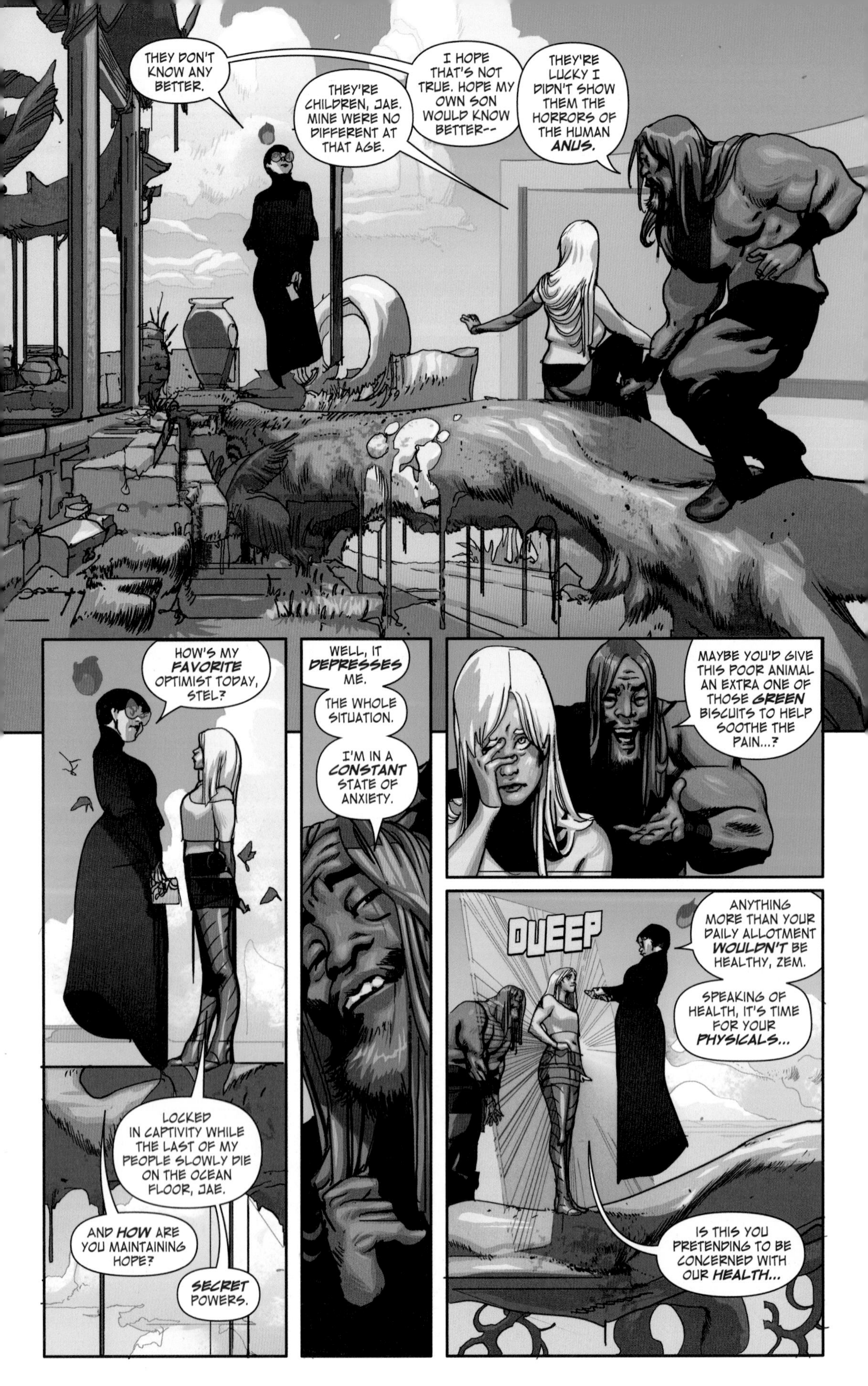
THEY DON'T KNOW ANY BETTER.
THEY'RE CHILDREN, JAE. MINE WERE NO DIFFERENT AT THAT AGE.
I HOPE THAT'S NOT TRUE. HOPE MY OWN SON WOULD KNOW BETTER--
THEY'RE LUCKY I DIDN'T SHOW THEM THE HORRORS OF THE HUMAN ANUS.
HOW'S MY FAVORITE OPTIMIST TODAY, STEL?
LOCKED IN CAPTIVITY WHILE THE LAST OF MY PEOPLE SLOWLY DIE ON THE OCEAN FLOOR, JAE.
AND HOW ARE YOU MAINTAINING HOPE?
SECRET POWERS.
WELL, IT DEPRESSES ME.
THE WHOLE SITUATION.
I'M IN A CONSTANT STATE OF ANXIETY.
MAYBE YOU'D GIVE THIS POOR ANIMAL AN EXTRA ONE OF THOSE GREEN BISCUITS TO HELP SOOTHE THE PAIN...?
DUEEP
ANYTHING MORE THAN YOUR DAILY ALLOTMENT WOULDN'T BE HEALTHY, ZEM.
SPEAKING OF HEALTH, IT'S TIME FOR YOUR PHYSICALS...
IS THIS YOU PRETENDING TO BE CONCERNED WITH OUR HEALTH...

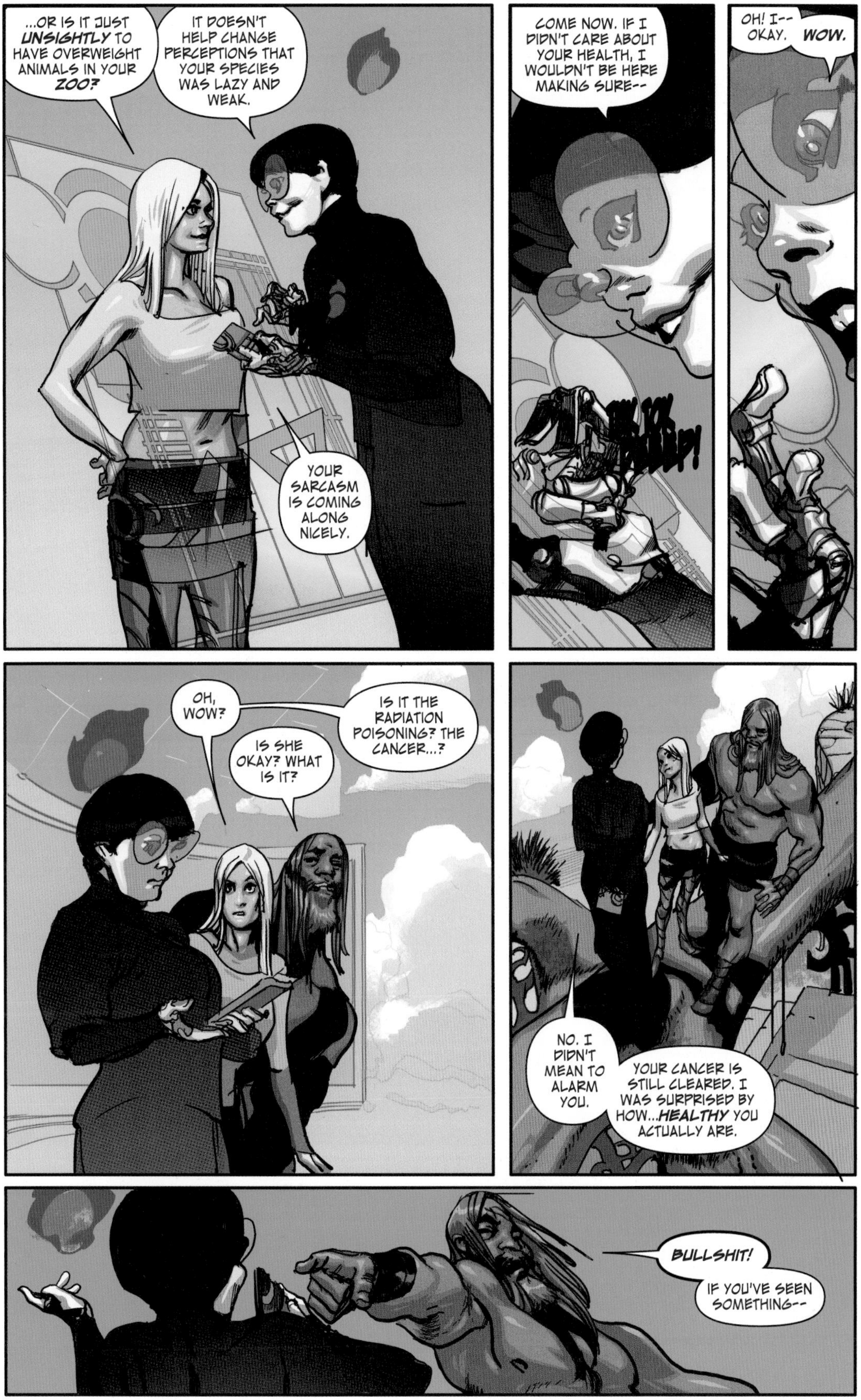

...OR IS IT JUST *UNSIGHTLY* TO HAVE OVERWEIGHT ANIMALS IN YOUR *ZOO?*
IT DOESN'T HELP CHANGE PERCEPTIONS THAT YOUR SPECIES WAS LAZY AND WEAK.
YOUR SARCASM IS COMING ALONG NICELY.
COME NOW. IF I DIDN'T CARE ABOUT YOUR HEALTH, I WOULDN'T BE HERE MAKING SURE--
OH! I-- OKAY.
WOW.
OH, WOW?
IS SHE OKAY? WHAT IS IT?
IS IT THE RADIATION POISONING? THE CANCER...?
NO. I DIDN'T MEAN TO ALARM YOU.
YOUR CANCER IS STILL CLEARED. I WAS SURPRISED BY HOW...*HEALTHY* YOU ACTUALLY ARE.
BULLSHIT!
IF YOU'VE SEEN SOMETHING--

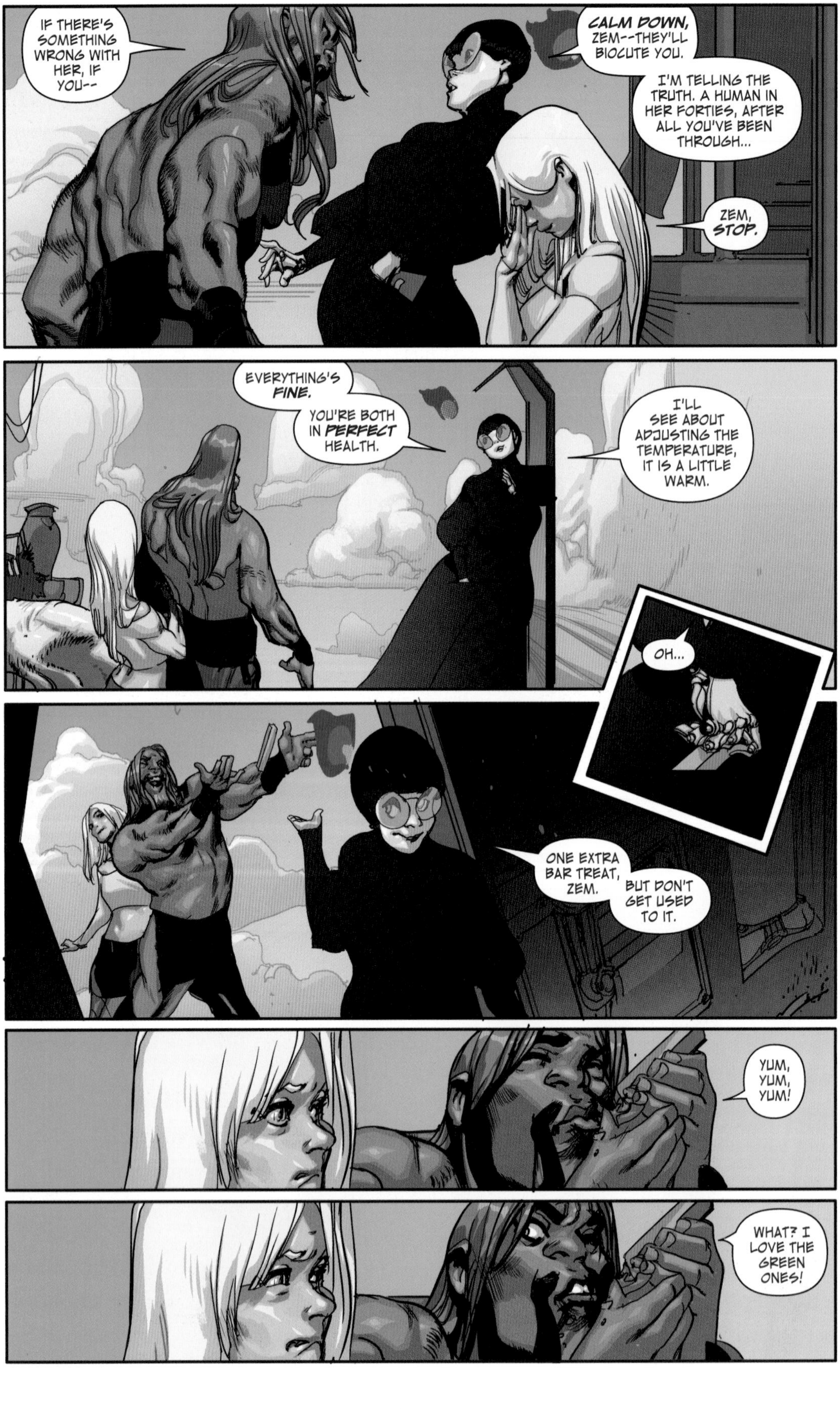
IF THERE'S SOMETHING WRONG WITH HER, IF YOU--
CALM DOWN, ZEM--THEY'LL BIOCUTE YOU.
I'M TELLING THE TRUTH. A HUMAN IN HER FORTIES, AFTER ALL YOU'VE BEEN THROUGH...
ZEM, STOP.
EVERYTHING'S FINE.
YOU'RE BOTH IN PERFECT HEALTH.
I'LL SEE ABOUT ADJUSTING THE TEMPERATURE, IT IS A LITTLE WARM.
OH...
ONE EXTRA BAR TREAT, ZEM.
BUT DON'T GET USED TO IT.
YUM, YUM, YUM!
WHAT? I LOVE THE GREEN ONES!

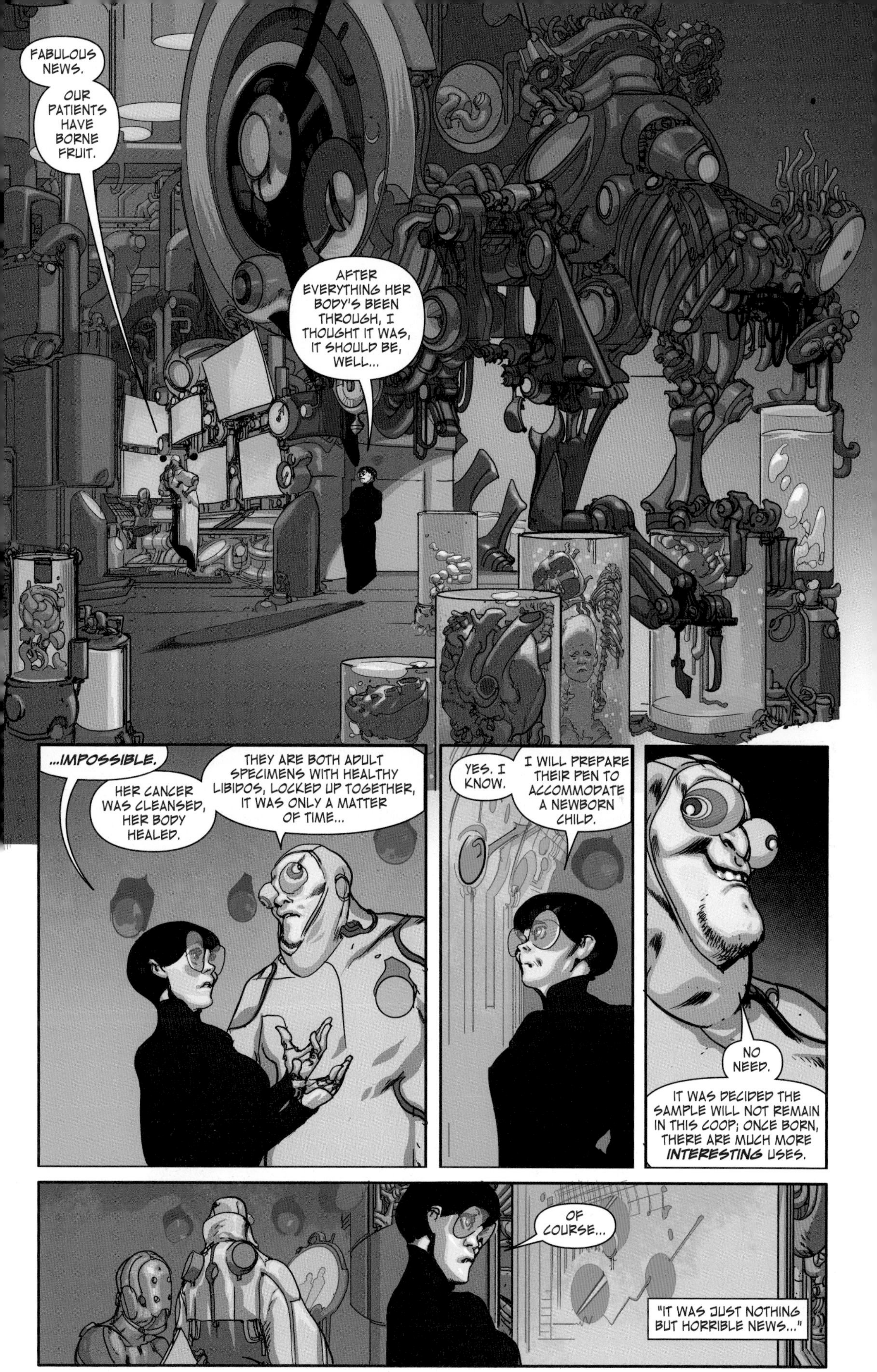
FABULOUS NEWS.
OUR PATIENTS HAVE BORNE FRUIT.
AFTER EVERYTHING HER BODY'S BEEN THROUGH, I THOUGHT IT WAS, IT SHOULD BE, WELL...
...IMPOSSIBLE.
HER CANCER WAS CLEANSED, HER BODY HEALED.
THEY ARE BOTH ADULT SPECIMENS WITH HEALTHY LIBIDOS, LOCKED UP TOGETHER, IT WAS ONLY A MATTER OF TIME...
YES. I KNOW.
I WILL PREPARE THEIR PEN TO ACCOMMODATE A NEWBORN CHILD.
NO NEED.
IT WAS DECIDED THE SAMPLE WILL NOT REMAIN IN THIS COOP; ONCE BORN, THERE ARE MUCH MORE INTERESTING USES.
OF COURSE...
"IT WAS JUST NOTHING BUT HORRIBLE NEWS..."

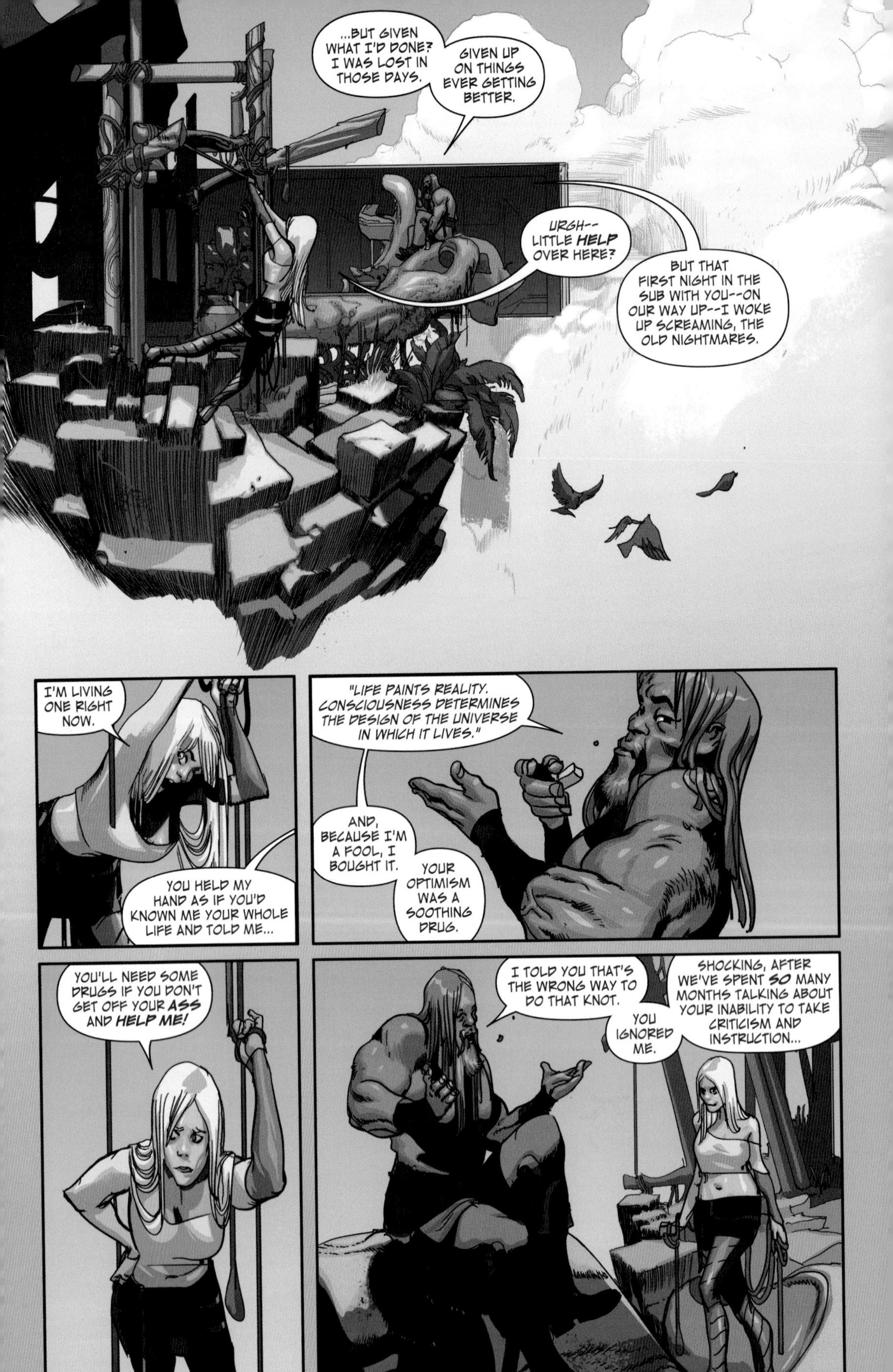
...BUT GIVEN WHAT I'D DONE? I WAS LOST IN THOSE DAYS.
GIVEN UP ON THINGS EVER GETTING BETTER.
URGH-- LITTLE HELP OVER HERE?
BUT THAT FIRST NIGHT IN THE SUB WITH YOU--ON OUR WAY UP--I WOKE UP SCREAMING, THE OLD NIGHTMARES.
I'M LIVING ONE RIGHT NOW.
YOU HELD MY HAND AS IF YOU'D KNOWN ME YOUR WHOLE LIFE AND TOLD ME...
"LIFE PAINTS REALITY. CONSCIOUSNESS DETERMINES THE DESIGN OF THE UNIVERSE IN WHICH IT LIVES."
AND, BECAUSE I'M A FOOL, I BOUGHT IT.
YOUR OPTIMISM WAS A SOOTHING DRUG.
YOU'LL NEED SOME DRUGS IF YOU DON'T GET OFF YOUR ASS AND HELP ME!
I TOLD YOU THAT'S THE WRONG WAY TO DO THAT KNOT.
YOU IGNORED ME.
SHOCKING, AFTER WE'VE SPENT SO MANY MONTHS TALKING ABOUT YOUR INABILITY TO TAKE CRITICISM AND INSTRUCTION...

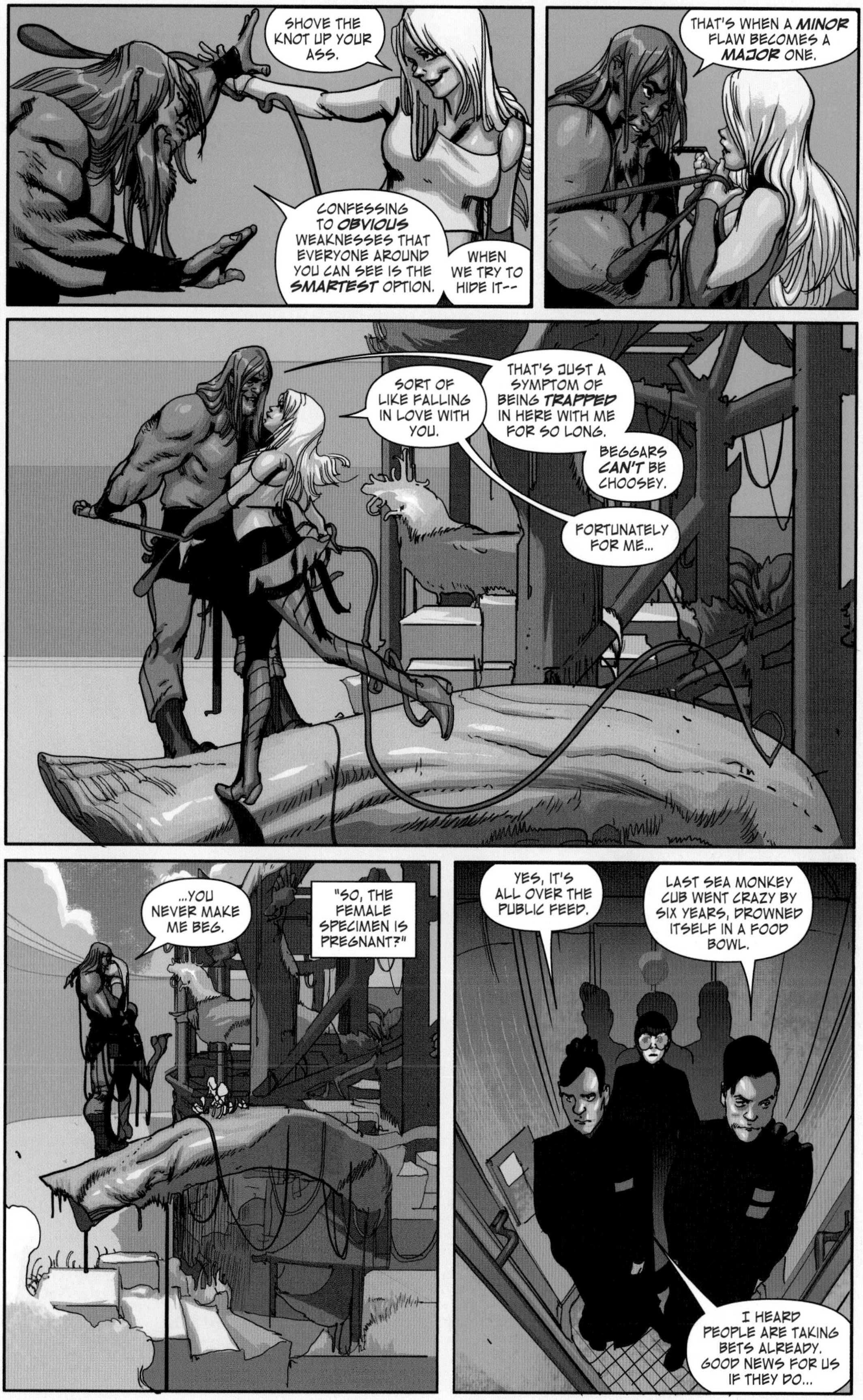
SHOVE THE KNOT UP YOUR ASS.
CONFESSING TO OBVIOUS WEAKNESSES THAT EVERYONE AROUND YOU CAN SEE IS THE SMARTEST OPTION.
WHEN WE TRY TO HIDE IT--
THAT'S WHEN A MINOR FLAW BECOMES A MAJOR ONE.
SORT OF LIKE FALLING IN LOVE WITH YOU.
THAT'S JUST A SYMPTOM OF BEING TRAPPED IN HERE WITH ME FOR SO LONG.
BEGGARS CAN'T BE CHOOSEY.
FORTUNATELY FOR ME...
...YOU NEVER MAKE ME BEG.
"SO, THE FEMALE SPECIMEN IS PREGNANT?"
YES, IT'S ALL OVER THE PUBLIC FEED.
LAST SEA MONKEY CUB WENT CRAZY BY SIX YEARS, DROWNED ITSELF IN A FOOD BOWL.
I HEARD PEOPLE ARE TAKING BETS ALREADY. GOOD NEWS FOR US IF THEY DO...

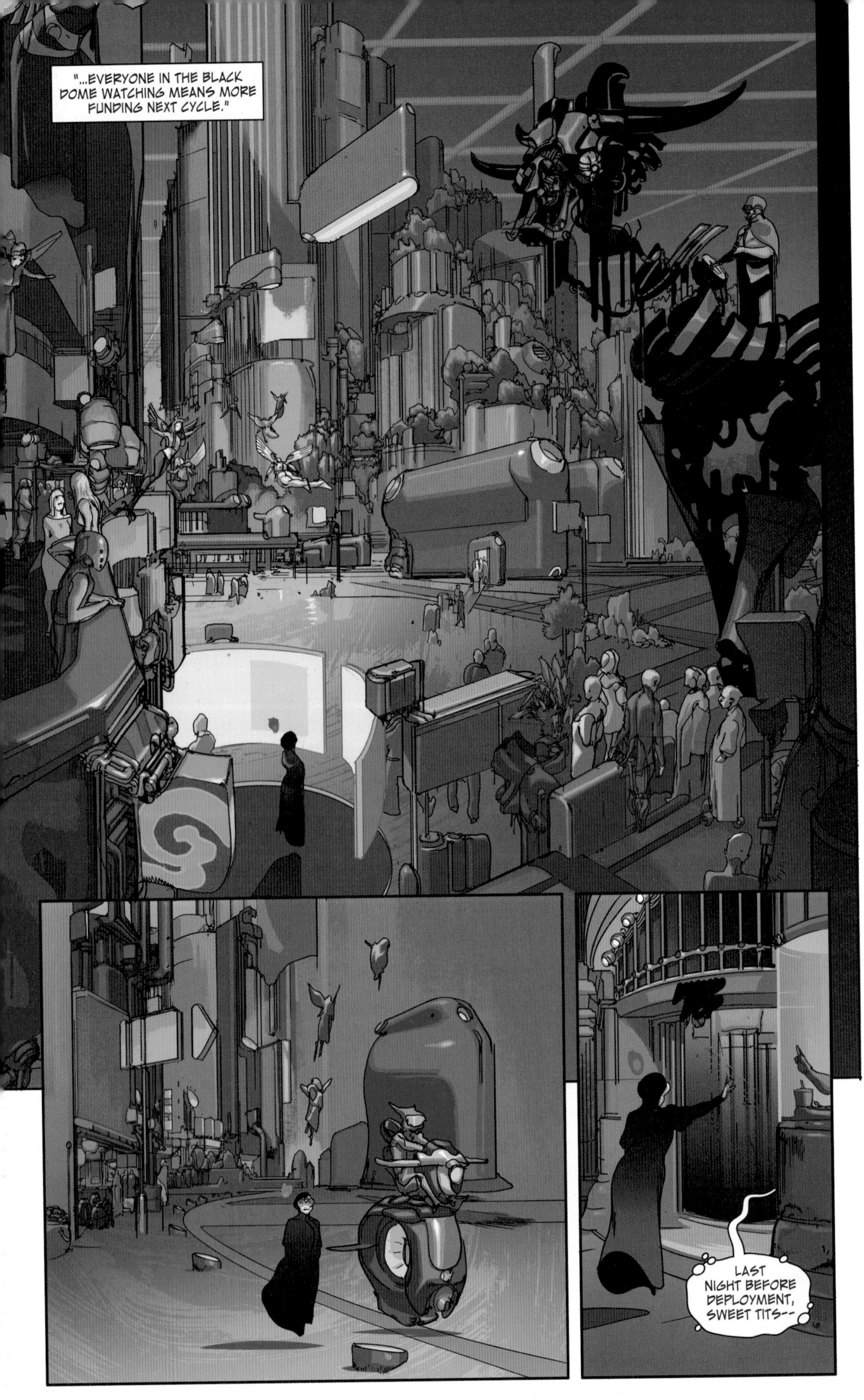
"...EVERYONE IN THE BLACK DOME WATCHING MEANS MORE FUNDING NEXT CYCLE."
LAST NIGHT BEFORE DEPLOYMENT, SWEET TITS--

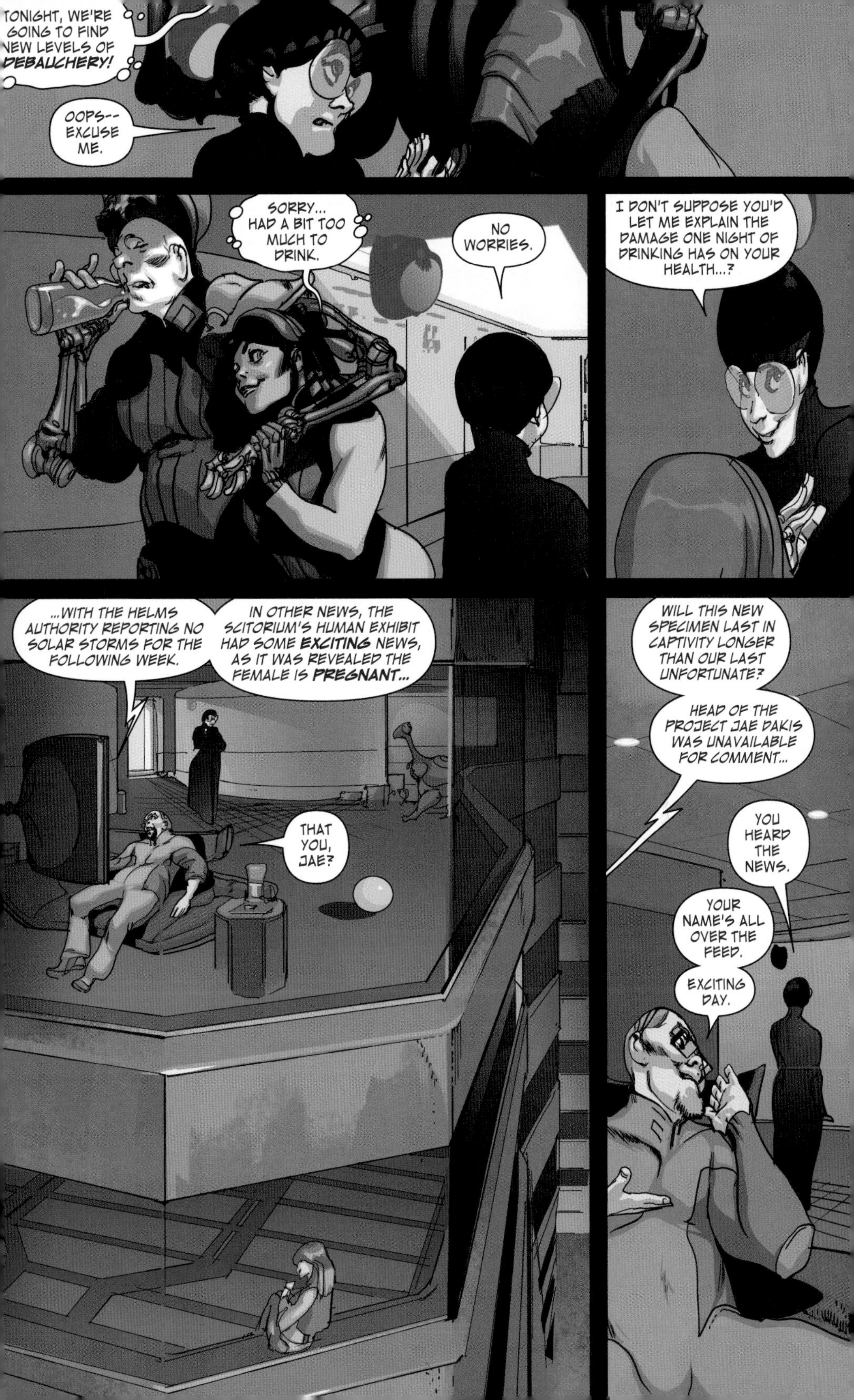
TONIGHT, WE'RE GOING TO FIND NEW LEVELS OF DEBAUCHERY!
OOPS-- EXCUSE ME.
SORRY... HAD A BIT TOO MUCH TO DRINK.
NO WORRIES.
I DON'T SUPPOSE YOU'D LET ME EXPLAIN THE DAMAGE ONE NIGHT OF DRINKING HAS ON YOUR HEALTH...?
...WITH THE HELMS AUTHORITY REPORTING NO SOLAR STORMS FOR THE FOLLOWING WEEK.
IN OTHER NEWS, THE SCITORIUM'S HUMAN EXHIBIT HAD SOME EXCITING NEWS, AS IT WAS REVEALED THE FEMALE IS PREGNANT...
THAT YOU, JAE?
WILL THIS NEW SPECIMEN LAST IN CAPTIVITY LONGER THAN OUR LAST UNFORTUNATE?
HEAD OF THE PROJECT JAE DAKIS WAS UNAVAILABLE FOR COMMENT...
YOU HEARD THE NEWS.
YOUR NAME'S ALL OVER THE FEED.
EXCITING DAY.

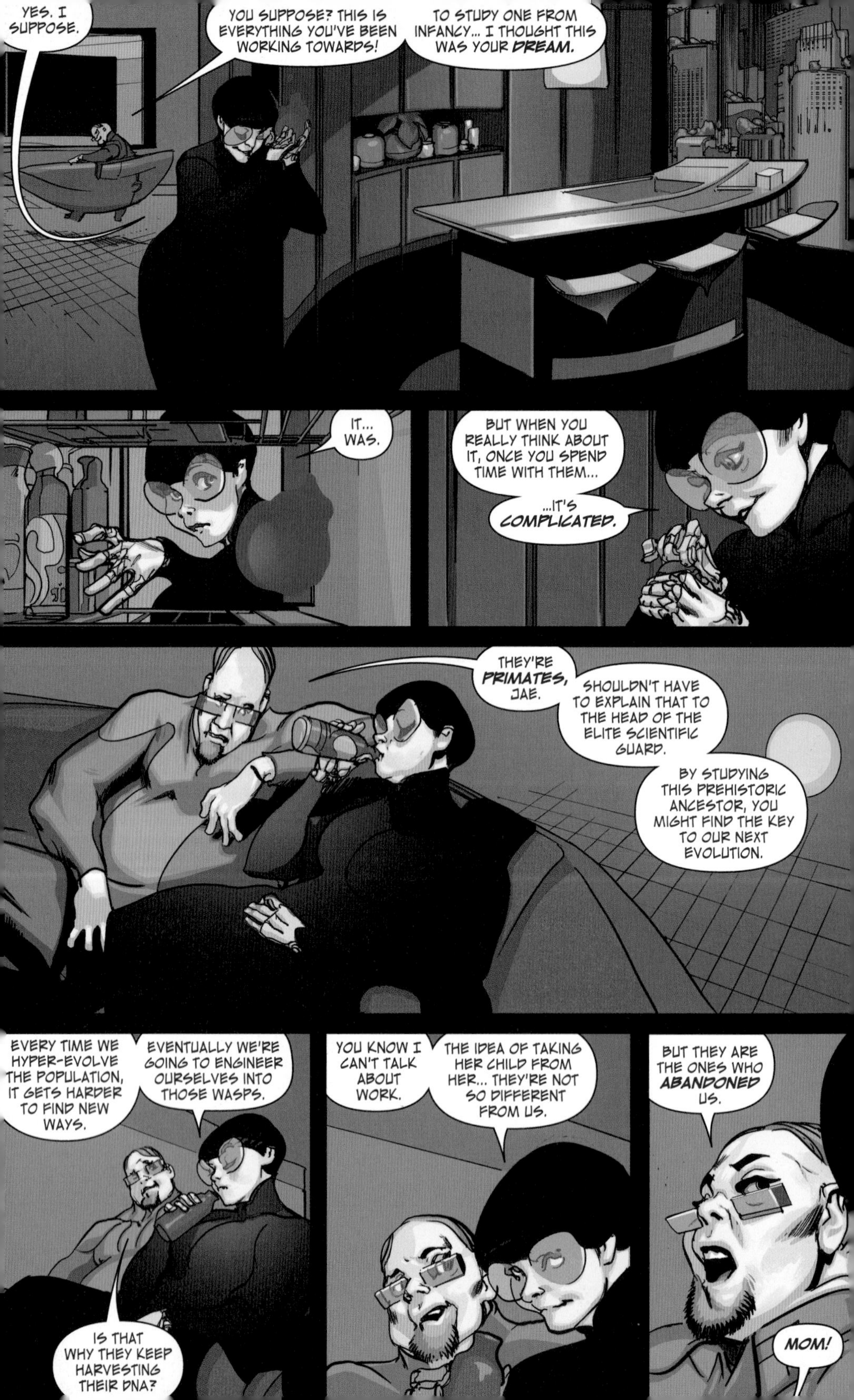
YES. I SUPPOSE.
YOU SUPPOSE? THIS IS EVERYTHING YOU'VE BEEN WORKING TOWARDS!
TO STUDY ONE FROM INFANCY... I THOUGHT THIS WAS YOUR DREAM.
IT... WAS.
BUT WHEN YOU REALLY THINK ABOUT IT, ONCE YOU SPEND TIME WITH THEM...
...IT'S COMPLICATED.
THEY'RE PRIMATES, JAE.
SHOULDN'T HAVE TO EXPLAIN THAT TO THE HEAD OF THE ELITE SCIENTIFIC GUARD.
BY STUDYING THIS PREHISTORIC ANCESTOR, YOU MIGHT FIND THE KEY TO OUR NEXT EVOLUTION.
EVERY TIME WE HYPER-EVOLVE THE POPULATION, IT GETS HARDER TO FIND NEW WAYS.
EVENTUALLY WE'RE GOING TO ENGINEER OURSELVES INTO THOSE WASPS.
IS THAT WHY THEY KEEP HARVESTING THEIR DNA?
YOU KNOW I CAN'T TALK ABOUT WORK.
THE IDEA OF TAKING HER CHILD FROM HER... THEY'RE NOT SO DIFFERENT FROM US.
BUT THEY ARE THE ONES WHO ABANDONED US.
MOM!

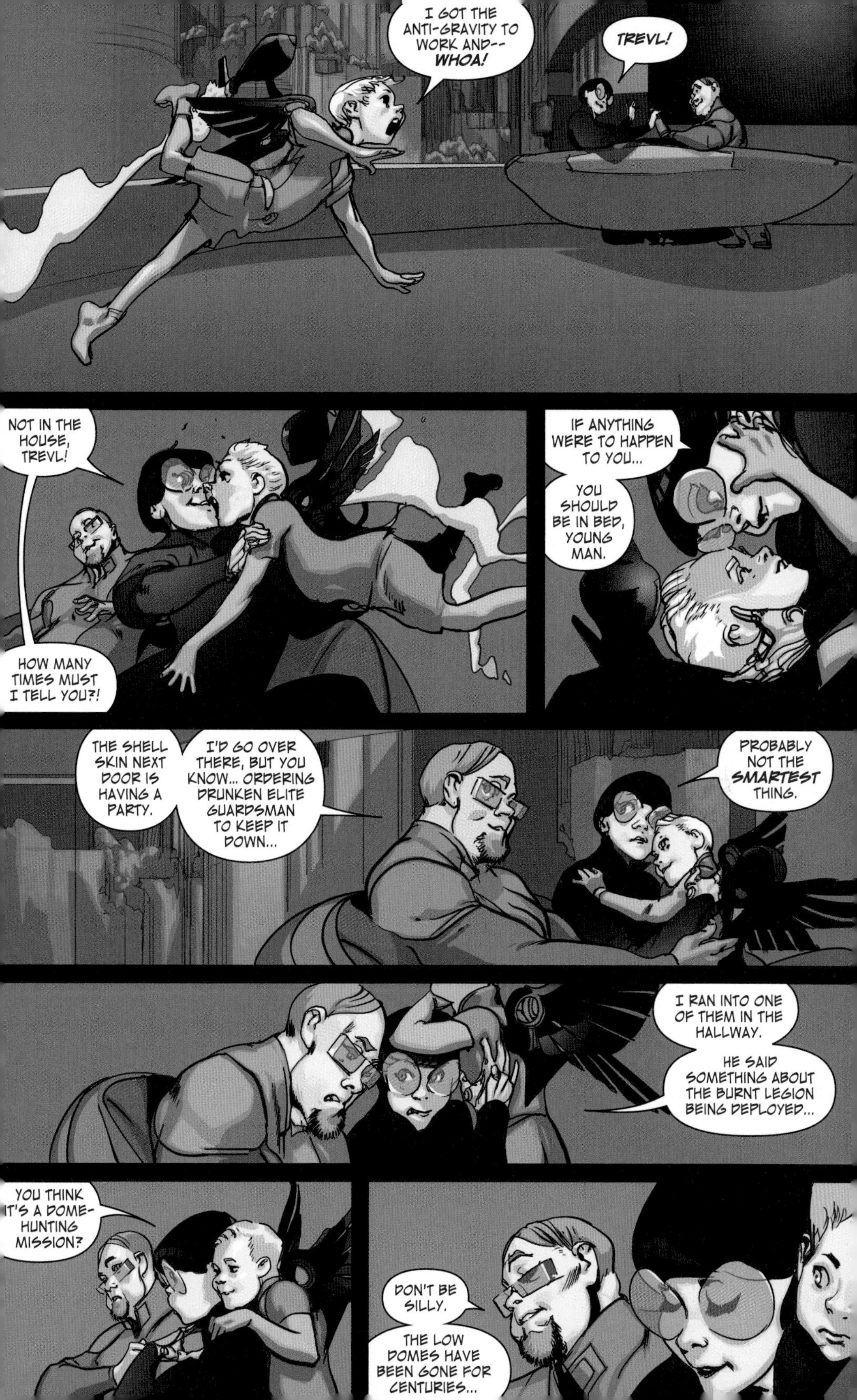
I GOT THE ANTI-GRAVITY TO WORK AND-- WHOA!
TREVL!
NOT IN THE HOUSE, TREVL!
HOW MANY TIMES MUST I TELL YOU?!
IF ANYTHING WERE TO HAPPEN TO YOU...
YOU SHOULD BE IN BED, YOUNG MAN.
THE SHELL SKIN NEXT DOOR IS HAVING A PARTY.
I'D GO OVER THERE, BUT YOU KNOW... ORDERING DRUNKEN ELITE GUARDSMAN TO KEEP IT DOWN...
PROBABLY NOT THE SMARTEST THING.
I RAN INTO ONE OF THEM IN THE HALLWAY.
HE SAID SOMETHING ABOUT THE BURNT LEGION BEING DEPLOYED...
YOU THINK IT'S A DOME-HUNTING MISSION?
DON'T BE SILLY.
THE LOW DOMES HAVE BEEN GONE FOR CENTURIES...

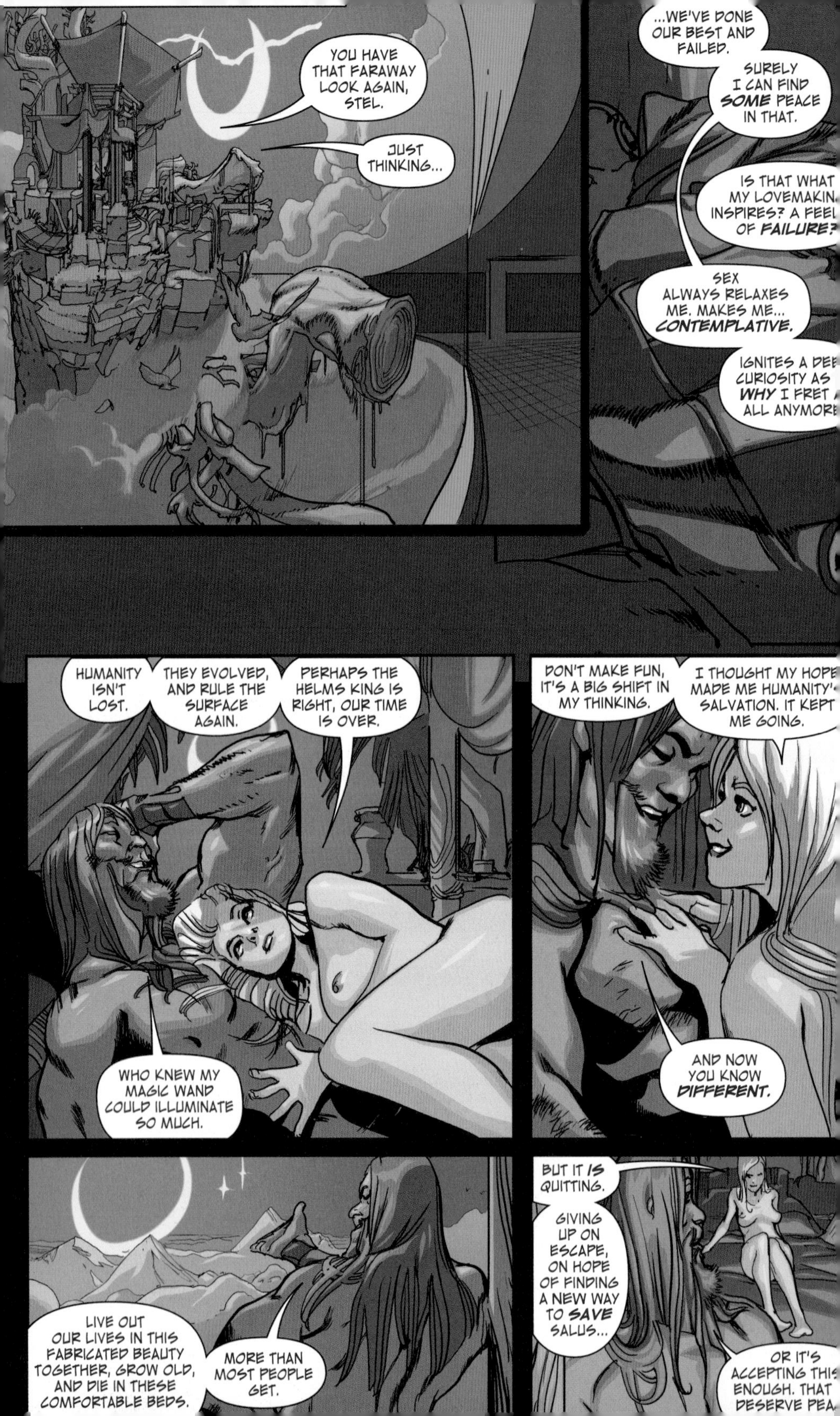

YOU HAVE THAT FARAWAY LOOK AGAIN, STEL.
JUST THINKING...
...WE'VE DONE OUR BEST AND FAILED.
SURELY I CAN FIND SOME PEACE IN THAT.
IS THAT WHAT MY LOVEMAKIN INSPIRES? A FEEL OF FAILURE?
SEX ALWAYS RELAXES ME. MAKES ME... CONTEMPLATIVE.
IGNITES A DEE CURIOSITY AS WHY I FRET ALL ANYMORE
HUMANITY ISN'T LOST.
THEY EVOLVED, AND RULE THE SURFACE AGAIN.
PERHAPS THE HELMS KING IS RIGHT, OUR TIME IS OVER.
WHO KNEW MY MAGIC WAND COULD ILLUMINATE SO MUCH.
DON'T MAKE FUN, IT'S A BIG SHIFT IN MY THINKING.
I THOUGHT MY HOPE MADE ME HUMANITY' SALVATION. IT KEPT ME GOING.
AND NOW YOU KNOW DIFFERENT.
LIVE OUT OUR LIVES IN THIS FABRICATED BEAUTY TOGETHER, GROW OLD, AND DIE IN THESE COMFORTABLE BEDS.
MORE THAN MOST PEOPLE GET.
BUT IT IS QUITTING.
GIVING UP ON ESCAPE, ON HOPE OF FINDING A NEW WAY TO SAVE SALUS...
OR IT'S ACCEPTING THIS ENOUGH. THAT DESERVE PEA

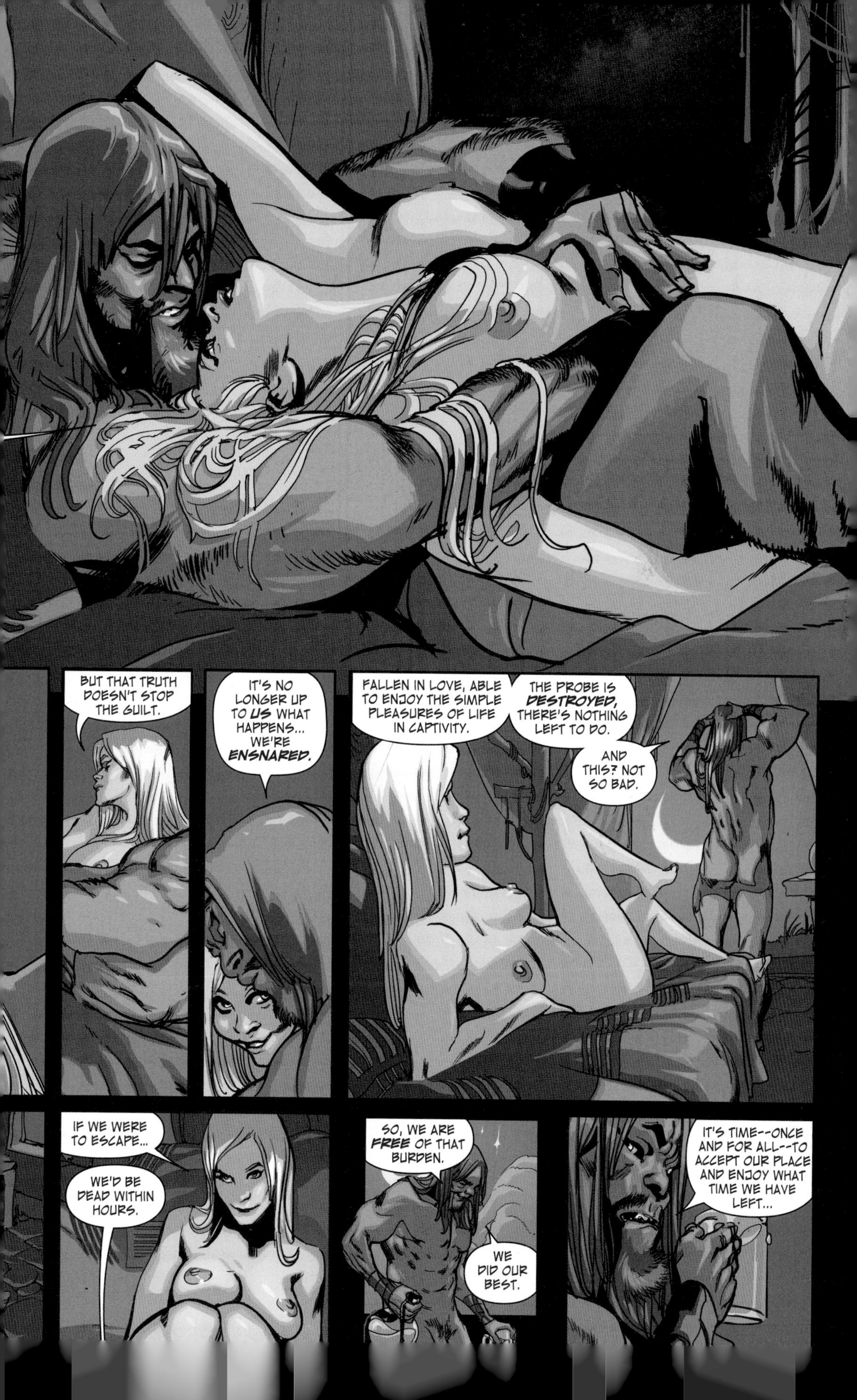

BUT THAT TRUTH DOESN'T STOP THE GUILT.
IT'S NO LONGER UP TO US WHAT HAPPENS... WE'RE ENSNARED.
FALLEN IN LOVE, ABLE TO ENJOY THE SIMPLE PLEASURES OF LIFE IN CAPTIVITY.
THE PROBE IS DESTROYED, THERE'S NOTHING LEFT TO DO.
AND THIS? NOT SO BAD.
IF WE WERE TO ESCAPE...
WE'D BE DEAD WITHIN HOURS.
SO, WE ARE FREE OF THAT BURDEN.
WE DID OUR BEST.
IT'S TIME--ONCE AND FOR ALL--TO ACCEPT OUR PLACE AND ENJOY WHAT TIME WE HAVE LEFT...

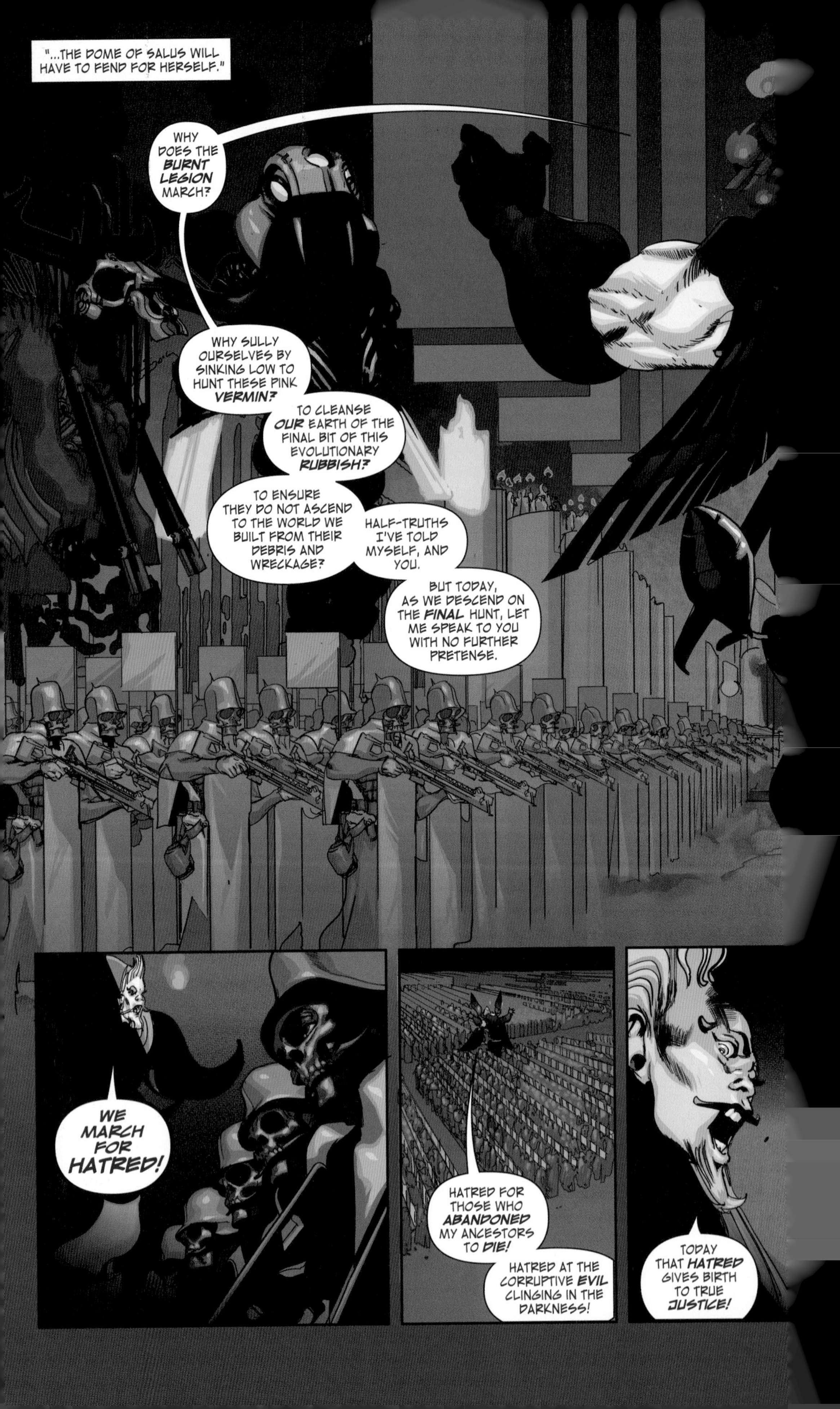
"...THE DOME OF SALUS WILL HAVE TO FEND FOR HERSELF."
WHY DOES THE BURNT LEGION MARCH?
WHY SULLY OURSELVES BY SINKING LOW TO HUNT THESE PINK VERMIN?
TO CLEANSE OUR EARTH OF THE FINAL BIT OF THIS EVOLUTIONARY RUBBISH?
TO ENSURE THEY DO NOT ASCEND TO THE WORLD WE BUILT FROM THEIR DEBRIS AND WRECKAGE?
HALF-TRUTHS I'VE TOLD MYSELF, AND YOU.
BUT TODAY, AS WE DESCEND ON THE FINAL HUNT, LET ME SPEAK TO YOU WITH NO FURTHER PRETENSE.
WE MARCH FOR HATRED!
HATRED FOR THOSE WHO ABANDONED MY ANCESTORS TO DIE!
HATRED AT THE CORRUPTIVE EVIL CLINGING IN THE DARKNESS!
TODAY THAT HATRED GIVES BIRTH TO TRUE JUSTICE!

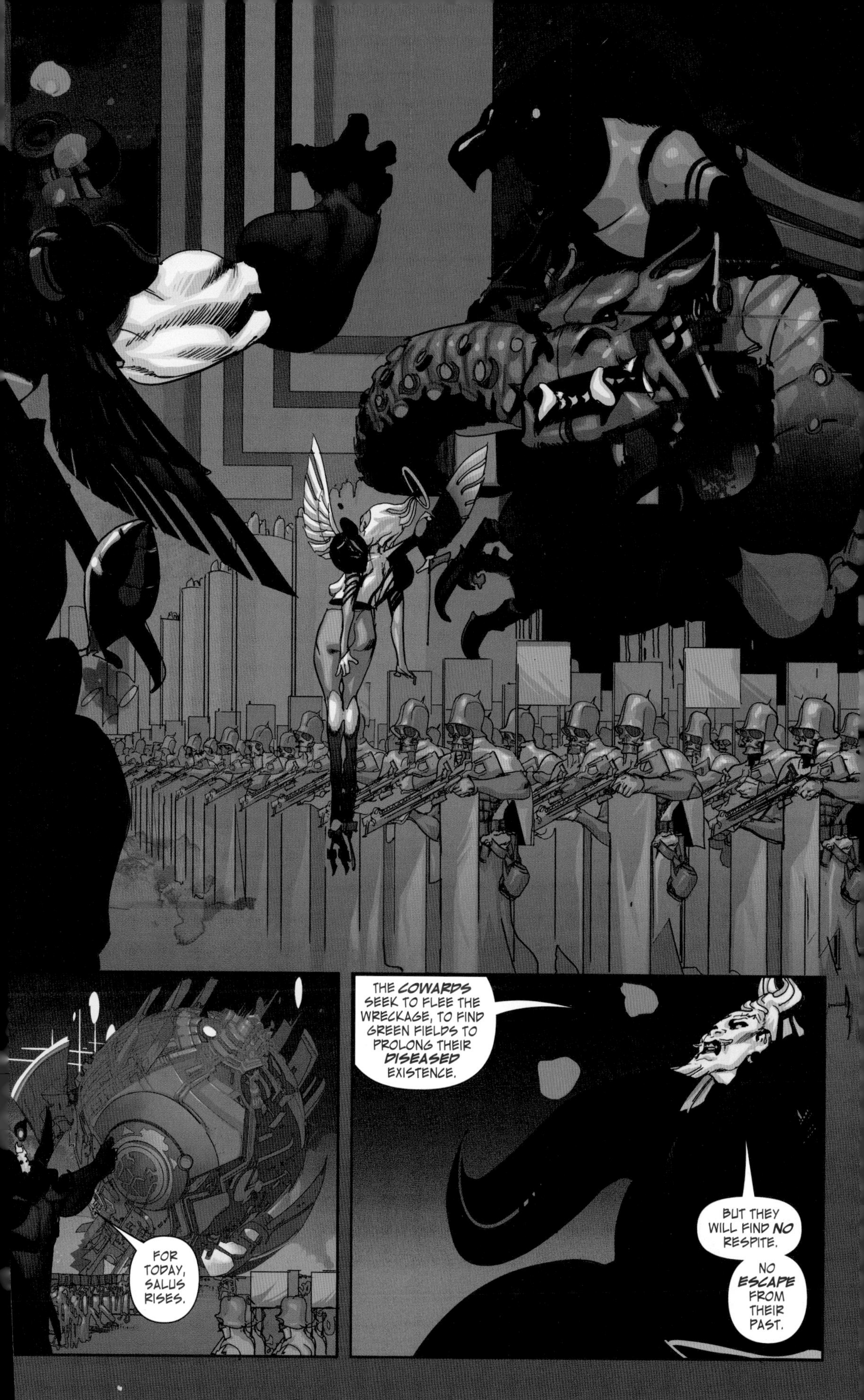
FOR TODAY, SALUS RISES.
THE COWARDS SEEK TO FLEE THE WRECKAGE, TO FIND GREEN FIELDS TO PROLONG THEIR DISEASED EXISTENCE.
BUT THEY WILL FIND NO RESPITE.
NO ESCAPE FROM THEIR PAST.

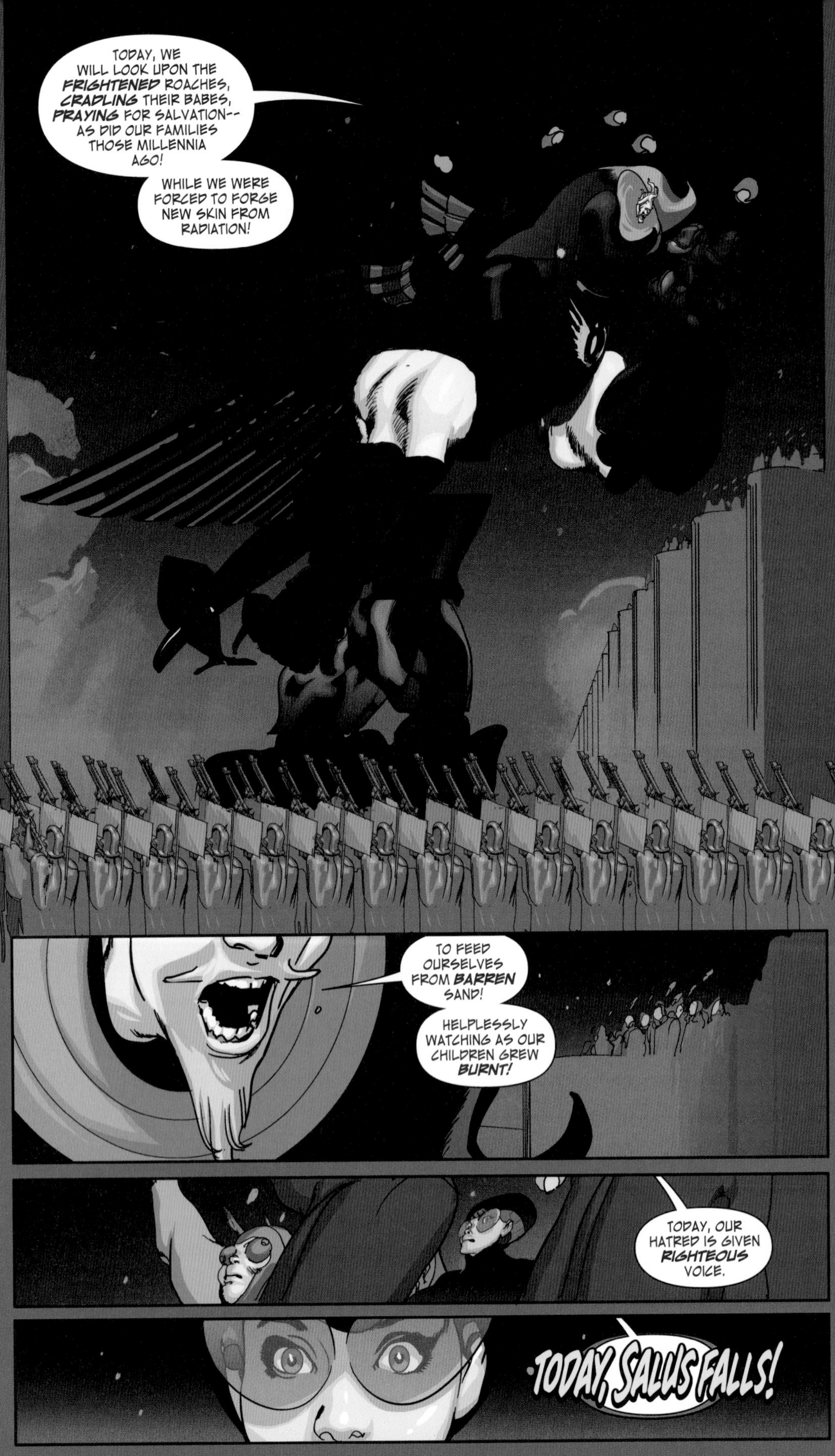

TODAY, WE WILL LOOK UPON THE FRIGHTENED ROACHES, CRADLING THEIR BABES, PRAYING FOR SALVATION-- AS DID OUR FAMILIES THOSE MILLENNIA AGO!
WHILE WE WERE FORCED TO FORGE NEW SKIN FROM RADIATION!
TO FEED OURSELVES FROM BARREN SAND!
HELPLESSLY WATCHING AS OUR CHILDREN GREW BURNT!
TODAY, OUR HATRED IS GIVEN RIGHTEOUS VOICE.
TODAY, SALUS FALLS!

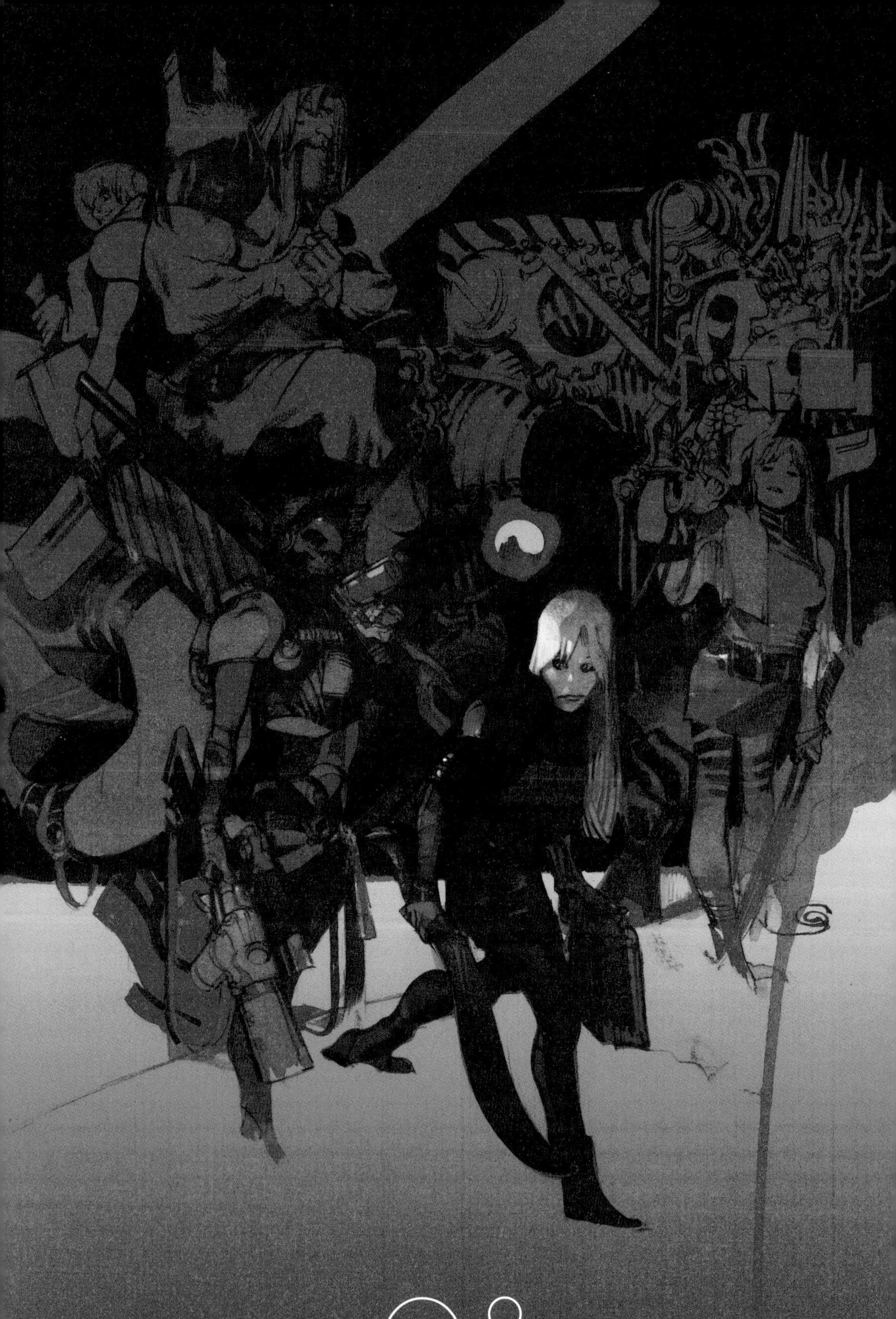

22

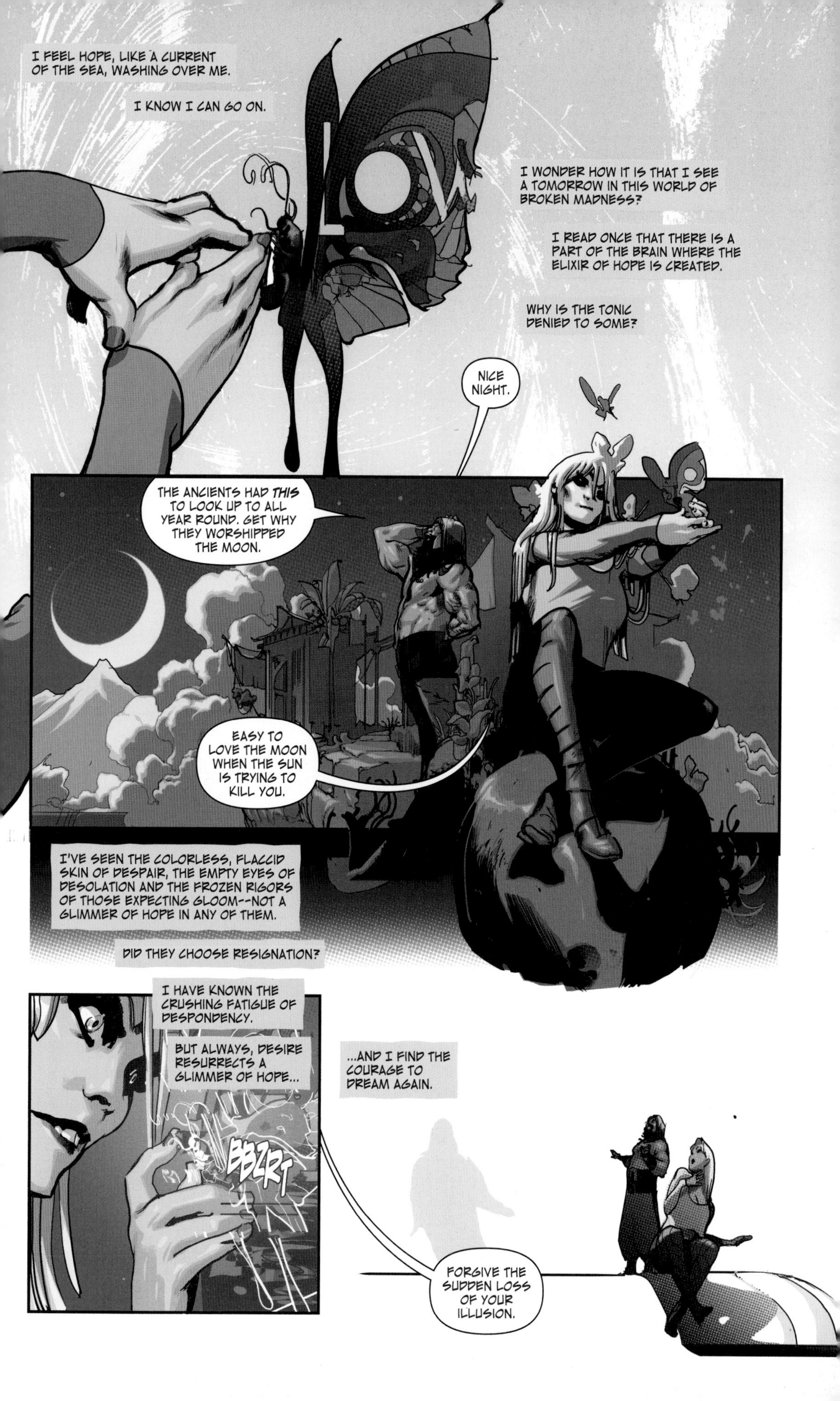
I FEEL HOPE, LIKE A CURRENT OF THE SEA, WASHING OVER ME.
I KNOW I CAN GO ON.
I WONDER HOW IT IS THAT I SEE A TOMORROW IN THIS WORLD OF BROKEN MADNESS?
I READ ONCE THAT THERE IS A PART OF THE BRAIN WHERE THE ELIXIR OF HOPE IS CREATED.
WHY IS THE TONIC DENIED TO SOME?
NICE NIGHT.
THE ANCIENTS HAD *THIS* TO LOOK UP TO ALL YEAR ROUND. GET WHY THEY WORSHIPPED THE MOON.
EASY TO LOVE THE MOON WHEN THE SUN IS TRYING TO KILL YOU.
I'VE SEEN THE COLORLESS, FLACCID SKIN OF DESPAIR, THE EMPTY EYES OF DESOLATION AND THE FROZEN RIGORS OF THOSE EXPECTING GLOOM--NOT A GLIMMER OF HOPE IN ANY OF THEM.
DID THEY CHOOSE RESIGNATION?
I HAVE KNOWN THE CRUSHING FATIGUE OF DESPONDENCY.
BUT ALWAYS, DESIRE RESURRECTS A GLIMMER OF HOPE...
BBZRT
...AND I FIND THE COURAGE TO DREAM AGAIN.
FORGIVE THE SUDDEN LOSS OF YOUR ILLUSION.

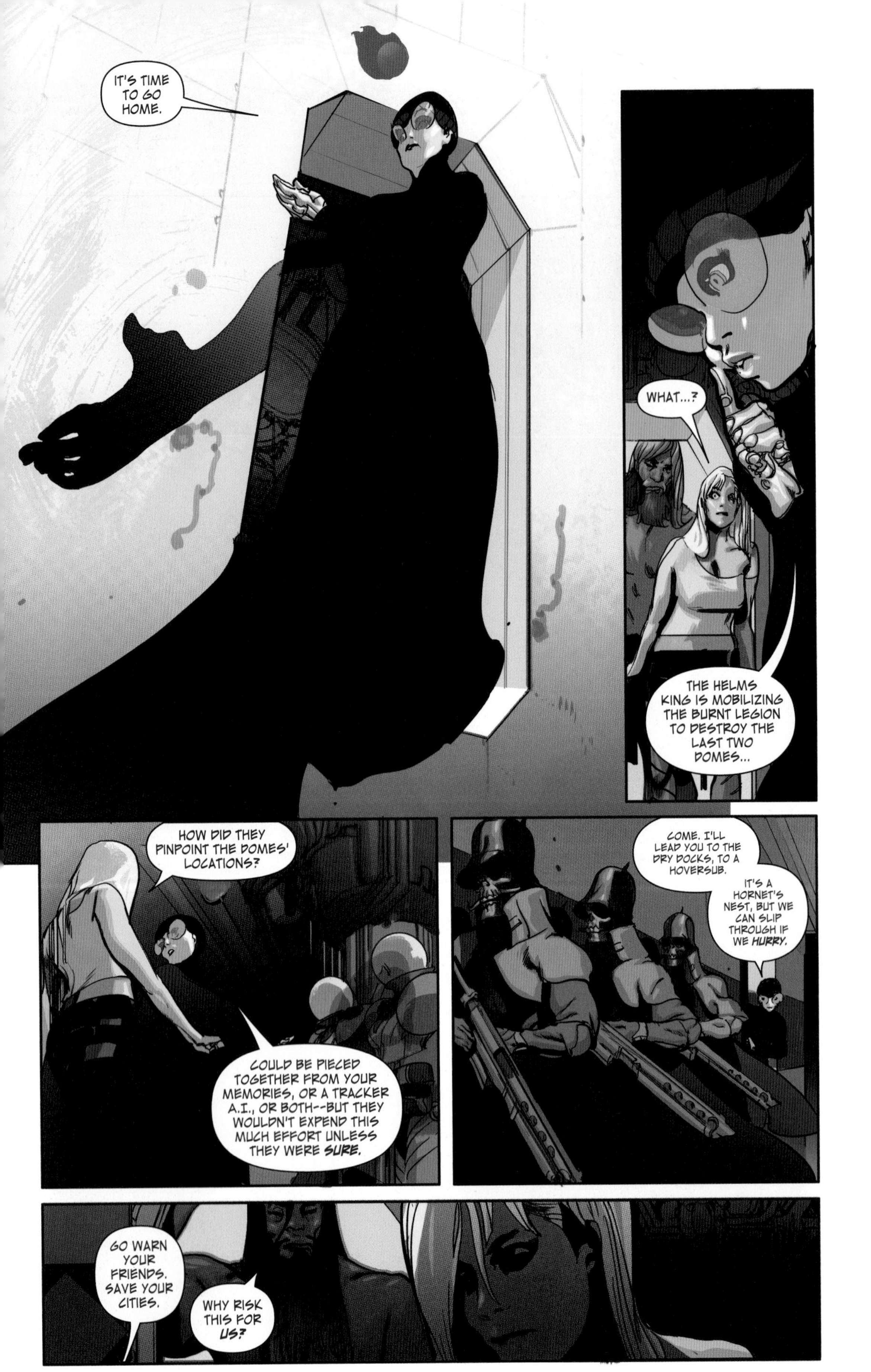
IT'S TIME TO GO HOME.
WHAT...?
THE HELMS KING IS MOBILIZING THE BURNT LEGION TO DESTROY THE LAST TWO DOMES...
HOW DID THEY PINPOINT THE DOMES' LOCATIONS?
COULD BE PIECED TOGETHER FROM YOUR MEMORIES, OR A TRACKER A.I., OR BOTH--BUT THEY WOULDN'T EXPEND THIS MUCH EFFORT UNLESS THEY WERE SURE.
COME. I'LL LEAD YOU TO THE DRY DOCKS, TO A HOVERSUB.
IT'S A HORNET'S NEST, BUT WE CAN SLIP THROUGH IF WE HURRY.
GO WARN YOUR FRIENDS. SAVE YOUR CITIES.
WHY RISK THIS FOR US?

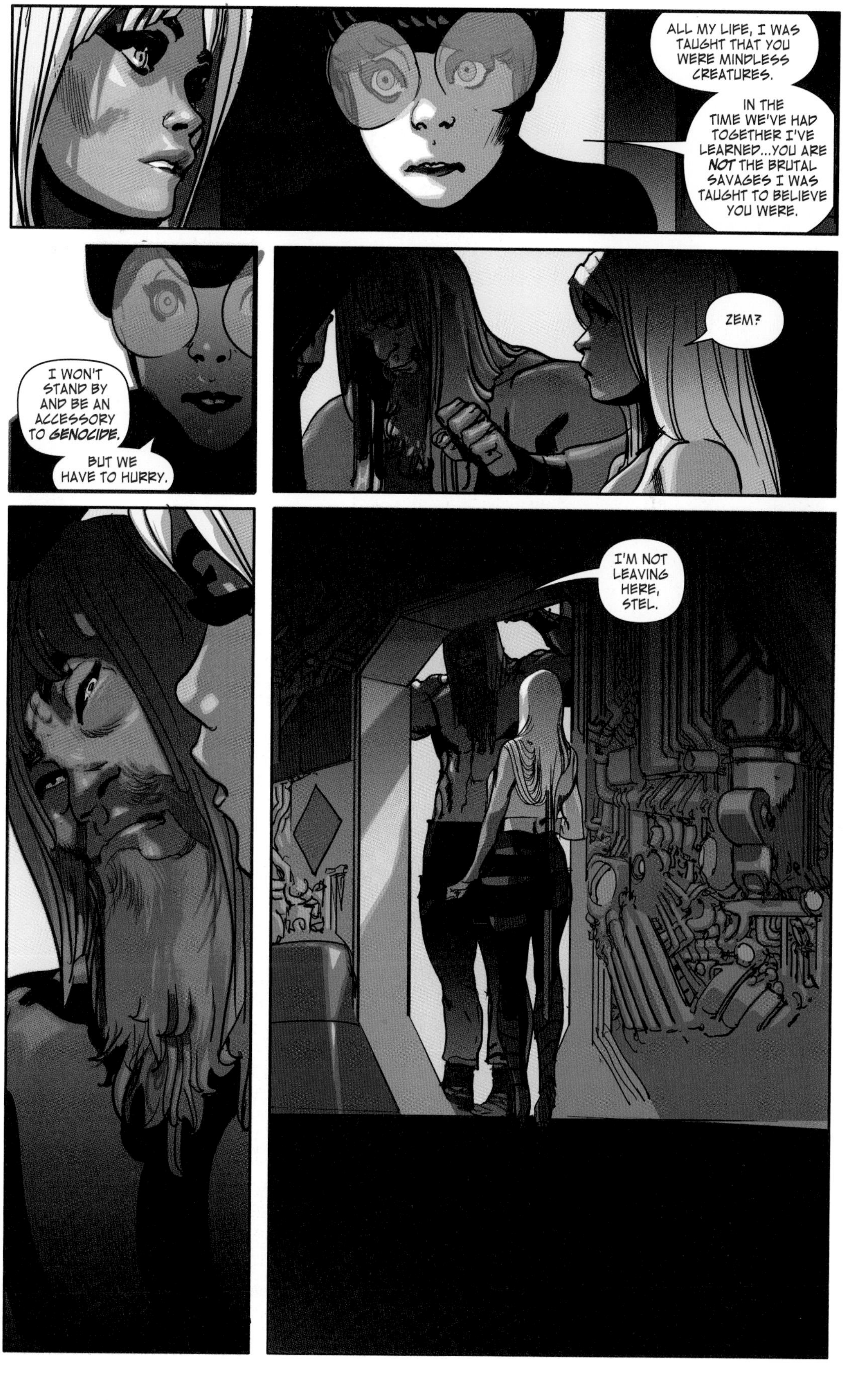
ALL MY LIFE, I WAS TAUGHT THAT YOU WERE MINDLESS CREATURES.
IN THE TIME WE'VE HAD TOGETHER I'VE LEARNED...YOU ARE *NOT* THE BRUTAL SAVAGES I WAS TAUGHT TO BELIEVE YOU WERE.
I WON'T STAND BY AND BE AN ACCESSORY TO *GENOCIDE*.
BUT WE HAVE TO HURRY.
ZEM?
I'M NOT LEAVING HERE, STEL.

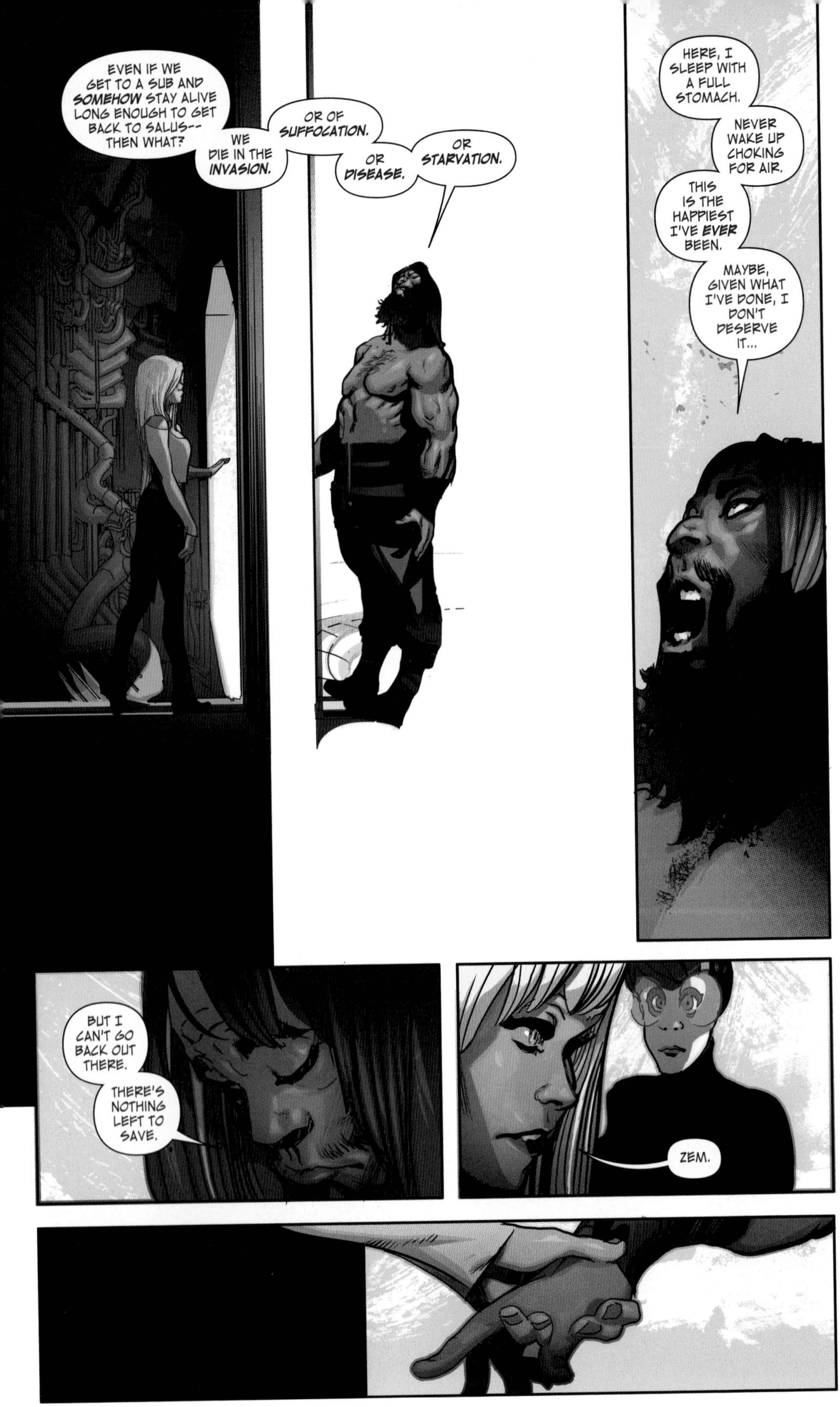
EVEN IF WE GET TO A SUB AND SOMEHOW STAY ALIVE LONG ENOUGH TO GET BACK TO SALUS-- THEN WHAT?
WE DIE IN THE INVASION.
OR OF SUFFOCATION.
OR DISEASE.
OR STARVATION.
HERE, I SLEEP WITH A FULL STOMACH.
NEVER WAKE UP CHOKING FOR AIR.
THIS IS THE HAPPIEST I'VE EVER BEEN.
MAYBE, GIVEN WHAT I'VE DONE, I DON'T DESERVE IT...
BUT I CAN'T GO BACK OUT THERE.
THERE'S NOTHING LEFT TO SAVE.
ZEM.

THERE
IS.

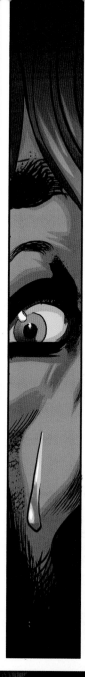

ALL RIGHT,
DOCTOR.

MY
HUSBAND
AND I
TALKED IT
OVER...

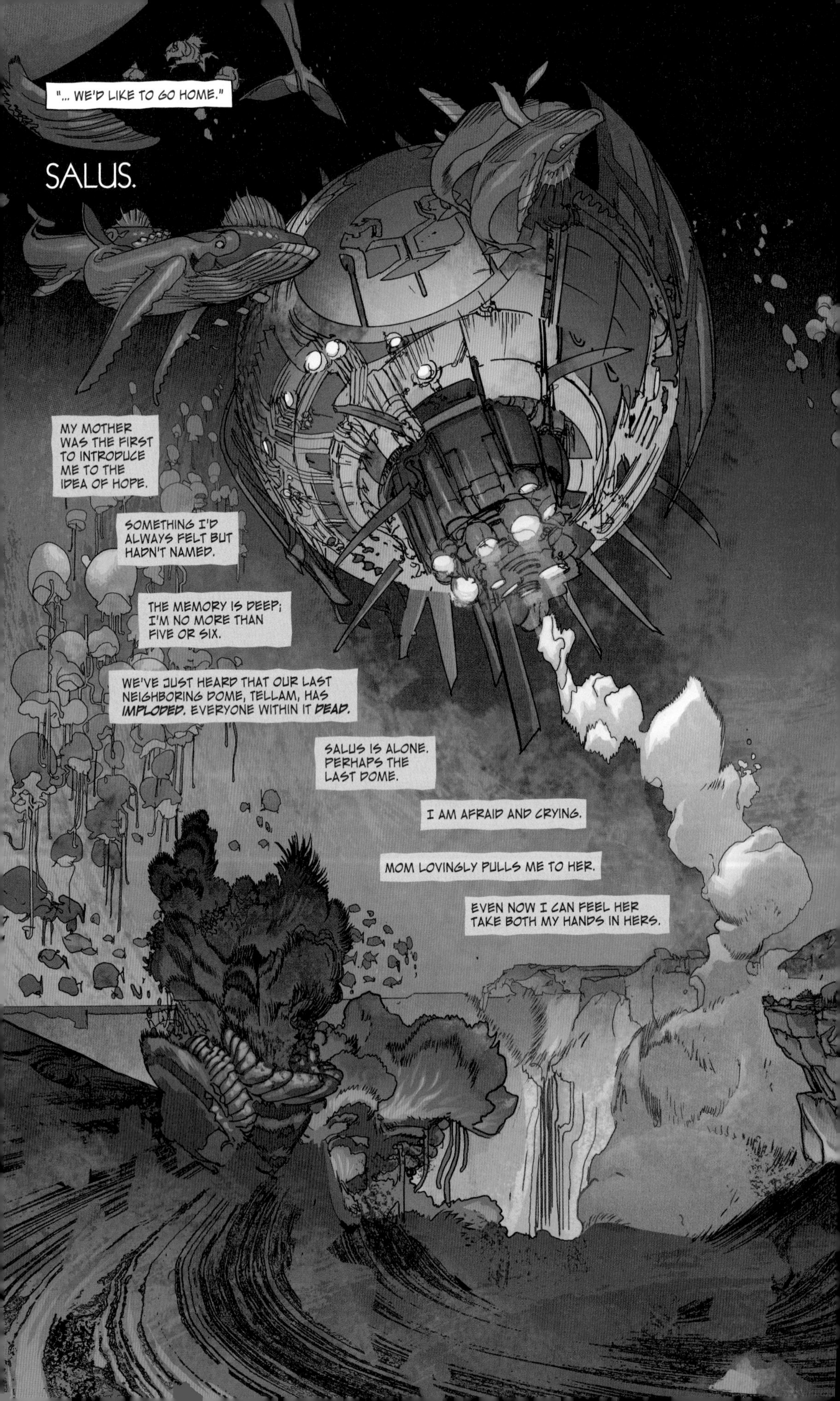
"... WE'D LIKE TO GO HOME."
SALUS.
MY MOTHER WAS THE FIRST TO INTRODUCE ME TO THE IDEA OF HOPE.
SOMETHING I'D ALWAYS FELT BUT HADN'T NAMED.
THE MEMORY IS DEEP; I'M NO MORE THAN FIVE OR SIX.
WE'VE JUST HEARD THAT OUR LAST NEIGHBORING DOME, TELLAM, HAS *IMPLODED*. EVERYONE WITHIN IT *DEAD*.
SALUS IS ALONE. PERHAPS THE LAST DOME.
I AM AFRAID AND CRYING.
MOM LOVINGLY PULLS ME TO HER.
EVEN NOW I CAN FEEL HER TAKE BOTH MY HANDS IN HERS.

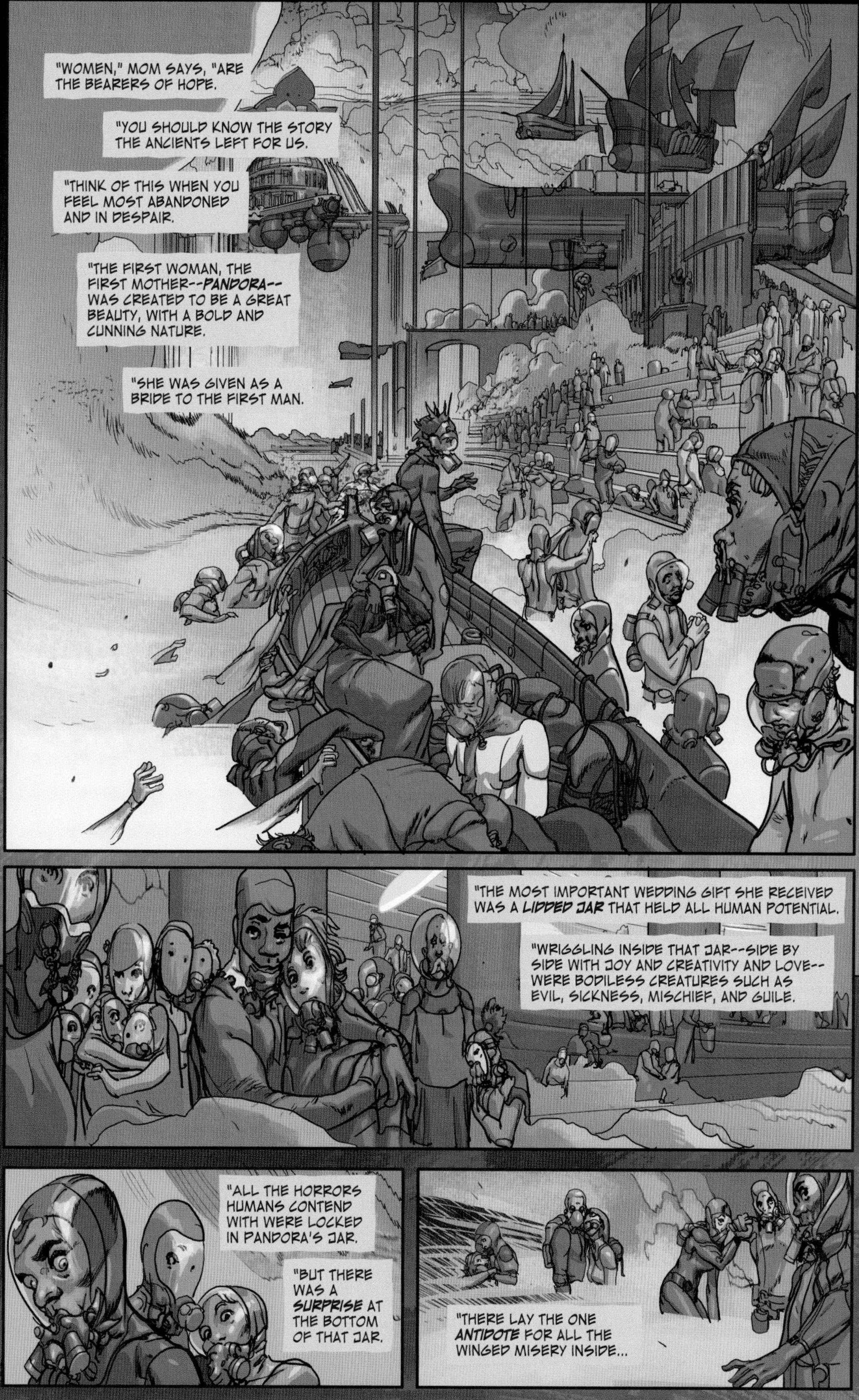
"WOMEN," MOM SAYS, "ARE THE BEARERS OF HOPE.
"YOU SHOULD KNOW THE STORY THE ANCIENTS LEFT FOR US.
"THINK OF THIS WHEN YOU FEEL MOST ABANDONED AND IN DESPAIR.
"THE FIRST WOMAN, THE FIRST MOTHER--PANDORA--WAS CREATED TO BE A GREAT BEAUTY, WITH A BOLD AND CUNNING NATURE.
"SHE WAS GIVEN AS A BRIDE TO THE FIRST MAN.
"THE MOST IMPORTANT WEDDING GIFT SHE RECEIVED WAS A LIDDED JAR THAT HELD ALL HUMAN POTENTIAL.
"WRIGGLING INSIDE THAT JAR--SIDE BY SIDE WITH JOY AND CREATIVITY AND LOVE--WERE BODILESS CREATURES SUCH AS EVIL, SICKNESS, MISCHIEF, AND GUILE.
"ALL THE HORRORS HUMANS CONTEND WITH WERE LOCKED IN PANDORA'S JAR.
"BUT THERE WAS A SURPRISE AT THE BOTTOM OF THAT JAR.
"THERE LAY THE ONE ANTIDOTE FOR ALL THE WINGED MISERY INSIDE...

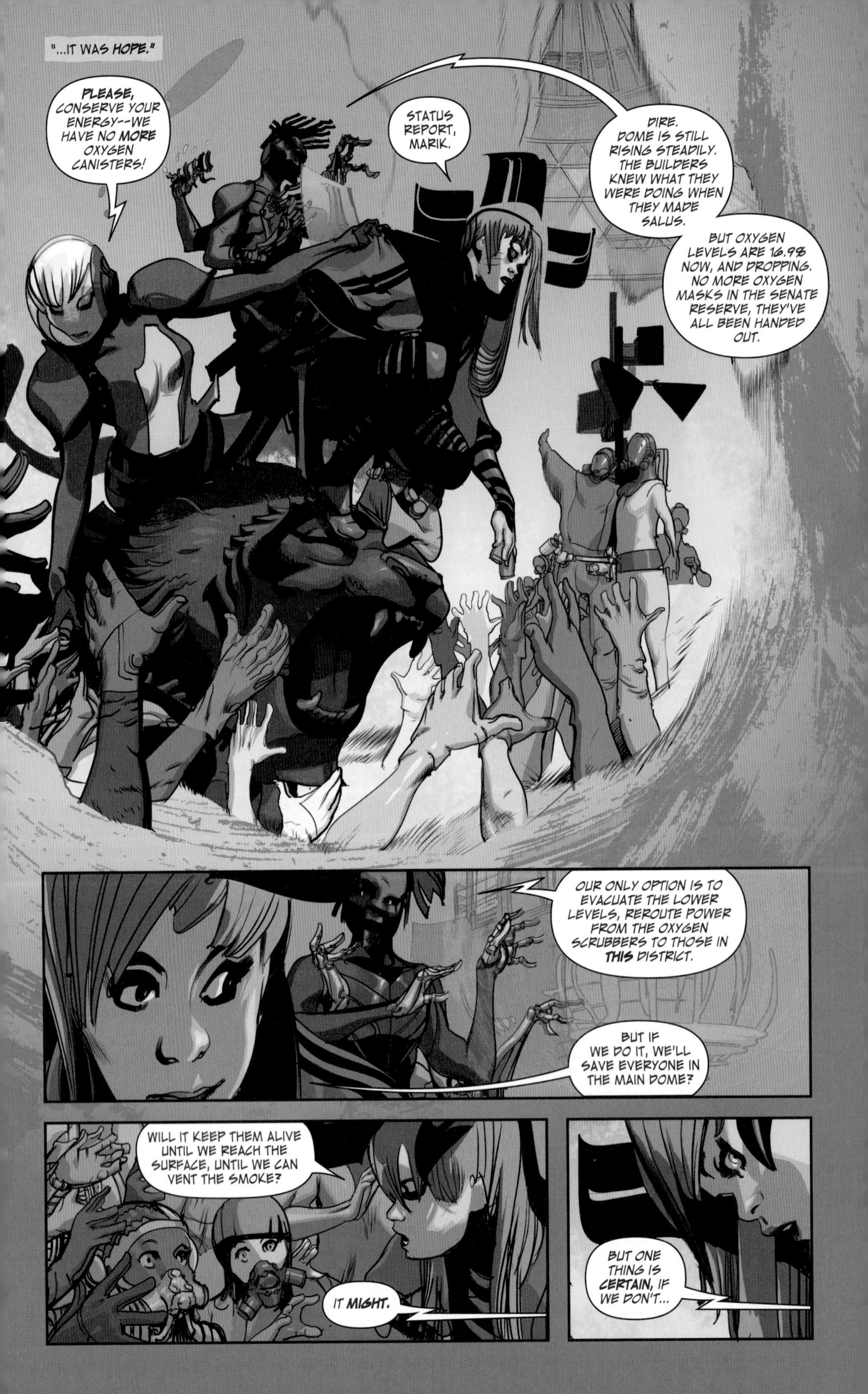
"...IT WAS HOPE."
PLEASE, CONSERVE YOUR ENERGY--WE HAVE NO MORE OXYGEN CANISTERS!
STATUS REPORT, MARIK.
DIRE. DOME IS STILL RISING STEADILY. THE BUILDERS KNEW WHAT THEY WERE DOING WHEN THEY MADE SALUS.
BUT OXYGEN LEVELS ARE 16.98 NOW, AND DROPPING. NO MORE OXYGEN MASKS IN THE SENATE RESERVE, THEY'VE ALL BEEN HANDED OUT.
OUR ONLY OPTION IS TO EVACUATE THE LOWER LEVELS, REROUTE POWER FROM THE OXYGEN SCRUBBERS TO THOSE IN THIS DISTRICT.
BUT IF WE DO IT, WE'LL SAVE EVERYONE IN THE MAIN DOME?
WILL IT KEEP THEM ALIVE UNTIL WE REACH THE SURFACE, UNTIL WE CAN VENT THE SMOKE?
IT MIGHT.
BUT ONE THING IS CERTAIN, IF WE DON'T...

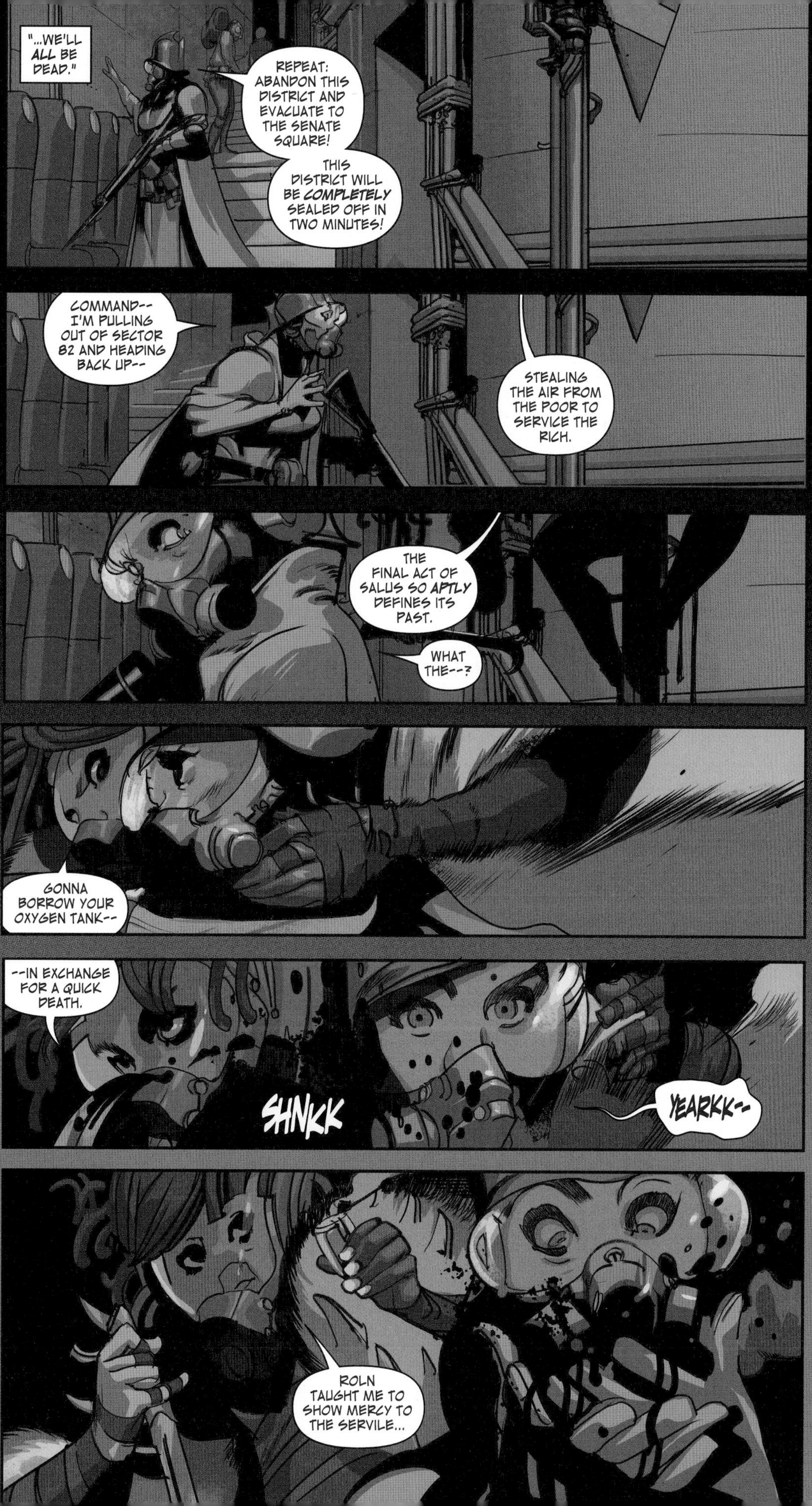
"...WE'LL ALL BE DEAD."
REPEAT: ABANDON THIS DISTRICT AND EVACUATE TO THE SENATE SQUARE!
THIS DISTRICT WILL BE COMPLETELY SEALED OFF IN TWO MINUTES!
COMMAND-- I'M PULLING OUT OF SECTOR B2 AND HEADING BACK UP--
STEALING THE AIR FROM THE POOR TO SERVICE THE RICH.
THE FINAL ACT OF SALUS SO APTLY DEFINES ITS PAST.
WHAT THE--?
GONNA BORROW YOUR OXYGEN TANK--
--IN EXCHANGE FOR A QUICK DEATH.
SHNKK
YEARKK--
ROLN TAUGHT ME TO SHOW MERCY TO THE SERVILE...

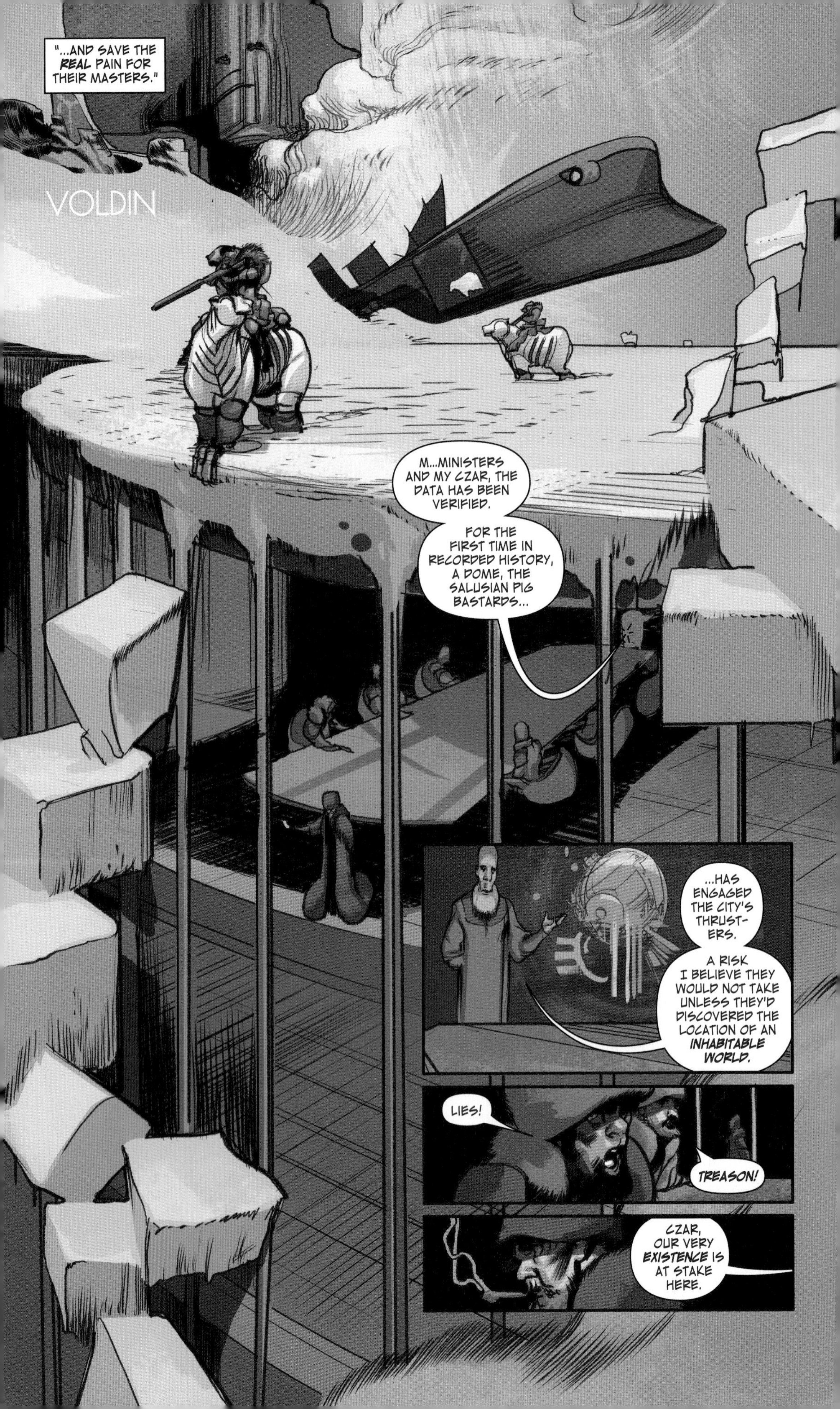
"...AND SAVE THE REAL PAIN FOR THEIR MASTERS."
VOLDIN
M...MINISTERS AND MY CZAR, THE DATA HAS BEEN VERIFIED.
FOR THE FIRST TIME IN RECORDED HISTORY, A DOME, THE SALUSIAN PIG BASTARDS...
...HAS ENGAGED THE CITY'S THRUST-ERS.
A RISK I BELIEVE THEY WOULD NOT TAKE UNLESS THEY'D DISCOVERED THE LOCATION OF AN INHABITABLE WORLD.
LIES!
TREASON!
CZAR, OUR VERY EXISTENCE IS AT STAKE HERE.

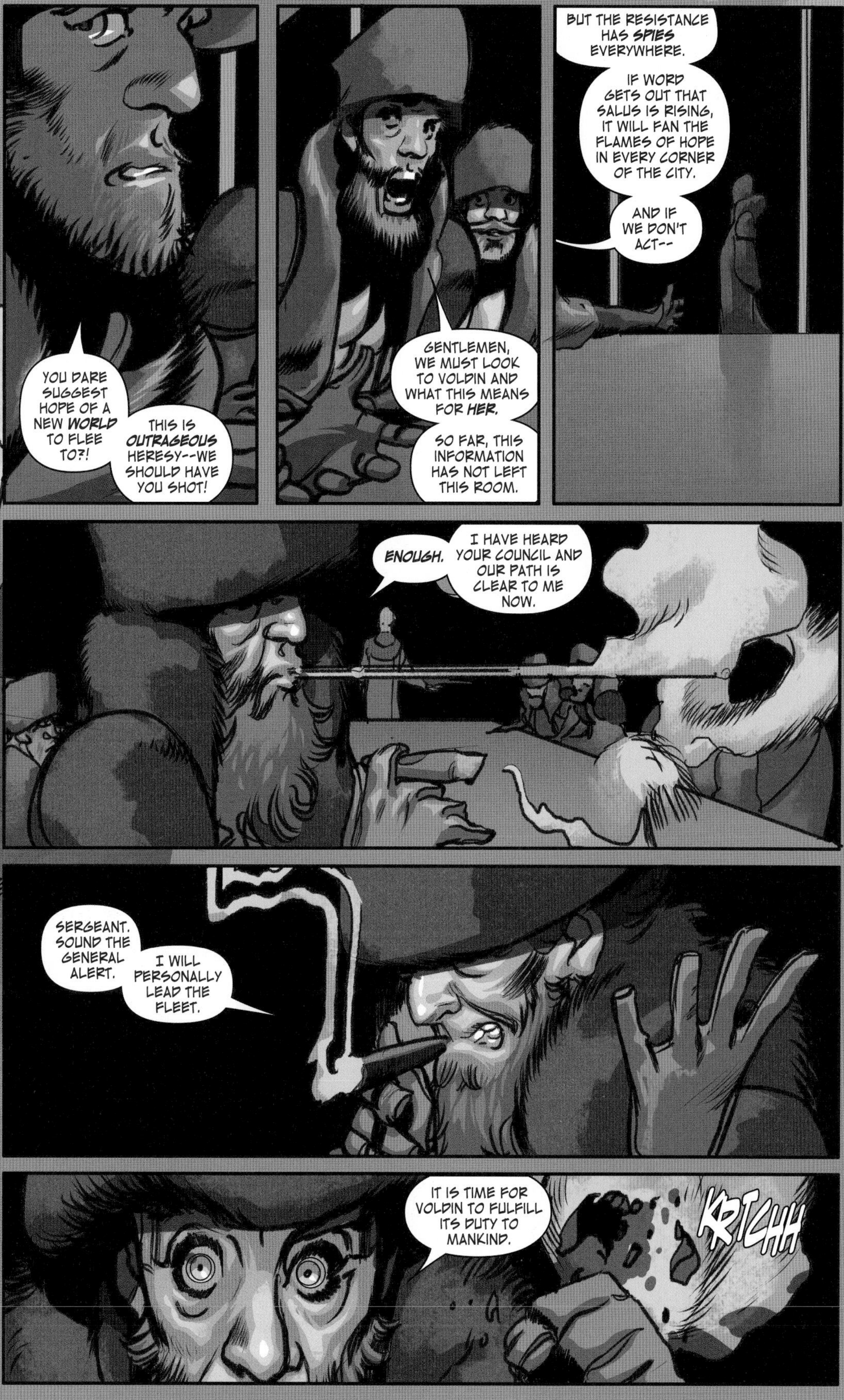
YOU DARE SUGGEST HOPE OF A NEW WORLD TO FLEE TO?!
THIS IS OUTRAGEOUS HERESY--WE SHOULD HAVE YOU SHOT!
GENTLEMEN, WE MUST LOOK TO VOLDIN AND WHAT THIS MEANS FOR HER.
SO FAR, THIS INFORMATION HAS NOT LEFT THIS ROOM.
BUT THE RESISTANCE HAS SPIES EVERYWHERE.
IF WORD GETS OUT THAT SALUS IS RISING, IT WILL FAN THE FLAMES OF HOPE IN EVERY CORNER OF THE CITY.
AND IF WE DON'T ACT--
ENOUGH.
I HAVE HEARD YOUR COUNCIL AND OUR PATH IS CLEAR TO ME NOW.
SERGEANT. SOUND THE GENERAL ALERT.
I WILL PERSONALLY LEAD THE FLEET.
IT IS TIME FOR VOLDIN TO FULFILL ITS DUTY TO MANKIND.
KRTCHH

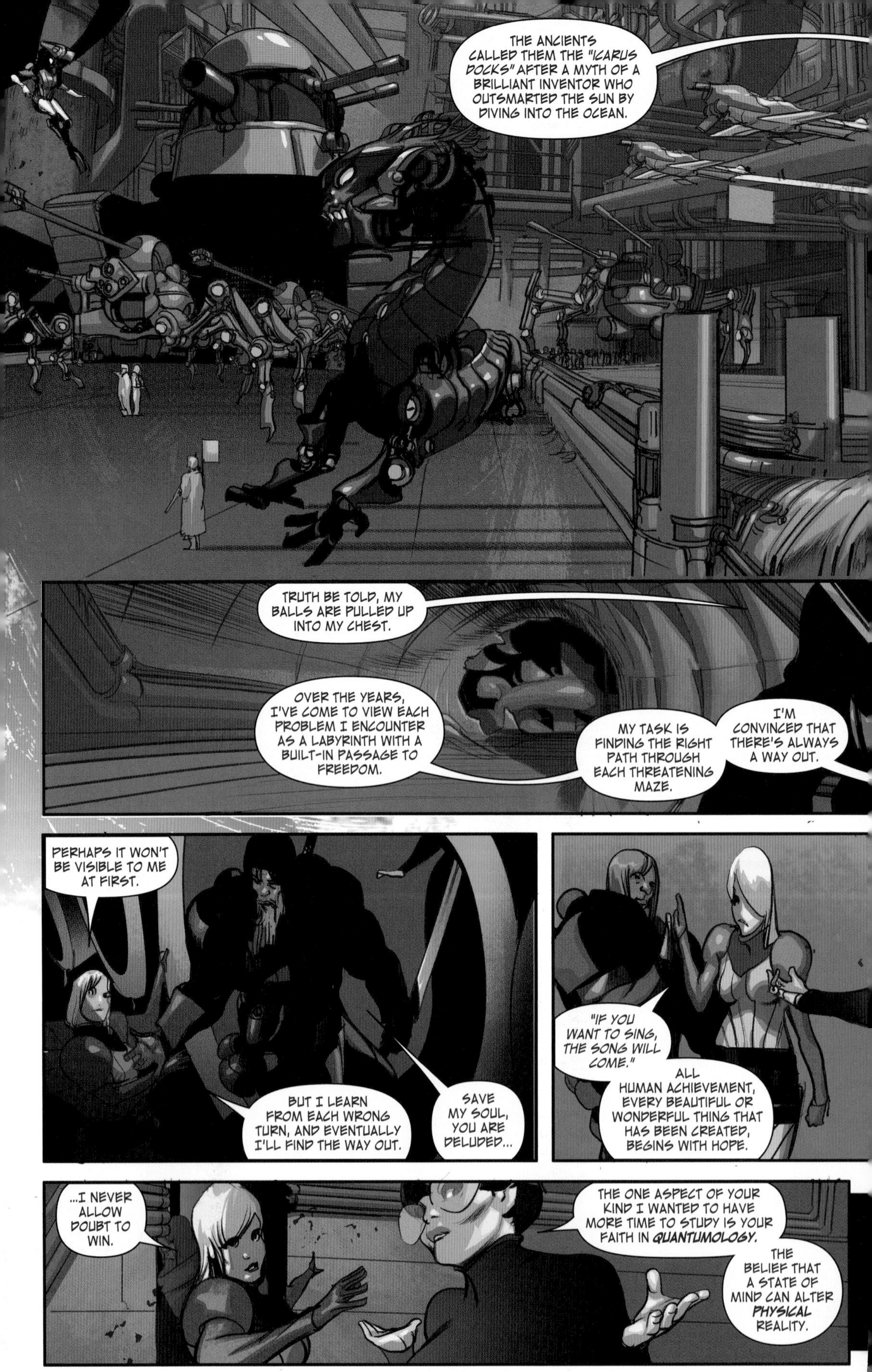
THE ANCIENTS CALLED THEM THE "ICARUS DOCKS" AFTER A MYTH OF A BRILLIANT INVENTOR WHO OUTSMARTED THE SUN BY DIVING INTO THE OCEAN.
TRUTH BE TOLD, MY BALLS ARE PULLED UP INTO MY CHEST.
OVER THE YEARS, I'VE COME TO VIEW EACH PROBLEM I ENCOUNTER AS A LABYRINTH WITH A BUILT-IN PASSAGE TO FREEDOM.
MY TASK IS FINDING THE RIGHT PATH THROUGH EACH THREATENING MAZE.
I'M CONVINCED THAT THERE'S ALWAYS A WAY OUT.
PERHAPS IT WON'T BE VISIBLE TO ME AT FIRST.
BUT I LEARN FROM EACH WRONG TURN, AND EVENTUALLY I'LL FIND THE WAY OUT.
SAVE MY SOUL, YOU ARE DELUDED...
"IF YOU WANT TO SING, THE SONG WILL COME."
ALL HUMAN ACHIEVEMENT, EVERY BEAUTIFUL OR WONDERFUL THING THAT HAS BEEN CREATED, BEGINS WITH HOPE.
...I NEVER ALLOW DOUBT TO WIN.
THE ONE ASPECT OF YOUR KIND I WANTED TO HAVE MORE TIME TO STUDY IS YOUR FAITH IN ***QUANTUMOLOGY.***
THE BELIEF THAT A STATE OF MIND CAN ALTER ***PHYSICAL*** REALITY.

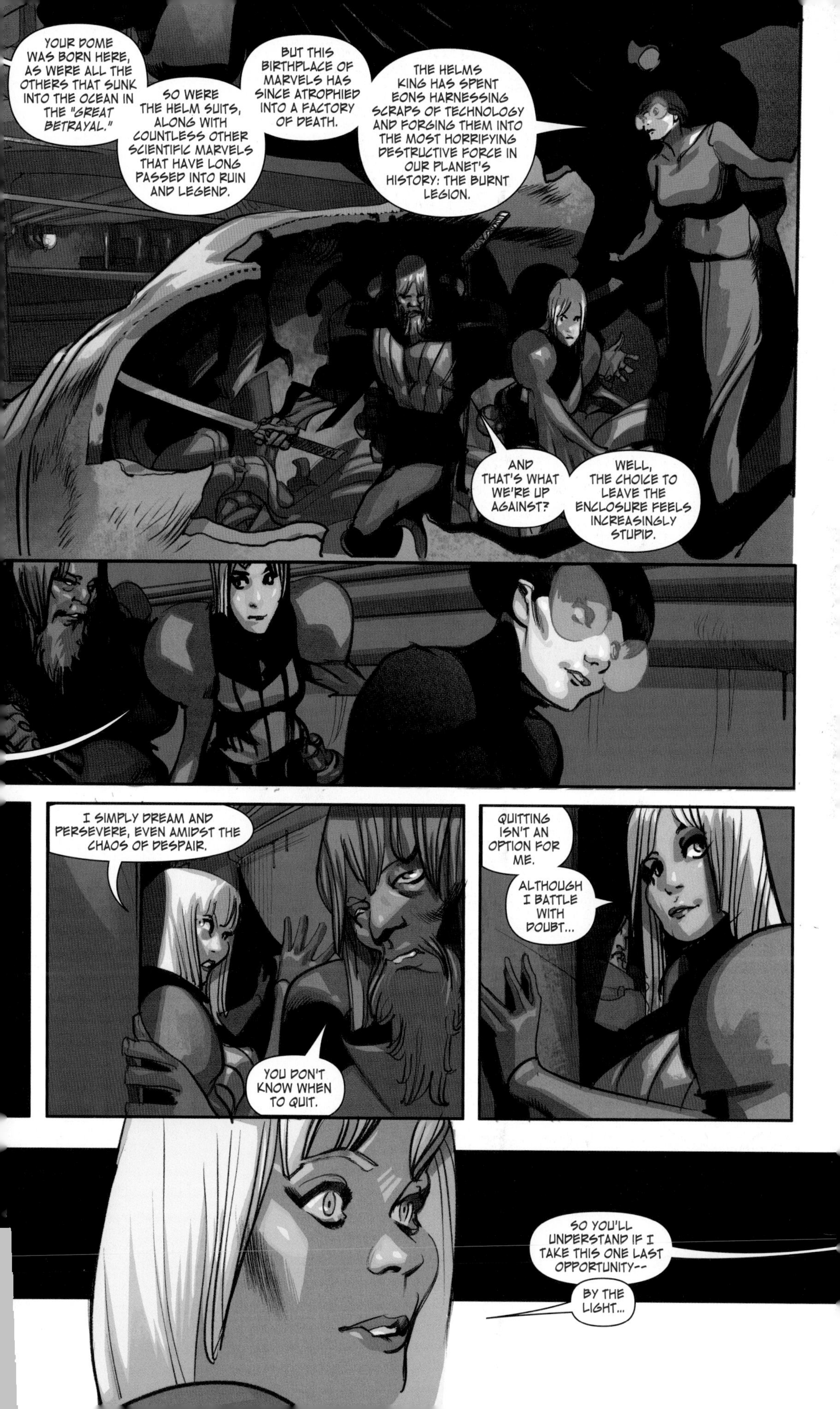

YOUR DOME WAS BORN HERE, AS WERE ALL THE OTHERS THAT SUNK INTO THE OCEAN IN THE "GREAT BETRAYAL."
SO WERE THE HELM SUITS, ALONG WITH COUNTLESS OTHER SCIENTIFIC MARVELS THAT HAVE LONG PASSED INTO RUIN AND LEGEND.
BUT THIS BIRTHPLACE OF MARVELS HAS SINCE ATROPHIED INTO A FACTORY OF DEATH.
THE HELMS KING HAS SPENT EONS HARNESSING SCRAPS OF TECHNOLOGY AND FORGING THEM INTO THE MOST HORRIFYING DESTRUCTIVE FORCE IN OUR PLANET'S HISTORY: THE BURNT LEGION.
AND THAT'S WHAT WE'RE UP AGAINST?
WELL, THE CHOICE TO LEAVE THE ENCLOSURE FEELS INCREASINGLY STUPID.
I SIMPLY DREAM AND PERSEVERE, EVEN AMIDST THE CHAOS OF DESPAIR.
YOU DON'T KNOW WHEN TO QUIT.
QUITTING ISN'T AN OPTION FOR ME.
ALTHOUGH I BATTLE WITH DOUBT...
SO YOU'LL UNDERSTAND IF I TAKE THIS ONE LAST OPPORTUNITY--
BY THE LIGHT...

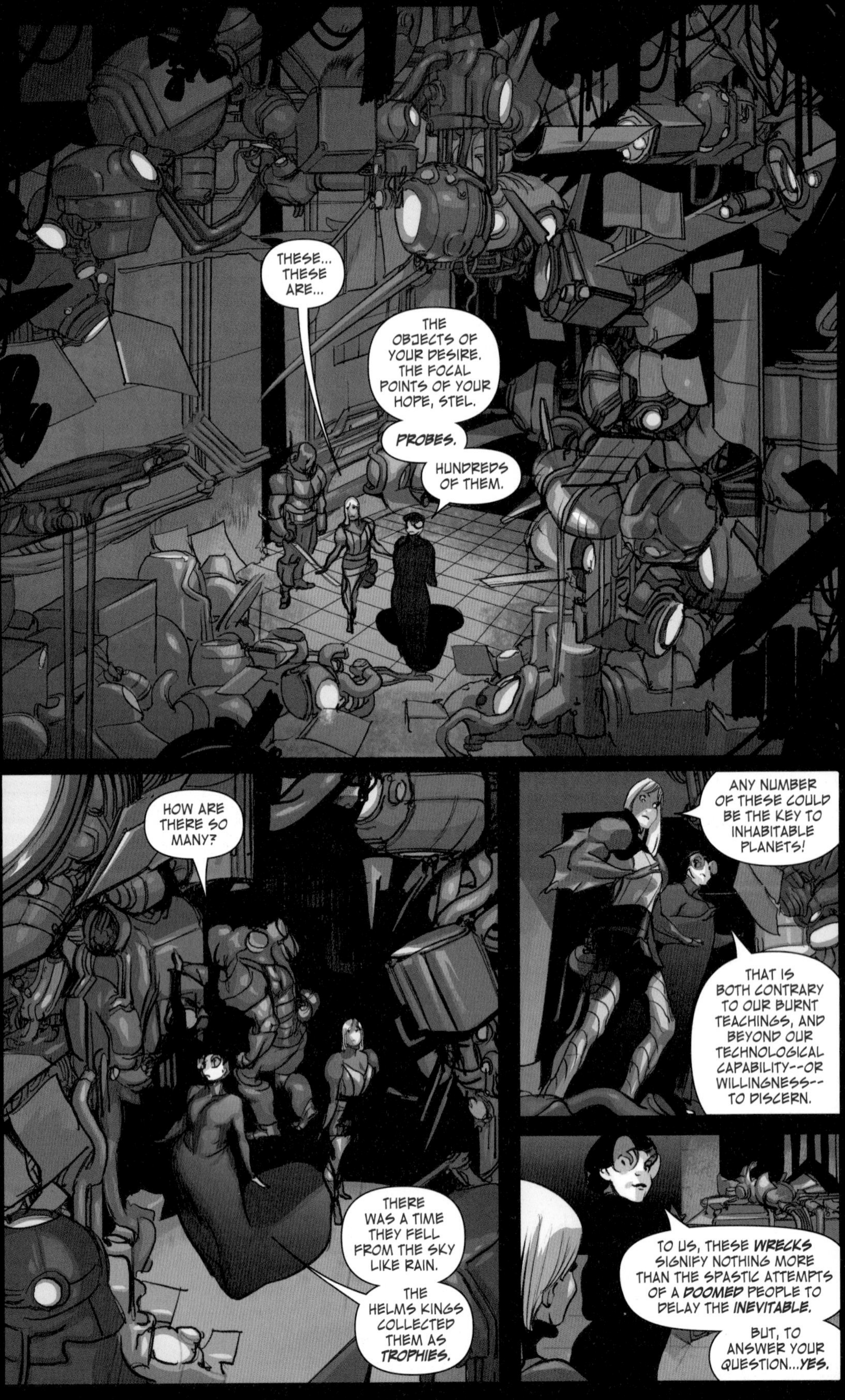

THESE... THESE ARE...
THE OBJECTS OF YOUR DESIRE. THE FOCAL POINTS OF YOUR HOPE, STEL.
PROBES.
HUNDREDS OF THEM.
HOW ARE THERE SO MANY?
THERE WAS A TIME THEY FELL FROM THE SKY LIKE RAIN.
THE HELMS KINGS COLLECTED THEM AS TROPHIES.
ANY NUMBER OF THESE COULD BE THE KEY TO INHABITABLE PLANETS!
THAT IS BOTH CONTRARY TO OUR BURNT TEACHINGS, AND BEYOND OUR TECHNOLOGICAL CAPABILITY--OR WILLINGNESS--TO DISCERN.
TO US, THESE WRECKS SIGNIFY NOTHING MORE THAN THE SPASTIC ATTEMPTS OF A DOOMED PEOPLE TO DELAY THE INEVITABLE.
BUT, TO ANSWER YOUR QUESTION...YES.

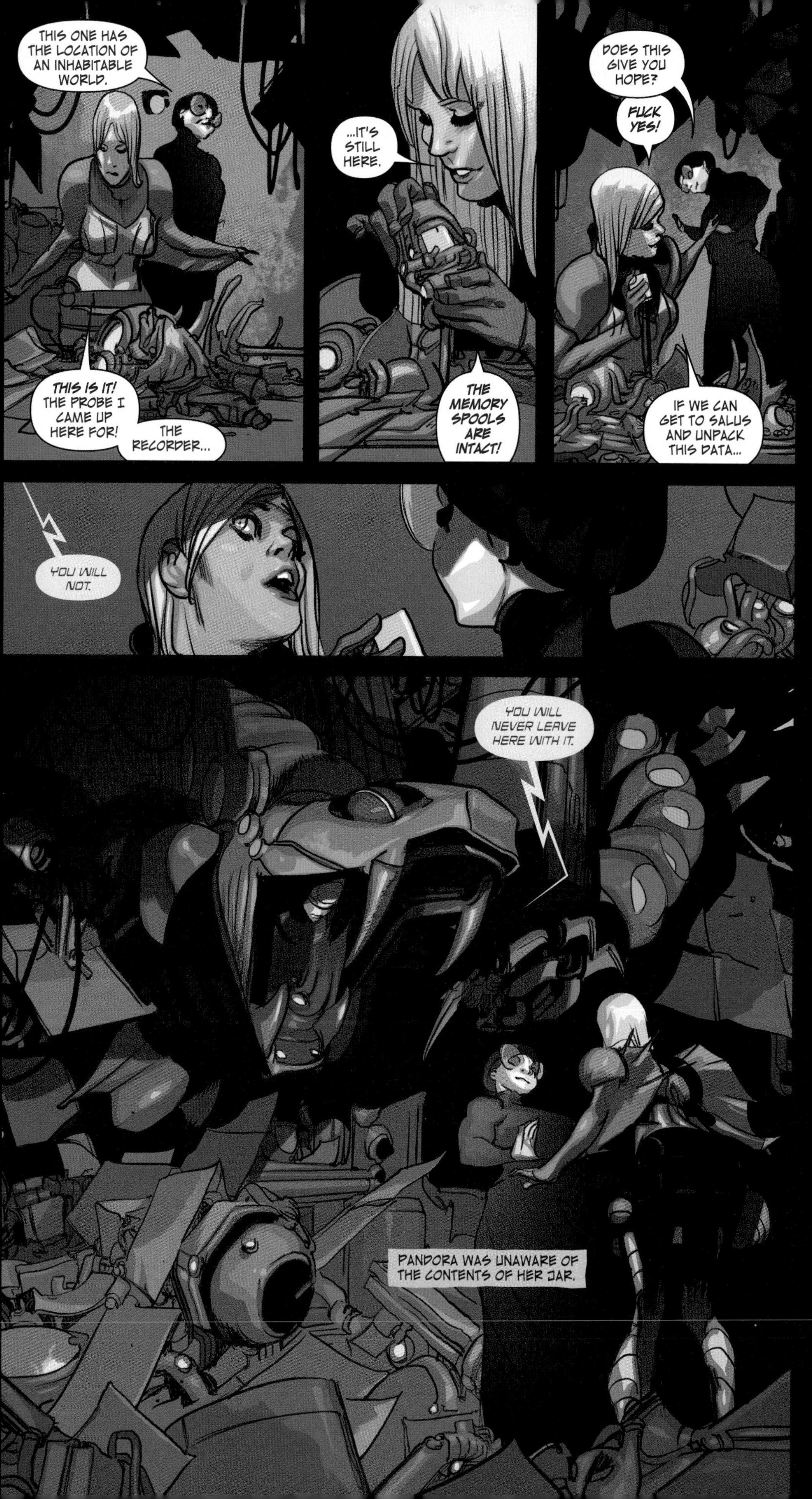
THIS ONE HAS THE LOCATION OF AN INHABITABLE WORLD.
THIS IS IT! THE PROBE I CAME UP HERE FOR!
THE RECORDER...
...IT'S STILL HERE.
THE MEMORY SPOOLS ARE INTACT!
DOES THIS GIVE YOU HOPE?
FUCK YES!
IF WE CAN GET TO SALUS AND UNPACK THIS DATA...
YOU WILL NOT.
YOU WILL NEVER LEAVE HERE WITH IT.
PANDORA WAS UNAWARE OF THE CONTENTS OF HER JAR.

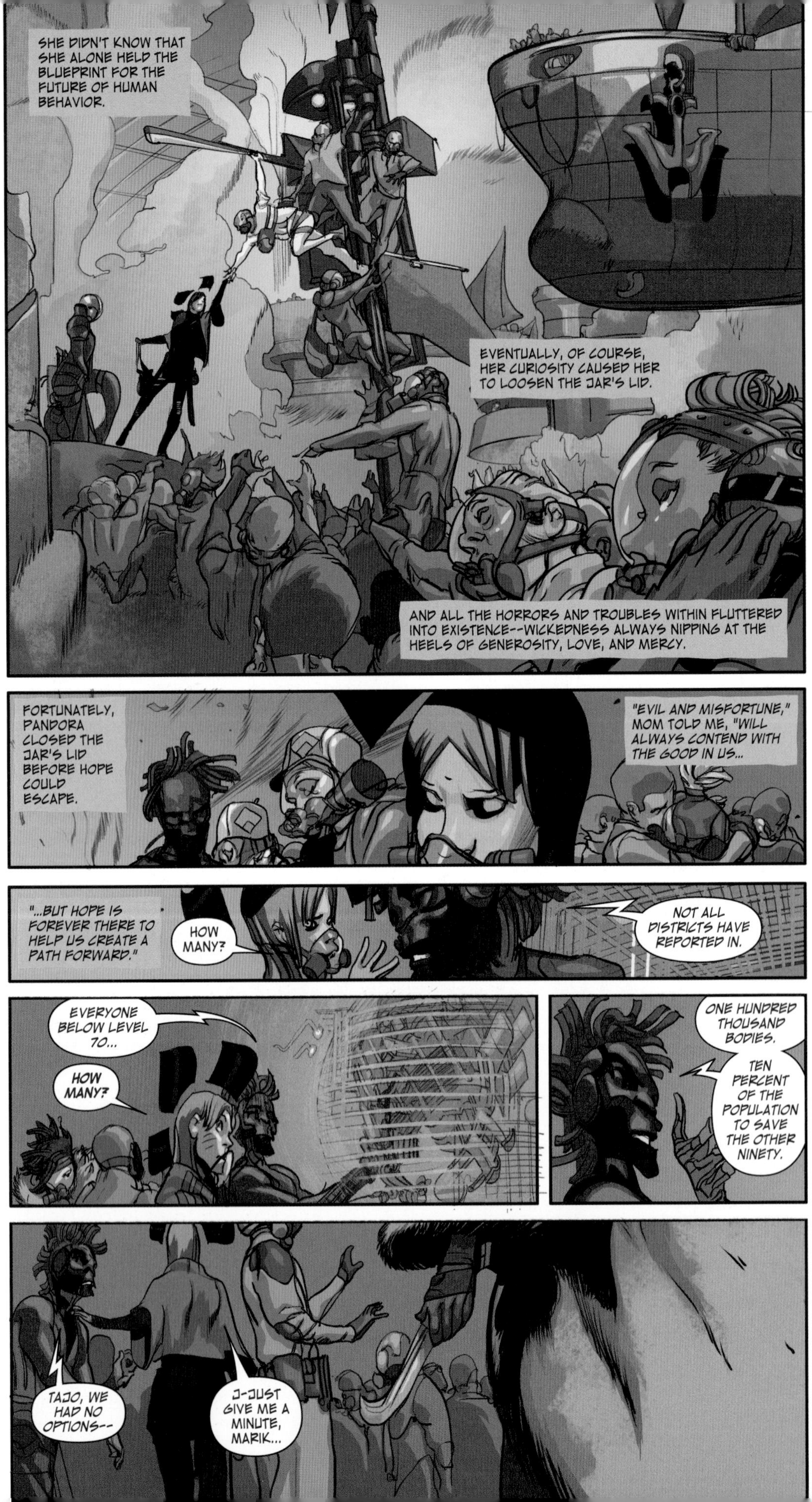
SHE DIDN'T KNOW THAT SHE ALONE HELD THE BLUEPRINT FOR THE FUTURE OF HUMAN BEHAVIOR.
EVENTUALLY, OF COURSE, HER CURIOSITY CAUSED HER TO LOOSEN THE JAR'S LID.
AND ALL THE HORRORS AND TROUBLES WITHIN FLUTTERED INTO EXISTENCE--WICKEDNESS ALWAYS NIPPING AT THE HEELS OF GENEROSITY, LOVE, AND MERCY.
FORTUNATELY, PANDORA CLOSED THE JAR'S LID BEFORE HOPE COULD ESCAPE.
"EVIL AND MISFORTUNE," MOM TOLD ME, "WILL ALWAYS CONTEND WITH THE GOOD IN US...
"...BUT HOPE IS FOREVER THERE TO HELP US CREATE A PATH FORWARD."
HOW MANY?
NOT ALL DISTRICTS HAVE REPORTED IN.
EVERYONE BELOW LEVEL 70...
HOW MANY?
ONE HUNDRED THOUSAND BODIES.
TEN PERCENT OF THE POPULATION TO SAVE THE OTHER NINETY.
TAJO, WE HAD NO OPTIONS--
J-JUST GIVE ME A MINUTE, MARIK...

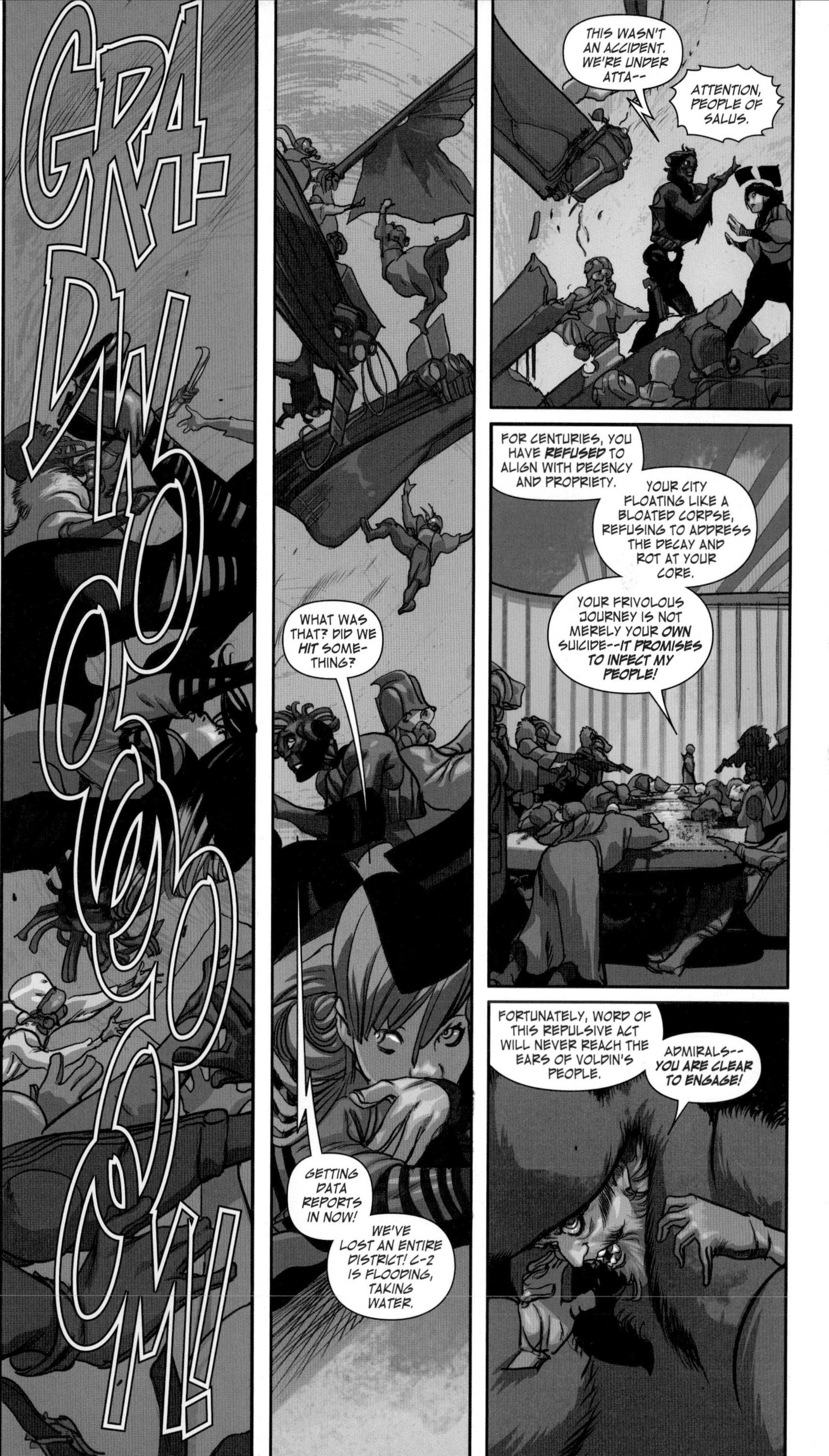
GRA-DWOOOOOM!
WHAT WAS THAT? DID WE HIT SOME-THING?
GETTING DATA REPORTS IN NOW!
WE'VE LOST AN ENTIRE DISTRICT! C-2 IS FLOODING, TAKING WATER.
THIS WASN'T AN ACCIDENT. WE'RE UNDER ATTA--
ATTENTION, PEOPLE OF SALUS.
FOR CENTURIES, YOU HAVE REFUSED TO ALIGN WITH DECENCY AND PROPRIETY.
YOUR CITY FLOATING LIKE A BLOATED CORPSE, REFUSING TO ADDRESS THE DECAY AND ROT AT YOUR CORE.
YOUR FRIVOLOUS JOURNEY IS NOT MERELY YOUR OWN SUICIDE--IT PROMISES TO INFECT MY PEOPLE!
FORTUNATELY, WORD OF THIS REPULSIVE ACT WILL NEVER REACH THE EARS OF VOLDIN'S PEOPLE.
ADMIRALS--YOU ARE CLEAR TO ENGAGE!

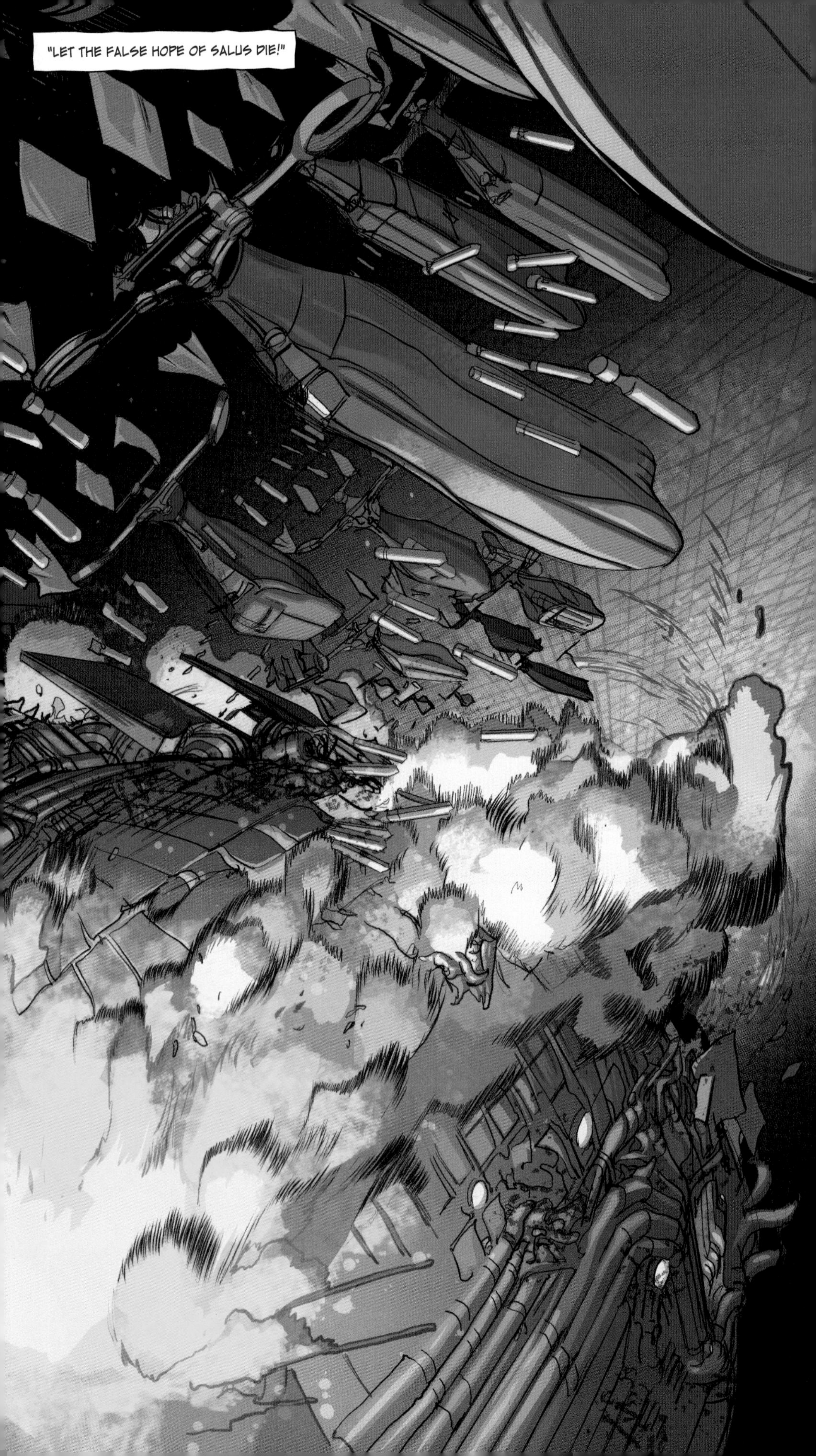
"LET THE FALSE HOPE OF SALUS DIE!"

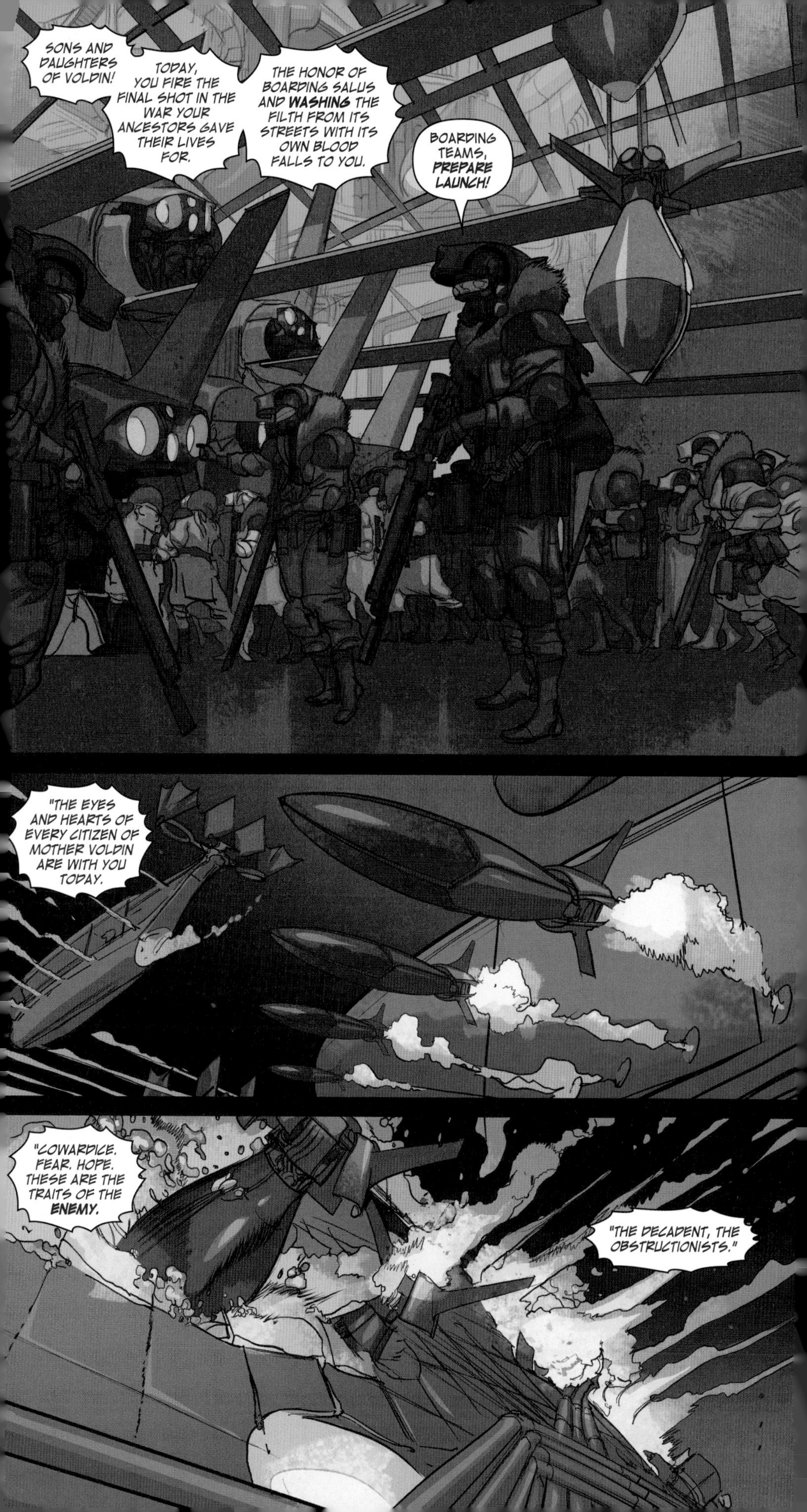
SONS AND DAUGHTERS OF VOLDIN!
TODAY, YOU FIRE THE FINAL SHOT IN THE WAR YOUR ANCESTORS GAVE THEIR LIVES FOR.
THE HONOR OF BOARDING SALUS AND WASHING THE FILTH FROM ITS STREETS WITH ITS OWN BLOOD FALLS TO YOU.
BOARDING TEAMS, PREPARE LAUNCH!
"THE EYES AND HEARTS OF EVERY CITIZEN OF MOTHER VOLDIN ARE WITH YOU TODAY.
"COWARDICE. FEAR. HOPE. THESE ARE THE TRAITS OF THE ENEMY.
"THE DECADENT, THE OBSTRUCTIONISTS."

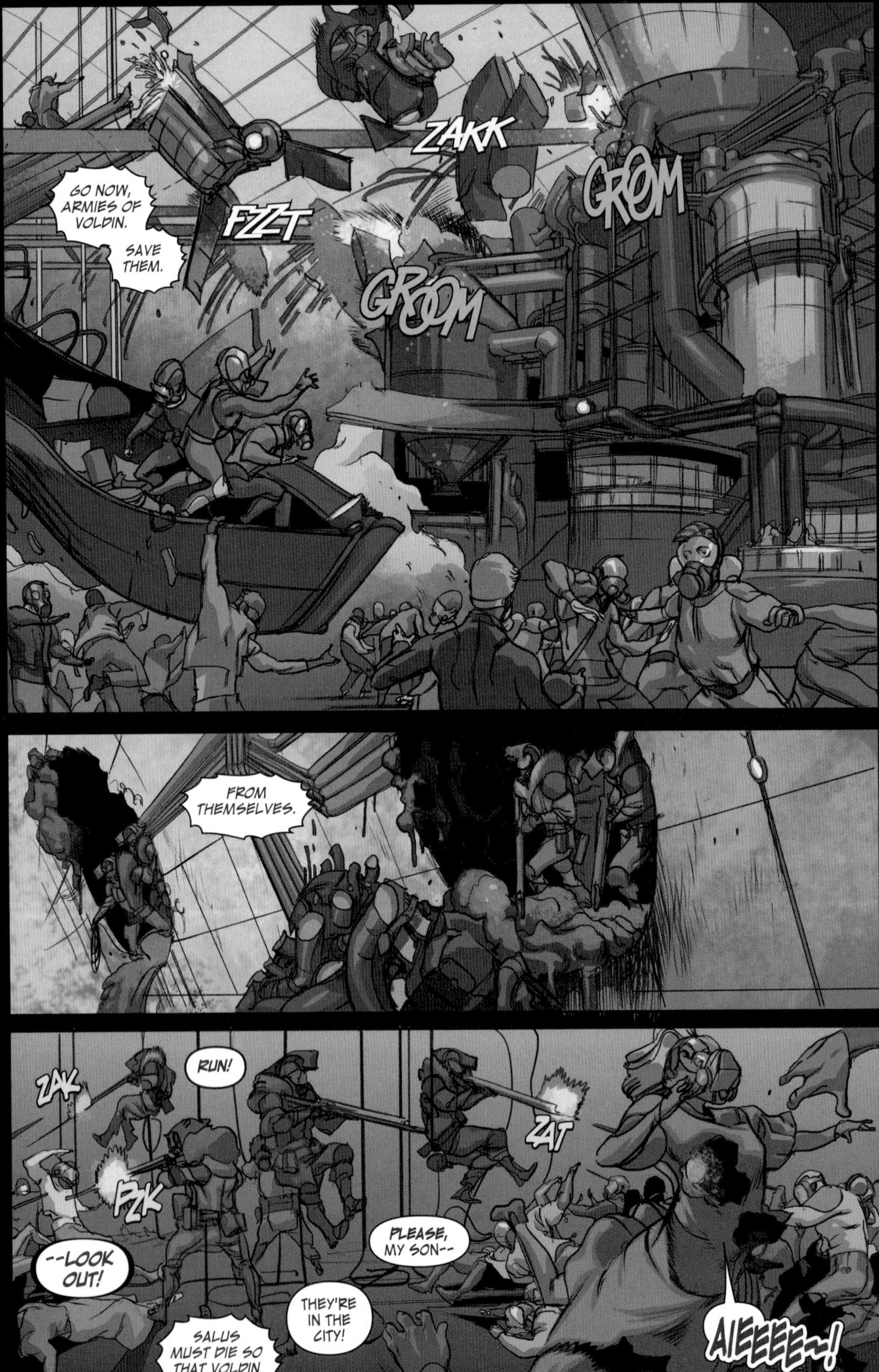
GO NOW, ARMIES OF VOLDIN.
SAVE THEM.
FZZT
ZAKK
GROM
GROOM
FROM THEMSELVES.
ZAK
RUN!
ZAT
PZK
--LOOK OUT!
PLEASE, MY SON--
THEY'RE IN THE CITY!
SALUS MUST DIE SO THAT VOLDIN MAY LIVE!
AIEEEE--!

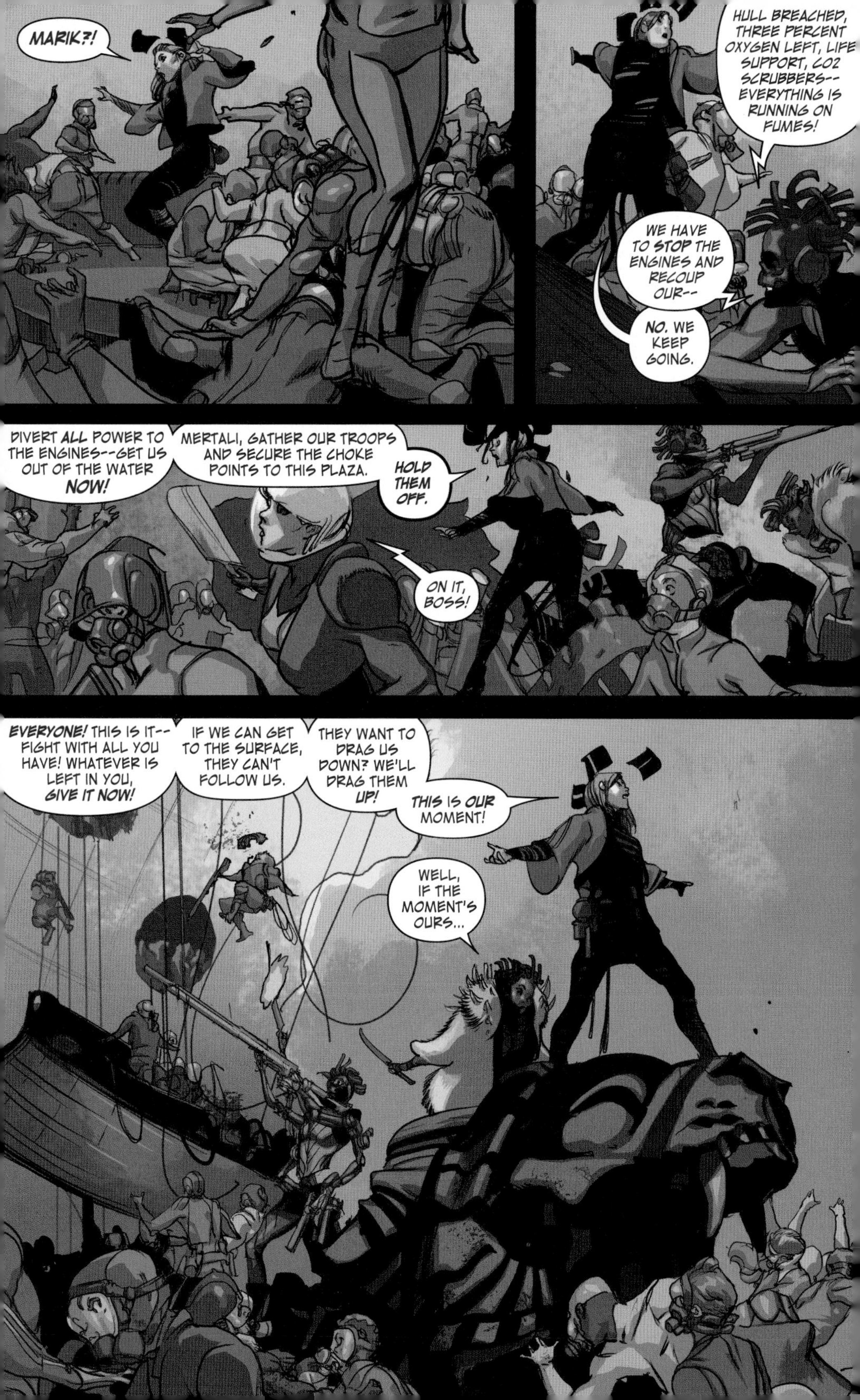
MARIK?!
HULL BREACHED, THREE PERCENT OXYGEN LEFT, LIFE SUPPORT, CO2 SCRUBBERS-- EVERYTHING IS RUNNING ON FUMES!
WE HAVE TO STOP THE ENGINES AND RECOUP OUR--
NO. WE KEEP GOING.
DIVERT ALL POWER TO THE ENGINES--GET US OUT OF THE WATER NOW!
MERTALI, GATHER OUR TROOPS AND SECURE THE CHOKE POINTS TO THIS PLAZA.
HOLD THEM OFF.
ON IT, BOSS!
EVERYONE! THIS IS IT-- FIGHT WITH ALL YOU HAVE! WHATEVER IS LEFT IN YOU, GIVE IT NOW!
IF WE CAN GET TO THE SURFACE, THEY CAN'T FOLLOW US.
THEY WANT TO DRAG US DOWN? WE'LL DRAG THEM UP!
THIS IS OUR MOMENT!
WELL, IF THE MOMENT'S OURS...

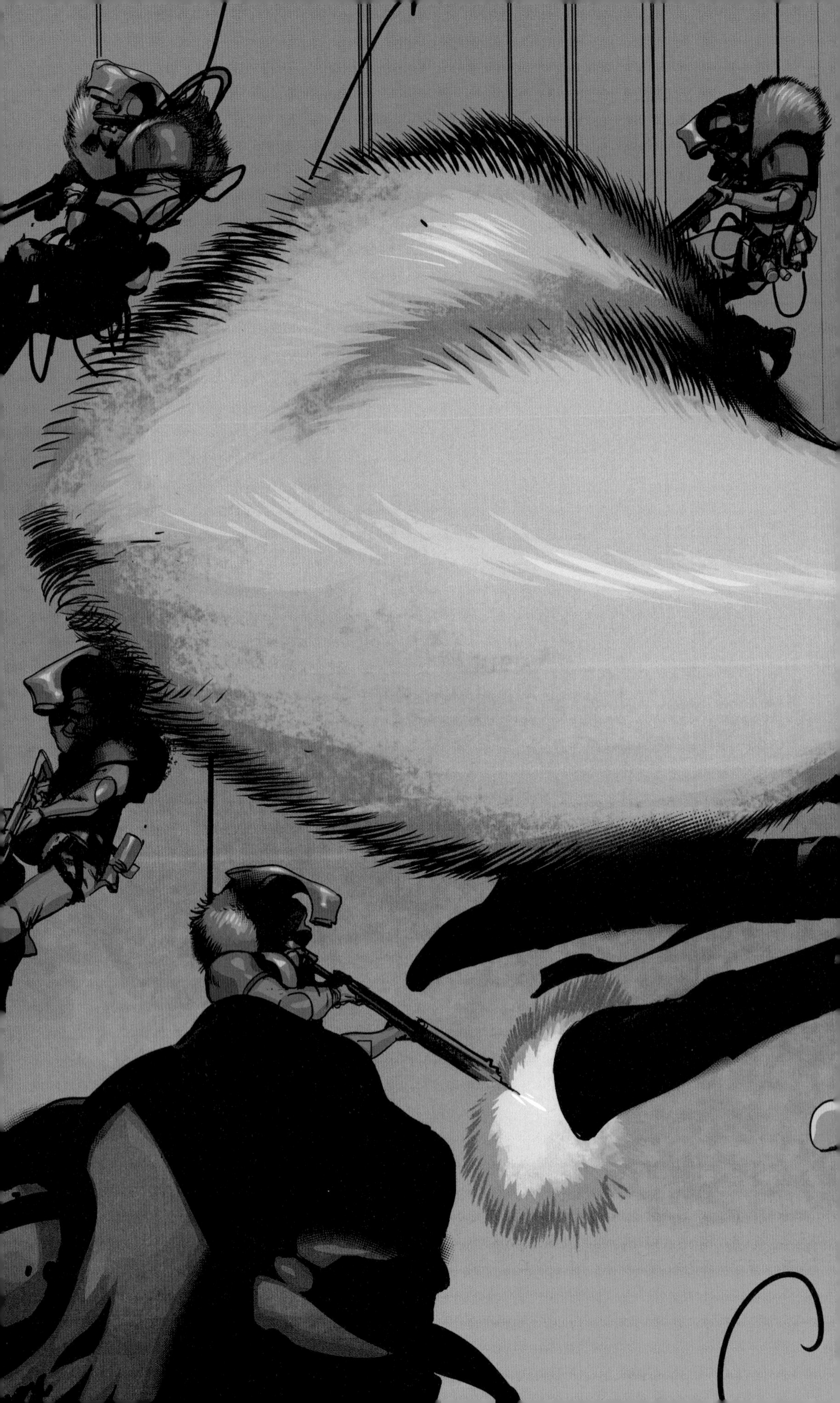

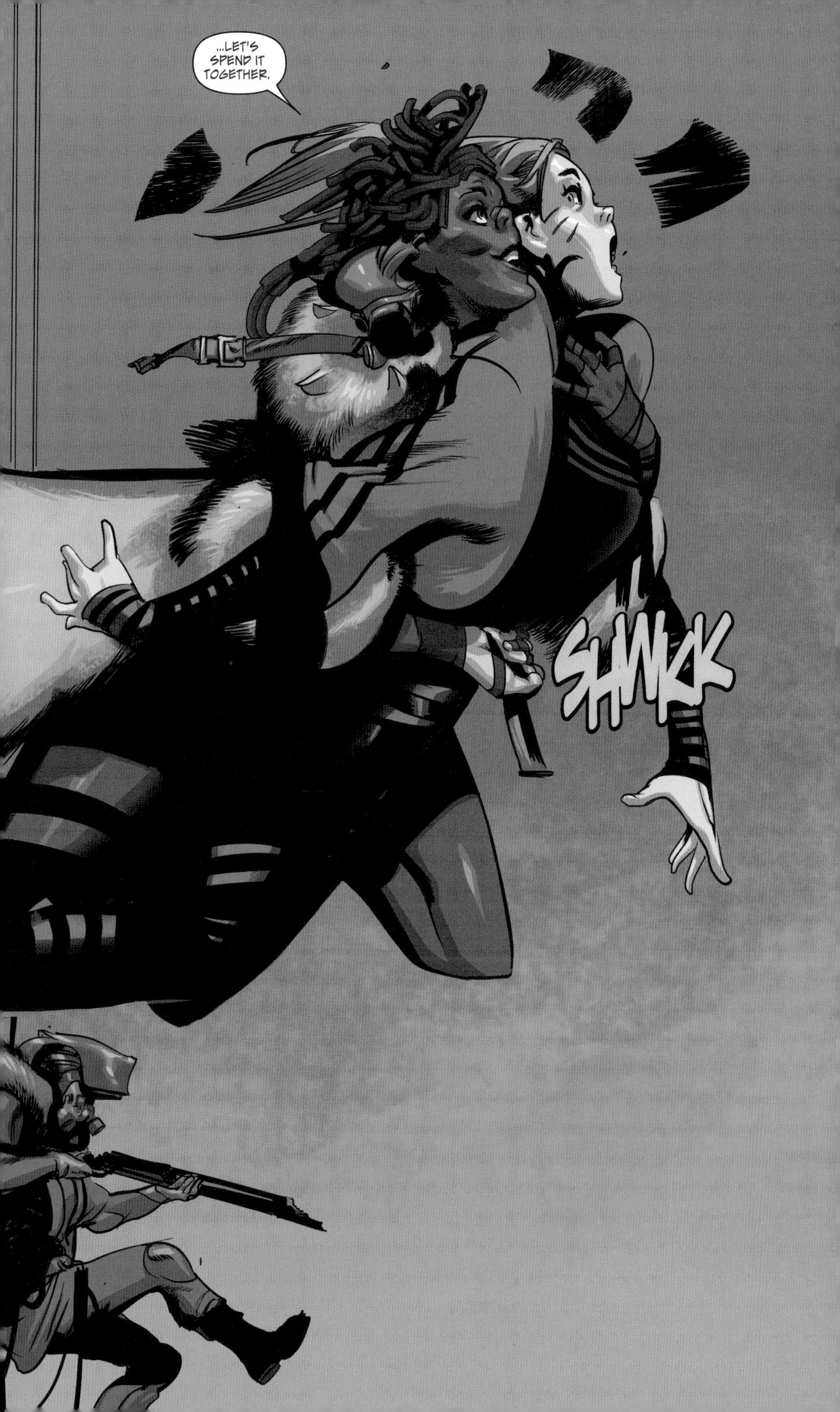
...LET'S SPEND IT TOGETHER.
SHNKK

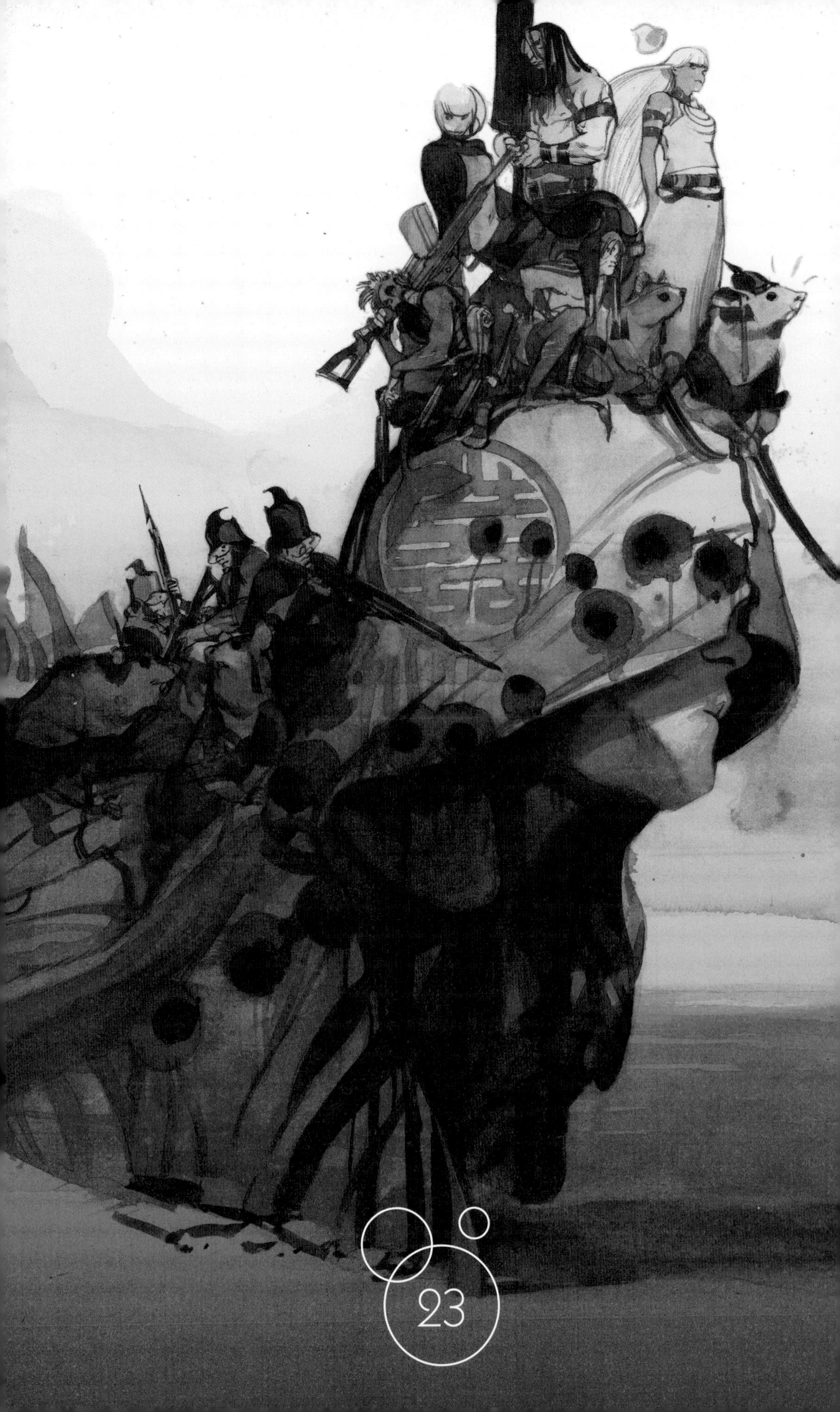

23

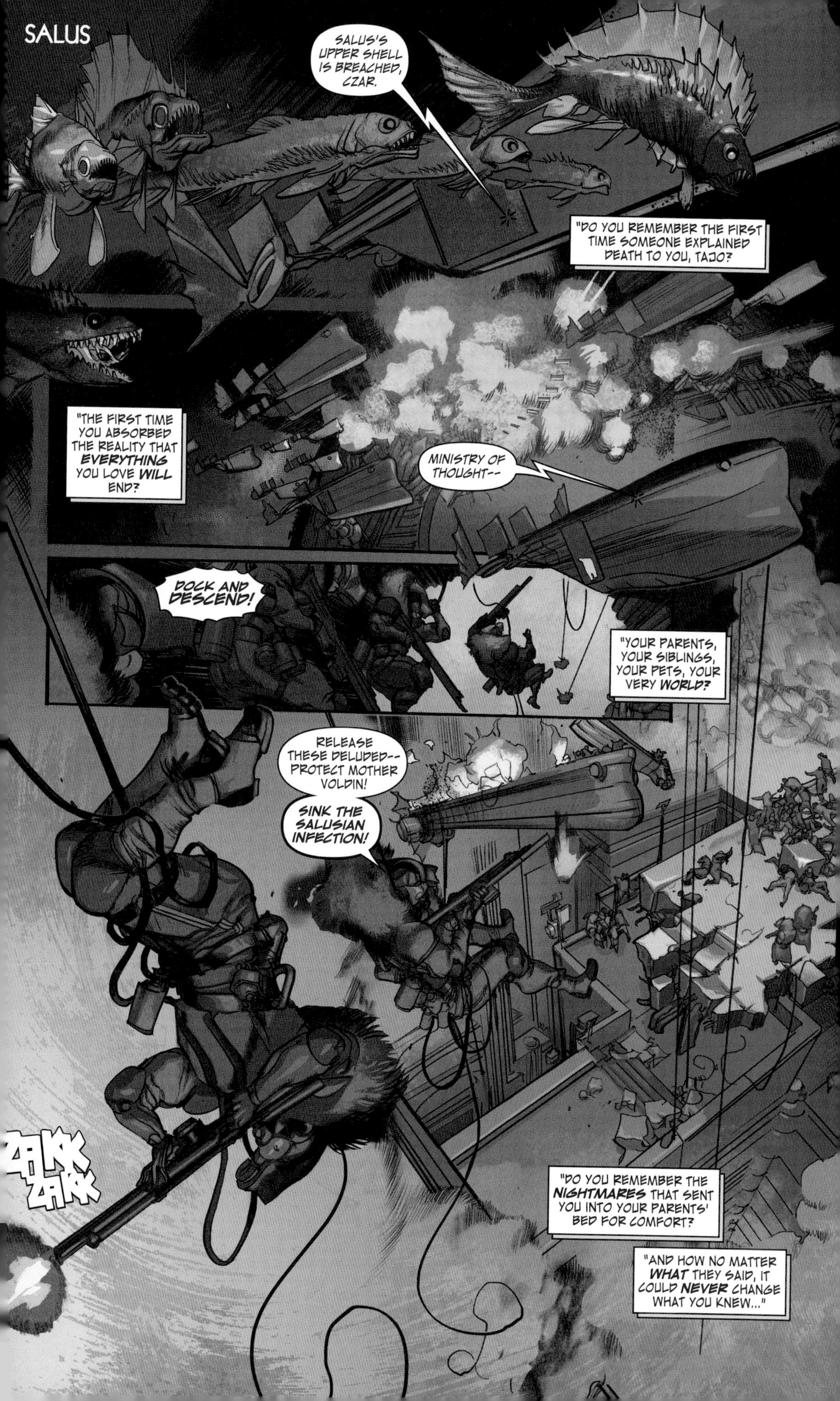
SALUS
SALUS'S UPPER SHELL IS BREACHED, CZAR.
"DO YOU REMEMBER THE FIRST TIME SOMEONE EXPLAINED DEATH TO YOU, TAJO?
"THE FIRST TIME YOU ABSORBED THE REALITY THAT EVERYTHING YOU LOVE WILL END?
MINISTRY OF THOUGHT--
DOCK AND DESCEND!
"YOUR PARENTS, YOUR SIBLINGS, YOUR PETS, YOUR VERY WORLD?
RELEASE THESE DELUDED--PROTECT MOTHER VOLDIN!
SINK THE SALUSIAN INFECTION!
ZAKK ZAKK
"DO YOU REMEMBER THE NIGHTMARES THAT SENT YOU INTO YOUR PARENTS' BED FOR COMFORT?
"AND HOW NO MATTER WHAT THEY SAID, IT COULD NEVER CHANGE WHAT YOU KNEW..."

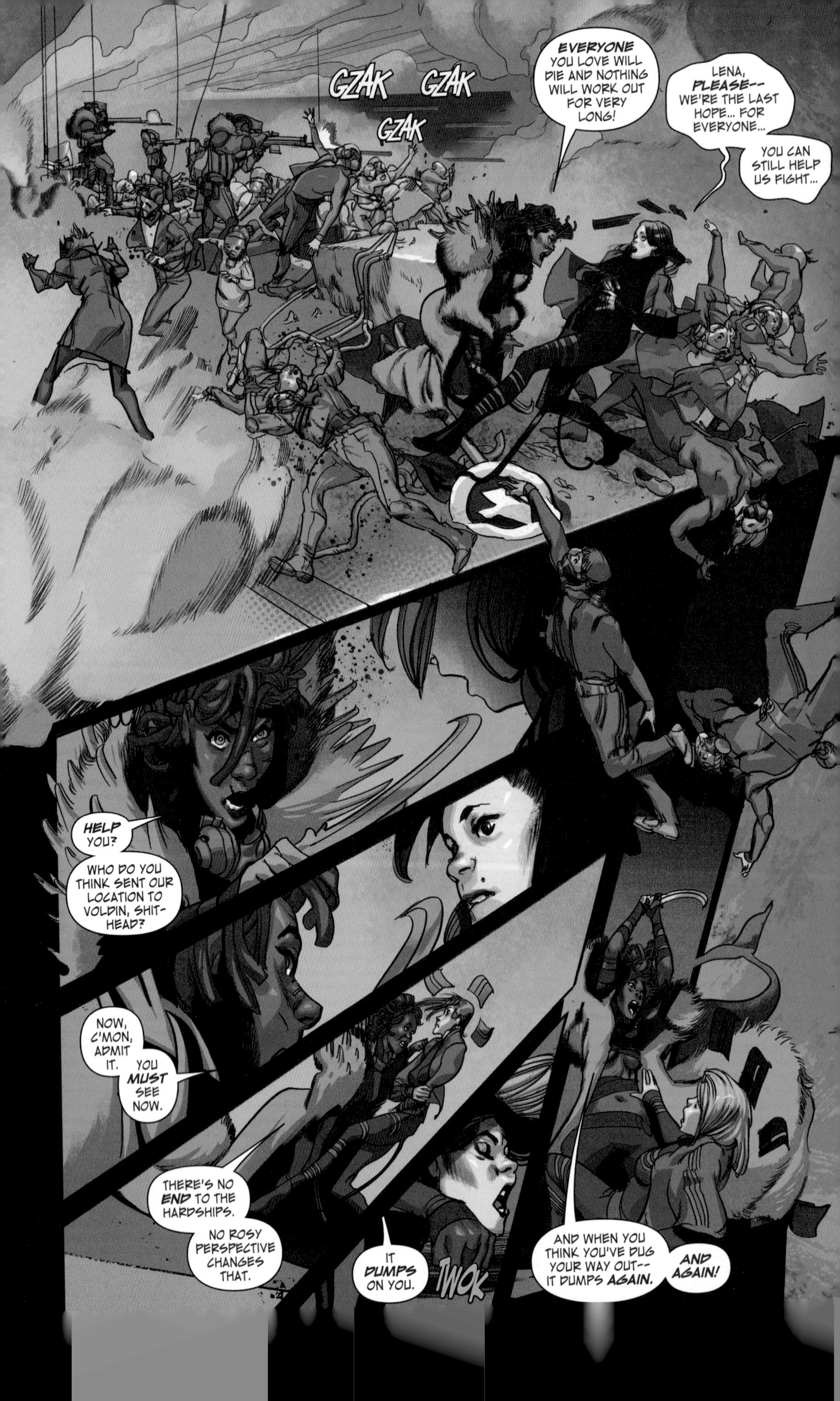

GZAK GZAK
GZAK
EVERYONE YOU LOVE WILL DIE AND NOTHING WILL WORK OUT FOR VERY LONG!
LENA, PLEASE-- WE'RE THE LAST HOPE... FOR EVERYONE...
YOU CAN STILL HELP US FIGHT...
HELP YOU?
WHO DO YOU THINK SENT OUR LOCATION TO VOLDIN, SHIT-HEAD?
NOW, C'MON, ADMIT IT.
YOU MUST SEE NOW.
THERE'S NO END TO THE HARDSHIPS.
NO ROSY PERSPECTIVE CHANGES THAT.
IT DUMPS ON YOU.
TWOK
AND WHEN YOU THINK YOU'VE DUG YOUR WAY OUT-- IT DUMPS AGAIN.
AND AGAIN!

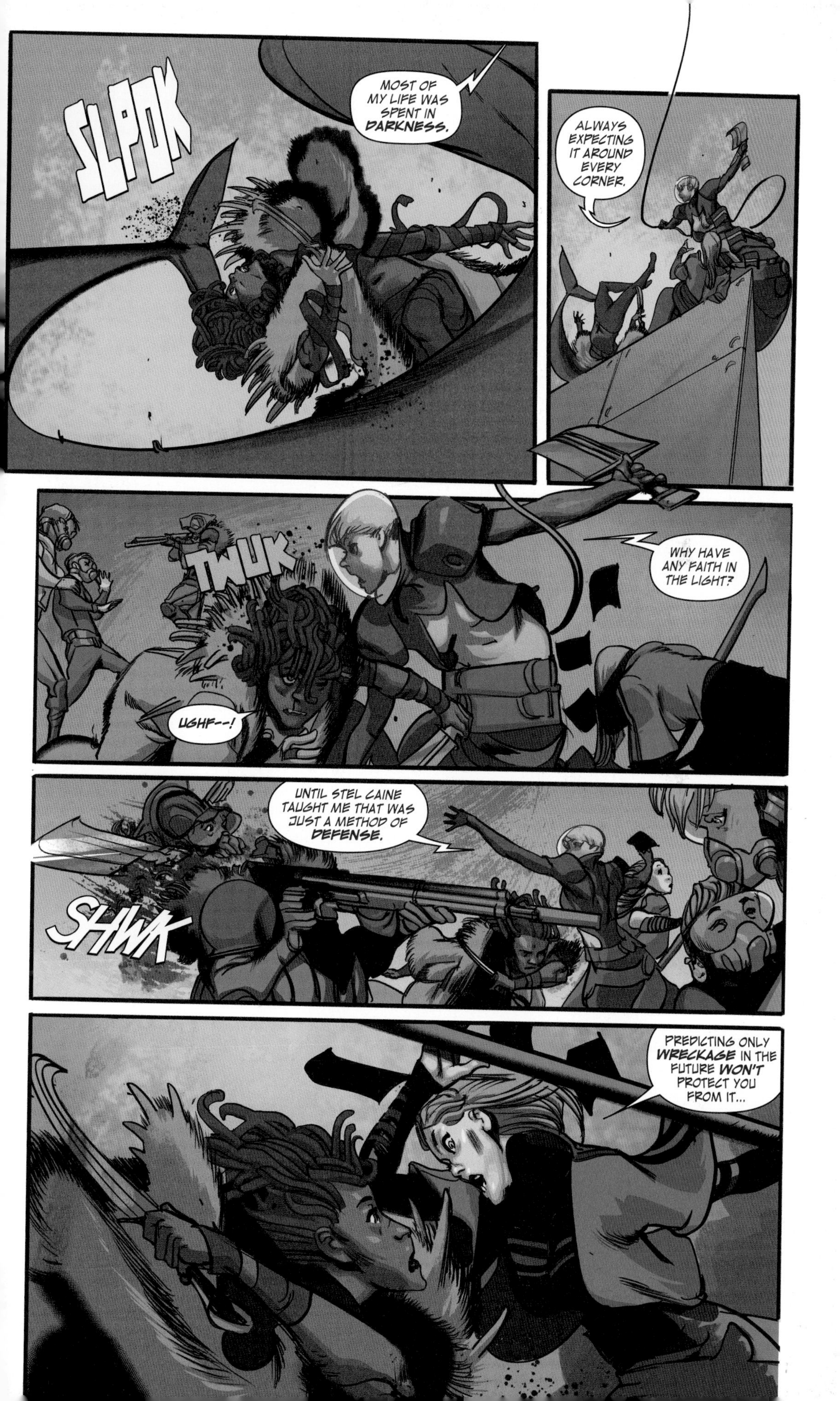
SLPOK
MOST OF MY LIFE WAS SPENT IN DARKNESS.
ALWAYS EXPECTING IT AROUND EVERY CORNER.
TWUK
WHY HAVE ANY FAITH IN THE LIGHT?
UGHF--!
UNTIL STEL CAINE TAUGHT ME THAT WAS JUST A METHOD OF DEFENSE.
SHWK
PREDICTING ONLY WRECKAGE IN THE FUTURE WON'T PROTECT YOU FROM IT...

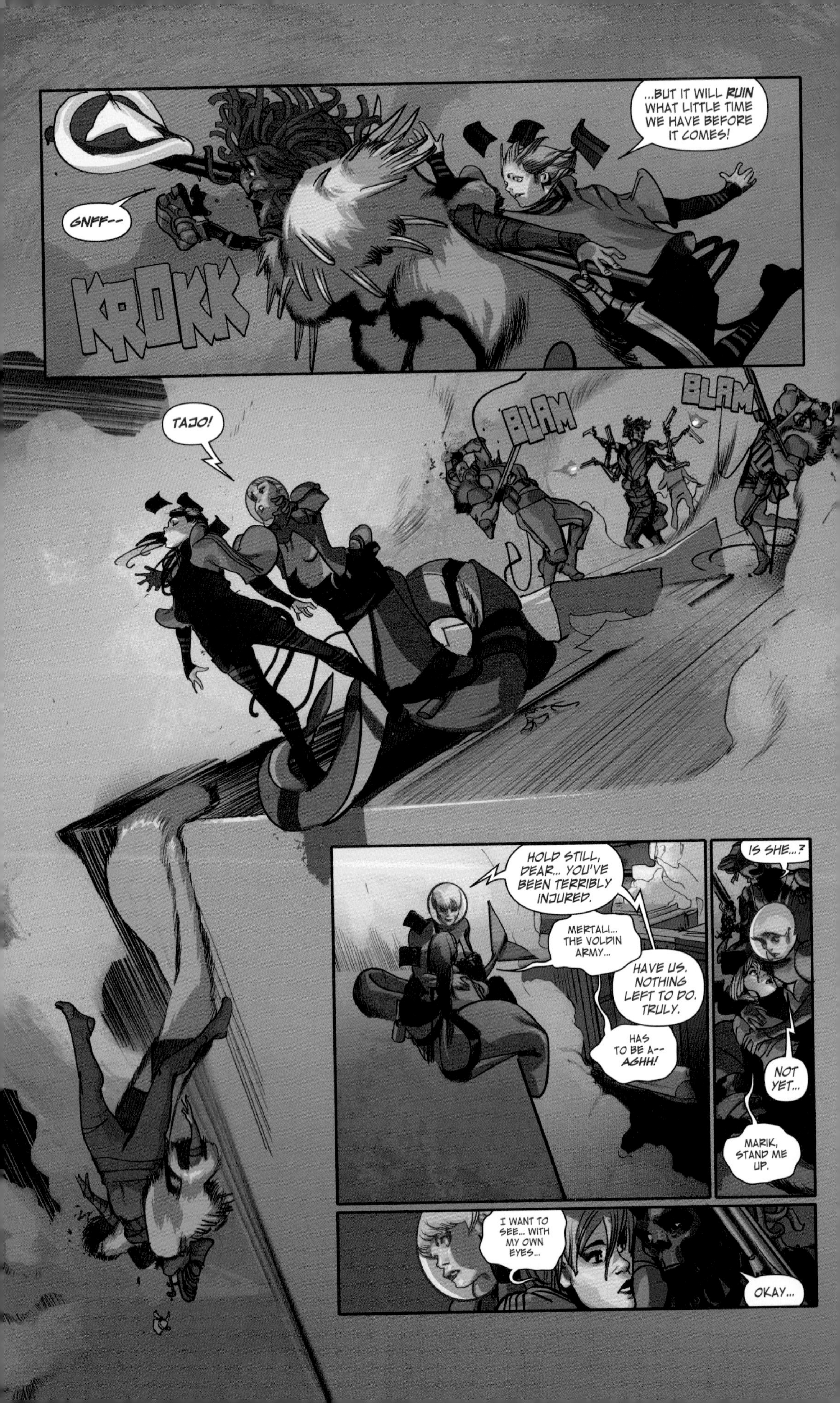

...BUT IT WILL RUIN WHAT LITTLE TIME WE HAVE BEFORE IT COMES!
GNFF--
KROKK
TAJO!
BLAM
BLAM
HOLD STILL, DEAR... YOU'VE BEEN TERRIBLY INJURED.
MERTALI... THE VOLDIN ARMY...
HAVE US. NOTHING LEFT TO DO. TRULY.
HAS TO BE A-- AGHH!
IS SHE...?
NOT YET...
MARIK, STAND ME UP.
I WANT TO SEE... WITH MY OWN EYES...
OKAY...

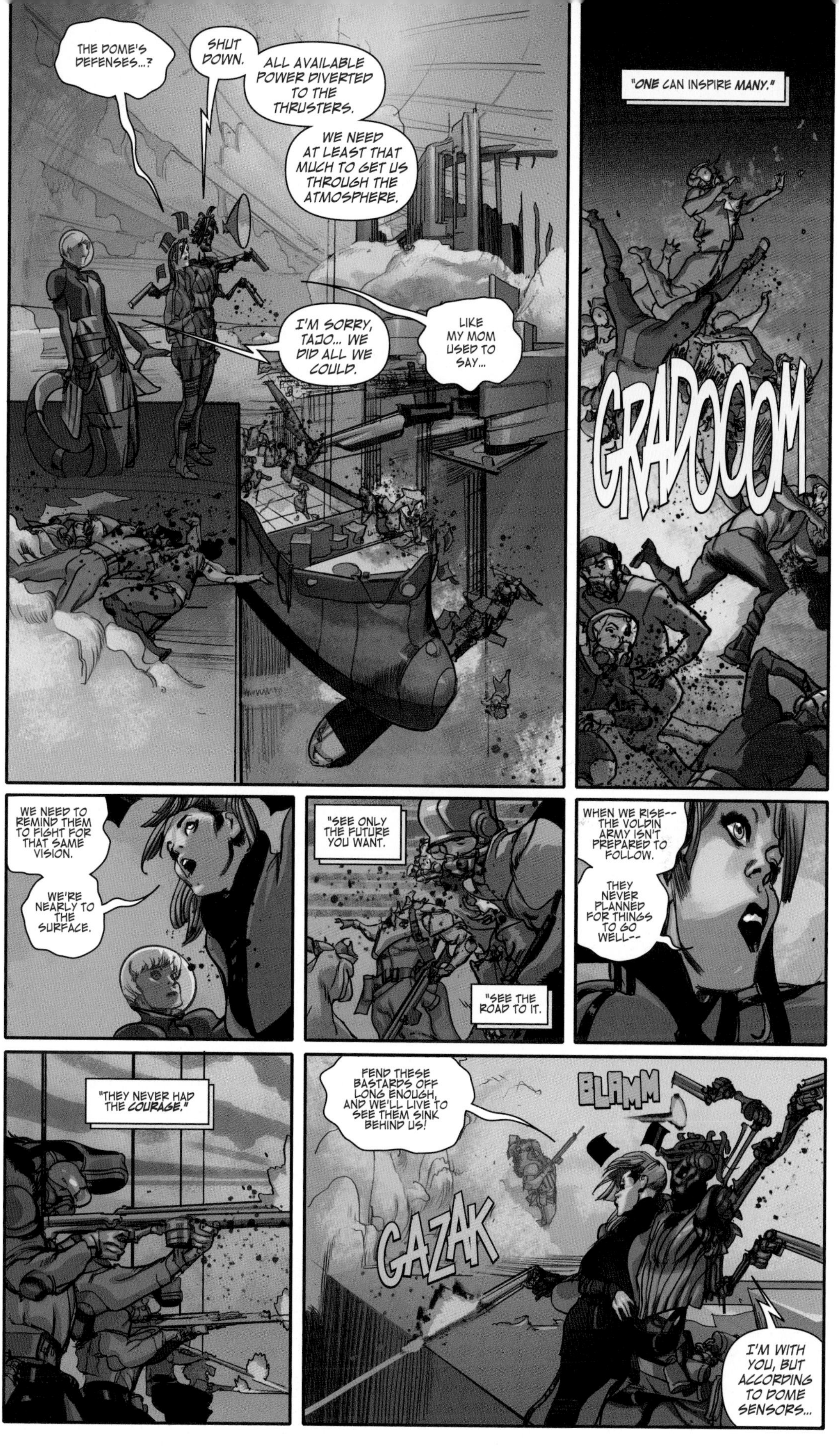

THE DOME'S DEFENSES...?
SHUT DOWN.
ALL AVAILABLE POWER DIVERTED TO THE THRUSTERS.
WE NEED AT LEAST THAT MUCH TO GET US THROUGH THE ATMOSPHERE.
I'M SORRY, TAJO... WE DID ALL WE COULD.
LIKE MY MOM USED TO SAY...
"ONE CAN INSPIRE MANY."
GRADOOOM
WE NEED TO REMIND THEM TO FIGHT FOR THAT SAME VISION.
WE'RE NEARLY TO THE SURFACE.
"SEE ONLY THE FUTURE YOU WANT.
"SEE THE ROAD TO IT.
WHEN WE RISE-- THE VOLDIN ARMY ISN'T PREPARED TO FOLLOW.
THEY NEVER PLANNED FOR THINGS TO GO WELL--
"THEY NEVER HAD THE COURAGE."
FEND THESE BASTARDS OFF LONG ENOUGH, AND WE'LL LIVE TO SEE THEM SINK BEHIND US!
BLAMM
GAZAK
I'M WITH YOU, BUT ACCORDING TO DOME SENSORS...

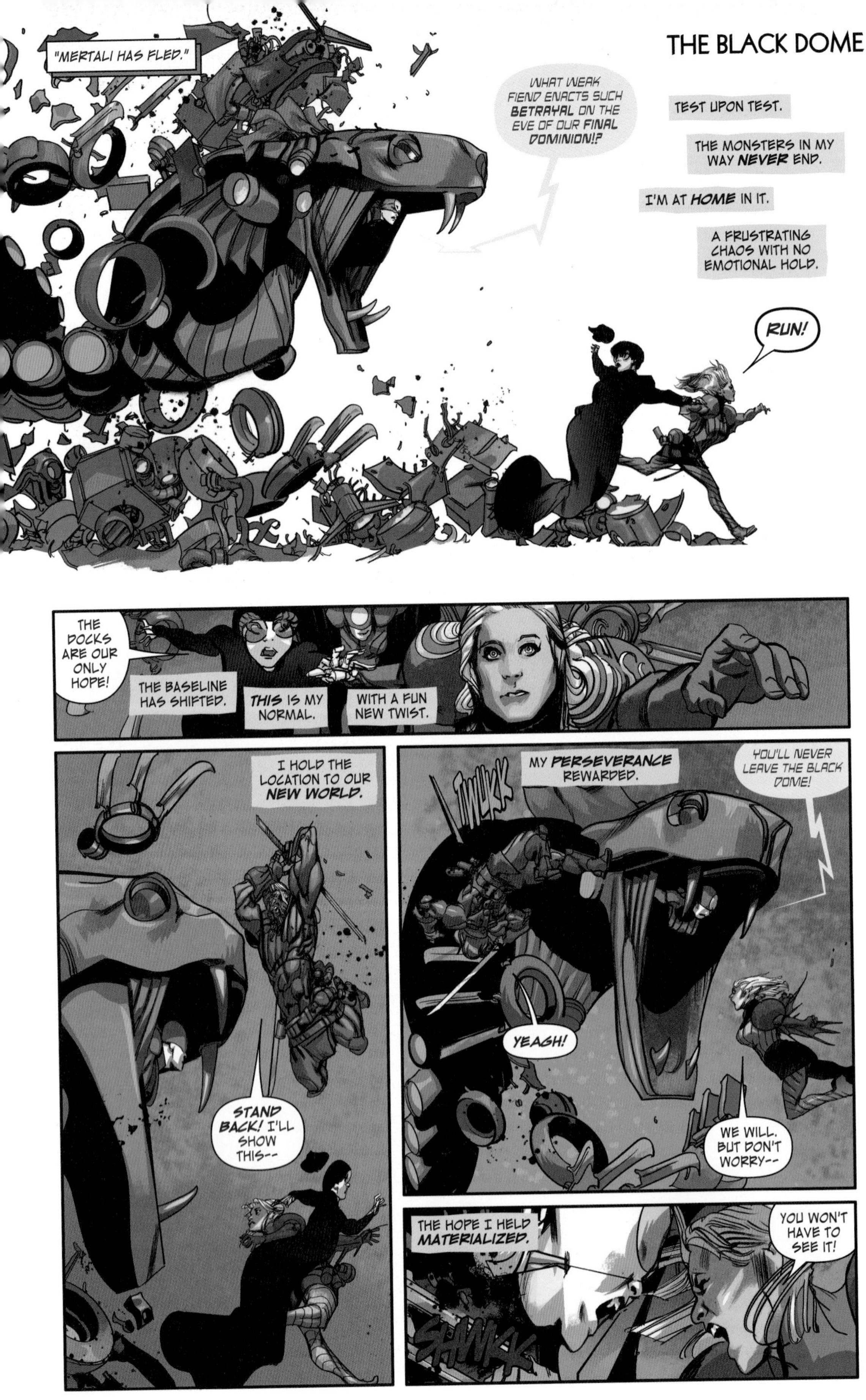
"MERTALI HAS FLED."
WHAT WEAK FIEND ENACTS SUCH BETRAYAL ON THE EVE OF OUR FINAL DOMINION!?
TEST UPON TEST.
THE MONSTERS IN MY WAY NEVER END.
I'M AT HOME IN IT.
A FRUSTRATING CHAOS WITH NO EMOTIONAL HOLD.
RUN!
THE DOCKS ARE OUR ONLY HOPE!
THE BASELINE HAS SHIFTED.
THIS IS MY NORMAL.
WITH A FUN NEW TWIST.
I HOLD THE LOCATION TO OUR NEW WORLD.
STAND BACK! I'LL SHOW THIS--
MY PERSEVERANCE REWARDED.
YOU'LL NEVER LEAVE THE BLACK DOME!
YEAGH!
WE WILL. BUT DON'T WORRY--
THE HOPE I HELD MATERIALIZED.
YOU WON'T HAVE TO SEE IT!
SHNKK

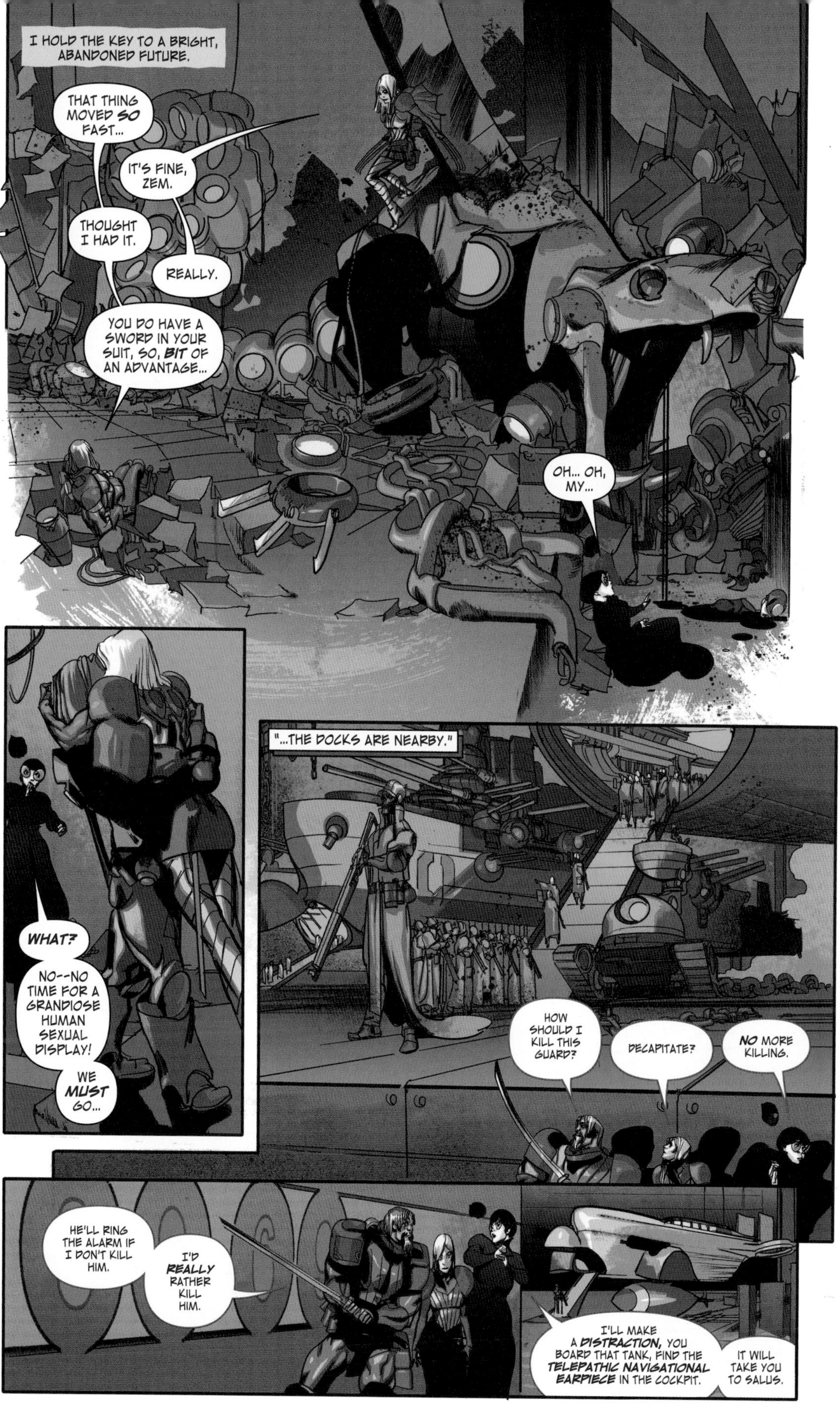
I HOLD THE KEY TO A BRIGHT, ABANDONED FUTURE.
THAT THING MOVED **SO** FAST...
IT'S FINE, ZEM.
THOUGHT I HAD IT.
REALLY.
YOU DO HAVE A SWORD IN YOUR SUIT, SO, **BIT** OF AN ADVANTAGE...
OH... OH, MY...
WHAT?
NO--NO TIME FOR A GRANDIOSE HUMAN SEXUAL DISPLAY!
WE **MUST** GO...
"...THE DOCKS ARE NEARBY."
HOW SHOULD I KILL THIS GUARD?
DECAPITATE?
NO MORE KILLING.
HE'LL RING THE ALARM IF I DON'T KILL HIM.
I'D **REALLY** RATHER KILL HIM.
I'LL MAKE A **DISTRACTION,** YOU BOARD THAT TANK, FIND THE ***TELEPATHIC NAVIGATIONAL EARPIECE*** IN THE COCKPIT.
IT WILL TAKE YOU TO SALUS.

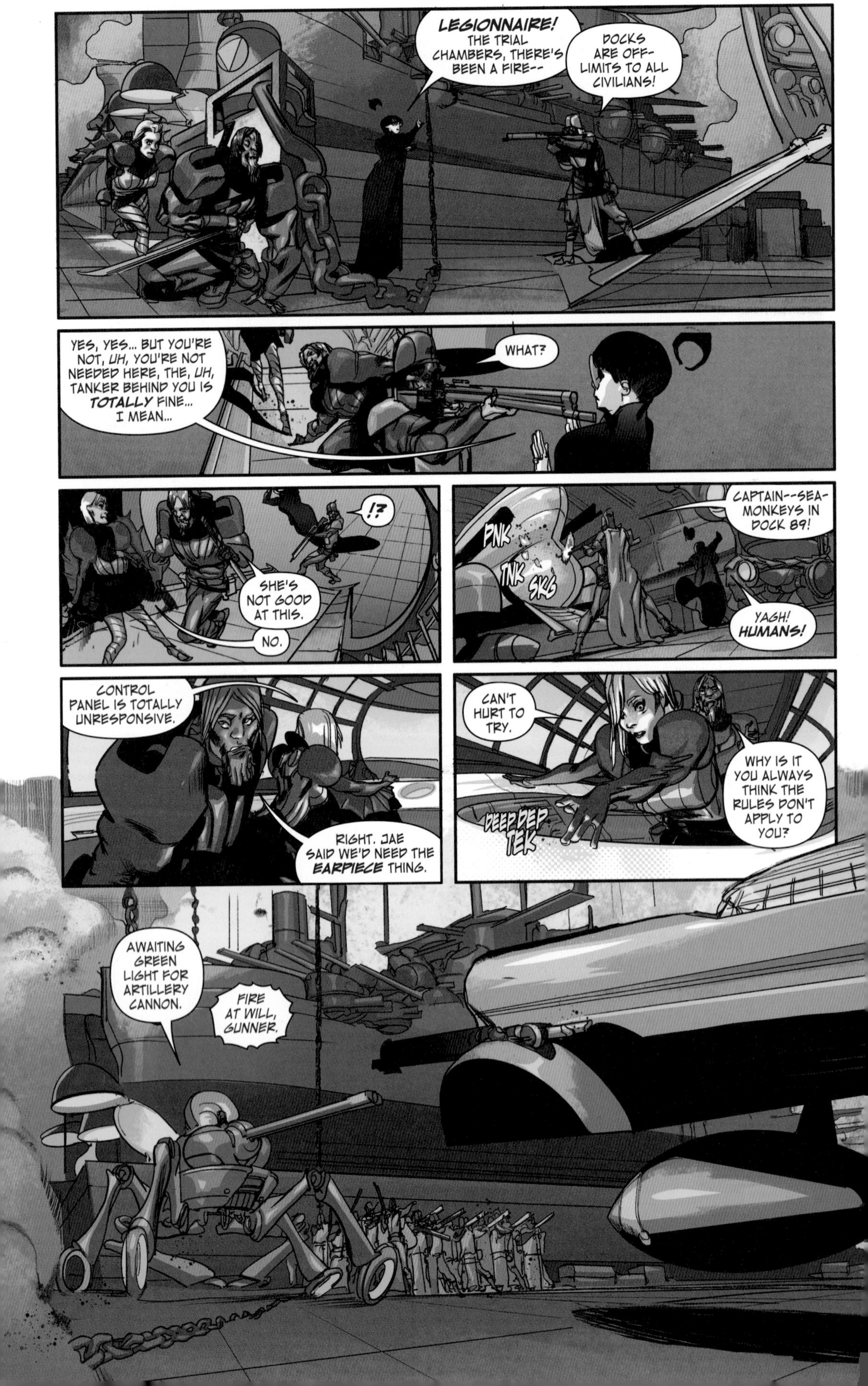
LEGIONNAIRE! THE TRIAL CHAMBERS, THERE'S BEEN A FIRE--
DOCKS ARE OFF-LIMITS TO ALL CIVILIANS!
YES, YES... BUT YOU'RE NOT, UH, YOU'RE NOT NEEDED HERE, THE, UH, TANKER BEHIND YOU IS TOTALLY FINE... I MEAN...
WHAT?
!?
SHE'S NOT GOOD AT THIS.
NO.
CAPTAIN--SEA-MONKEYS IN DOCK 89!
PNK
TNK
SKG
YAGH! HUMANS!
CONTROL PANEL IS TOTALLY UNRESPONSIVE.
RIGHT. JAE SAID WE'D NEED THE EARPIECE THING.
CAN'T HURT TO TRY.
DEEP DEP TEK
WHY IS IT YOU ALWAYS THINK THE RULES DON'T APPLY TO YOU?
AWAITING GREEN LIGHT FOR ARTILLERY CANNON.
FIRE AT WILL, GUNNER.

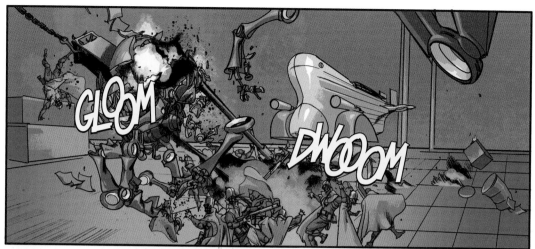

GLOOM

DWOOM

OOPS...

YOU-- AWAY FROM THE CONTROL BAY!

I'M SO SORRY! WAS TRYING TO HELP...

MAYBE NOT SO BAD.

SHE BOUGHT ME TIME TO FIND *THIS* THINGY.

ZAK ZAK ZAK

PNK SHK SNK TWG

YERAGH!

ESTABLISHING CEREBRAL LINK.

WHOA, I SEE THE CONTROLS IN MY HEAD!

NEAT. SO, MAYBE YOU COULD HELP JAE?

GO.

BE SAFE!

SAVE THEM!

I ALWAYS LIKED HER.

SHE ALWAYS GAVE YOU EXTRA *TREATS*.

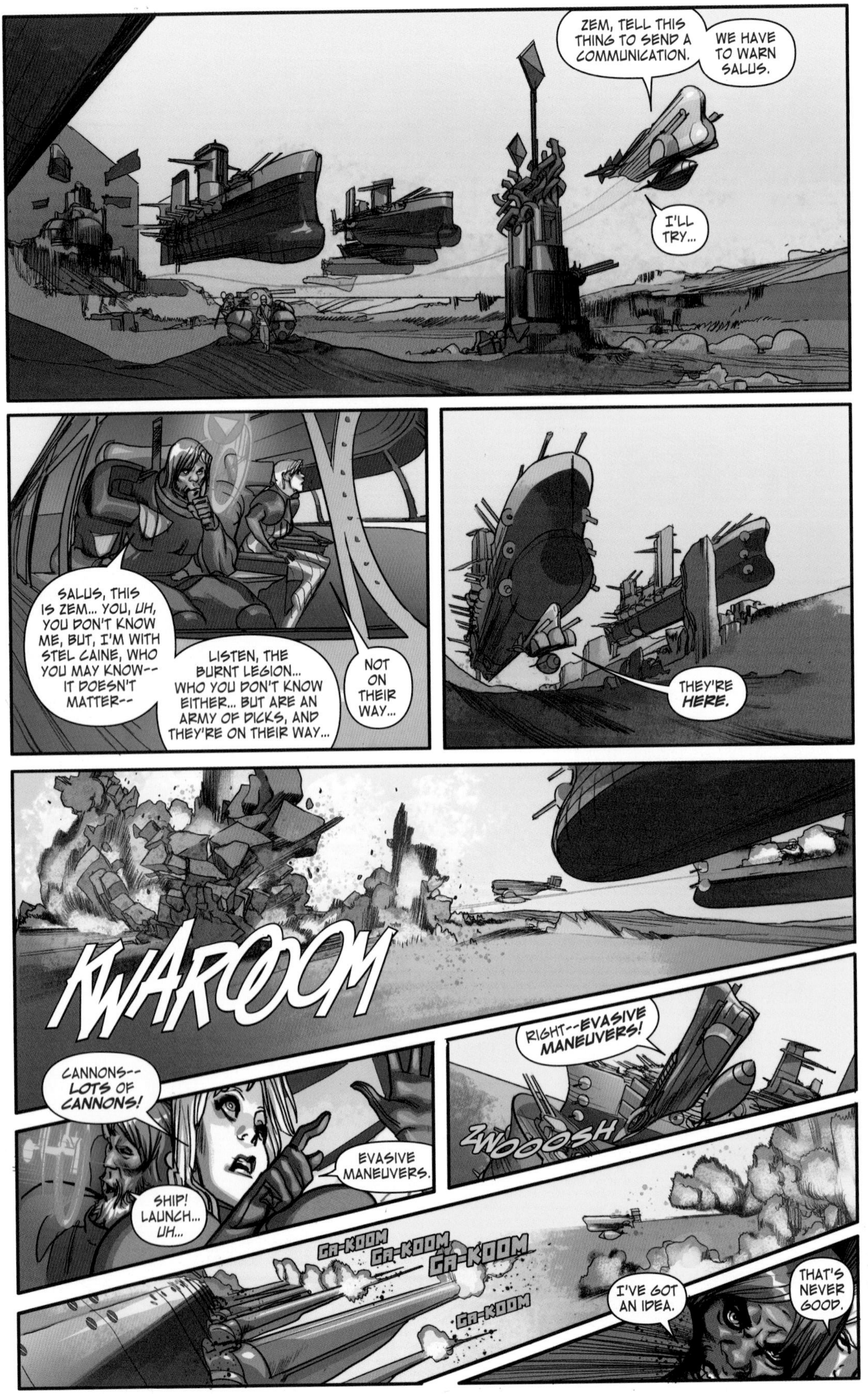
ZEM, TELL THIS THING TO SEND A COMMUNICATION.
WE HAVE TO WARN SALUS.
I'LL TRY...
SALUS, THIS IS ZEM... YOU, UH, YOU DON'T KNOW ME, BUT, I'M WITH STEL CAINE, WHO YOU MAY KNOW-- IT DOESN'T MATTER--
LISTEN, THE BURNT LEGION... WHO YOU DON'T KNOW EITHER... BUT ARE AN ARMY OF DICKS, AND THEY'RE ON THEIR WAY...
NOT ON THEIR WAY...
THEY'RE HERE.
KWAROOOM
CANNONS-- LOTS OF CANNONS!
EVASIVE MANEUVERS.
SHIP! LAUNCH... UH...
RIGHT--EVASIVE MANEUVERS!
ZWOOOSH
GA-KOOM
GA-KOOM
GA-KOOM
GA-KOOM
I'VE GOT AN IDEA.
THAT'S NEVER GOOD.

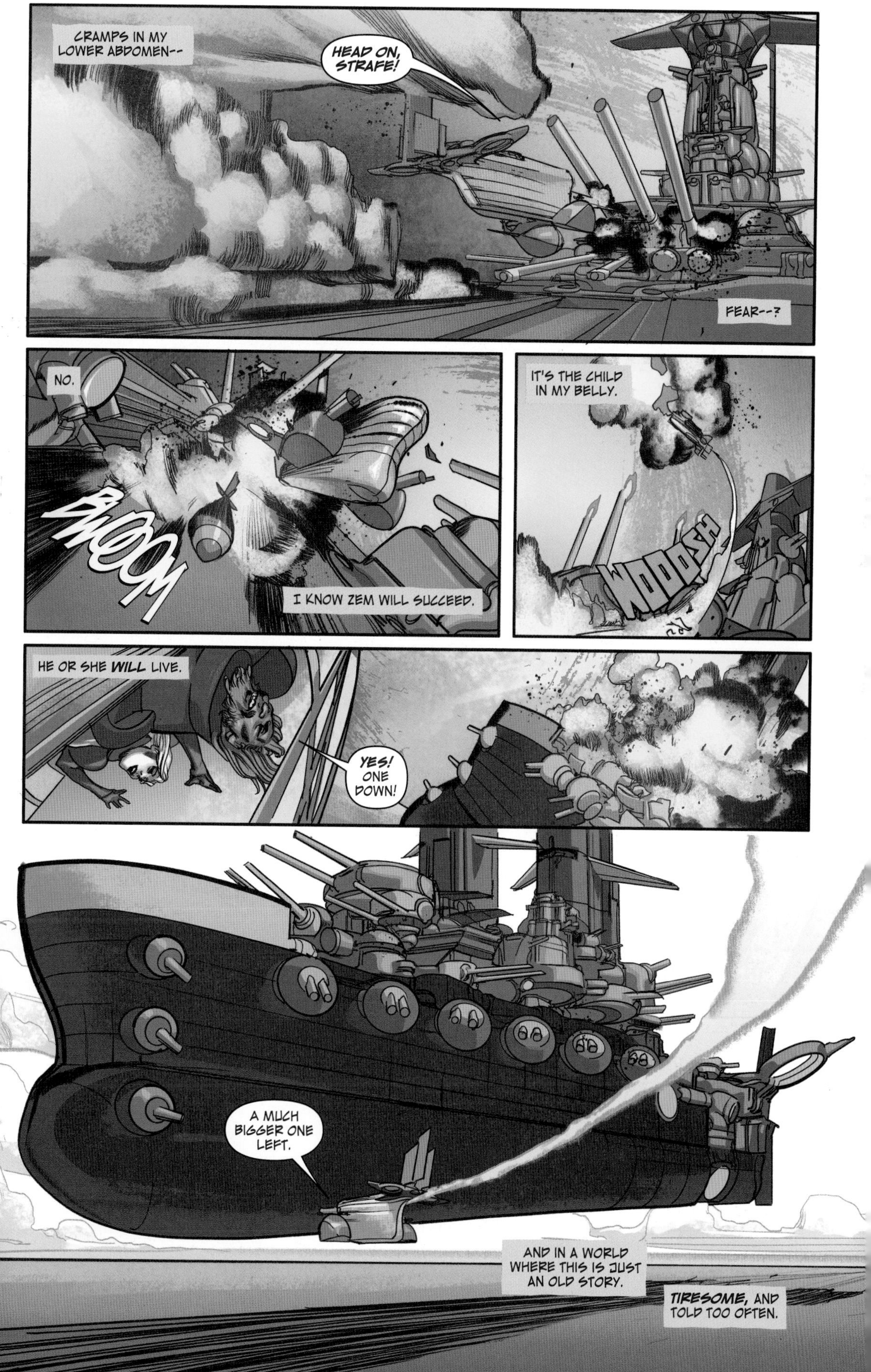

CRAMPS IN MY LOWER ABDOMEN--
HEAD ON, STRAFE!
FEAR--?
NO.
BWOOOM
I KNOW ZEM WILL SUCCEED.
IT'S THE CHILD IN MY BELLY.
WOOOSH
HE OR SHE WILL LIVE.
YES! ONE DOWN!
A MUCH BIGGER ONE LEFT.
AND IN A WORLD WHERE THIS IS JUST AN OLD STORY.
TIRESOME, AND TOLD TOO OFTEN.

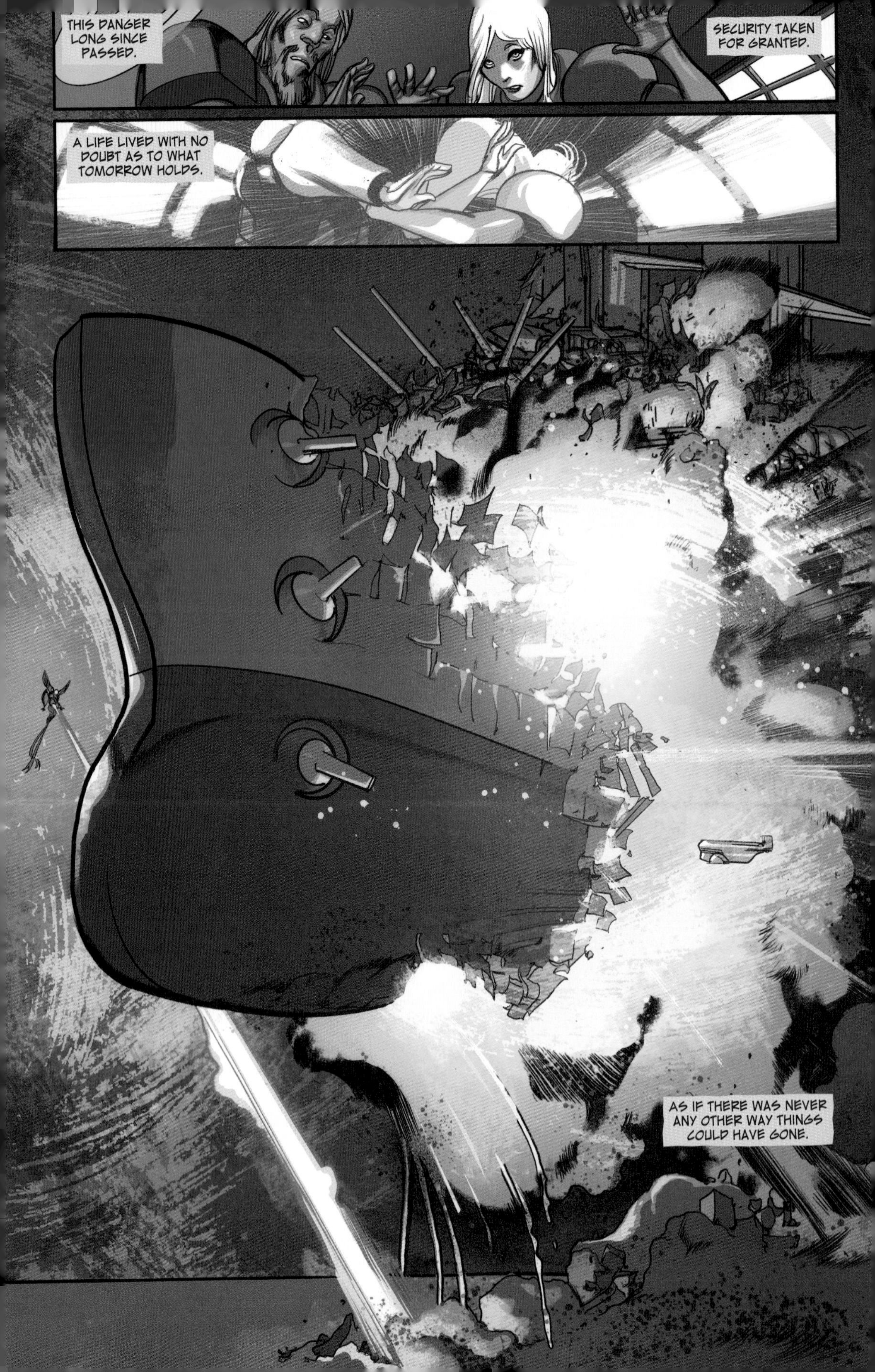
THIS DANGER LONG SINCE PASSED.
SECURITY TAKEN FOR GRANTED.
A LIFE LIVED WITH NO DOUBT AS TO WHAT TOMORROW HOLDS.
AS IF THERE WAS NEVER ANY OTHER WAY THINGS COULD HAVE GONE.

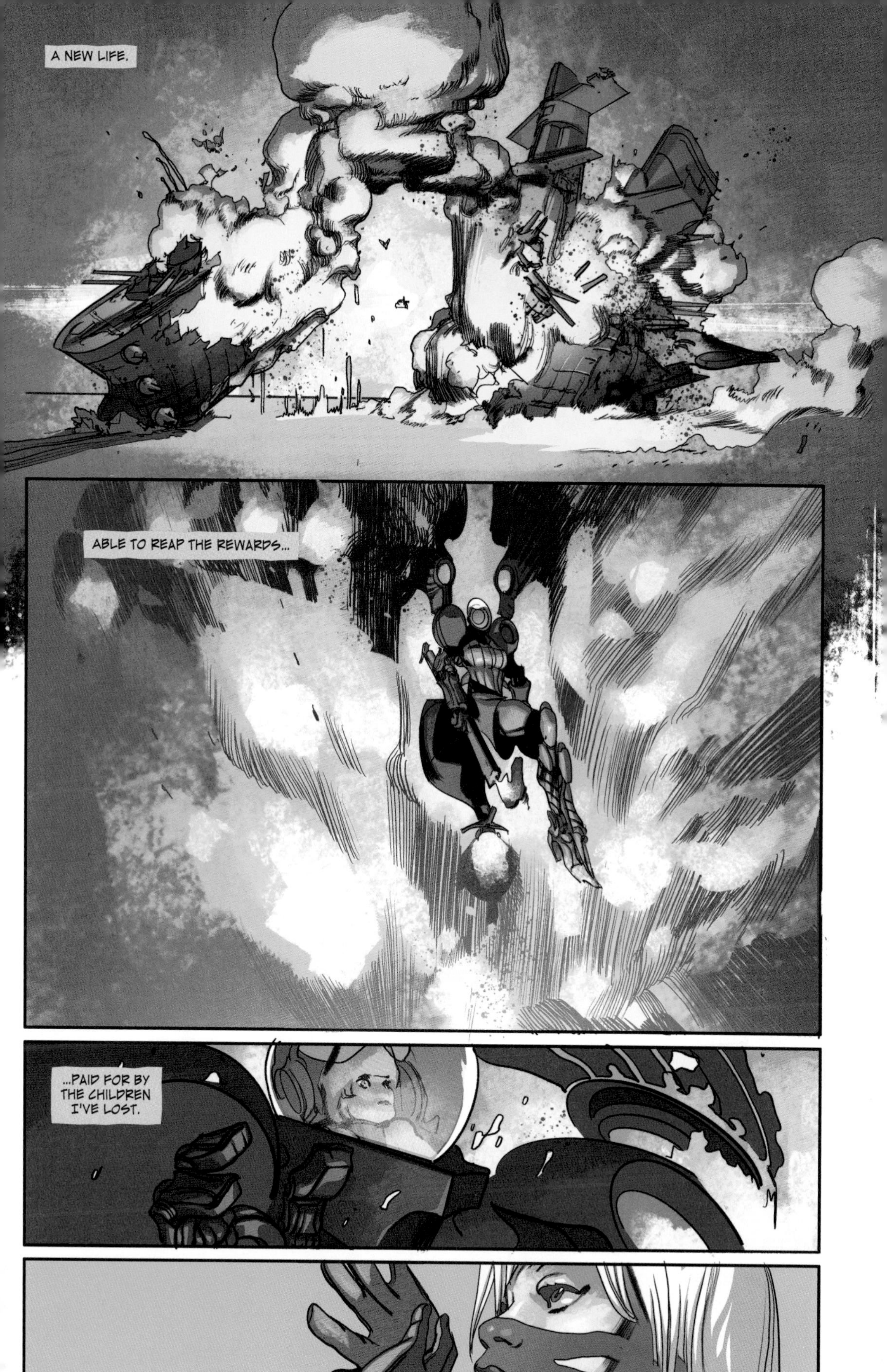
A NEW LIFE.
ABLE TO REAP THE REWARDS...
...PAID FOR BY THE CHILDREN I'VE LOST.

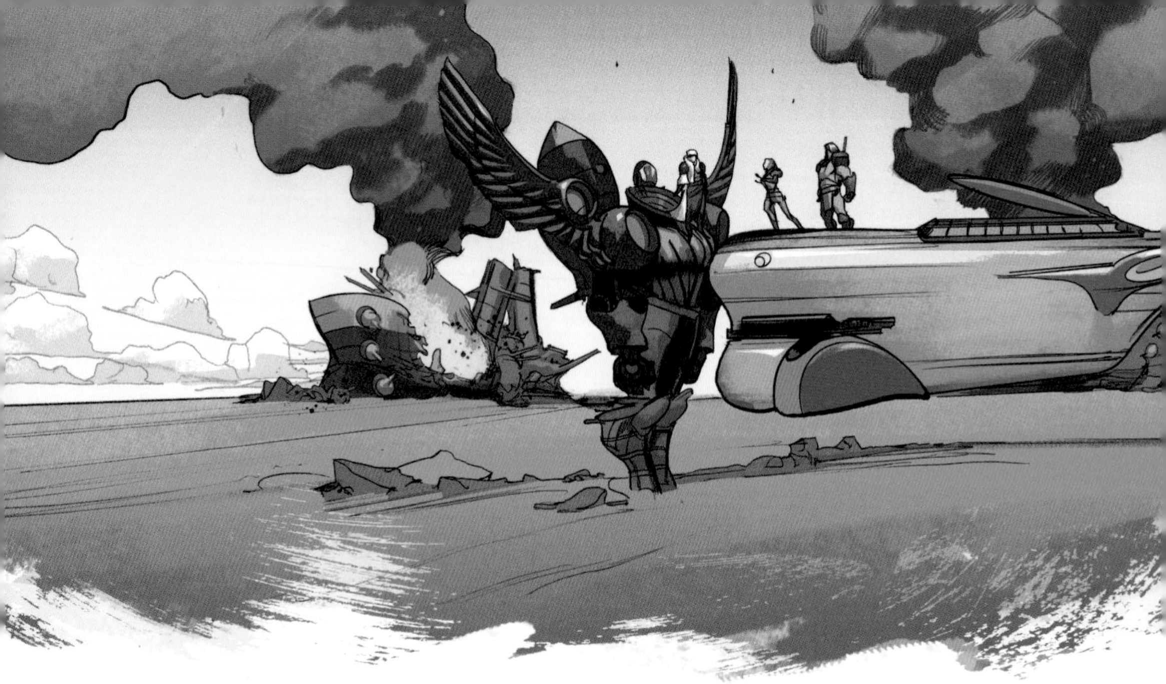

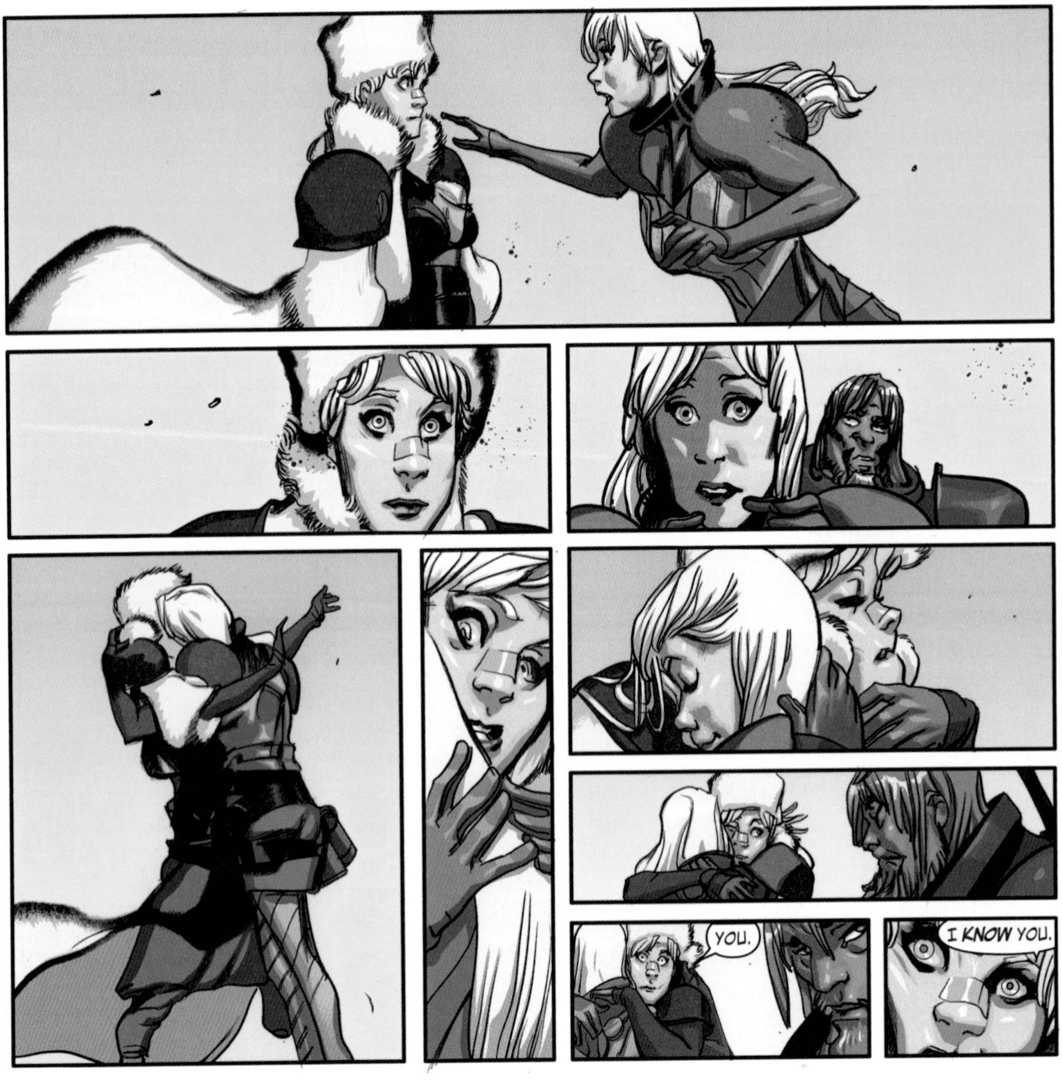

YOU.
I KNOW YOU.

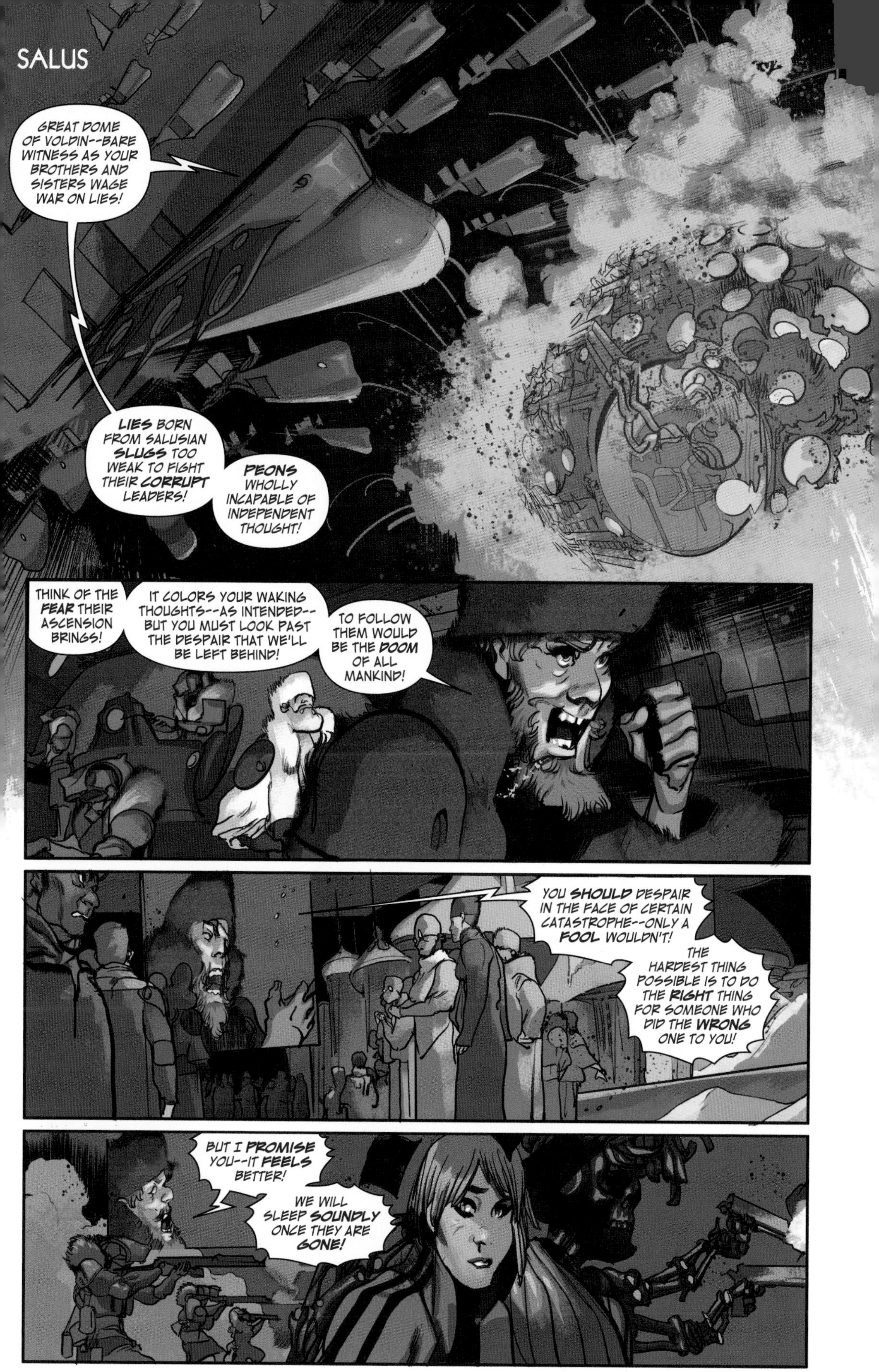
SALUS
GREAT DOME OF VOLDIN--BARE WITNESS AS YOUR BROTHERS AND SISTERS WAGE WAR ON LIES!
LIES BORN FROM SALUSIAN SLUGS TOO WEAK TO FIGHT THEIR CORRUPT LEADERS!
PEONS WHOLLY INCAPABLE OF INDEPENDENT THOUGHT!
THINK OF THE FEAR THEIR ASCENSION BRINGS!
IT COLORS YOUR WAKING THOUGHTS--AS INTENDED--BUT YOU MUST LOOK PAST THE DESPAIR THAT WE'LL BE LEFT BEHIND!
TO FOLLOW THEM WOULD BE THE DOOM OF ALL MANKIND!
YOU SHOULD DESPAIR IN THE FACE OF CERTAIN CATASTROPHE--ONLY A FOOL WOULDN'T!
THE HARDEST THING POSSIBLE IS TO DO THE RIGHT THING FOR SOMEONE WHO DID THE WRONG ONE TO YOU!
BUT I PROMISE YOU--IT FEELS BETTER!
WE WILL SLEEP SOUNDLY ONCE THEY ARE GONE!

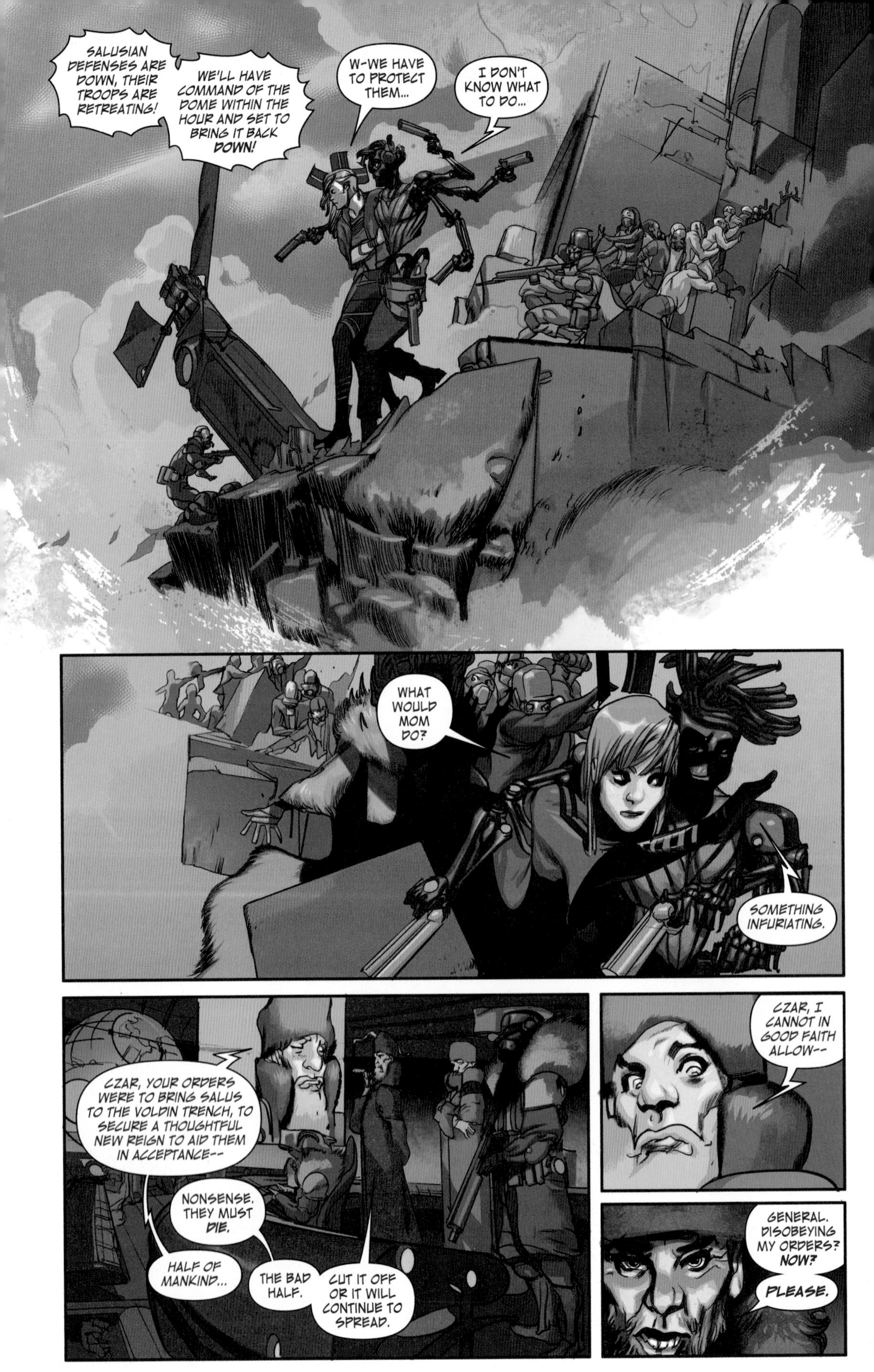
SALUSIAN DEFENSES ARE DOWN, THEIR TROOPS ARE RETREATING!
WE'LL HAVE COMMAND OF THE DOME WITHIN THE HOUR AND SET TO BRING IT BACK DOWN!
W-WE HAVE TO PROTECT THEM...
I DON'T KNOW WHAT TO DO...
WHAT WOULD MOM DO?
SOMETHING INFURIATING.
CZAR, YOUR ORDERS WERE TO BRING SALUS TO THE VOLDIN TRENCH, TO SECURE A THOUGHTFUL NEW REIGN TO AID THEM IN ACCEPTANCE--
NONSENSE. THEY MUST DIE.
HALF OF MANKIND...
THE BAD HALF.
CUT IT OFF OR IT WILL CONTINUE TO SPREAD.
CZAR, I CANNOT IN GOOD FAITH ALLOW--
GENERAL. DISOBEYING MY ORDERS? NOW?
PLEASE.

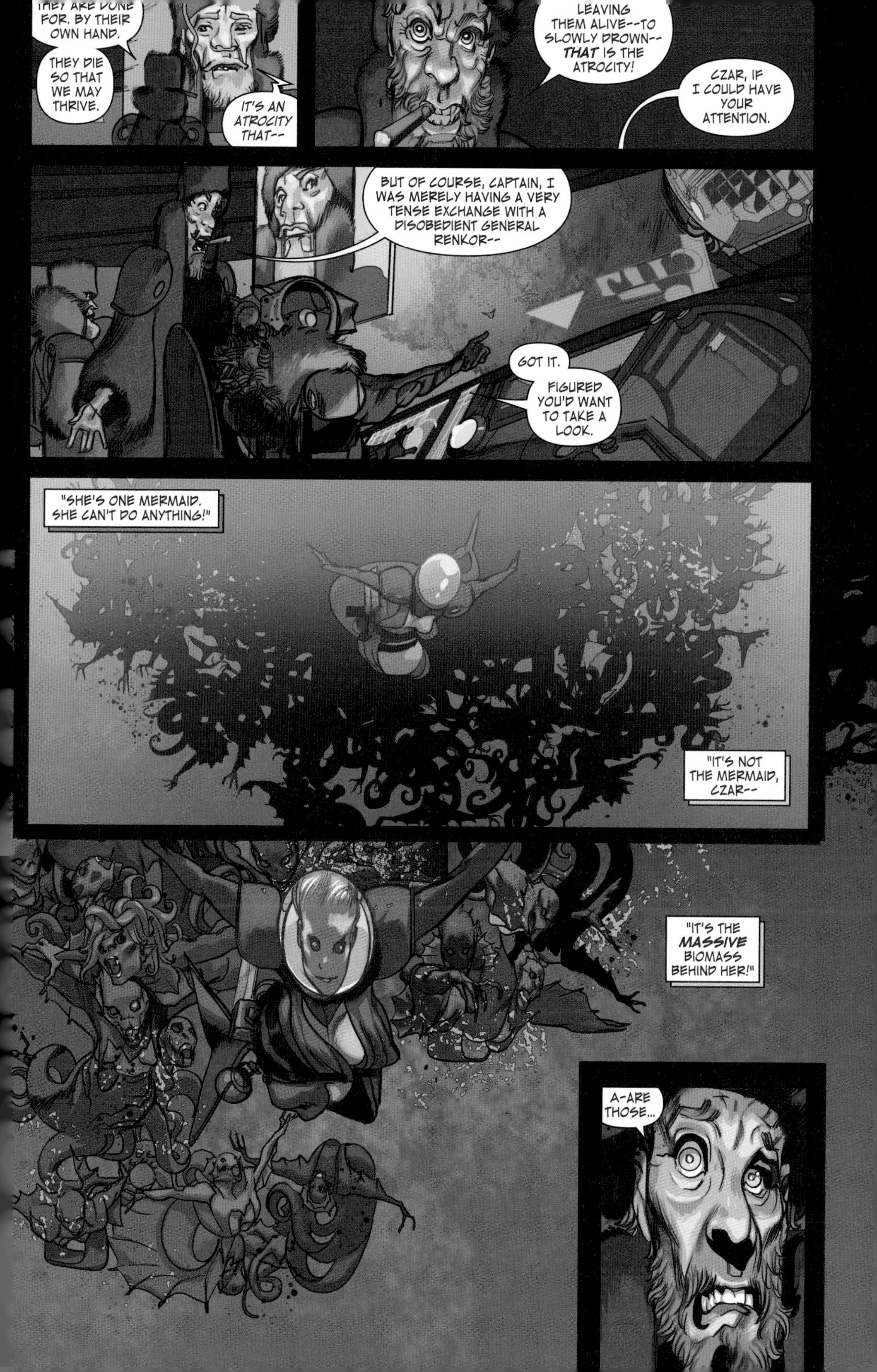
THEY ARE DONE FOR. BY THEIR OWN HAND.
THEY DIE SO THAT WE MAY THRIVE.
IT'S AN ATROCITY THAT--
LEAVING THEM ALIVE--TO SLOWLY DROWN-- THAT IS THE ATROCITY!
CZAR, IF I COULD HAVE YOUR ATTENTION.
BUT OF COURSE, CAPTAIN, I WAS MERELY HAVING A VERY TENSE EXCHANGE WITH A DISOBEDIENT GENERAL RENKOR--
GOT IT.
FIGURED YOU'D WANT TO TAKE A LOOK.
"SHE'S ONE MERMAID. SHE CAN'T DO ANYTHING!"
"IT'S NOT THE MERMAID, CZAR--
"IT'S THE MASSIVE BIOMASS BEHIND HER!"
A-ARE THOSE...

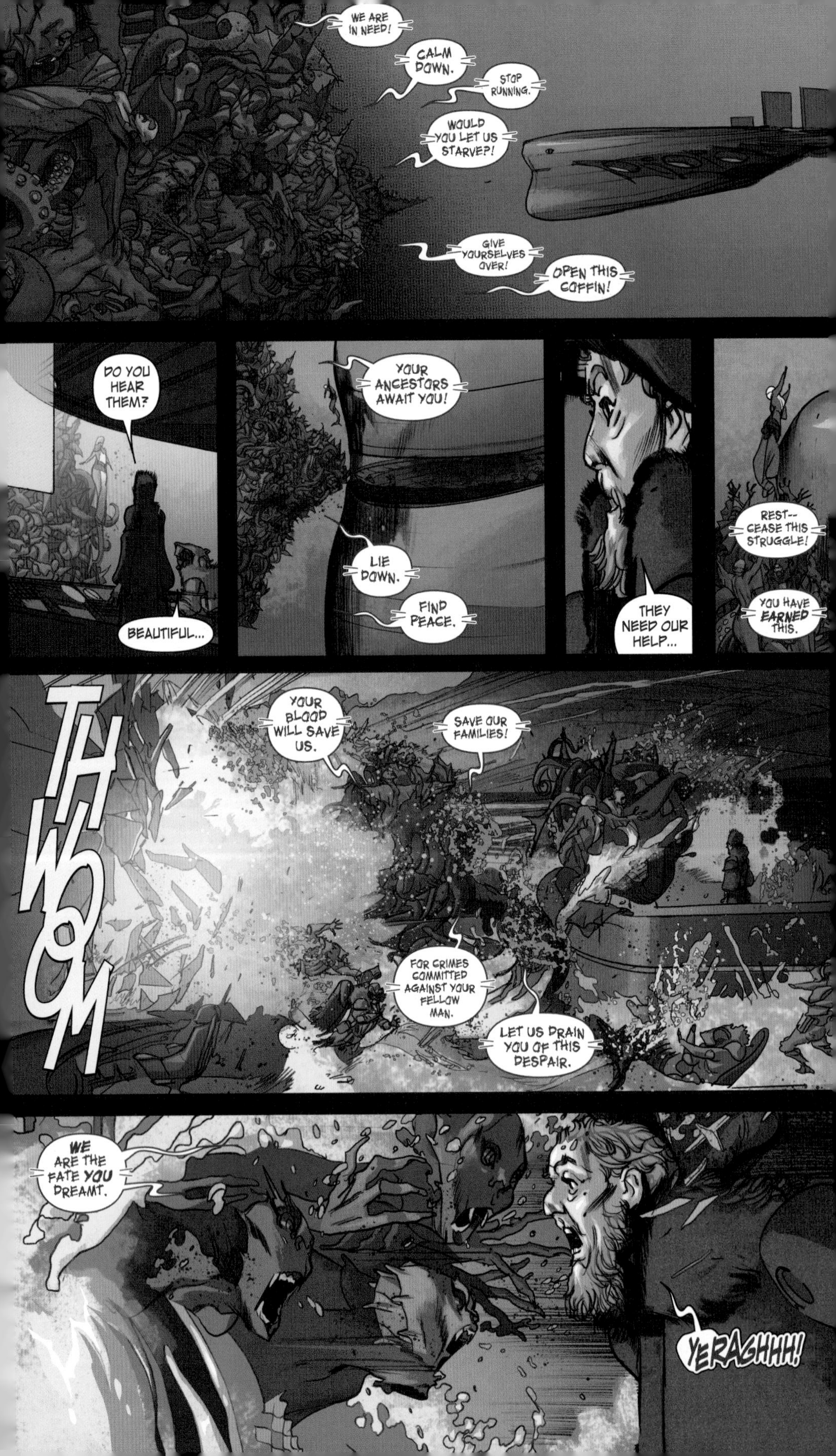
WE ARE IN NEED!
CALM DOWN.
STOP RUNNING.
WOULD YOU LET US STARVE?!
GIVE YOURSELVES OVER!
OPEN THIS COFFIN!
DO YOU HEAR THEM?
BEAUTIFUL...
YOUR ANCESTORS AWAIT YOU!
LIE DOWN.
FIND PEACE.
THEY NEED OUR HELP...
REST-- CEASE THIS STRUGGLE!
YOU HAVE EARNED THIS.
THWOOM
YOUR BLOOD WILL SAVE US.
SAVE OUR FAMILIES!
FOR CRIMES COMMITTED AGAINST YOUR FELLOW MAN.
LET US DRAIN YOU OF THIS DESPAIR.
WE ARE THE FATE YOU DREAMT.
YERAGHHH!

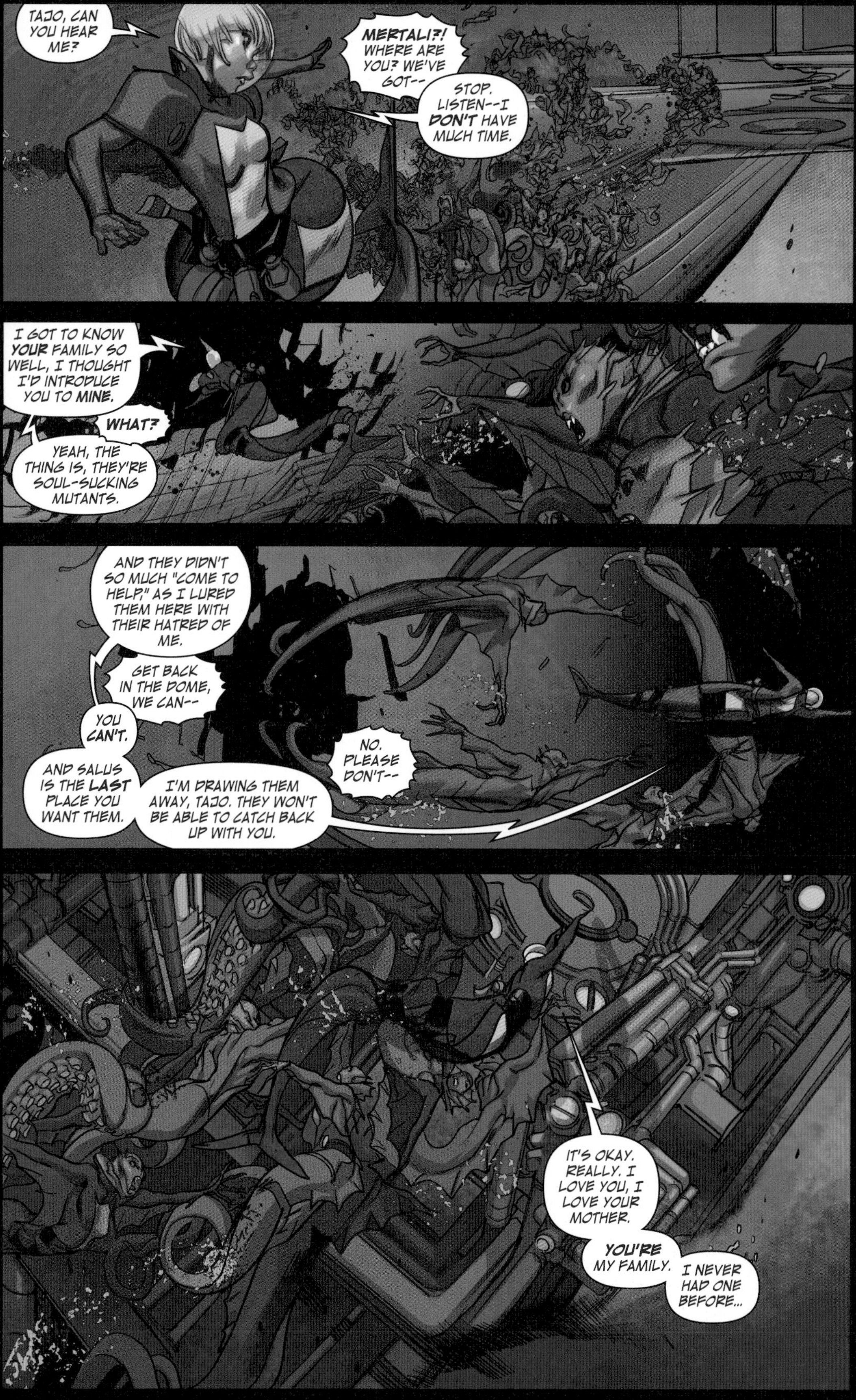
TAJO, CAN YOU HEAR ME?
MERTALI?! WHERE ARE YOU? WE'VE GOT--
STOP. LISTEN--I DON'T HAVE MUCH TIME.
I GOT TO KNOW YOUR FAMILY SO WELL, I THOUGHT I'D INTRODUCE YOU TO MINE.
WHAT?
YEAH, THE THING IS, THEY'RE SOUL-SUCKING MUTANTS.
AND THEY DIDN'T SO MUCH "COME TO HELP," AS I LURED THEM HERE WITH THEIR HATRED OF ME.
GET BACK IN THE DOME, WE CAN--
YOU CAN'T.
AND SALUS IS THE LAST PLACE YOU WANT THEM.
I'M DRAWING THEM AWAY, TAJO. THEY WON'T BE ABLE TO CATCH BACK UP WITH YOU.
NO. PLEASE DON'T--
IT'S OKAY. REALLY. I LOVE YOU, I LOVE YOUR MOTHER.
YOU'RE MY FAMILY.
I NEVER HAD ONE BEFORE...

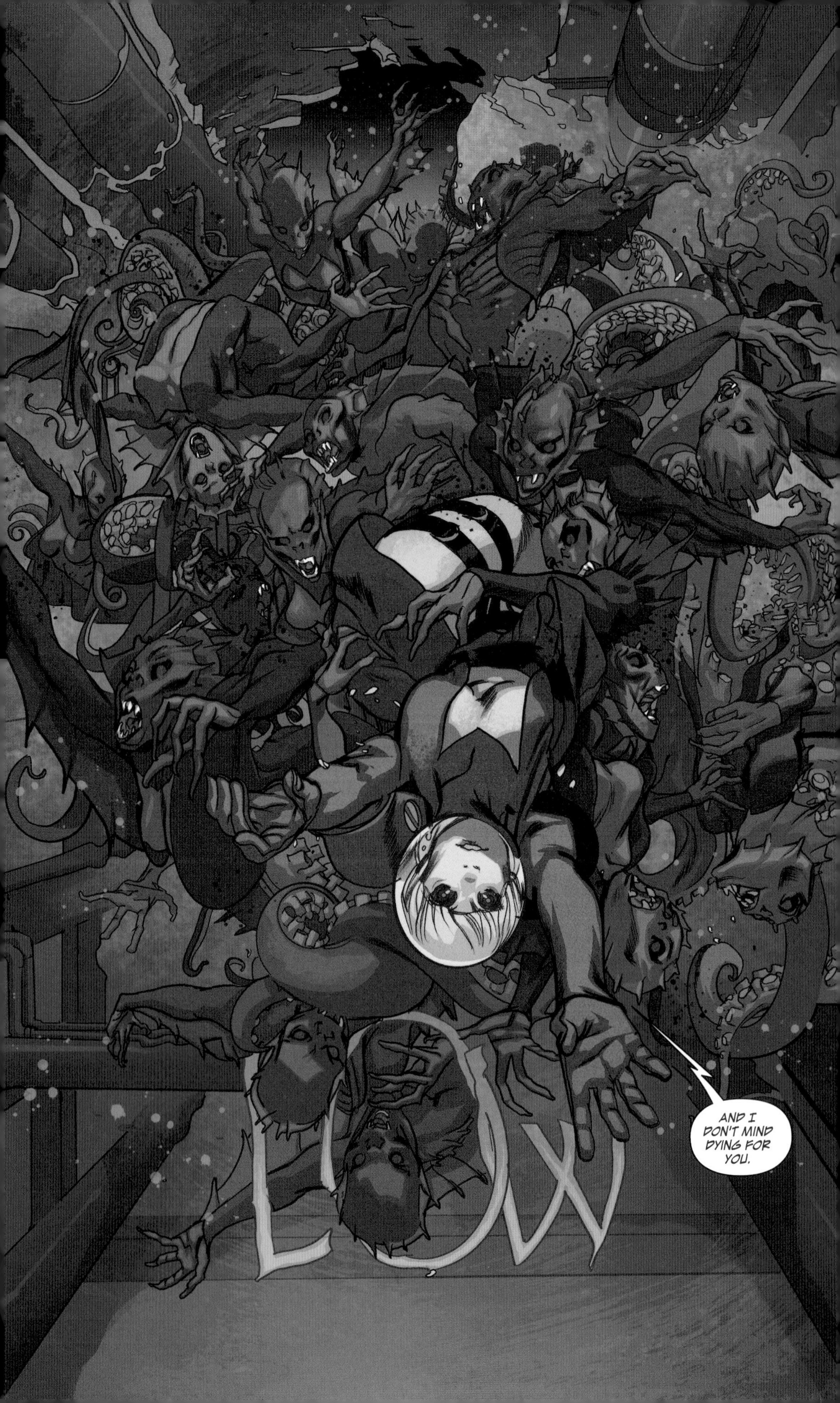
LOW
AND I DON'T MIND DYING FOR YOU.

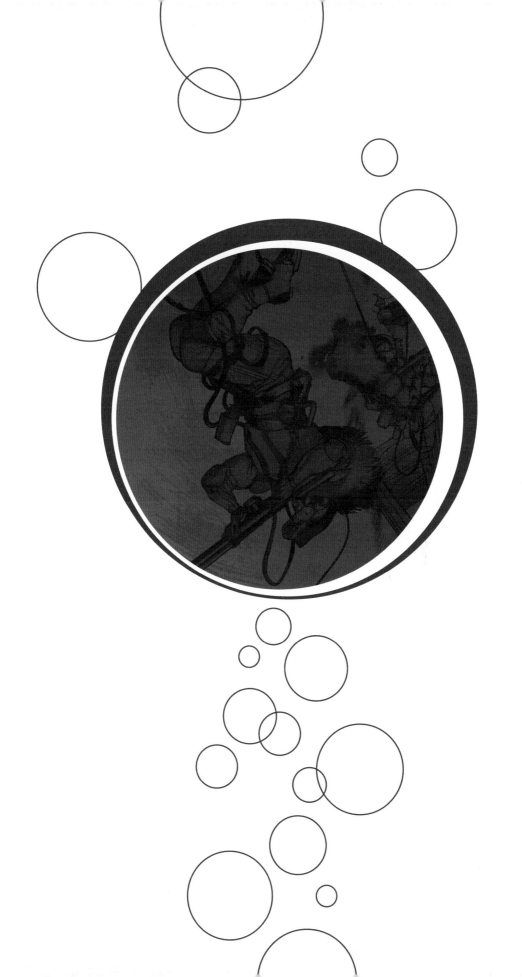

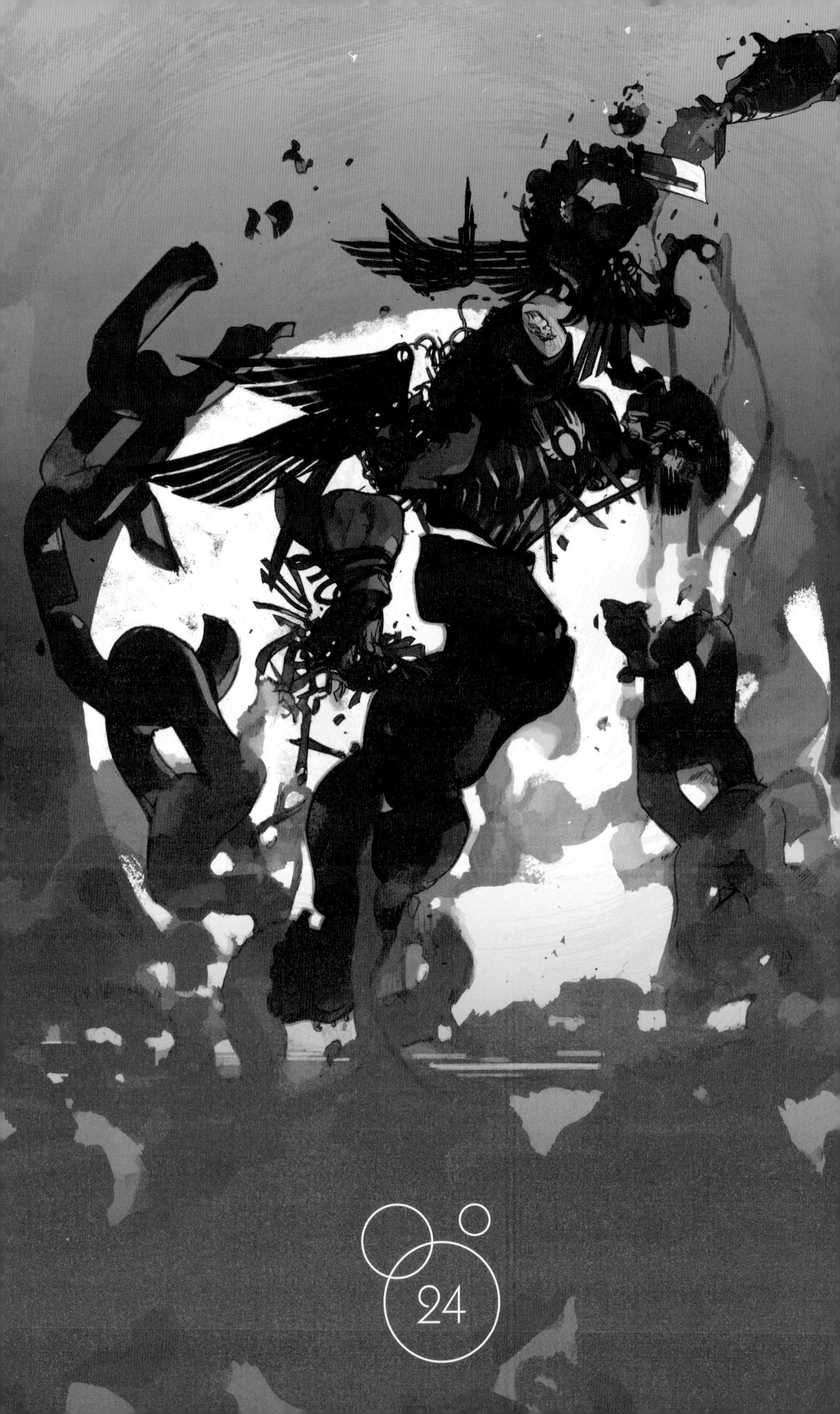

24

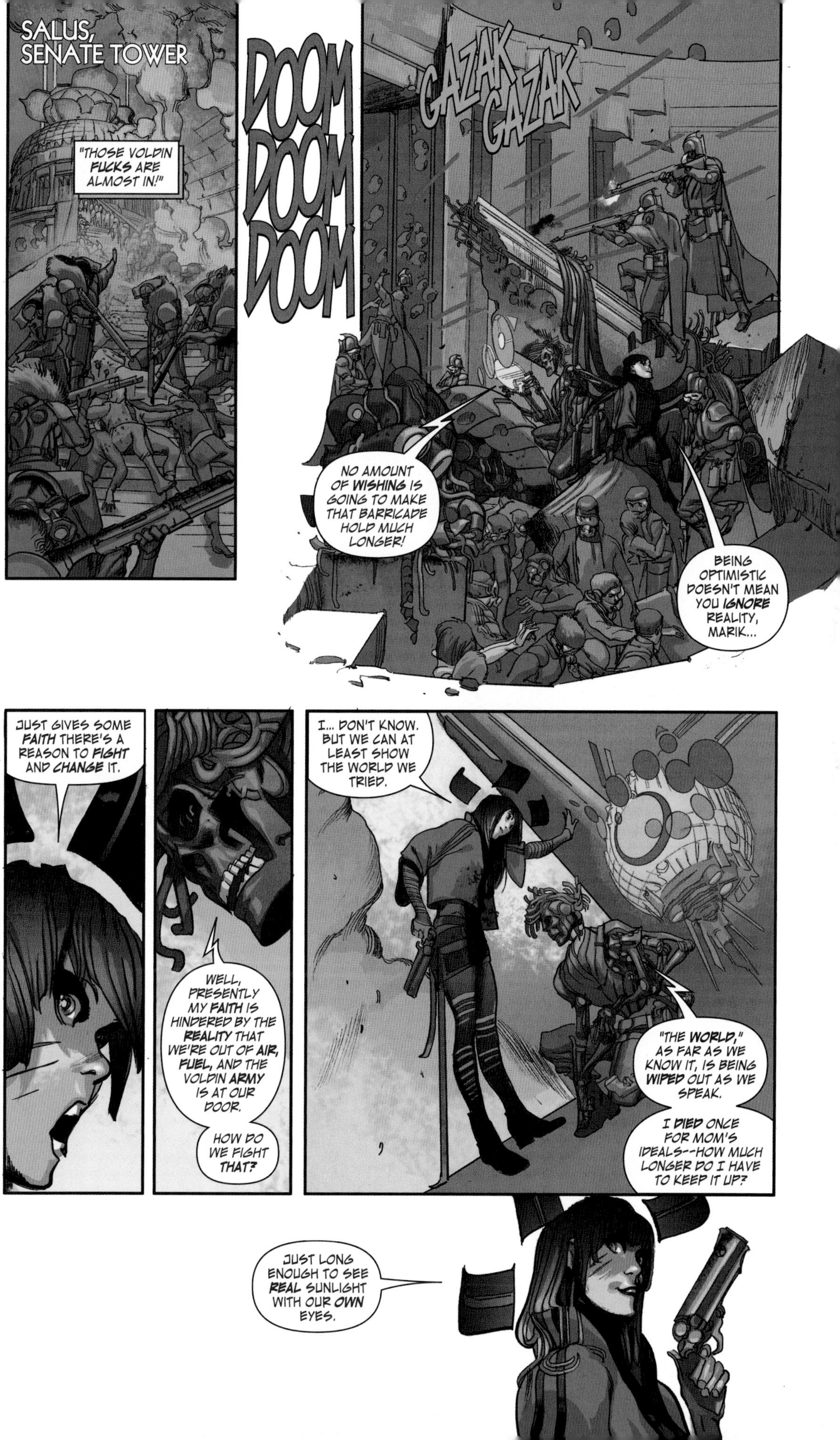
SALUS, SENATE TOWER
"THOSE VOLDIN FUCKS ARE ALMOST IN!"
DOOM DOOM DOOM
GAZAK GAZAK
NO AMOUNT OF WISHING IS GOING TO MAKE THAT BARRICADE HOLD MUCH LONGER!
BEING OPTIMISTIC DOESN'T MEAN YOU IGNORE REALITY, MARIK...
JUST GIVES SOME FAITH THERE'S A REASON TO FIGHT AND CHANGE IT.
WELL, PRESENTLY MY FAITH IS HINDERED BY THE REALITY THAT WE'RE OUT OF AIR, FUEL, AND THE VOLDIN ARMY IS AT OUR DOOR.
HOW DO WE FIGHT THAT?
I... DON'T KNOW. BUT WE CAN AT LEAST SHOW THE WORLD WE TRIED.
"THE WORLD," AS FAR AS WE KNOW IT, IS BEING WIPED OUT AS WE SPEAK.
I DIED ONCE FOR MOM'S IDEALS--HOW MUCH LONGER DO I HAVE TO KEEP IT UP?
JUST LONG ENOUGH TO SEE REAL SUNLIGHT WITH OUR OWN EYES.

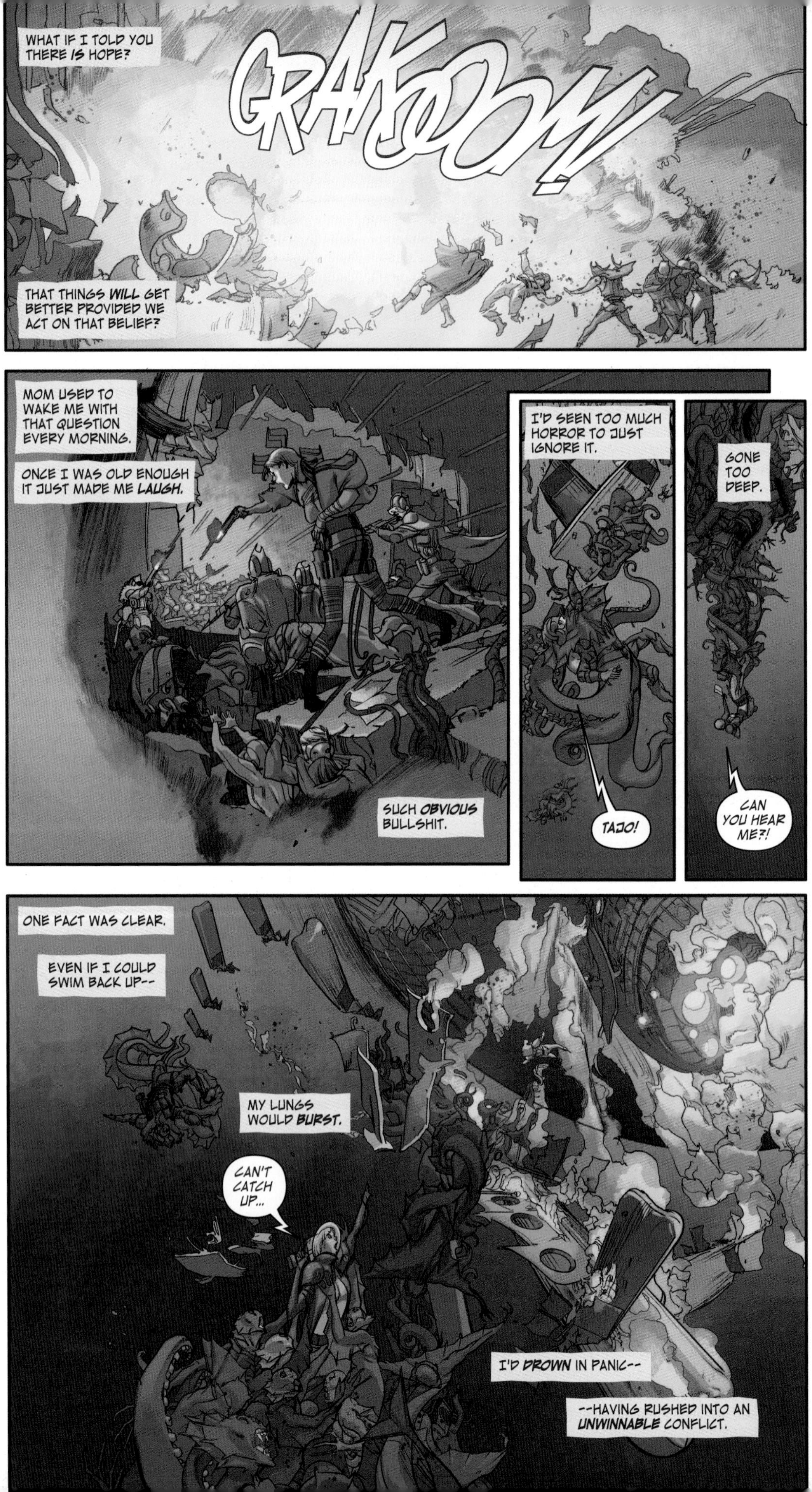
WHAT IF I TOLD YOU THERE IS HOPE?
GRAKOOOM!
THAT THINGS WILL GET BETTER PROVIDED WE ACT ON THAT BELIEF?
MOM USED TO WAKE ME WITH THAT QUESTION EVERY MORNING.
ONCE I WAS OLD ENOUGH IT JUST MADE ME LAUGH.
SUCH OBVIOUS BULLSHIT.
I'D SEEN TOO MUCH HORROR TO JUST IGNORE IT.
TAJO!
GONE TOO DEEP.
CAN YOU HEAR ME?!
ONE FACT WAS CLEAR.
EVEN IF I COULD SWIM BACK UP--
MY LUNGS WOULD BURST.
CAN'T CATCH UP...
I'D DROWN IN PANIC--
--HAVING RUSHED INTO AN UNWINNABLE CONFLICT.

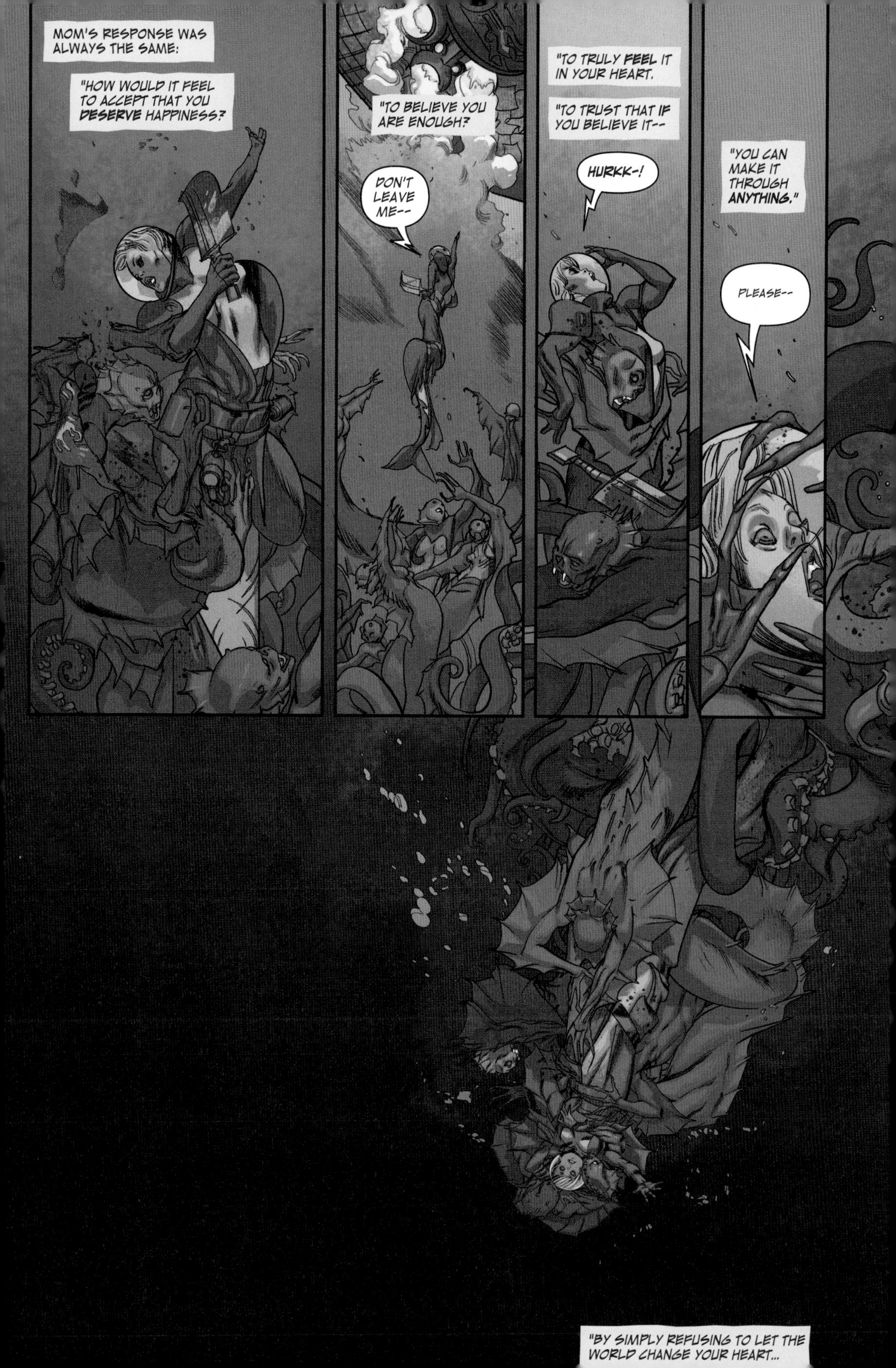
MOM'S RESPONSE WAS ALWAYS THE SAME:
"HOW WOULD IT FEEL TO ACCEPT THAT YOU DESERVE HAPPINESS?
"TO BELIEVE YOU ARE ENOUGH?
DON'T LEAVE ME--
"TO TRULY FEEL IT IN YOUR HEART.
"TO TRUST THAT IF YOU BELIEVE IT--
HURKK-!
"YOU CAN MAKE IT THROUGH ANYTHING."
PLEASE--
"BY SIMPLY REFUSING TO LET THE WORLD CHANGE YOUR HEART...

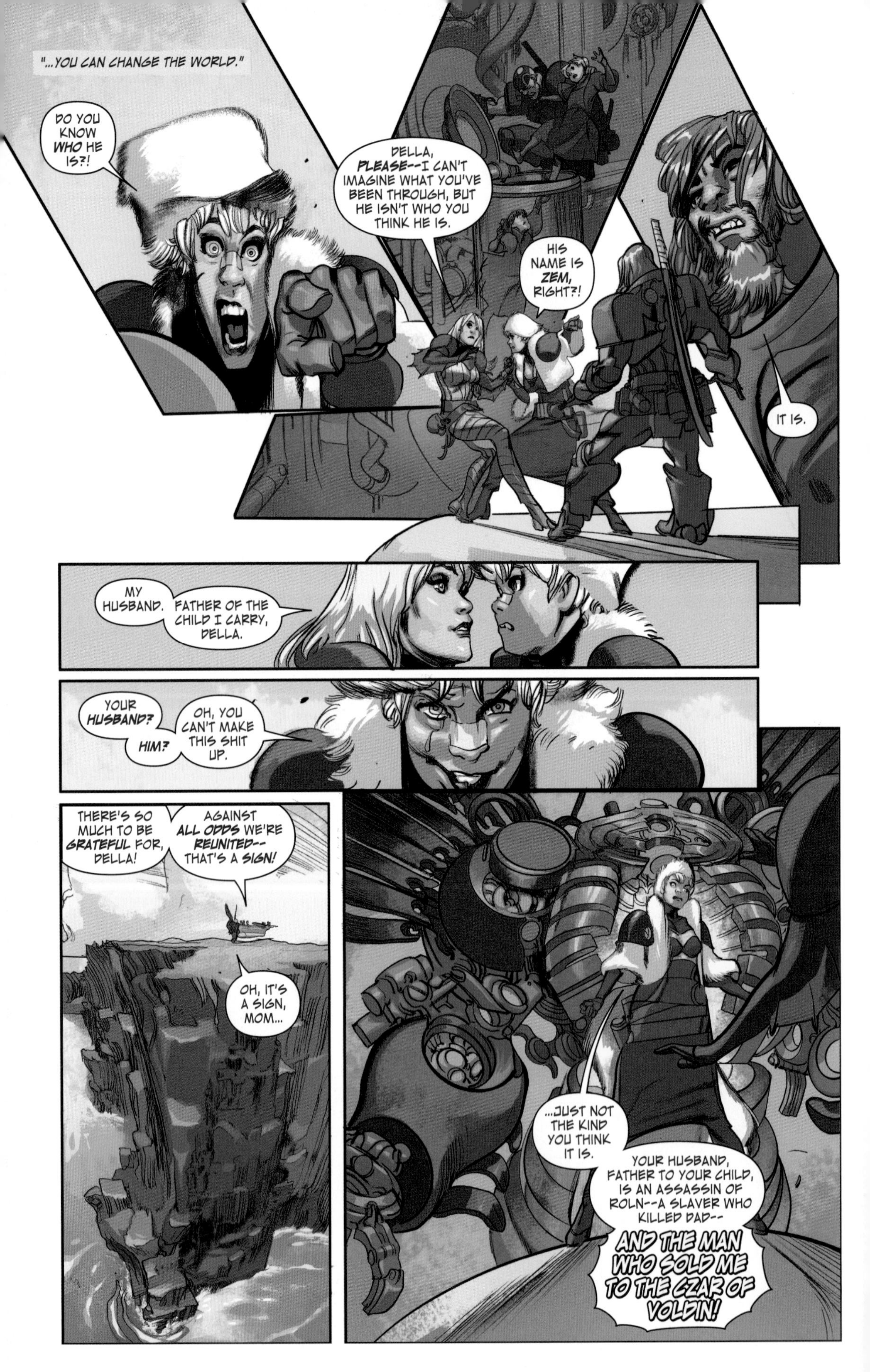
"...YOU CAN CHANGE THE WORLD."
DO YOU KNOW WHO HE IS?!
DELLA, PLEASE--I CAN'T IMAGINE WHAT YOU'VE BEEN THROUGH, BUT HE ISN'T WHO YOU THINK HE IS.
HIS NAME IS ZEM, RIGHT?!
IT IS.
MY HUSBAND.
FATHER OF THE CHILD I CARRY, DELLA.
YOUR HUSBAND?
HIM?
OH, YOU CAN'T MAKE THIS SHIT UP.
THERE'S SO MUCH TO BE GRATEFUL FOR, DELLA!
AGAINST ALL ODDS WE'RE REUNITED--THAT'S A SIGN!
OH, IT'S A SIGN, MOM...
...JUST NOT THE KIND YOU THINK IT IS.
YOUR HUSBAND, FATHER TO YOUR CHILD, IS AN ASSASSIN OF ROLN--A SLAVER WHO KILLED DAD--
AND THE MAN WHO SOLD ME TO THE CZAR OF VOLDIN!

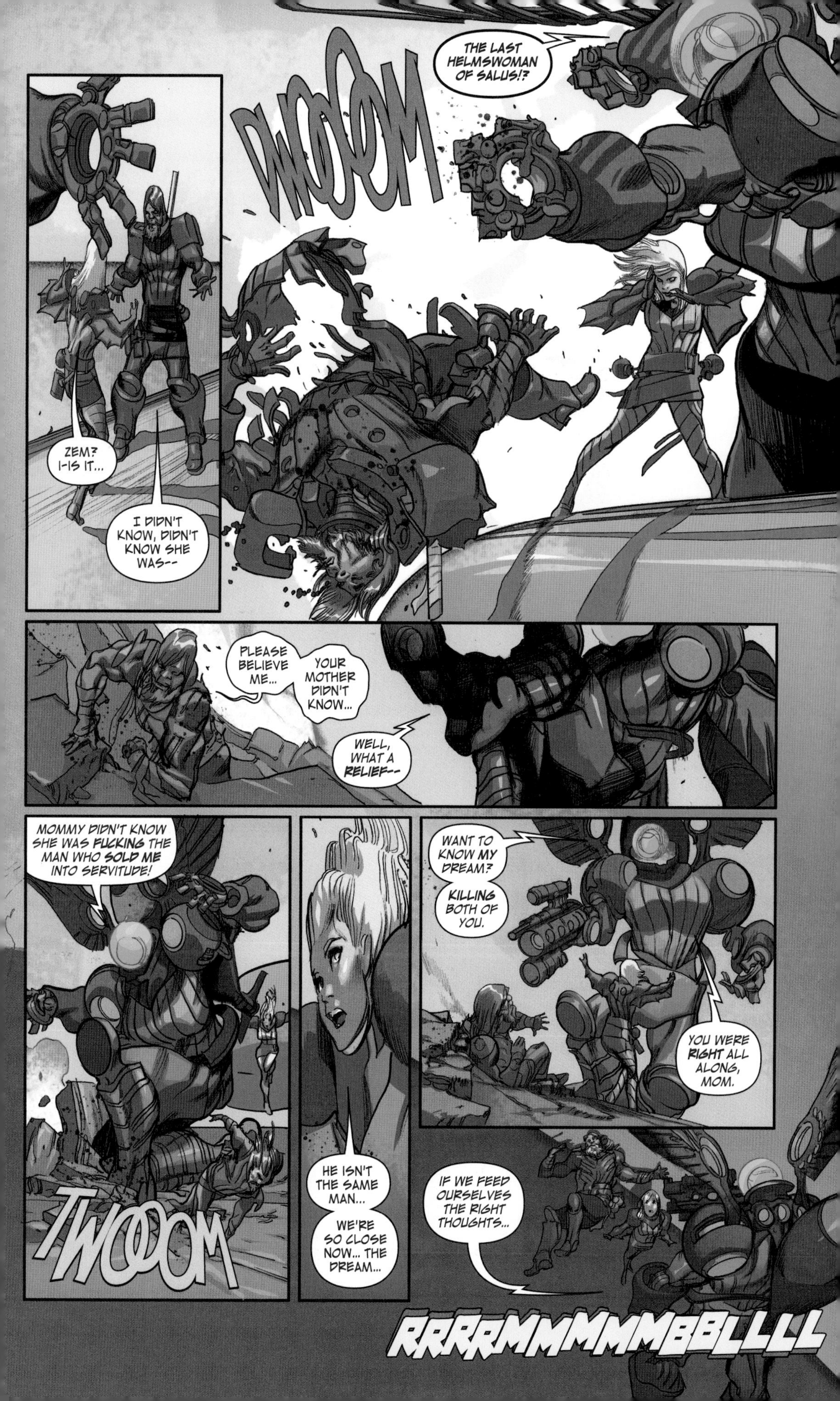
THE LAST HELMSWOMAN OF SALUS!?
DWOOOM
ZEM? I-IS IT...
I DIDN'T KNOW, DIDN'T KNOW SHE WAS--
PLEASE BELIEVE ME...
YOUR MOTHER DIDN'T KNOW...
WELL, WHAT A RELIEF--
MOMMY DIDN'T KNOW SHE WAS FUCKING THE MAN WHO SOLD ME INTO SERVITUDE!
TWOOOM
HE ISN'T THE SAME MAN...
WE'RE SO CLOSE NOW... THE DREAM...
WANT TO KNOW MY DREAM?
KILLING BOTH OF YOU.
YOU WERE RIGHT ALL ALONG, MOM.
IF WE FEED OURSELVES THE RIGHT THOUGHTS...
RRRRMMMMMMBBLLLL

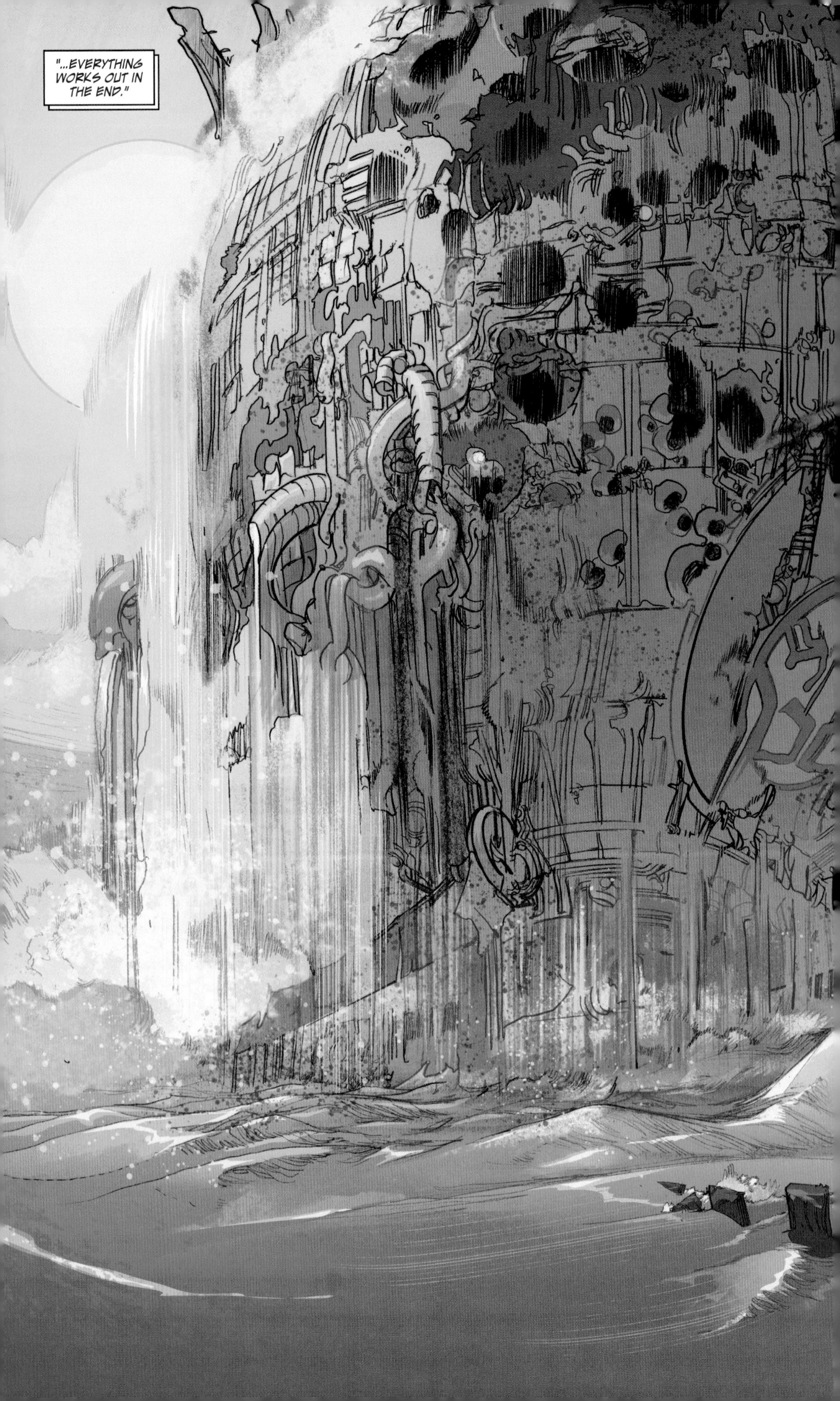
"...EVERYTHING WORKS OUT IN THE END."

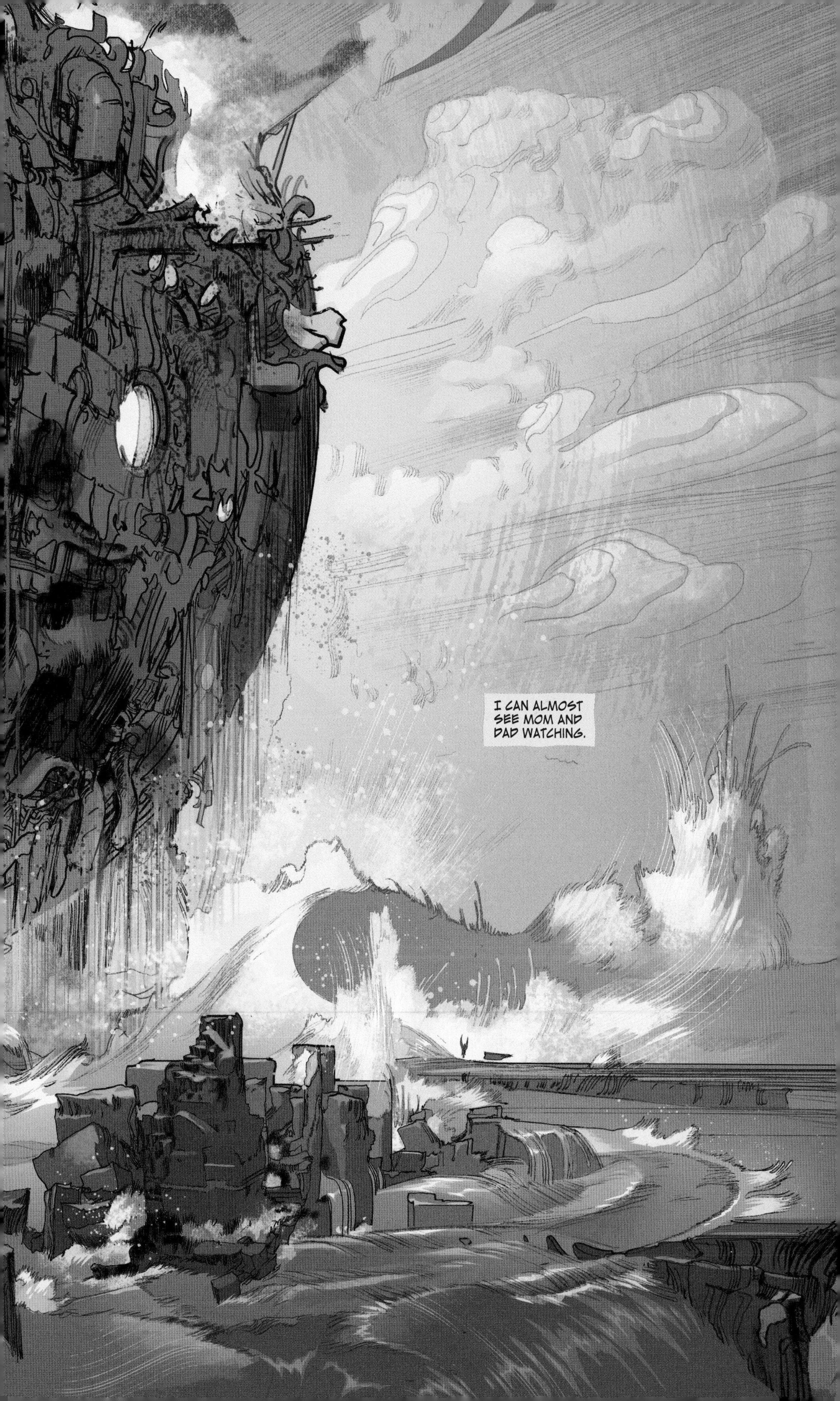
I CAN ALMOST
SEE MOM AND
DAD WATCHING.

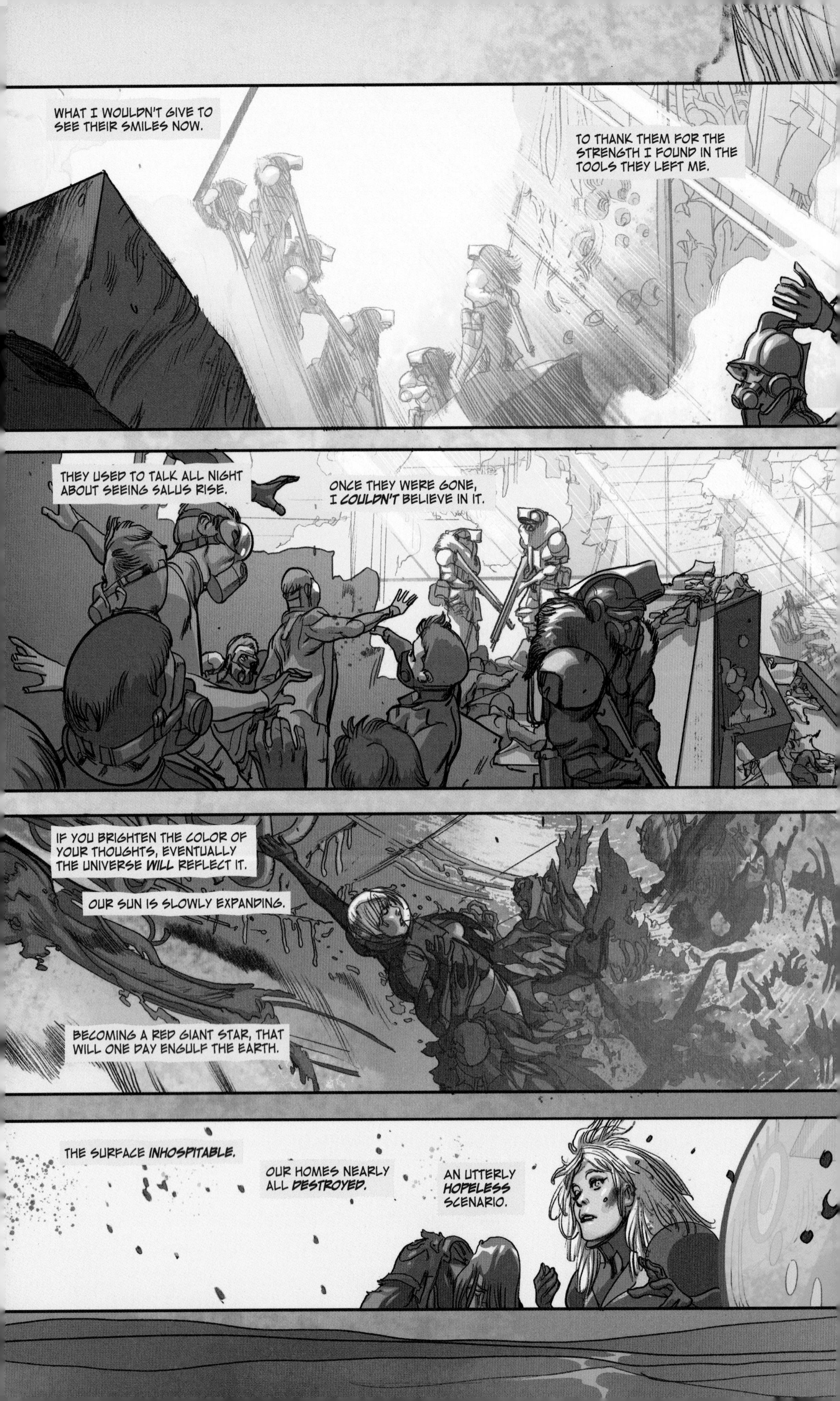
WHAT I WOULDN'T GIVE TO SEE THEIR SMILES NOW.
TO THANK THEM FOR THE STRENGTH I FOUND IN THE TOOLS THEY LEFT ME.
THEY USED TO TALK ALL NIGHT ABOUT SEEING SALUS RISE.
ONCE THEY WERE GONE, I *COULDN'T* BELIEVE IN IT.
IF YOU BRIGHTEN THE COLOR OF YOUR THOUGHTS, EVENTUALLY THE UNIVERSE *WILL* REFLECT IT.
OUR SUN IS SLOWLY EXPANDING.
BECOMING A RED GIANT STAR, THAT WILL ONE DAY ENGULF THE EARTH.
THE SURFACE *INHOSPITABLE*.
OUR HOMES NEARLY ALL *DESTROYED*.
AN UTTERLY *HOPELESS* SCENARIO.

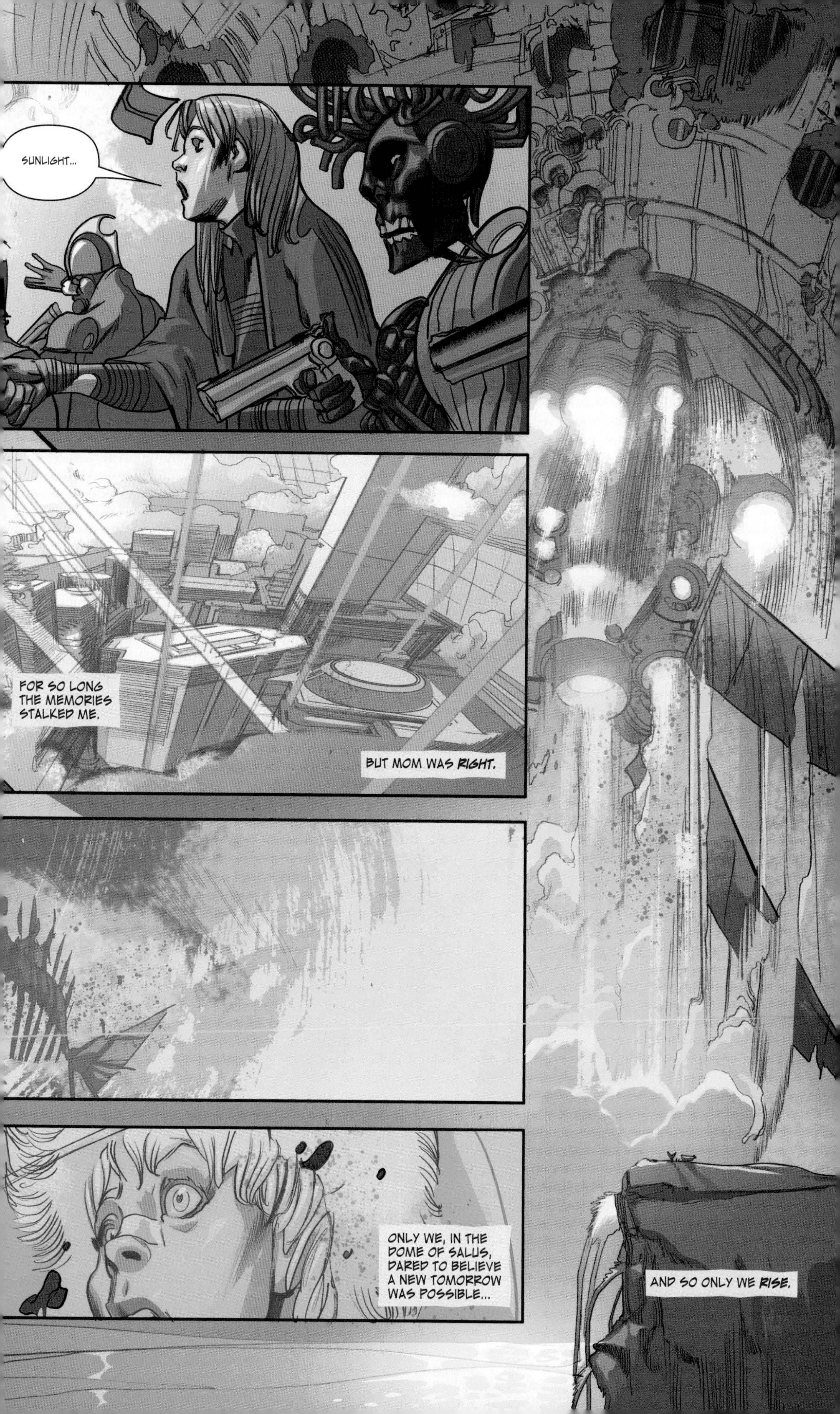
SUNLIGHT...
FOR SO LONG THE MEMORIES STALKED ME.
BUT MOM WAS RIGHT.
ONLY WE, IN THE DOME OF SALUS, DARED TO BELIEVE A NEW TOMORROW WAS POSSIBLE...
AND SO ONLY WE RISE.

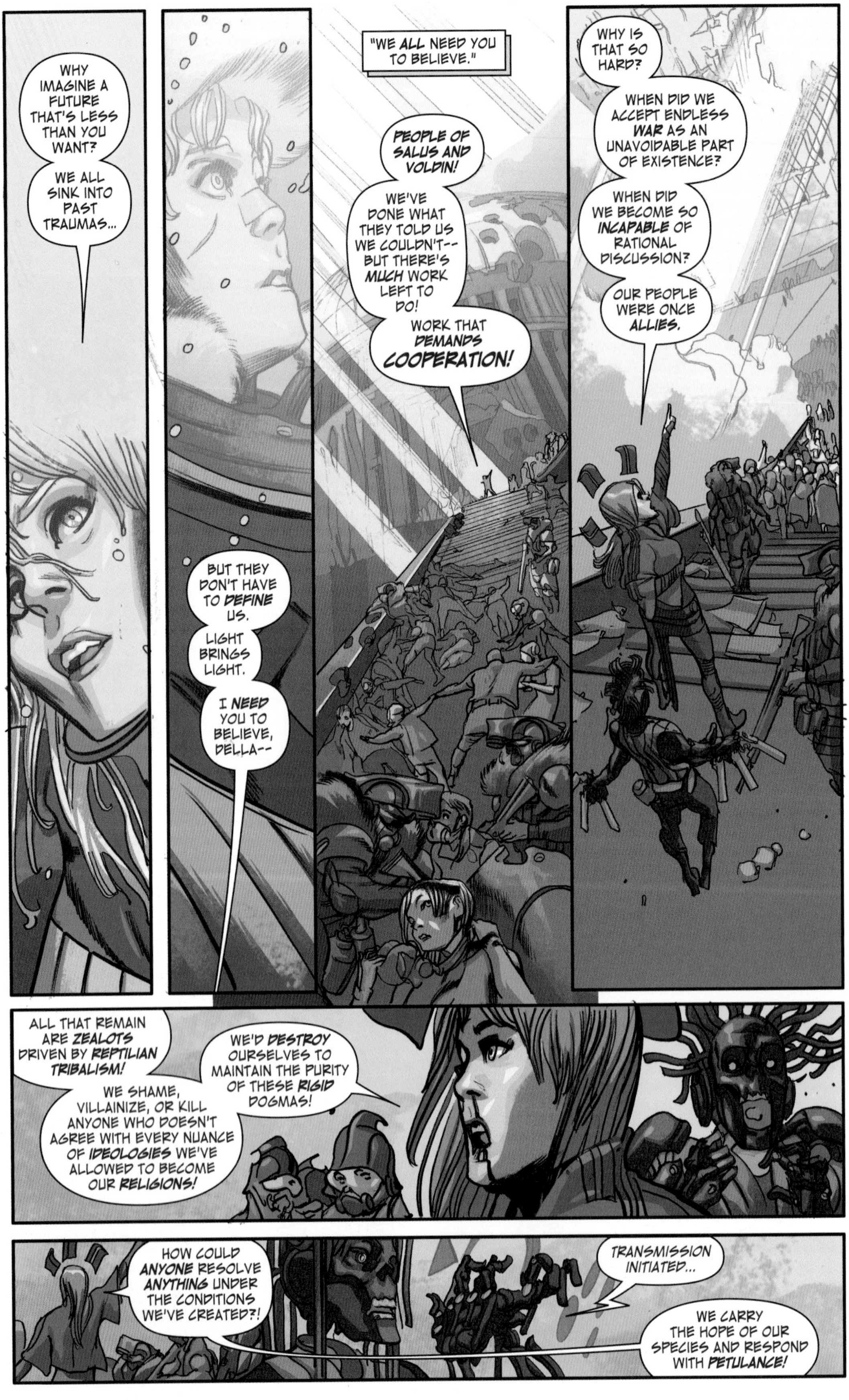

WHY IMAGINE A FUTURE THAT'S LESS THAN YOU WANT?
WE ALL SINK INTO PAST TRAUMAS...
BUT THEY DON'T HAVE TO DEFINE US.
LIGHT BRINGS LIGHT.
I NEED YOU TO BELIEVE, DELLA--
"WE ALL NEED YOU TO BELIEVE."
PEOPLE OF SALUS AND VOLDIN!
WE'VE DONE WHAT THEY TOLD US WE COULDN'T--BUT THERE'S MUCH WORK LEFT TO DO!
WORK THAT DEMANDS COOPERATION!
WHY IS THAT SO HARD?
WHEN DID WE ACCEPT ENDLESS WAR AS AN UNAVOIDABLE PART OF EXISTENCE?
WHEN DID WE BECOME SO INCAPABLE OF RATIONAL DISCUSSION?
OUR PEOPLE WERE ONCE ALLIES.
ALL THAT REMAIN ARE ZEALOTS DRIVEN BY REPTILIAN TRIBALISM!
WE SHAME, VILLAINIZE, OR KILL ANYONE WHO DOESN'T AGREE WITH EVERY NUANCE OF IDEOLOGIES WE'VE ALLOWED TO BECOME OUR RELIGIONS!
WE'D DESTROY OURSELVES TO MAINTAIN THE PURITY OF THESE RIGID DOGMAS!
HOW COULD ANYONE RESOLVE ANYTHING UNDER THE CONDITIONS WE'VE CREATED?!
TRANSMISSION INITIATED...
WE CARRY THE HOPE OF OUR SPECIES AND RESPOND WITH PETULANCE!

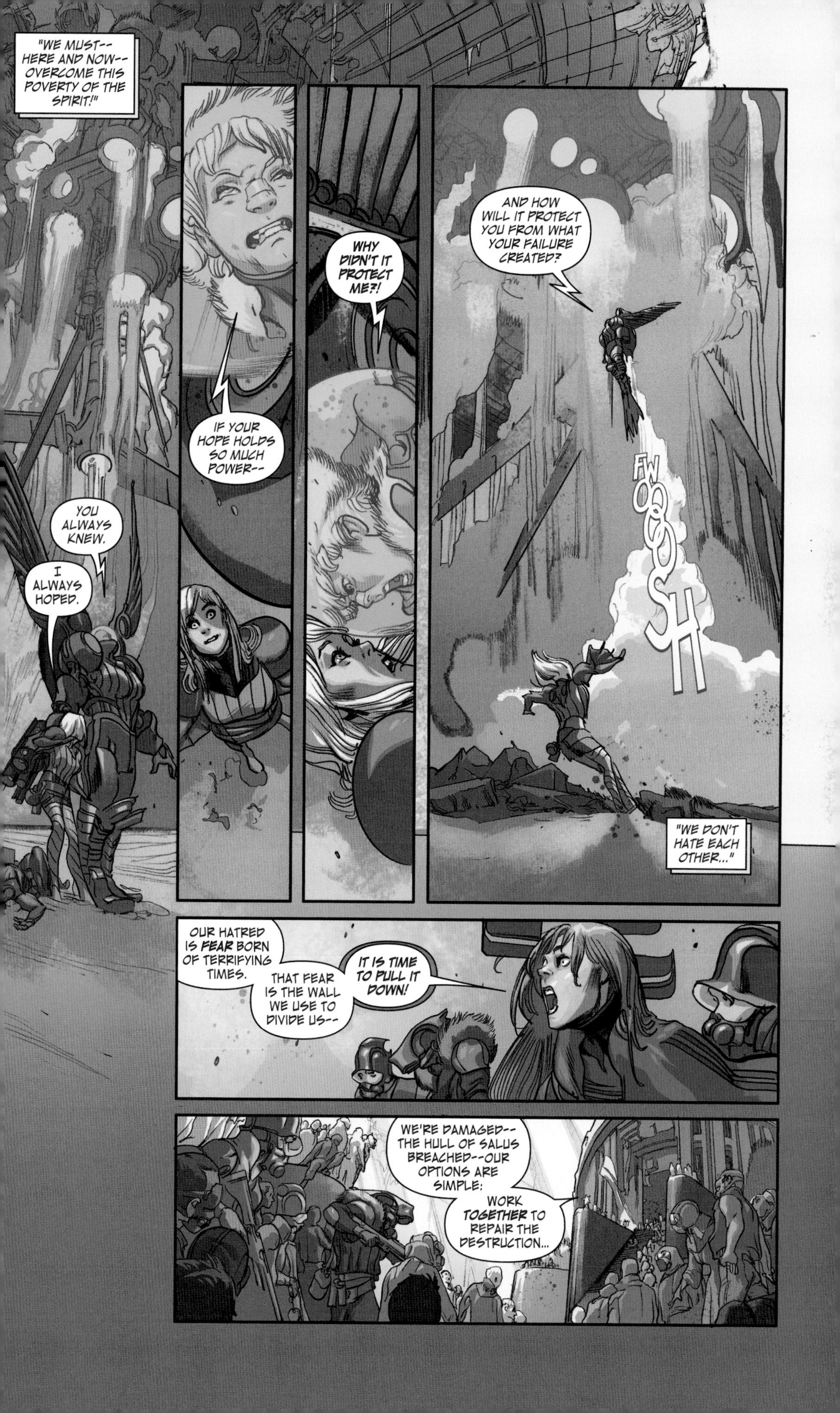
"WE MUST--
HERE AND NOW--
OVERCOME THIS
POVERTY OF THE
SPIRIT!"
IF YOUR
HOPE HOLDS
SO MUCH
POWER--
WHY
DIDN'T IT
PROTECT
ME?!
AND HOW
WILL IT PROTECT
YOU FROM WHAT
YOUR FAILURE
CREATED?
FWOOOSH
YOU
ALWAYS
KNEW.
I
ALWAYS
HOPED.
"WE DON'T
HATE EACH
OTHER..."
OUR HATRED
IS FEAR BORN
OF TERRIFYING
TIMES.
THAT FEAR
IS THE WALL
WE USE TO
DIVIDE US--
IT IS TIME
TO PULL IT
DOWN!
WE'RE DAMAGED--
THE HULL OF SALUS
BREACHED--OUR
OPTIONS ARE
SIMPLE:
WORK
TOGETHER TO
REPAIR THE
DESTRUCTION...

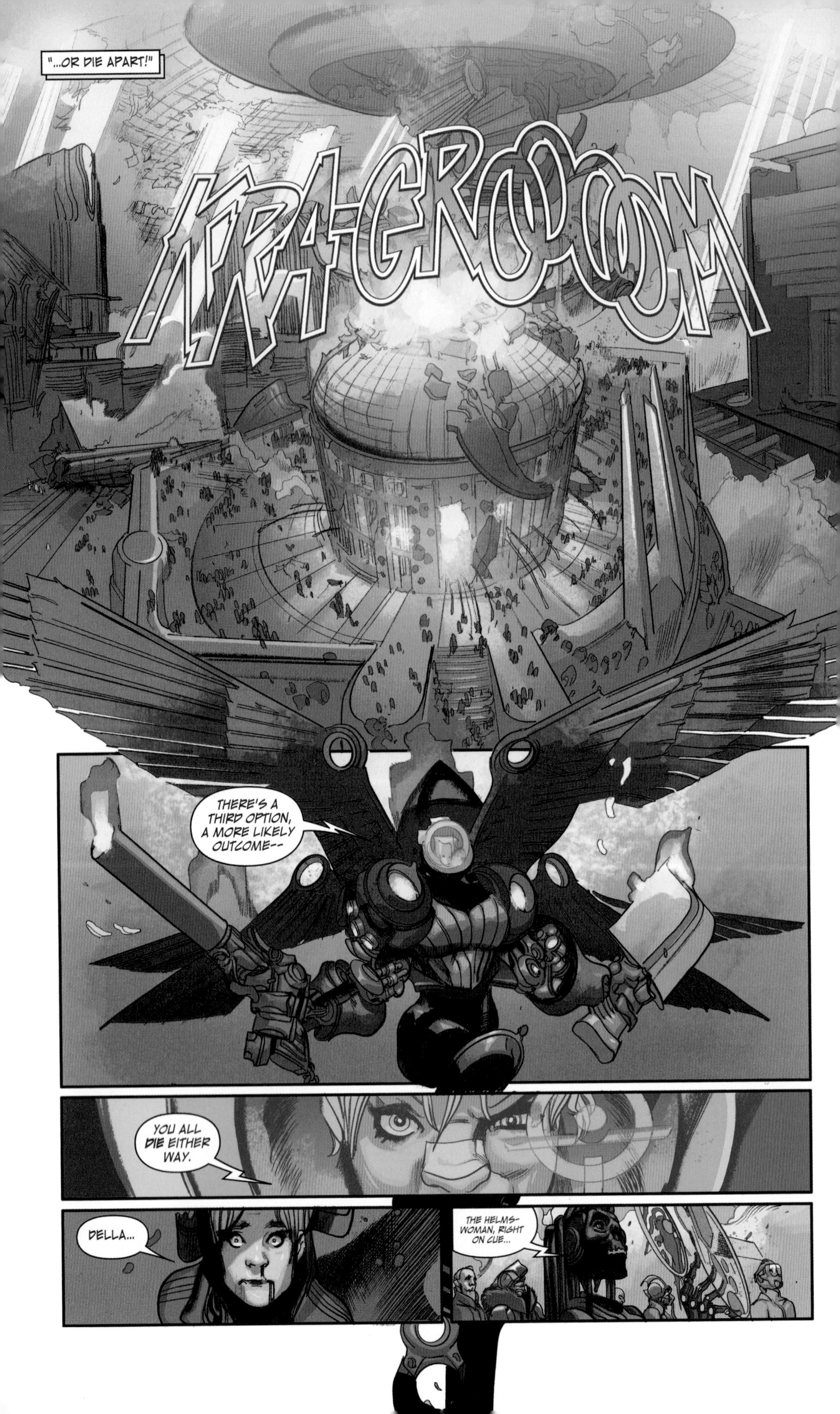
"...OR DIE APART!"
KRA-GROOOOOM
THERE'S A THIRD OPTION, A MORE LIKELY OUTCOME--
YOU ALL DIE EITHER WAY.
DELLA...
THE HELMS-WOMAN, RIGHT ON CUE...

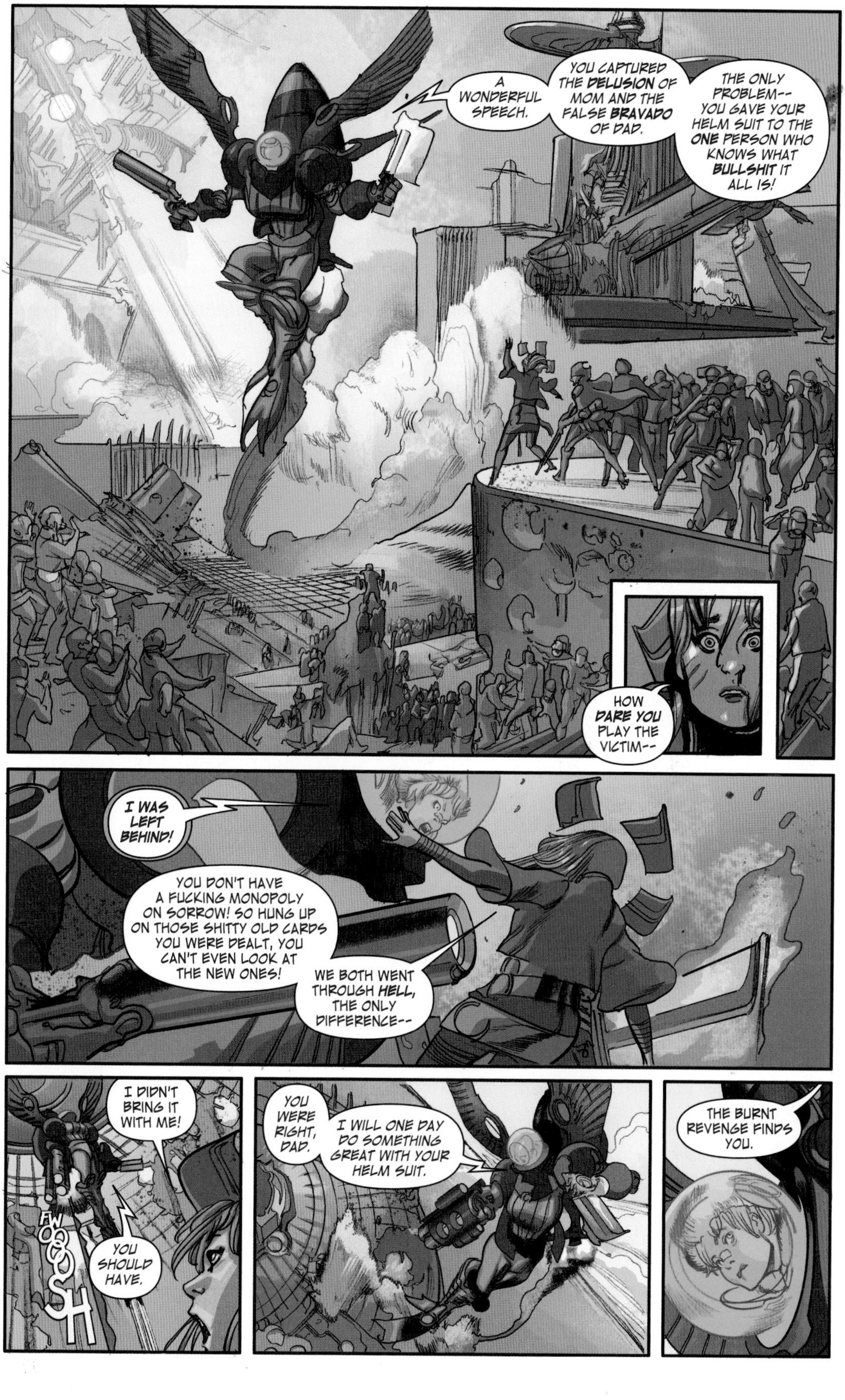

A WONDERFUL SPEECH.
YOU CAPTURED THE DELUSION OF MOM AND THE FALSE BRAVADO OF DAD.
THE ONLY PROBLEM-- YOU GAVE YOUR HELM SUIT TO THE ONE PERSON WHO KNOWS WHAT BULLSHIT IT ALL IS!
HOW DARE YOU PLAY THE VICTIM--
I WAS LEFT BEHIND!
YOU DON'T HAVE A FUCKING MONOPOLY ON SORROW! SO HUNG UP ON THOSE SHITTY OLD CARDS YOU WERE DEALT, YOU CAN'T EVEN LOOK AT THE NEW ONES!
WE BOTH WENT THROUGH HELL, THE ONLY DIFFERENCE--
I DIDN'T BRING IT WITH ME!
FWOOOSH
YOU SHOULD HAVE.
YOU WERE RIGHT, DAD.
I WILL ONE DAY DO SOMETHING GREAT WITH YOUR HELM SUIT.
THE BURNT REVENGE FINDS YOU.

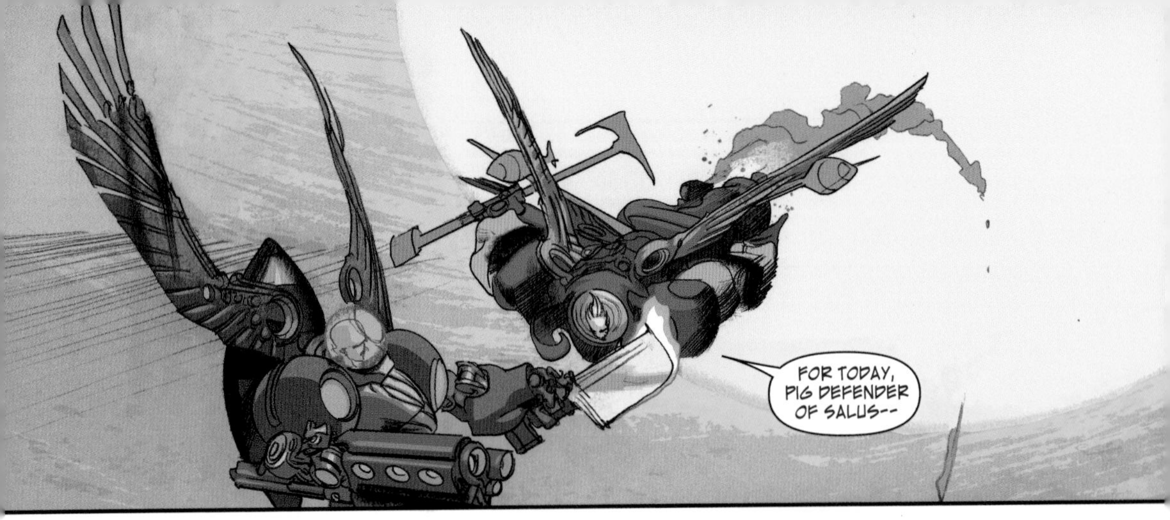
FOR TODAY, PIG DEFENDER OF SALUS--

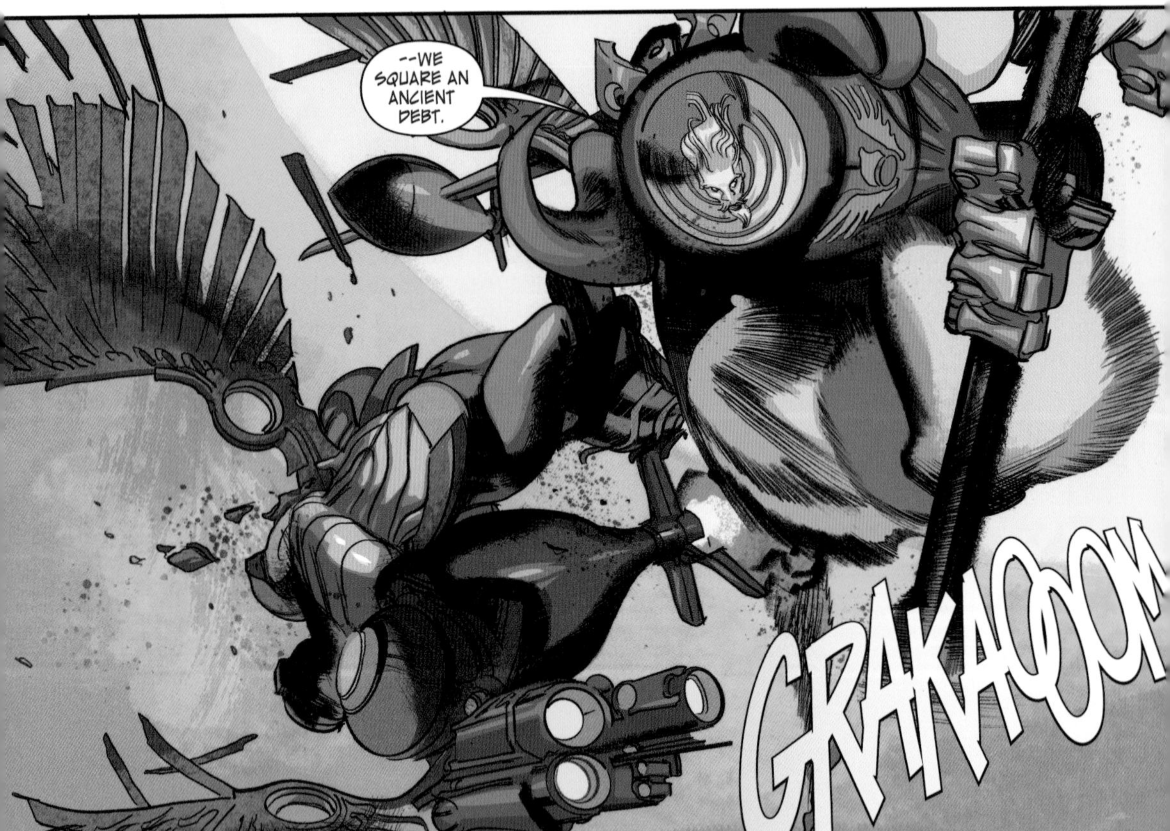
--WE SQUARE AN ANCIENT DEBT.
GRAKAOOOM

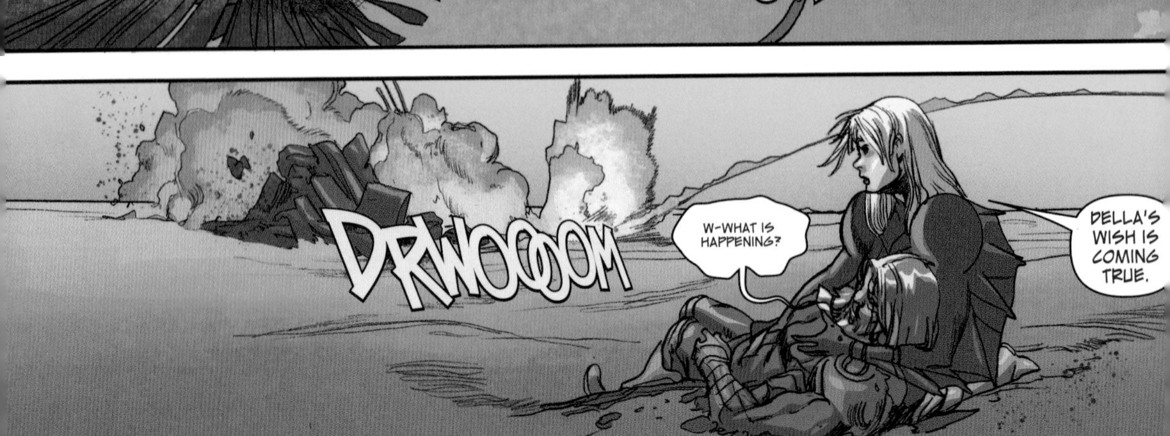
DRWOOOOM
W-WHAT IS HAPPENING?
DELLA'S WISH IS COMING TRUE.

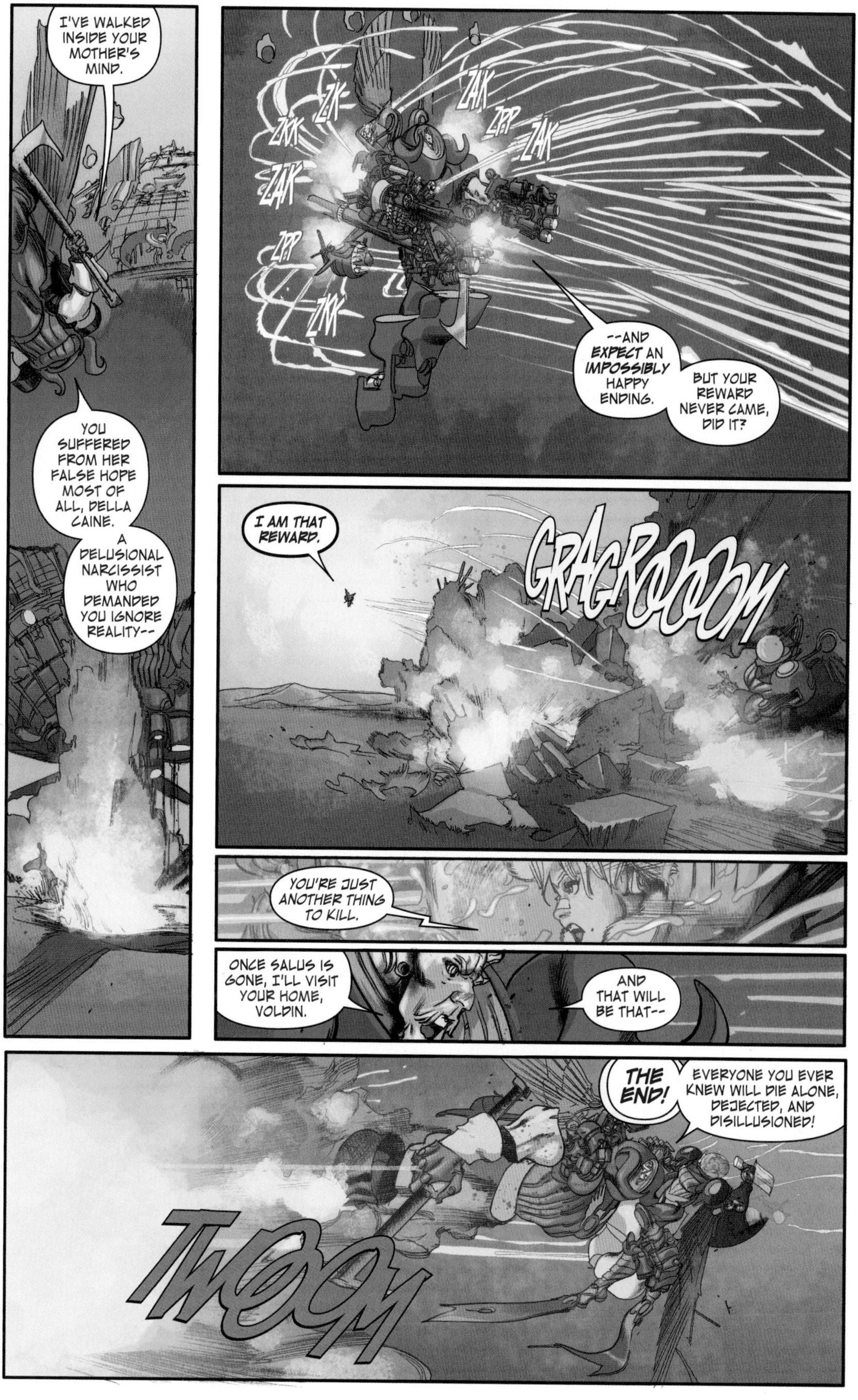

I'VE WALKED INSIDE YOUR MOTHER'S MIND.
ZKK
ZK
ZAK
ZPP
ZKK
ZAK
ZPP
ZAK
--AND EXPECT AN IMPOSSIBLY HAPPY ENDING.
BUT YOUR REWARD NEVER CAME, DID IT?
YOU SUFFERED FROM HER FALSE HOPE MOST OF ALL, DELLA CAINE.
A DELUSIONAL NARCISSIST WHO DEMANDED YOU IGNORE REALITY--
I AM THAT REWARD.
GRAGROOOOM
YOU'RE JUST ANOTHER THING TO KILL.
ONCE SALUS IS GONE, I'LL VISIT YOUR HOME, VOLDIN.
AND THAT WILL BE THAT--
THE END!
EVERYONE YOU EVER KNEW WILL DIE ALONE, DEJECTED, AND DISILLUSIONED!
TWOOOM

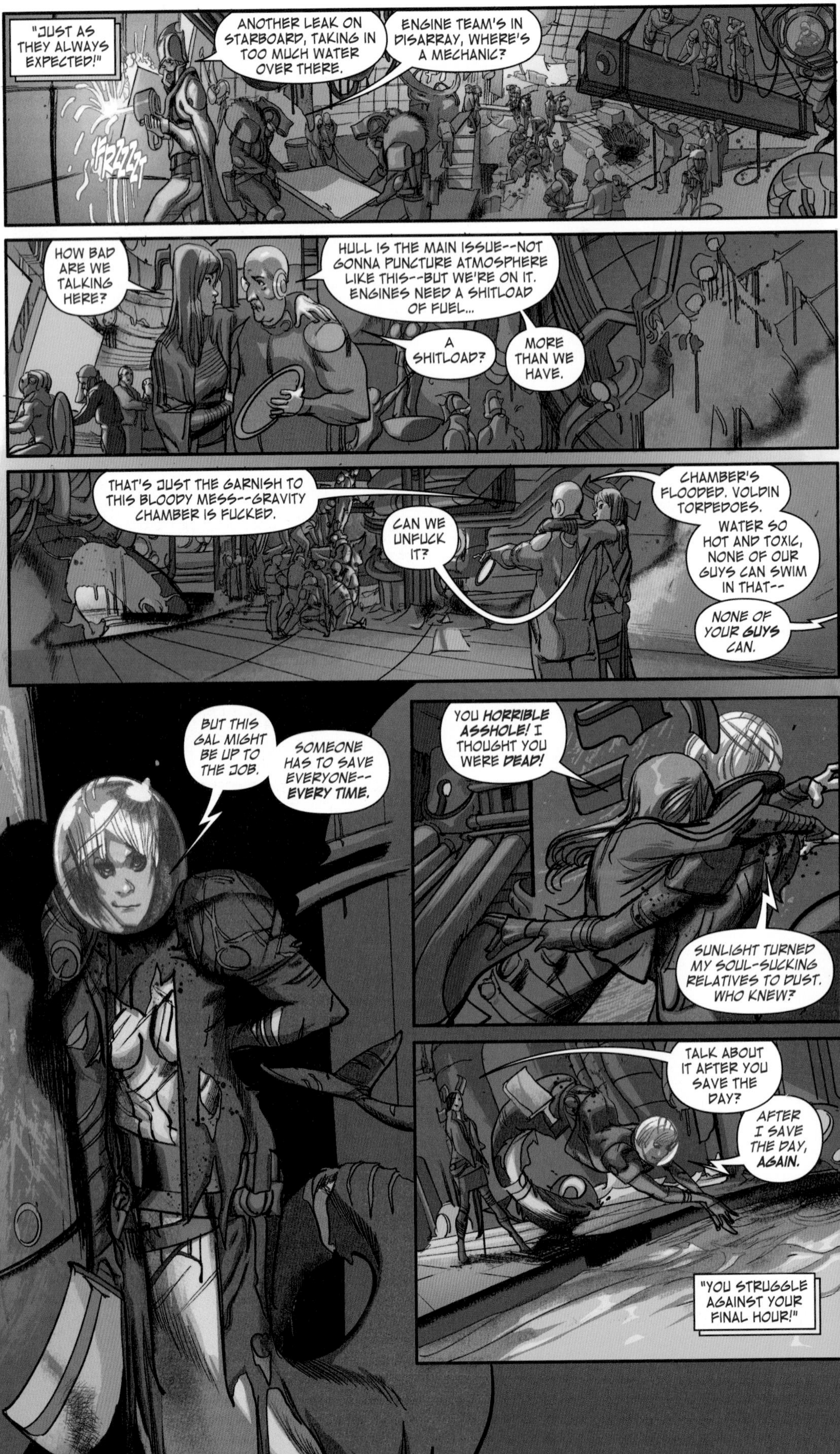
"JUST AS THEY ALWAYS EXPECTED!"
ANOTHER LEAK ON STARBOARD, TAKING IN TOO MUCH WATER OVER THERE.
ENGINE TEAM'S IN DISARRAY, WHERE'S A MECHANIC?
FRZZZT
HOW BAD ARE WE TALKING HERE?
HULL IS THE MAIN ISSUE--NOT GONNA PUNCTURE ATMOSPHERE LIKE THIS--BUT WE'RE ON IT. ENGINES NEED A SHITLOAD OF FUEL...
A SHITLOAD?
MORE THAN WE HAVE.
THAT'S JUST THE GARNISH TO THIS BLOODY MESS--GRAVITY CHAMBER IS FUCKED.
CAN WE UNFUCK IT?
CHAMBER'S FLOODED. VOLDIN TORPEDOES.
WATER SO HOT AND TOXIC, NONE OF OUR GUYS CAN SWIM IN THAT--
NONE OF YOUR GUYS CAN.
BUT THIS GAL MIGHT BE UP TO THE JOB.
SOMEONE HAS TO SAVE EVERYONE-- EVERY TIME.
YOU HORRIBLE ASSHOLE! I THOUGHT YOU WERE DEAD!
SUNLIGHT TURNED MY SOUL-SUCKING RELATIVES TO DUST. WHO KNEW?
TALK ABOUT IT AFTER YOU SAVE THE DAY?
AFTER I SAVE THE DAY, AGAIN.
"YOU STRUGGLE AGAINST YOUR FINAL HOUR!"

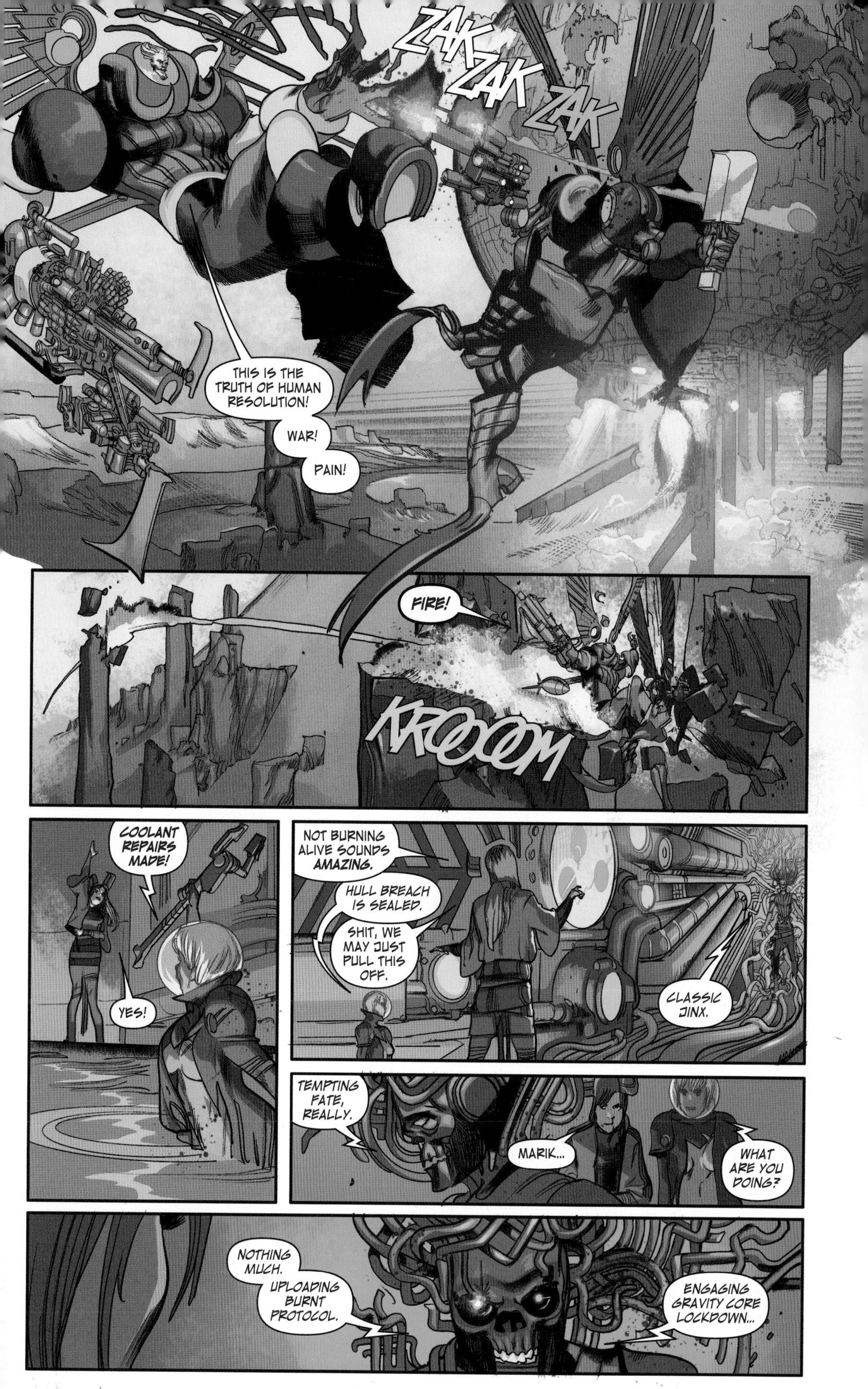
ZAK ZAK ZAK
THIS IS THE TRUTH OF HUMAN RESOLUTION!
WAR!
PAIN!
FIRE!
KROOOM
COOLANT REPAIRS MADE!
YES!
NOT BURNING ALIVE SOUNDS AMAZING.
HULL BREACH IS SEALED.
SHIT, WE MAY JUST PULL THIS OFF.
CLASSIC JINX.
TEMPTING FATE, REALLY.
MARIK...
WHAT ARE YOU DOING?
NOTHING MUCH.
UPLOADING BURNT PROTOCOL.
ENGAGING GRAVITY CORE LOCKDOWN...

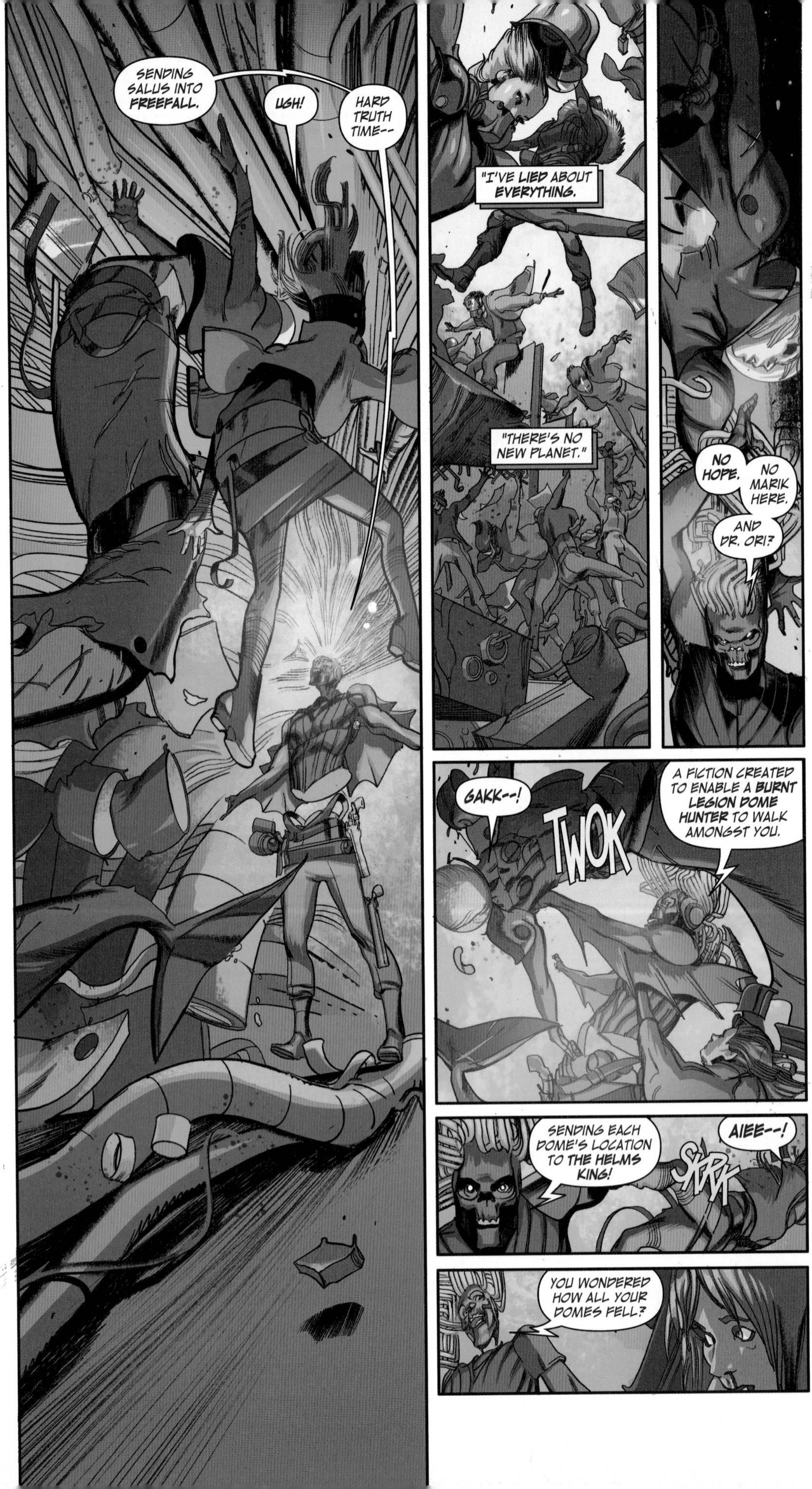
SENDING SALUS INTO FREEFALL.
UGH!
HARD TRUTH TIME--
"I'VE LIED ABOUT EVERYTHING.
"THERE'S NO NEW PLANET."
NO HOPE.
NO MARIK HERE.
AND DR. ORI?
GAKK--!
TWOK
A FICTION CREATED TO ENABLE A BURNT LEGION DOME HUNTER TO WALK AMONGST YOU.
SENDING EACH DOME'S LOCATION TO THE HELMS KING!
AIEE--!
YOU WONDERED HOW ALL YOUR DOMES FELL?

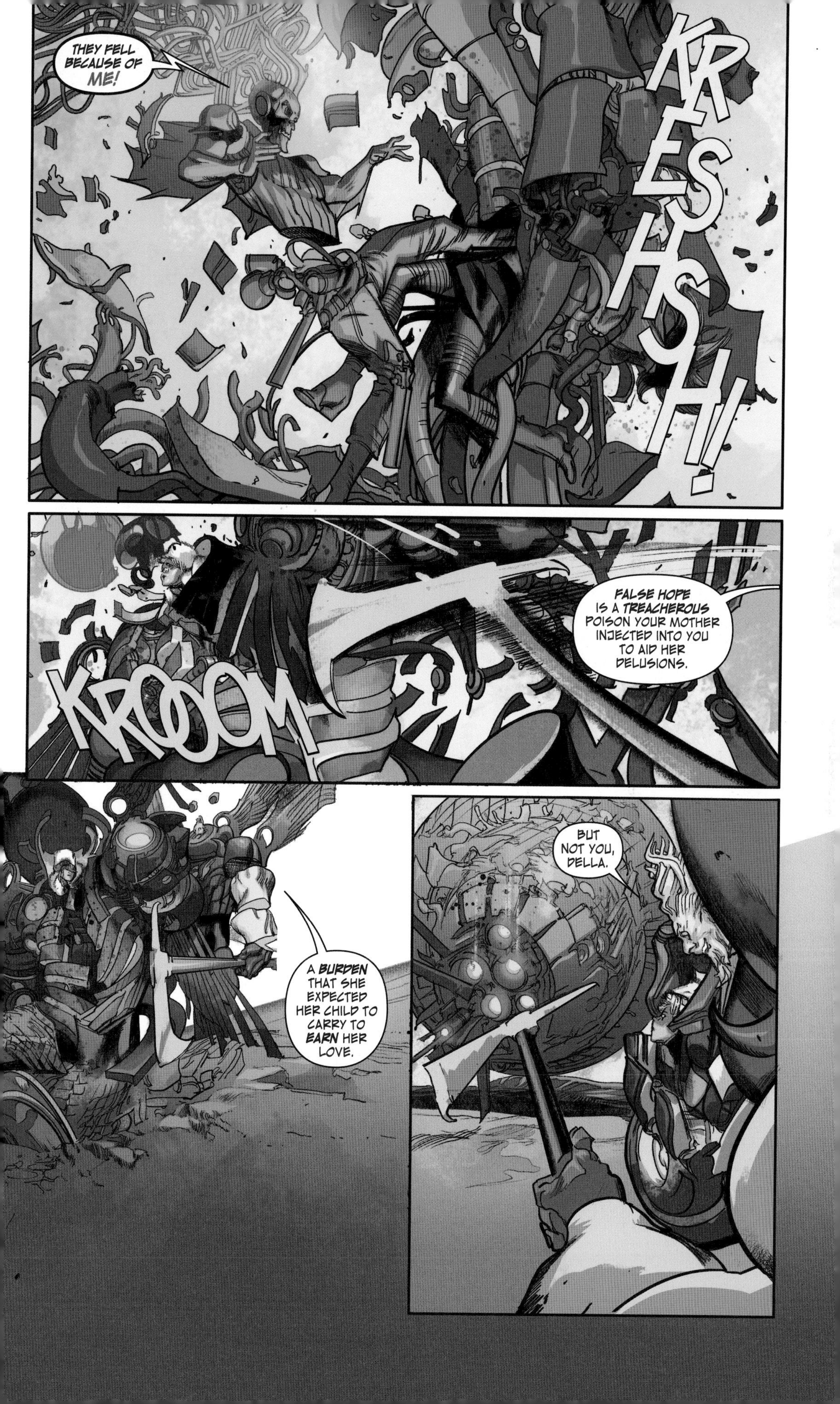
THEY FELL BECAUSE OF ME!
KRESHSH!!
FALSE HOPE IS A TREACHEROUS POISON YOUR MOTHER INJECTED INTO YOU TO AID HER DELUSIONS.
KROOOM
A BURDEN THAT SHE EXPECTED HER CHILD TO CARRY TO EARN HER LOVE.
BUT NOT YOU, DELLA.

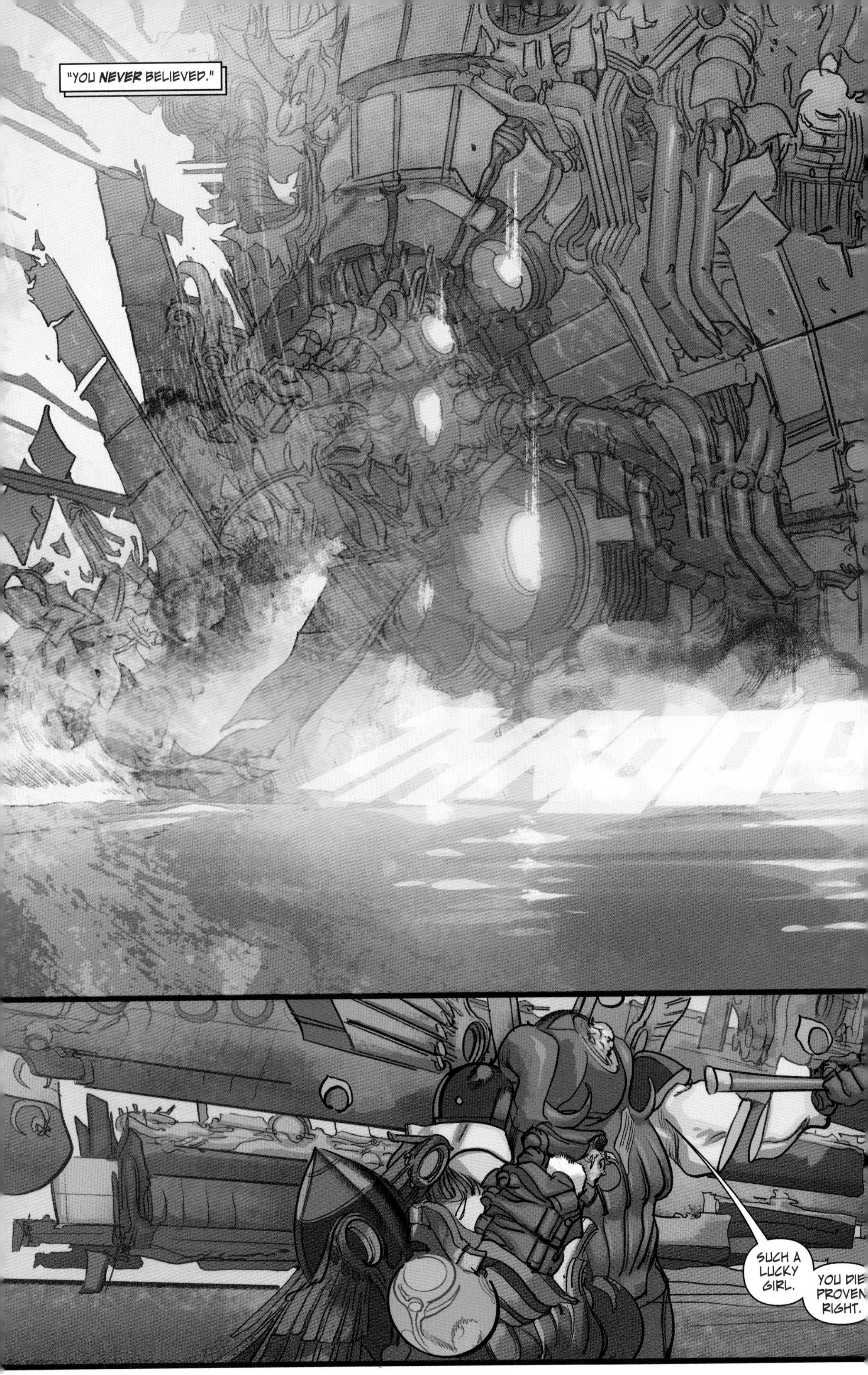
"YOU **NEVER** BELIEVED."
SUCH A LUCKY GIRL.
YOU DIE PROVEN RIGHT.

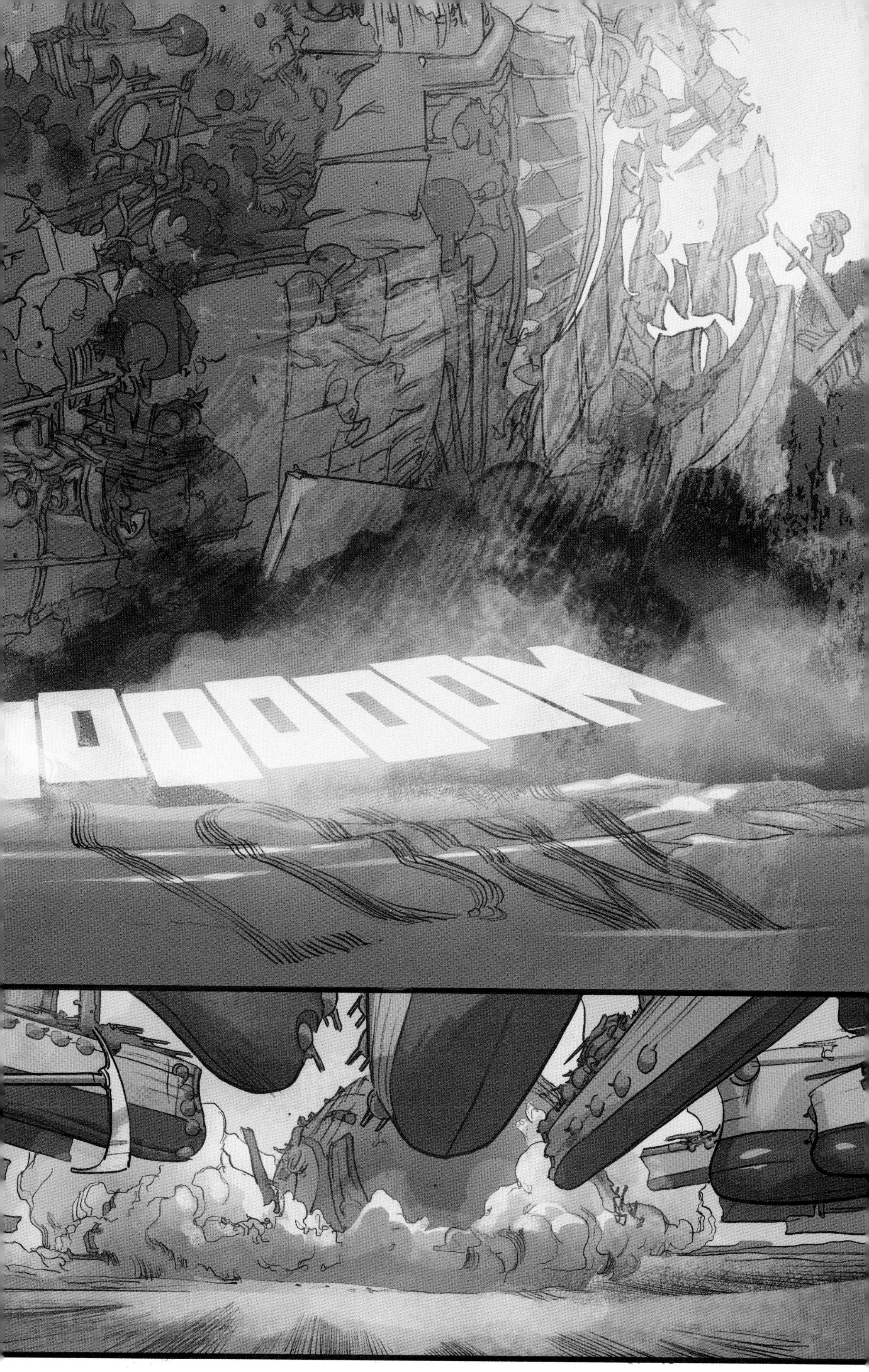
OOOOM

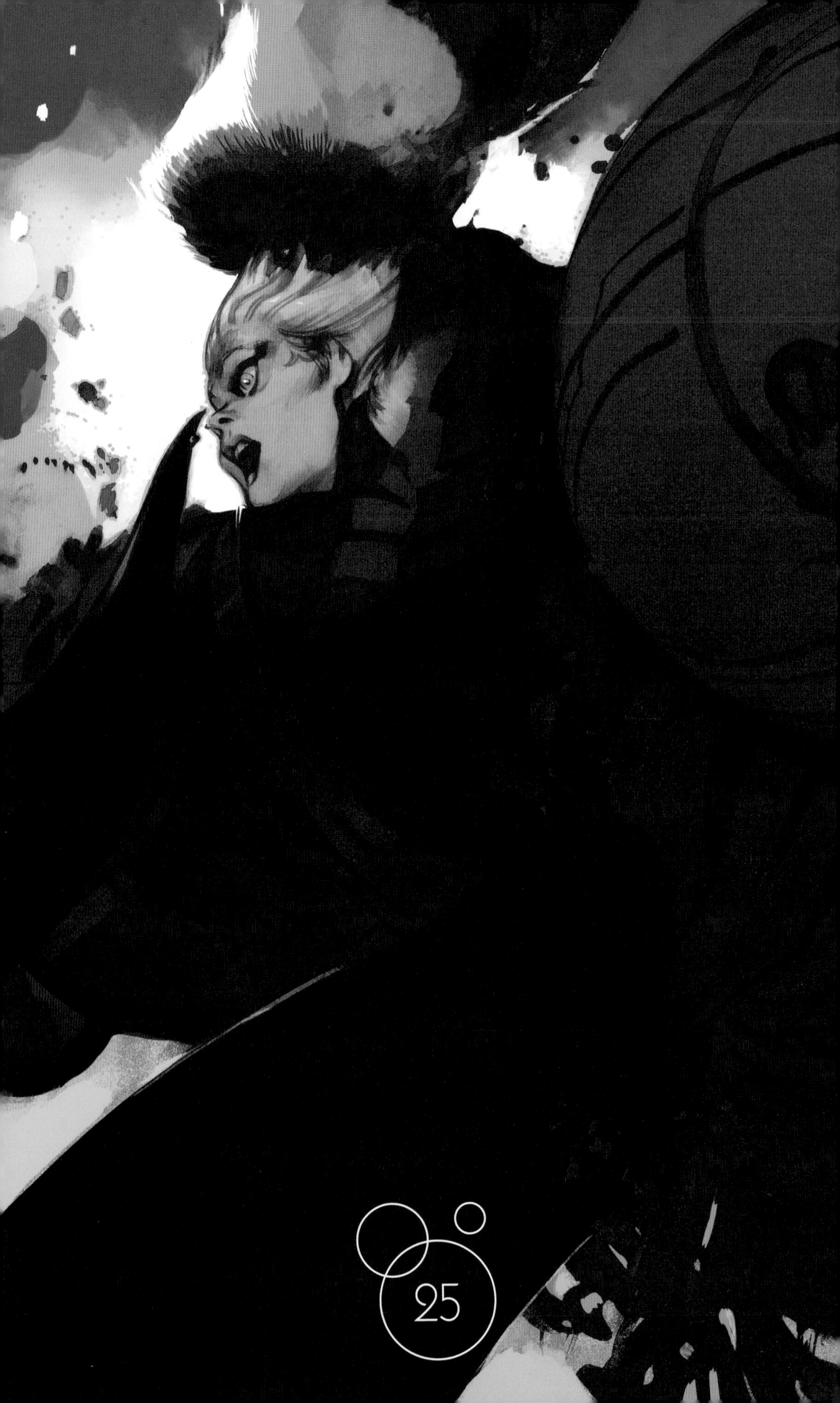

25

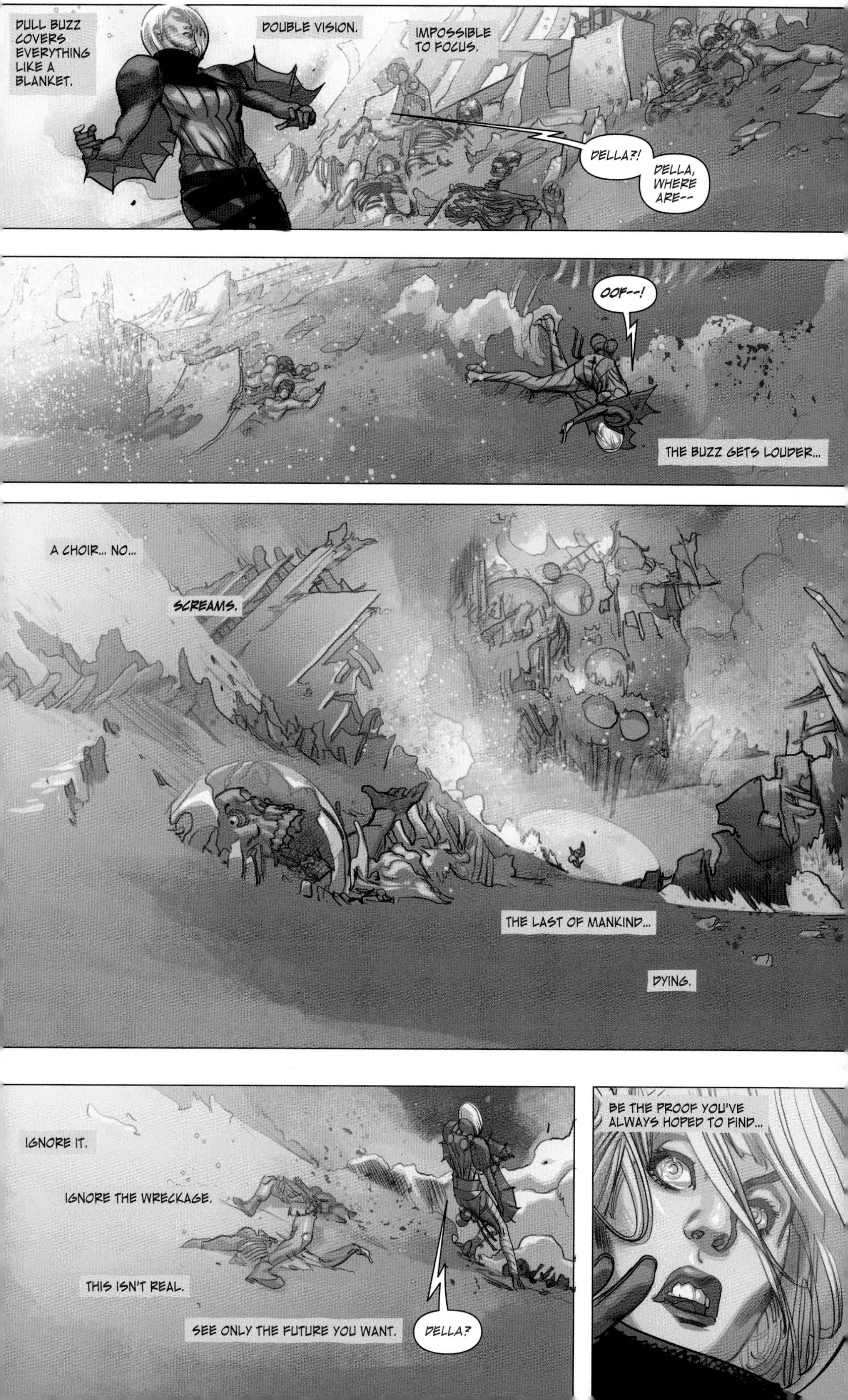
DULL BUZZ COVERS EVERYTHING LIKE A BLANKET.
DOUBLE VISION.
IMPOSSIBLE TO FOCUS.
DELLA?!
DELLA, WHERE ARE--
OOF--!
THE BUZZ GETS LOUDER...
A CHOIR... NO...
SCREAMS.
THE LAST OF MANKIND...
DYING.
IGNORE IT.
IGNORE THE WRECKAGE.
THIS ISN'T REAL.
SEE ONLY THE FUTURE YOU WANT.
DELLA?
BE THE PROOF YOU'VE ALWAYS HOPED TO FIND...

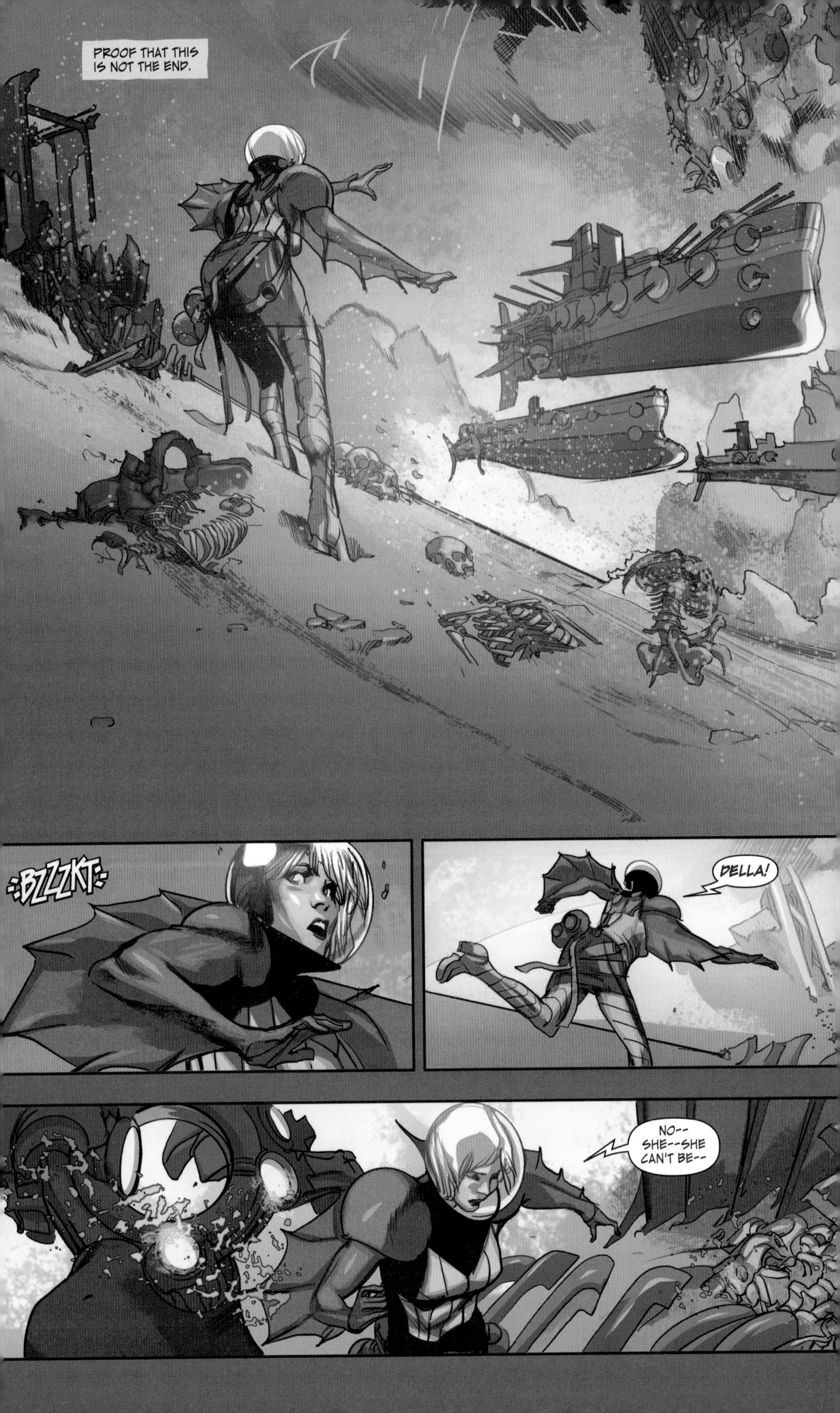
PROOF THAT THIS IS NOT THE END.
BZZZKT
DELLA!
NO--
SHE--SHE
CAN'T BE--

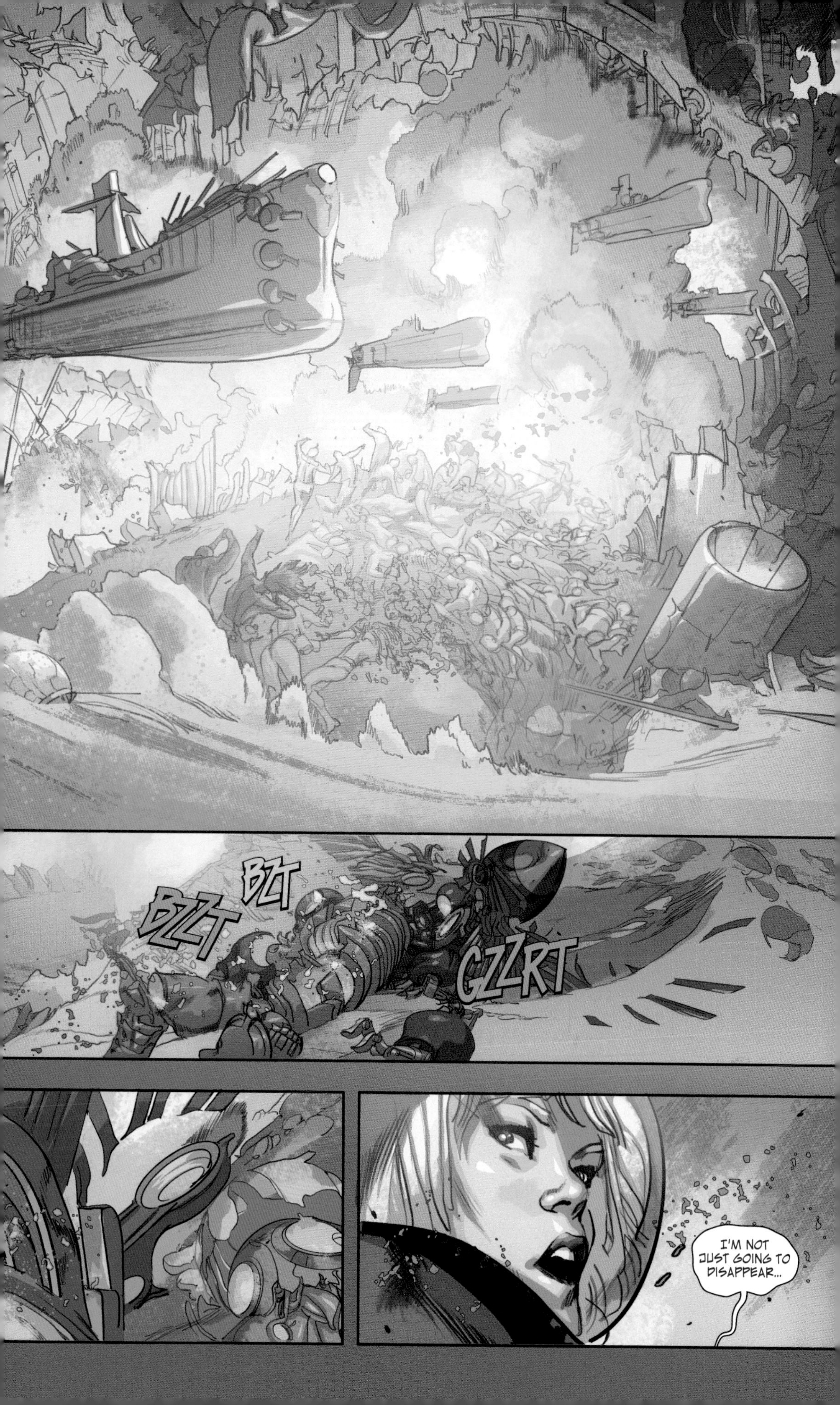
BZZT
BZT
GZZRT
I'M NOT JUST GOING TO DISAPPEAR...

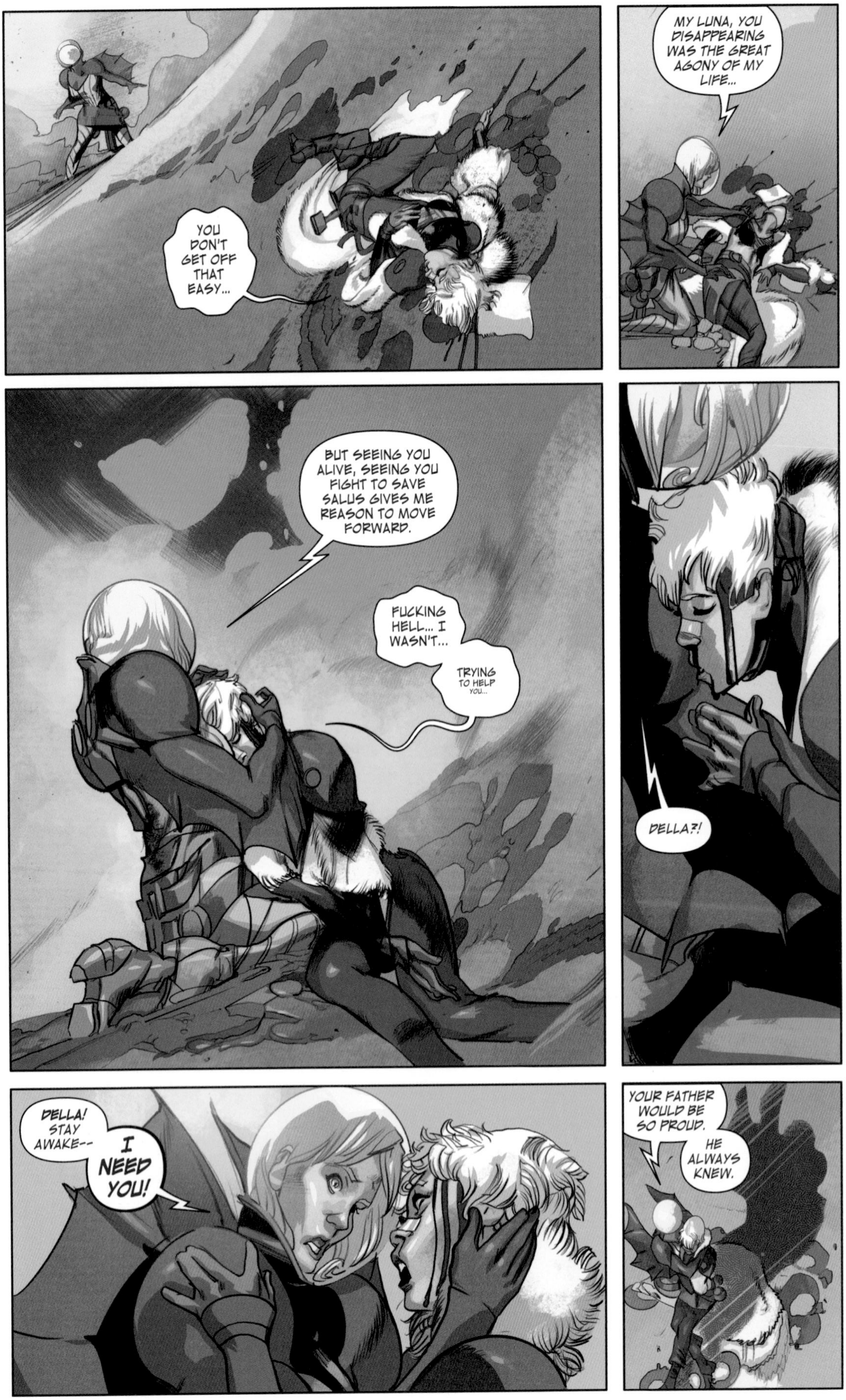

YOU DON'T GET OFF THAT EASY...
MY LUNA, YOU DISAPPEARING WAS THE GREAT AGONY OF MY LIFE...
BUT SEEING YOU ALIVE, SEEING YOU FIGHT TO SAVE SALUS GIVES ME REASON TO MOVE FORWARD.
FUCKING HELL... I WASN'T...
TRYING TO HELP YOU...
DELLA?!
DELLA! STAY AWAKE--
I NEED YOU!
YOUR FATHER WOULD BE SO PROUD.
HE ALWAYS KNEW.

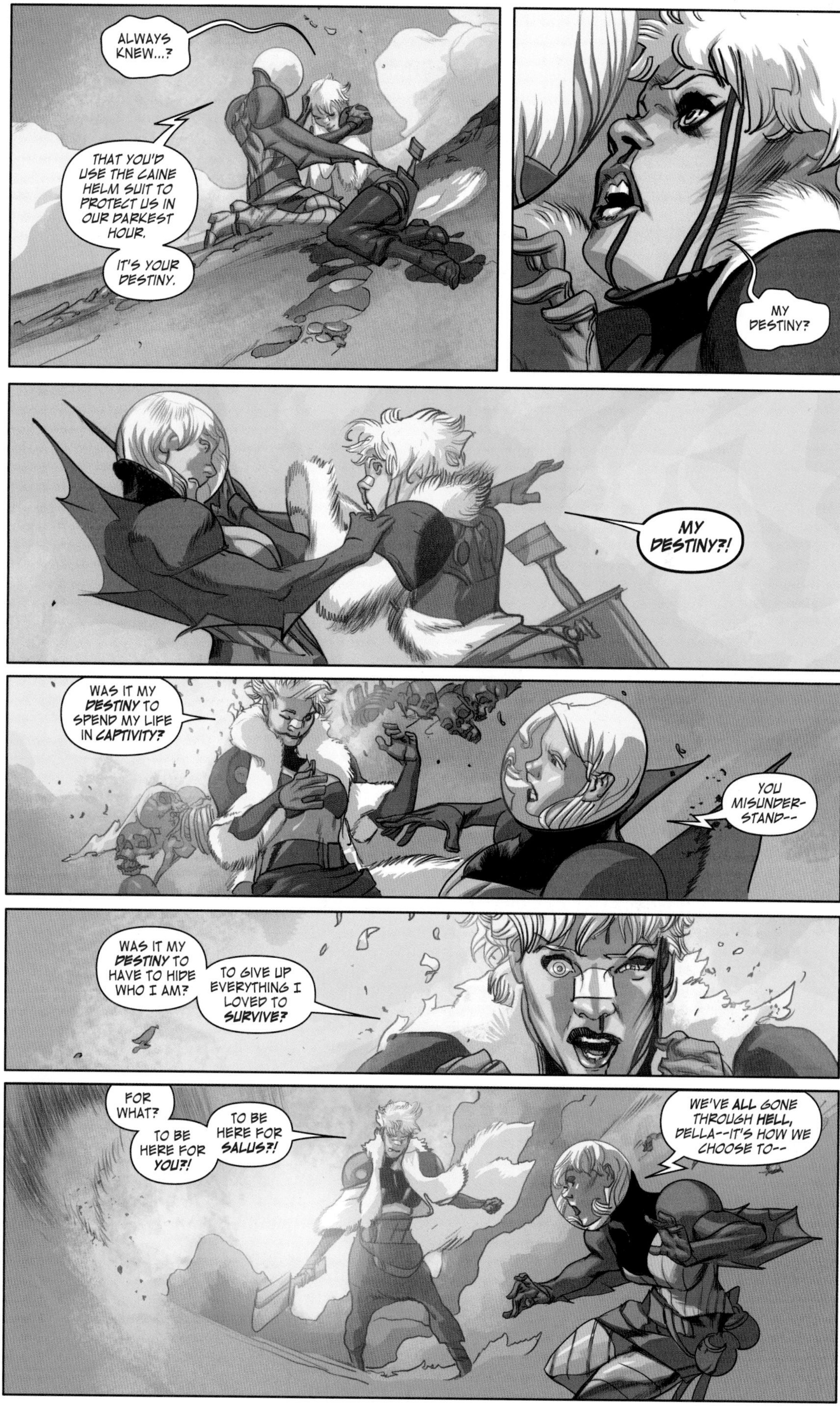
ALWAYS KNEW...?
THAT YOU'D USE THE CAINE HELM SUIT TO PROTECT US IN OUR DARKEST HOUR.
IT'S YOUR DESTINY.
MY DESTINY?
MY DESTINY?!
WAS IT MY DESTINY TO SPEND MY LIFE IN CAPTIVITY?
YOU MISUNDER-STAND--
WAS IT MY DESTINY TO HAVE TO HIDE WHO I AM?
TO GIVE UP EVERYTHING I LOVED TO SURVIVE?
FOR WHAT?
TO BE HERE FOR YOU?!
TO BE HERE FOR SALUS?!
WE'VE ALL GONE THROUGH HELL, DELLA--IT'S HOW WE CHOOSE TO--

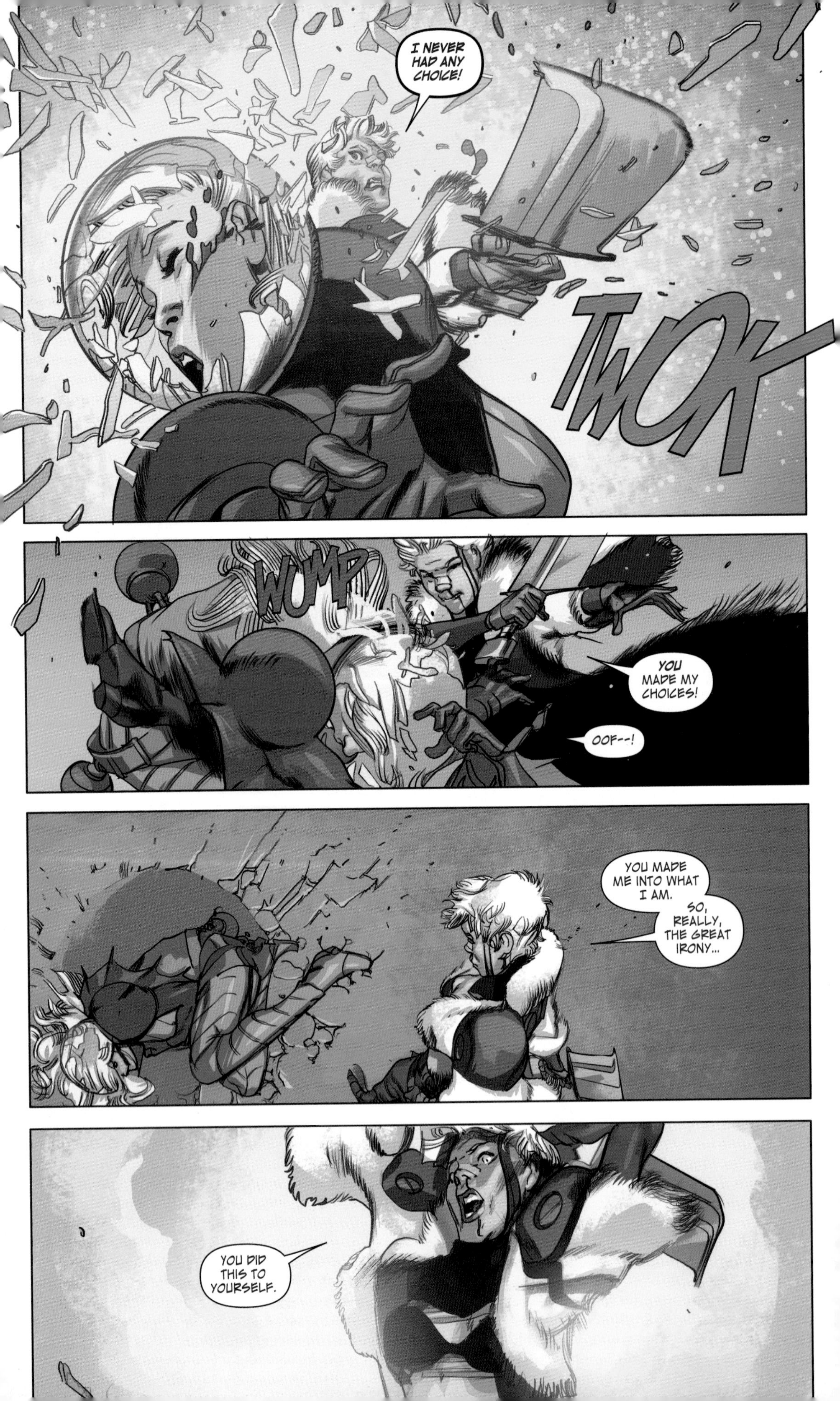
I NEVER HAD ANY CHOICE!
TWOK
WUMP
YOU MADE MY CHOICES!
OOF--!
YOU MADE ME INTO WHAT I AM.
SO, REALLY, THE GREAT IRONY...
YOU DID THIS TO YOURSELF.

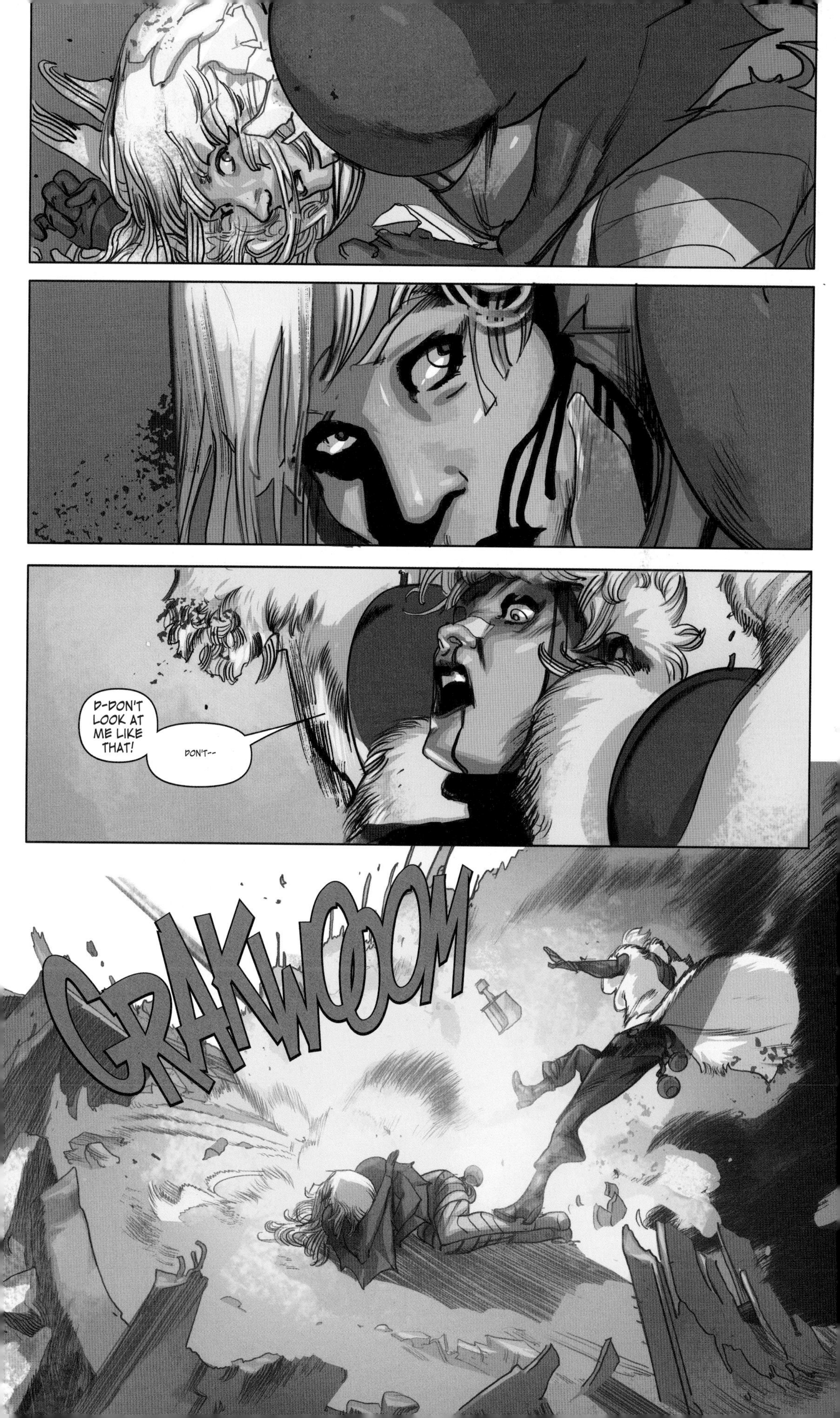
D-DON'T LOOK AT ME LIKE THAT!
DON'T--
GRAKWOOOM

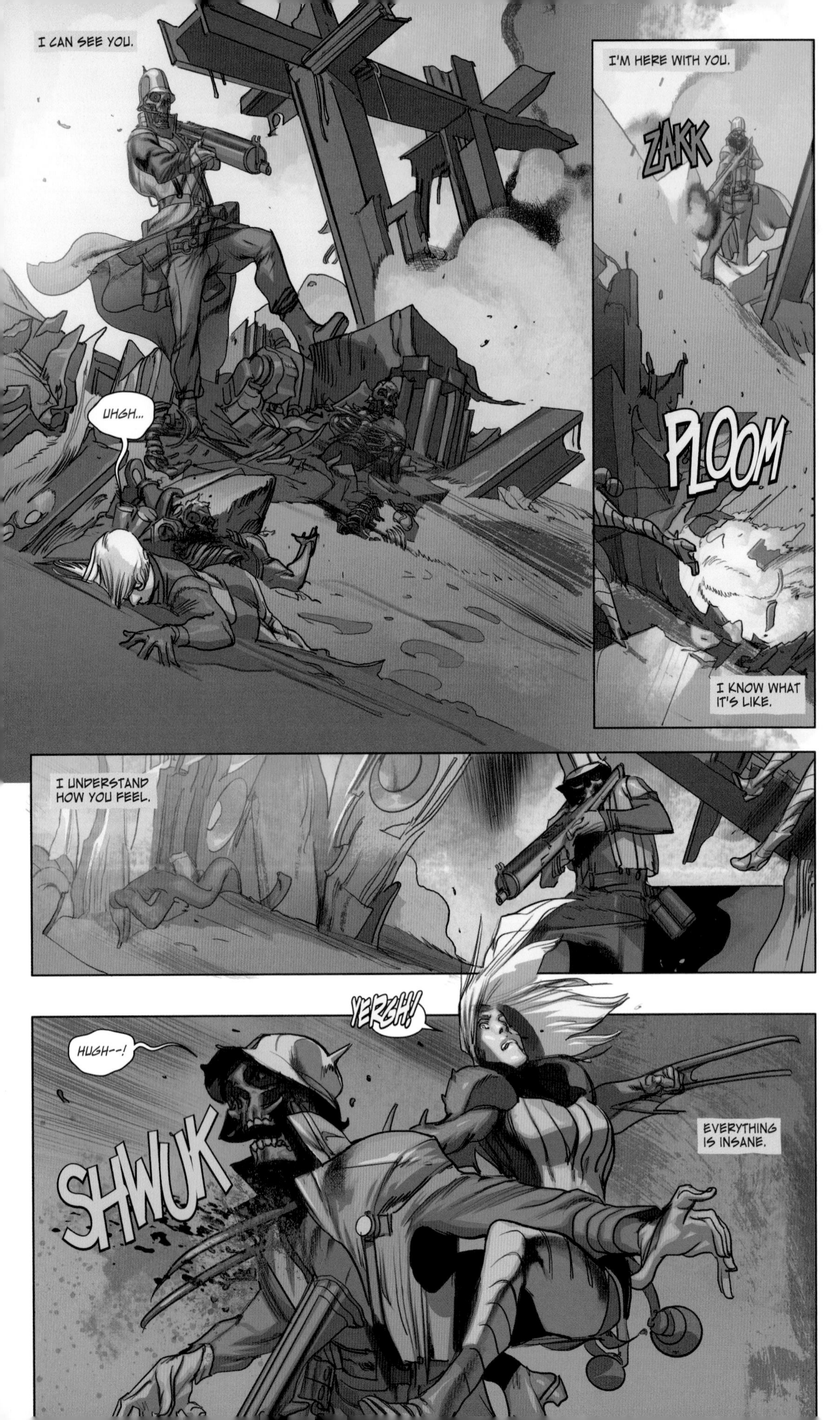

I CAN SEE YOU.
UHGH...
I'M HERE WITH YOU.
ZAKK
PLOOM
I KNOW WHAT IT'S LIKE.
I UNDERSTAND HOW YOU FEEL.
YERGH!
HUGH--!
SHWUK
EVERYTHING IS INSANE.

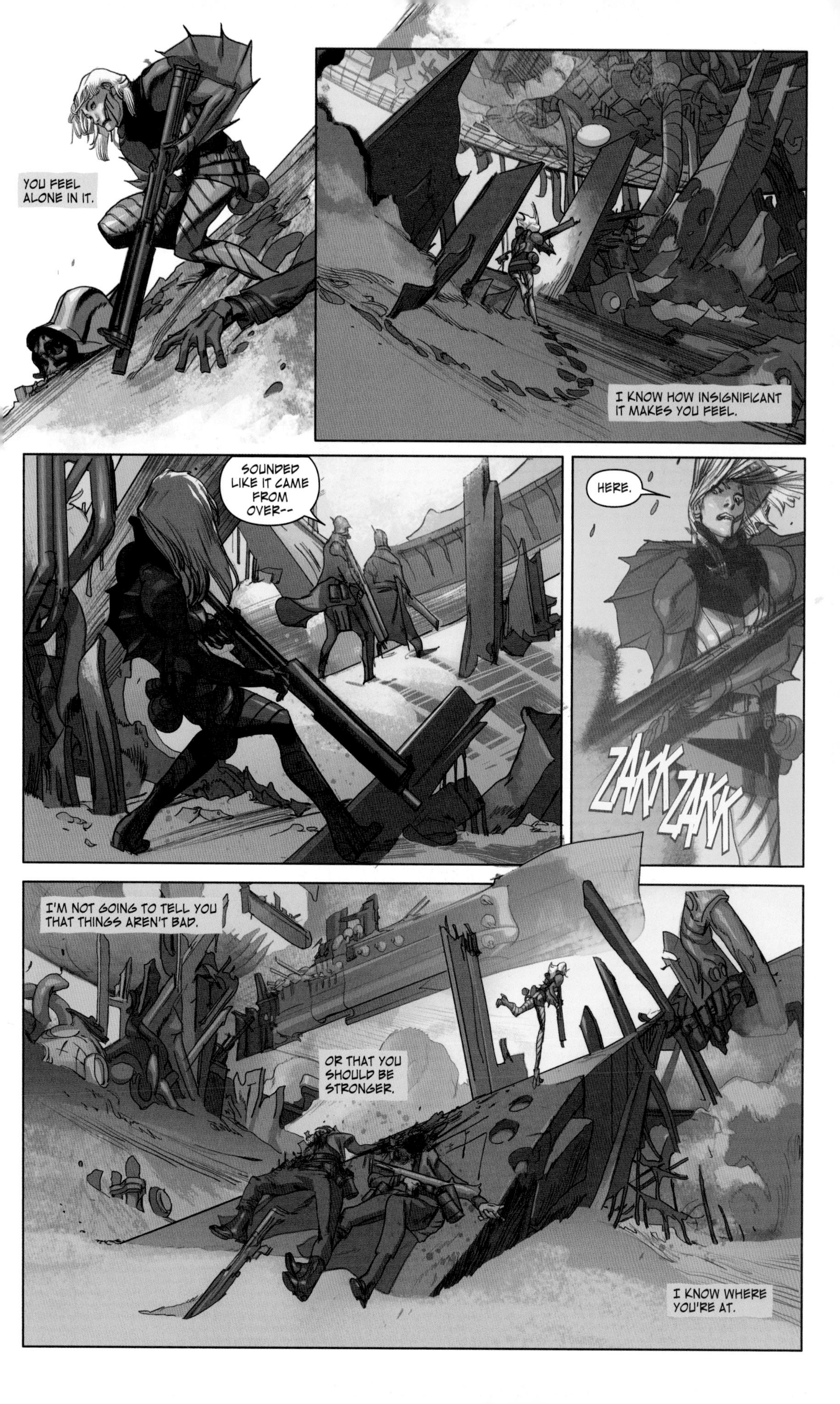
YOU FEEL ALONE IN IT.
I KNOW HOW INSIGNIFICANT IT MAKES YOU FEEL.
SOUNDED LIKE IT CAME FROM OVER--
HERE.
ZAKK ZAKK
I'M NOT GOING TO TELL YOU THAT THINGS AREN'T BAD.
OR THAT YOU SHOULD BE STRONGER.
I KNOW WHERE YOU'RE AT.

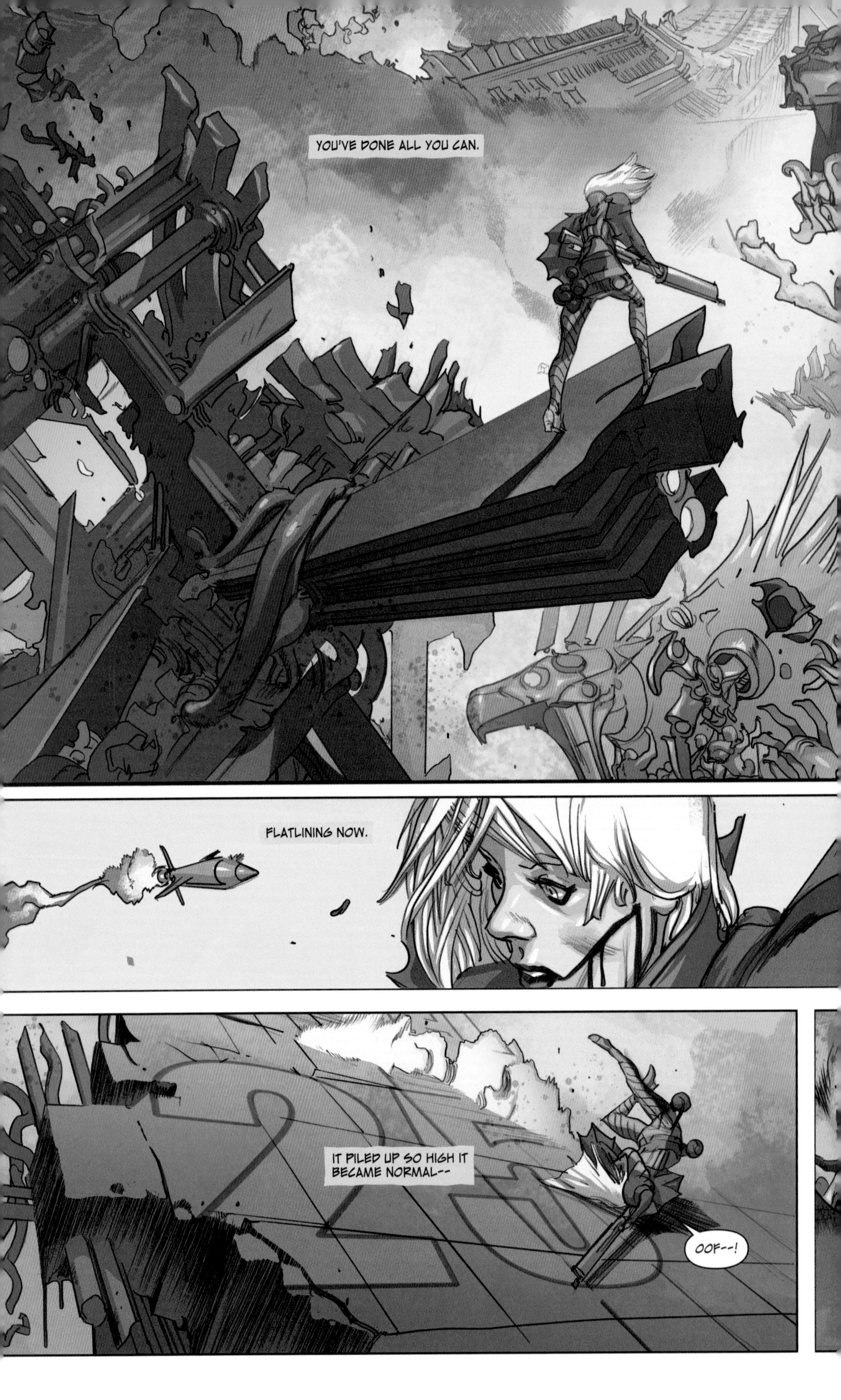
YOU'VE DONE ALL YOU CAN.
FLATLINING NOW.
IT PILED UP SO HIGH IT BECAME NORMAL--
OOF--!

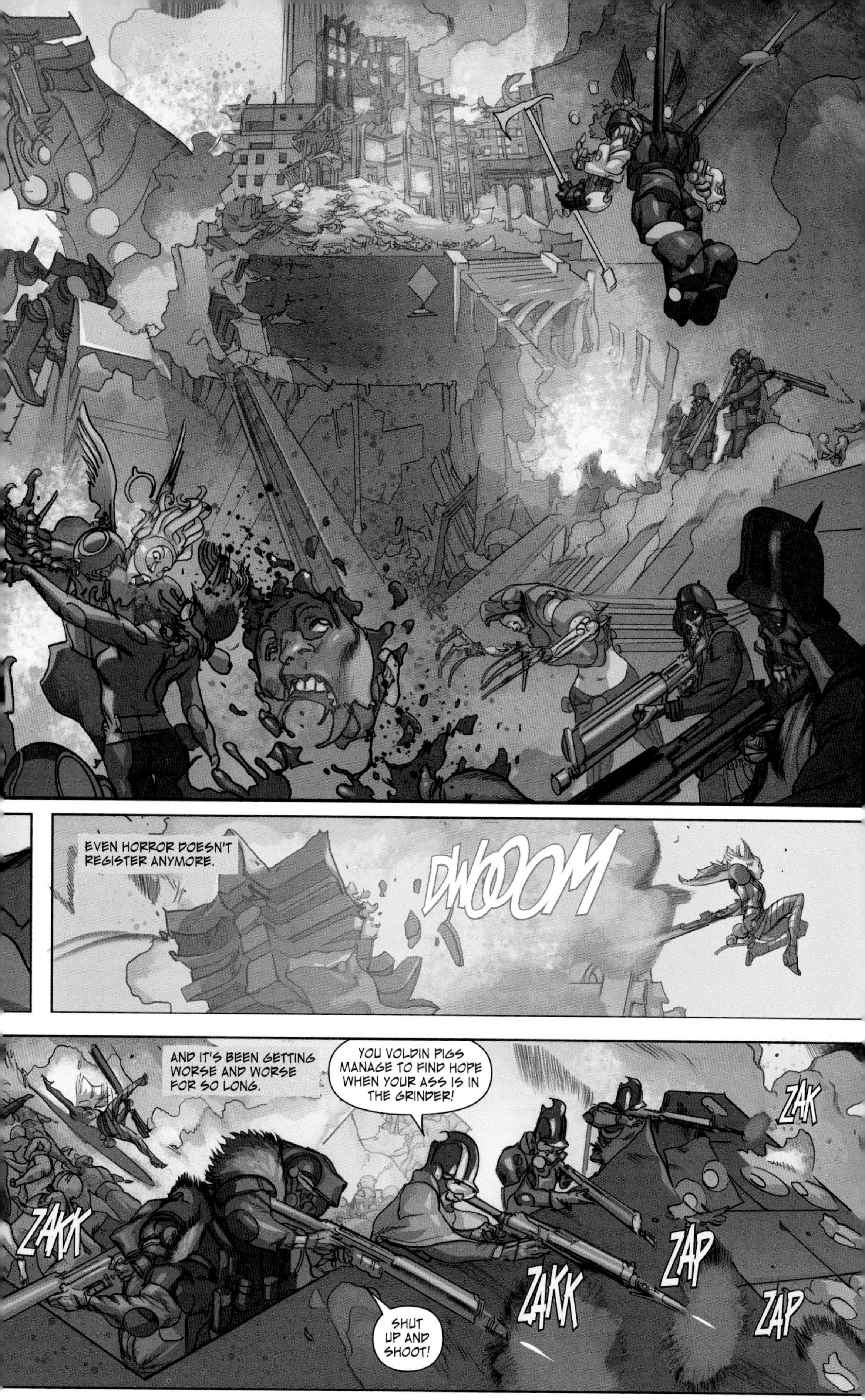
EVEN HORROR DOESN'T REGISTER ANYMORE.
DWOOOM
AND IT'S BEEN GETTING WORSE AND WORSE FOR SO LONG.
YOU VOLDIN PIGS MANAGE TO FIND HOPE WHEN YOUR ASS IS IN THE GRINDER!
ZAK
ZAKK
ZAKK
ZAP
ZAP
SHUT UP AND SHOOT!

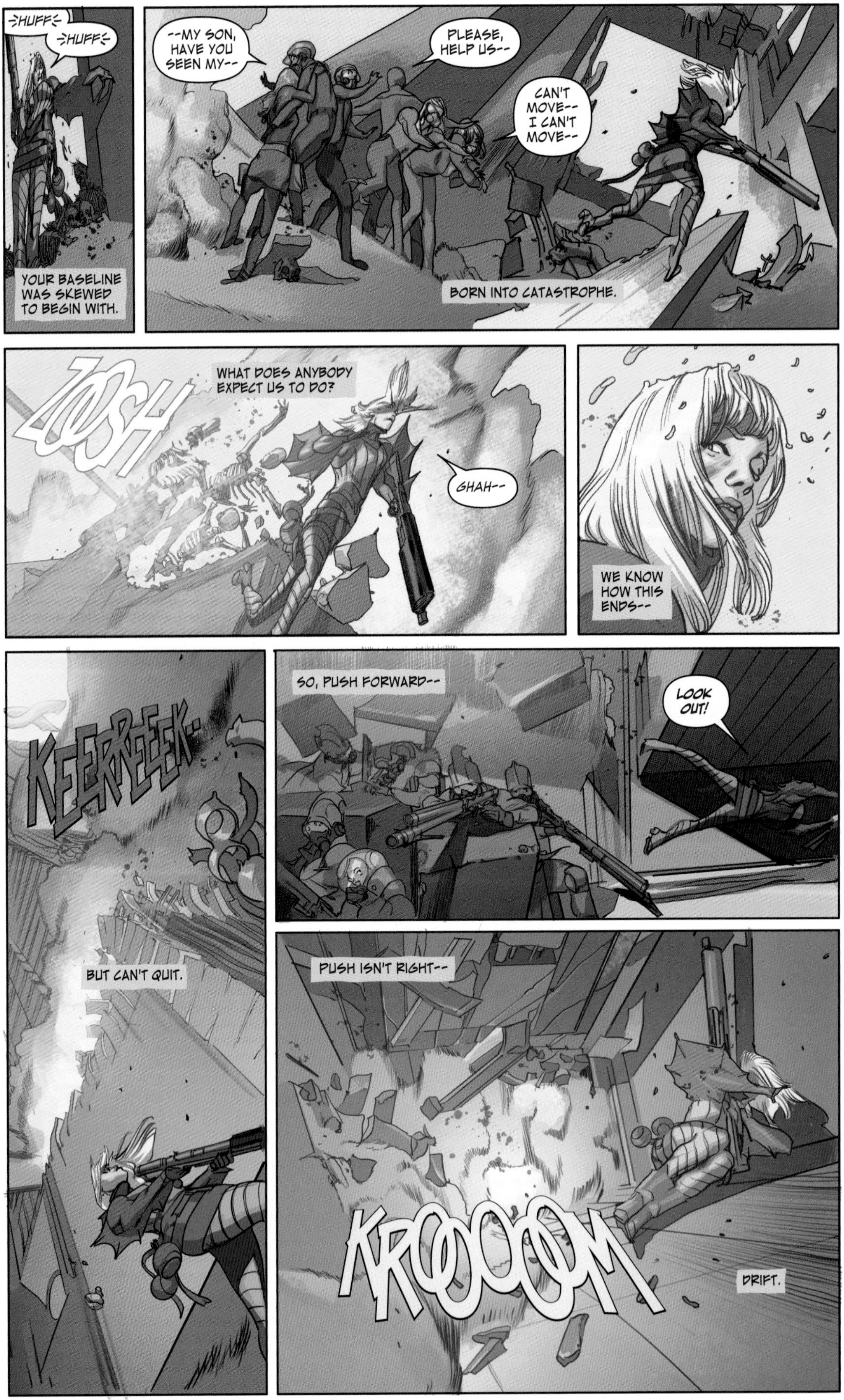

HUFF
HUFF
YOUR BASELINE WAS SKEWED TO BEGIN WITH.
--MY SON, HAVE YOU SEEN MY--
PLEASE, HELP US--
CAN'T MOVE-- I CAN'T MOVE--
BORN INTO CATASTROPHE.
ZOOSH
WHAT DOES ANYBODY EXPECT US TO DO?
GHAH--
WE KNOW HOW THIS ENDS--
KEERREEEK--
BUT CAN'T QUIT.
SO, PUSH FORWARD--
LOOK OUT!
PUSH ISN'T RIGHT--
KROOOOM
DRIFT.

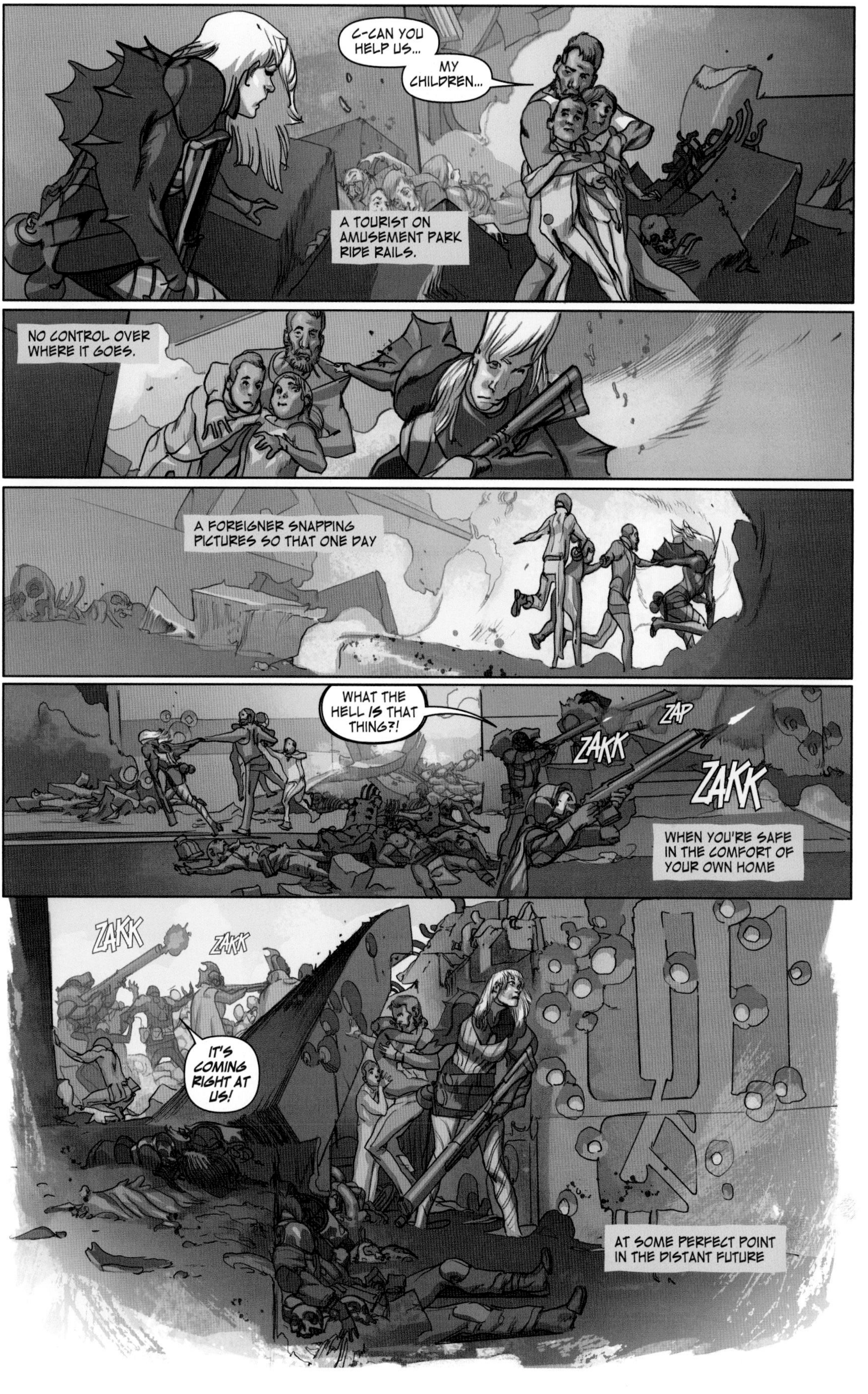
C-CAN YOU HELP US...
MY CHILDREN...
A TOURIST ON AMUSEMENT PARK RIDE RAILS.
NO CONTROL OVER WHERE IT GOES.
A FOREIGNER SNAPPING PICTURES SO THAT ONE DAY
WHAT THE HELL IS THAT THING?!
ZAP
ZAKK
ZAKK
WHEN YOU'RE SAFE IN THE COMFORT OF YOUR OWN HOME
ZAKK
ZAKK
IT'S COMING RIGHT AT US!
AT SOME PERFECT POINT IN THE DISTANT FUTURE

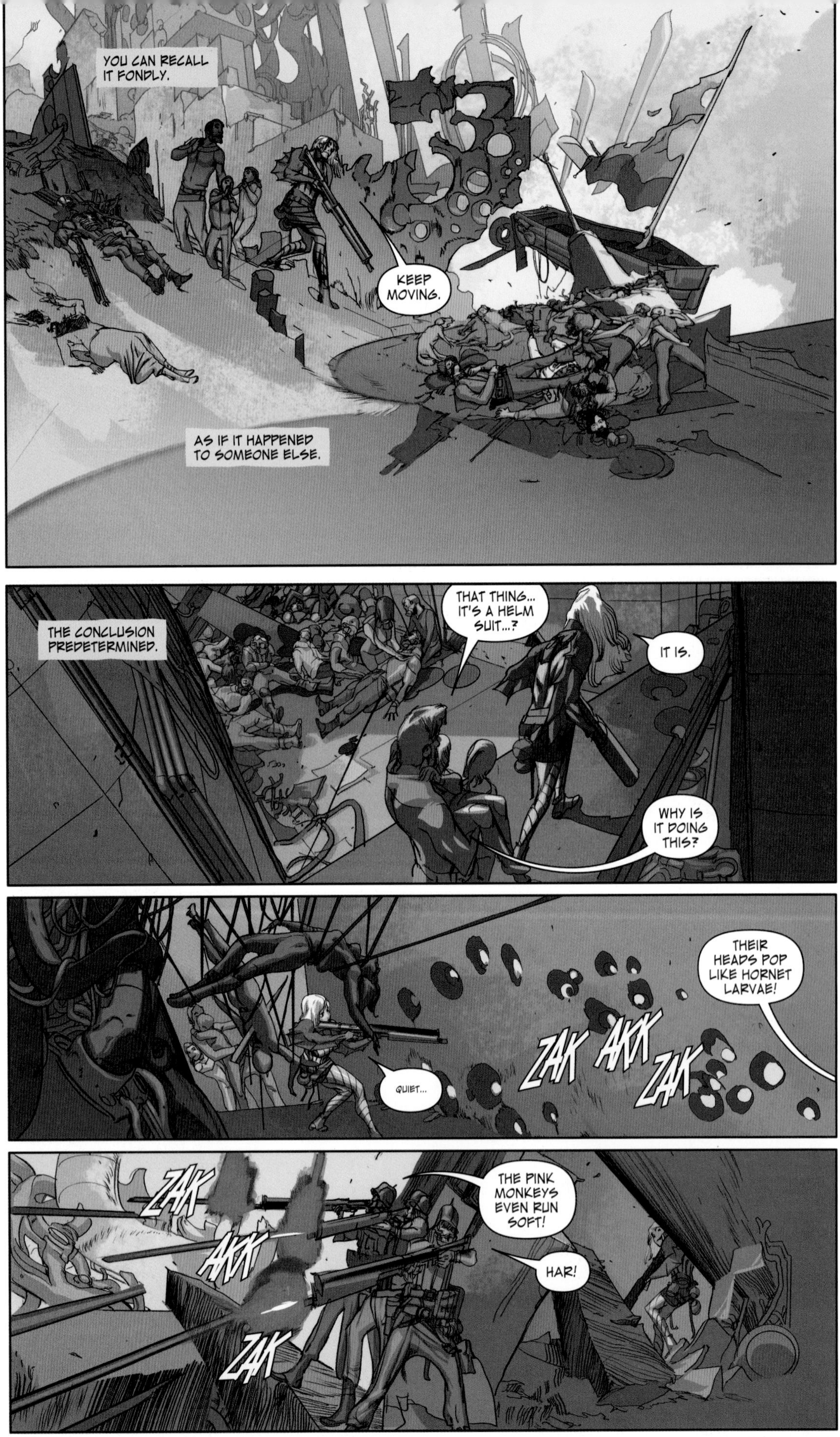
YOU CAN RECALL IT FONDLY.
KEEP MOVING.
AS IF IT HAPPENED TO SOMEONE ELSE.
THE CONCLUSION PREDETERMINED.
THAT THING... IT'S A HELM SUIT...?
IT IS.
WHY IS IT DOING THIS?
THEIR HEADS POP LIKE HORNET LARVAE!
ZAK AKK ZAK
QUIET...
ZAK
AKK
ZAK
THE PINK MONKEYS EVEN RUN SOFT!
HAR!

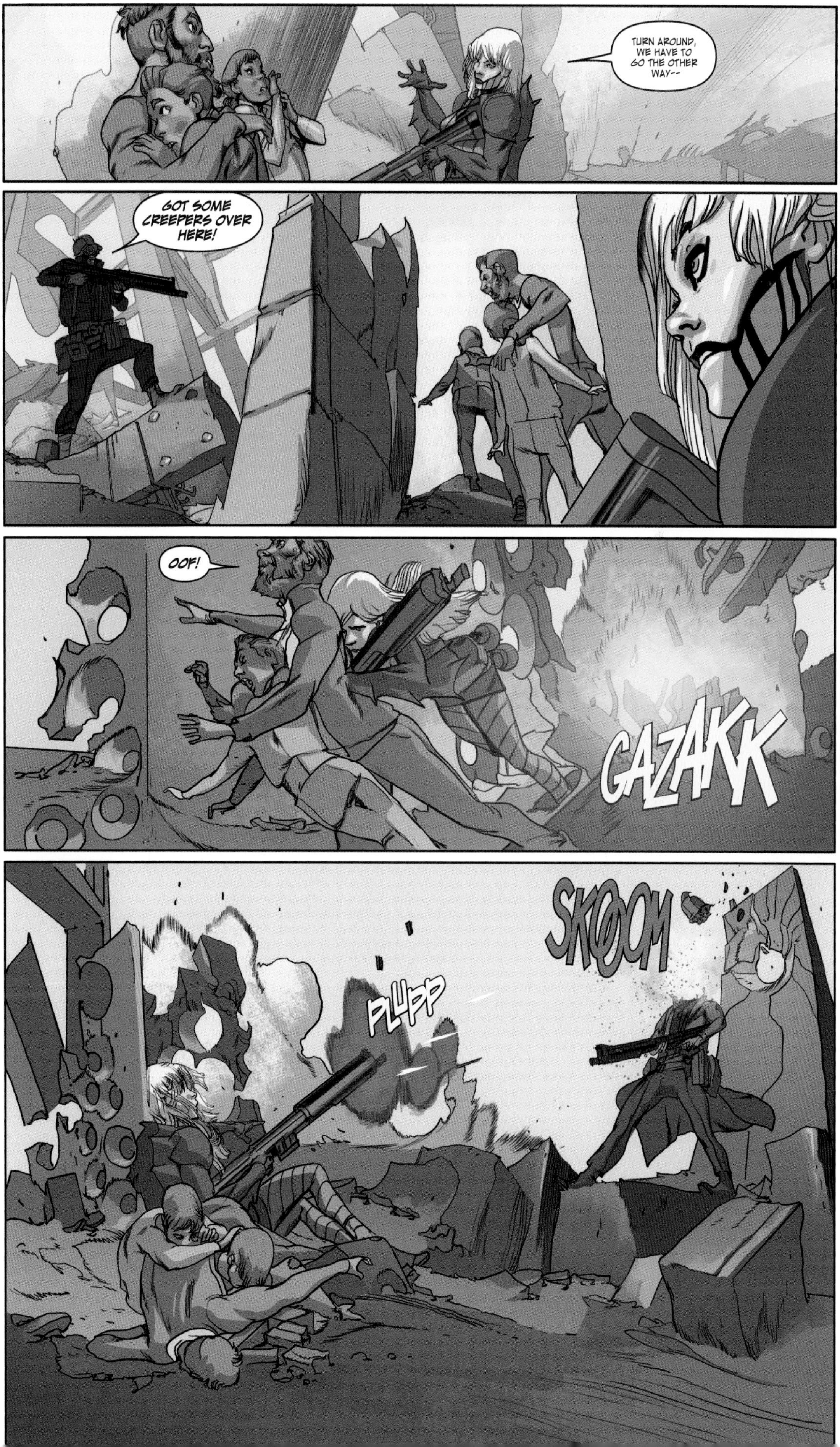
TURN AROUND, WE HAVE TO GO THE OTHER WAY--
GOT SOME CREEPERS OVER HERE!
OOF!
GAZAKK
SKOOM
PLUPP

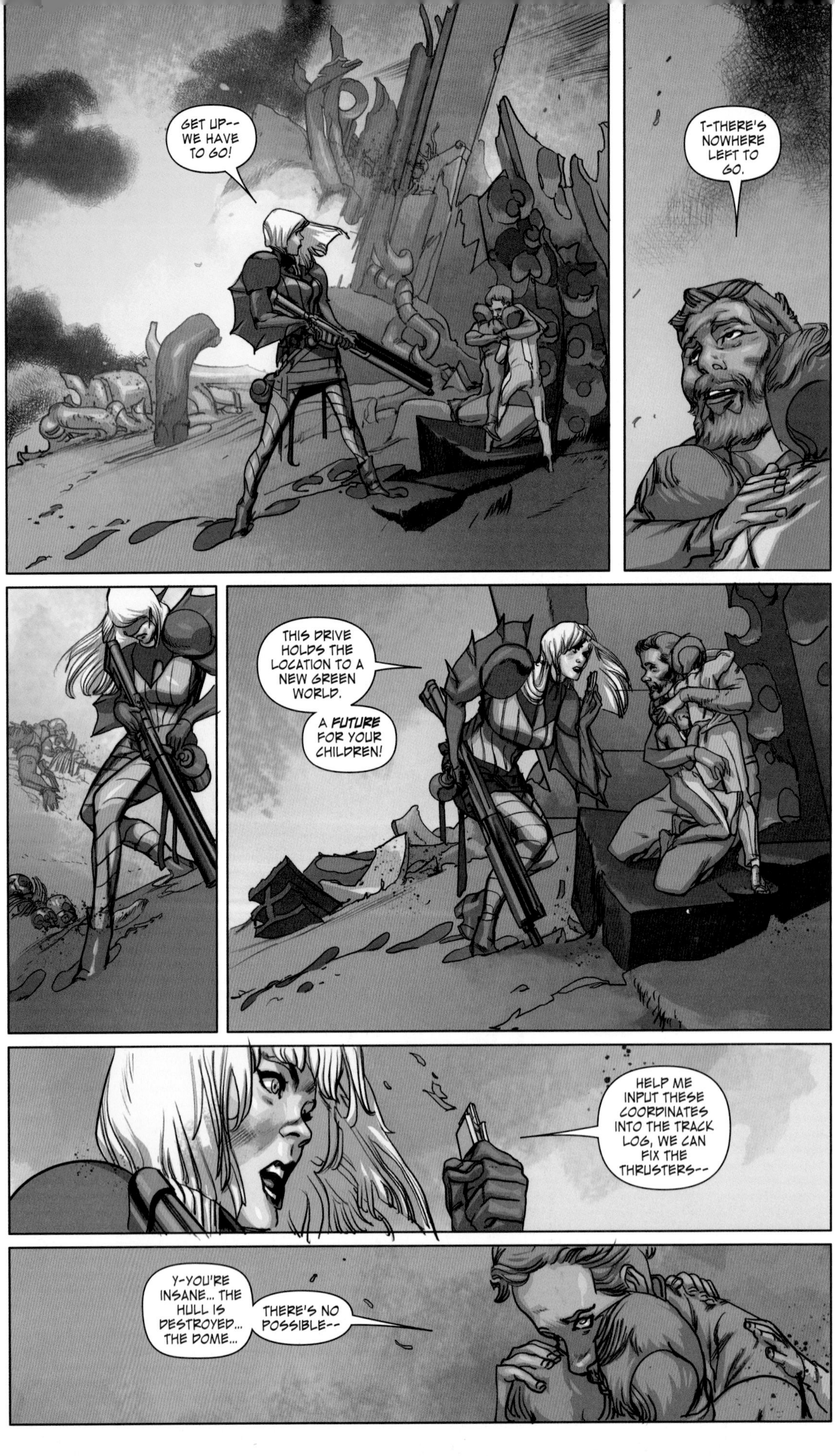
GET UP-- WE HAVE TO GO!
T-THERE'S NOWHERE LEFT TO GO.
THIS DRIVE HOLDS THE LOCATION TO A NEW GREEN WORLD.
A FUTURE FOR YOUR CHILDREN!
HELP ME INPUT THESE COORDINATES INTO THE TRACK LOG, WE CAN FIX THE THRUSTERS--
Y-YOU'RE INSANE... THE HULL IS DESTROYED... THE DOME...
THERE'S NO POSSIBLE--

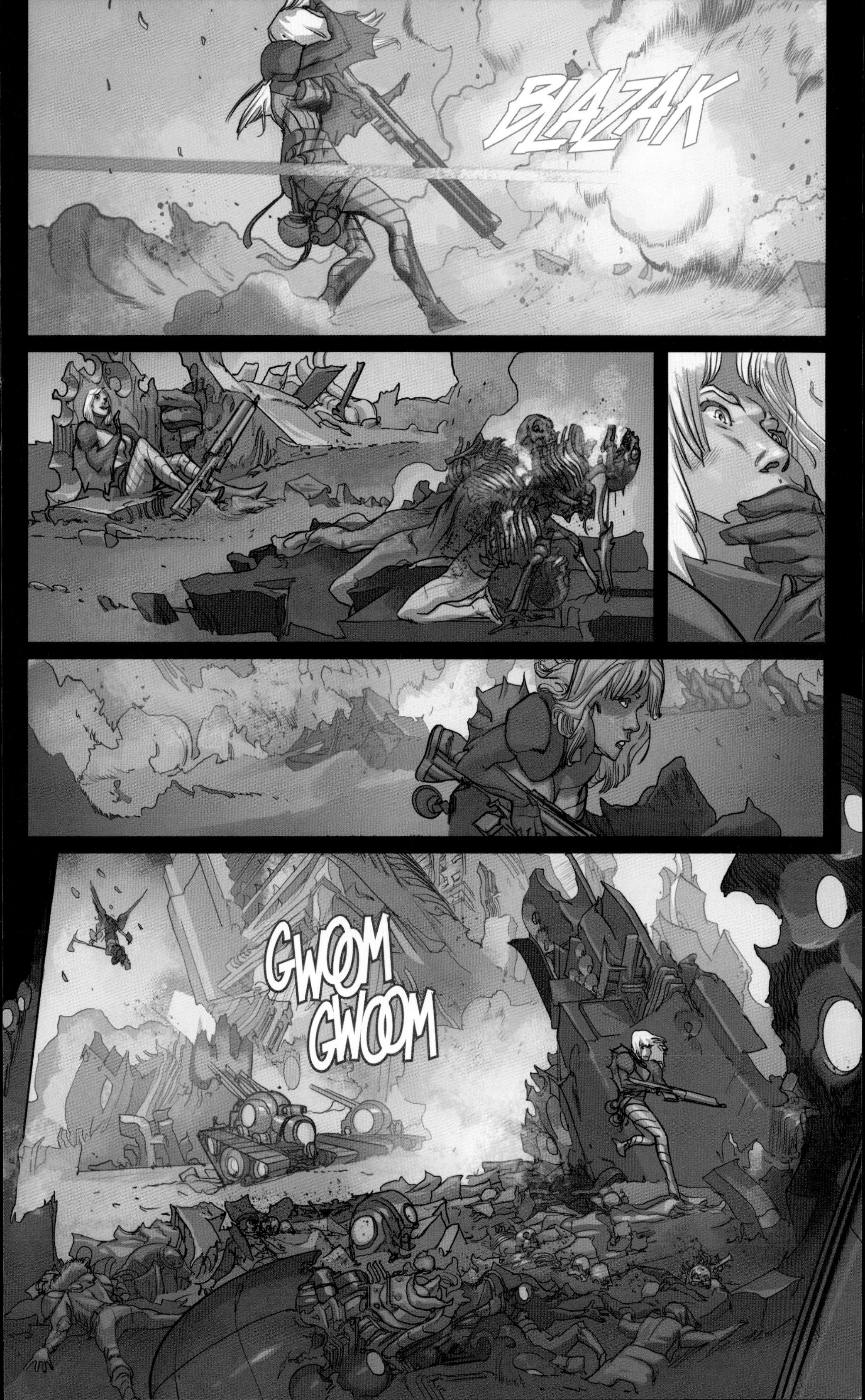
BLAZAK
GWOOM GWOOM

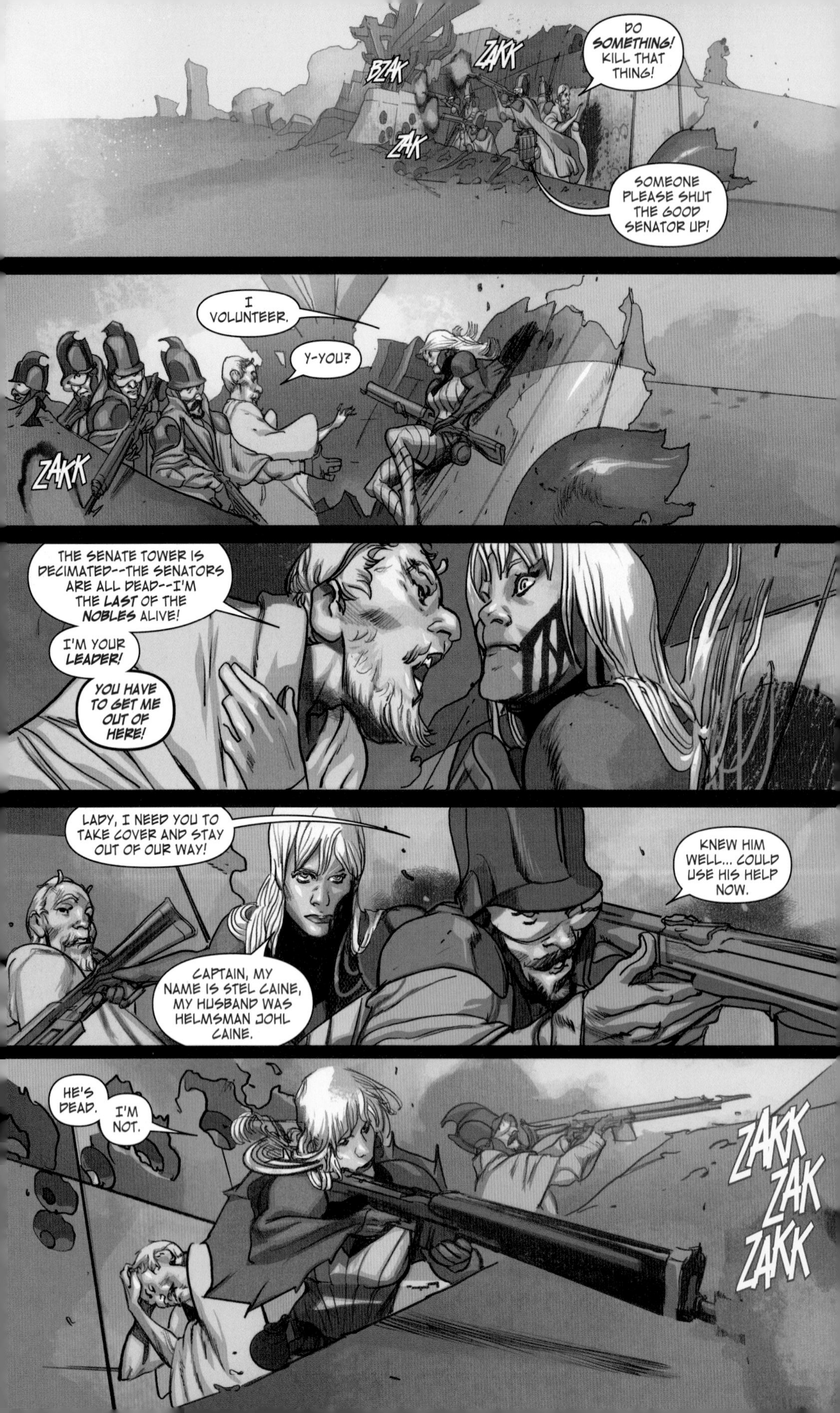
BZAK
ZAKK
ZAK
DO SOMETHING! KILL THAT THING!
SOMEONE PLEASE SHUT THE GOOD SENATOR UP!
I VOLUNTEER.
Y-YOU?
ZAKK
THE SENATE TOWER IS DECIMATED--THE SENATORS ARE ALL DEAD--I'M THE LAST OF THE NOBLES ALIVE!
I'M YOUR LEADER!
YOU HAVE TO GET ME OUT OF HERE!
LADY, I NEED YOU TO TAKE COVER AND STAY OUT OF OUR WAY!
CAPTAIN, MY NAME IS STEL CAINE, MY HUSBAND WAS HELMSMAN JOHL CAINE.
KNEW HIM WELL... COULD USE HIS HELP NOW.
HE'S DEAD.
I'M NOT.
ZAKK
ZAK
ZAKK

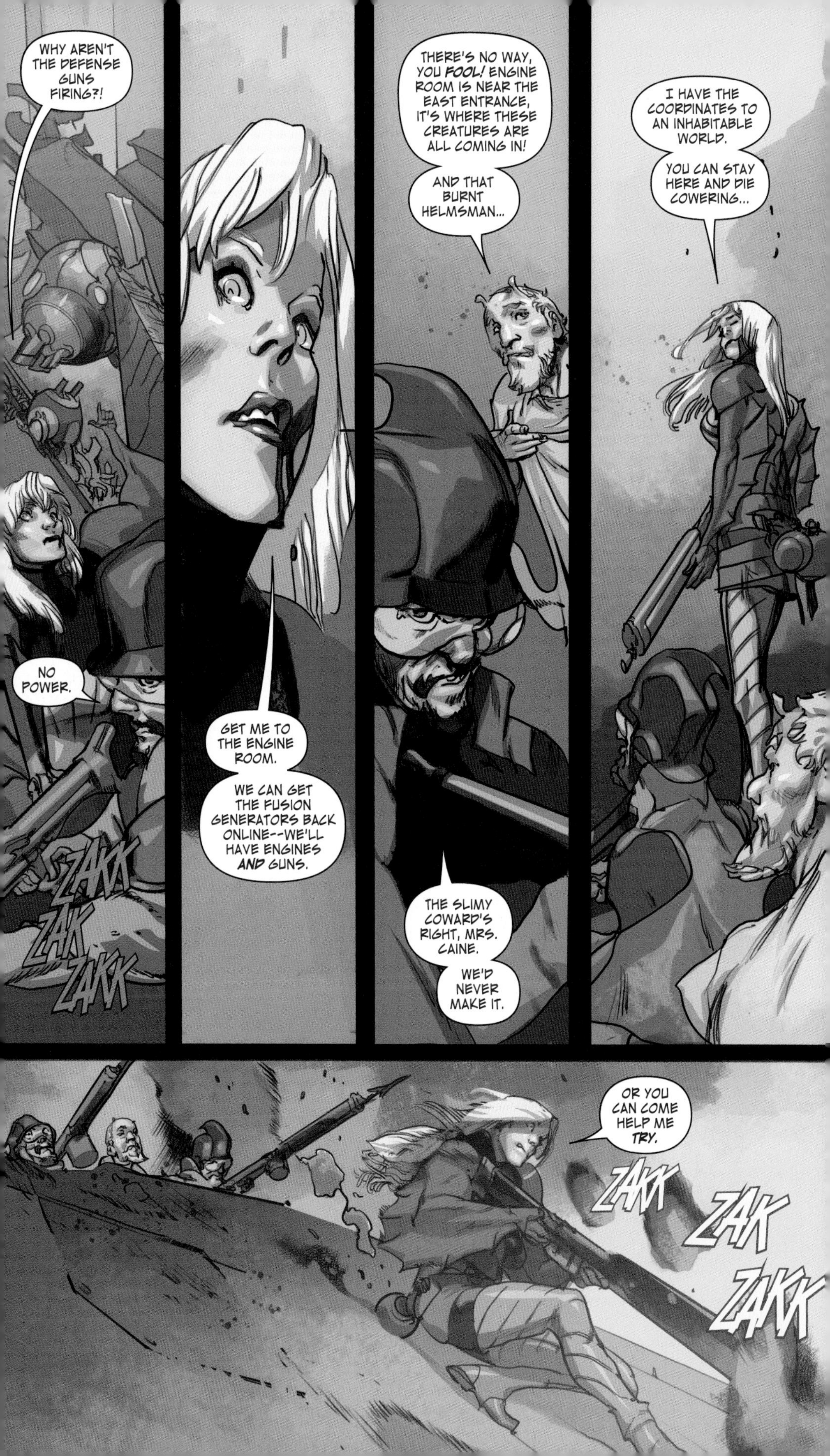

WHY AREN'T THE DEFENSE GUNS FIRING?!
NO POWER.
ZAKK ZAK ZAKK
GET ME TO THE ENGINE ROOM.
WE CAN GET THE FUSION GENERATORS BACK ONLINE--WE'LL HAVE ENGINES *AND* GUNS.
THERE'S NO WAY, YOU *FOOL!* ENGINE ROOM IS NEAR THE EAST ENTRANCE, IT'S WHERE THESE CREATURES ARE ALL COMING IN!
AND THAT BURNT HELMSMAN...
THE SLIMY COWARD'S RIGHT, MRS. CAINE.
WE'D NEVER MAKE IT.
I HAVE THE COORDINATES TO AN INHABITABLE WORLD.
YOU CAN STAY HERE AND DIE COWERING...
OR YOU CAN COME HELP ME *TRY.*
ZAKK ZAK ZAKK

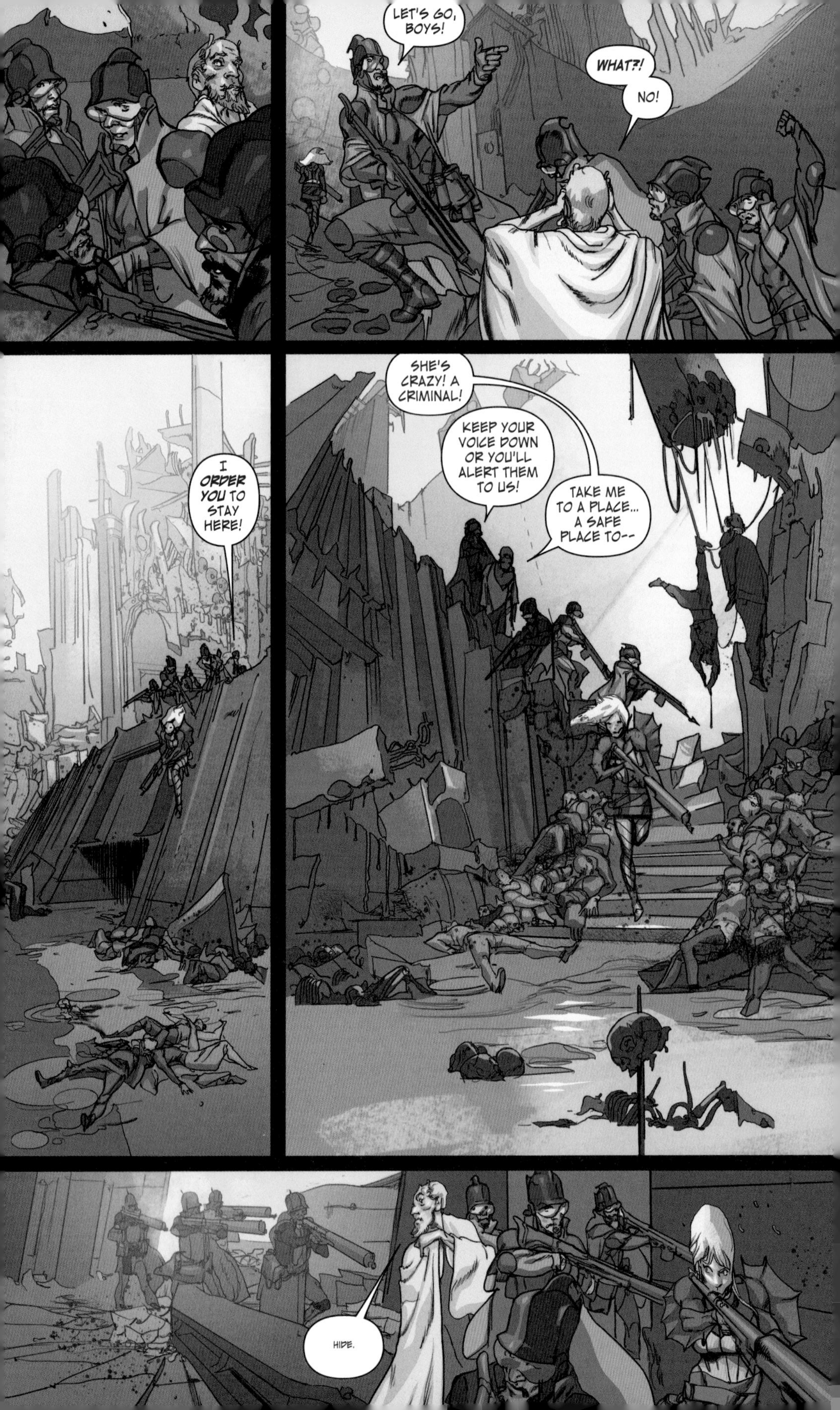
LET'S GO, BOYS!
WHAT?!
NO!
I ORDER YOU TO STAY HERE!
SHE'S CRAZY! A CRIMINAL!
KEEP YOUR VOICE DOWN OR YOU'LL ALERT THEM TO US!
TAKE ME TO A PLACE... A SAFE PLACE TO--
HIDE.

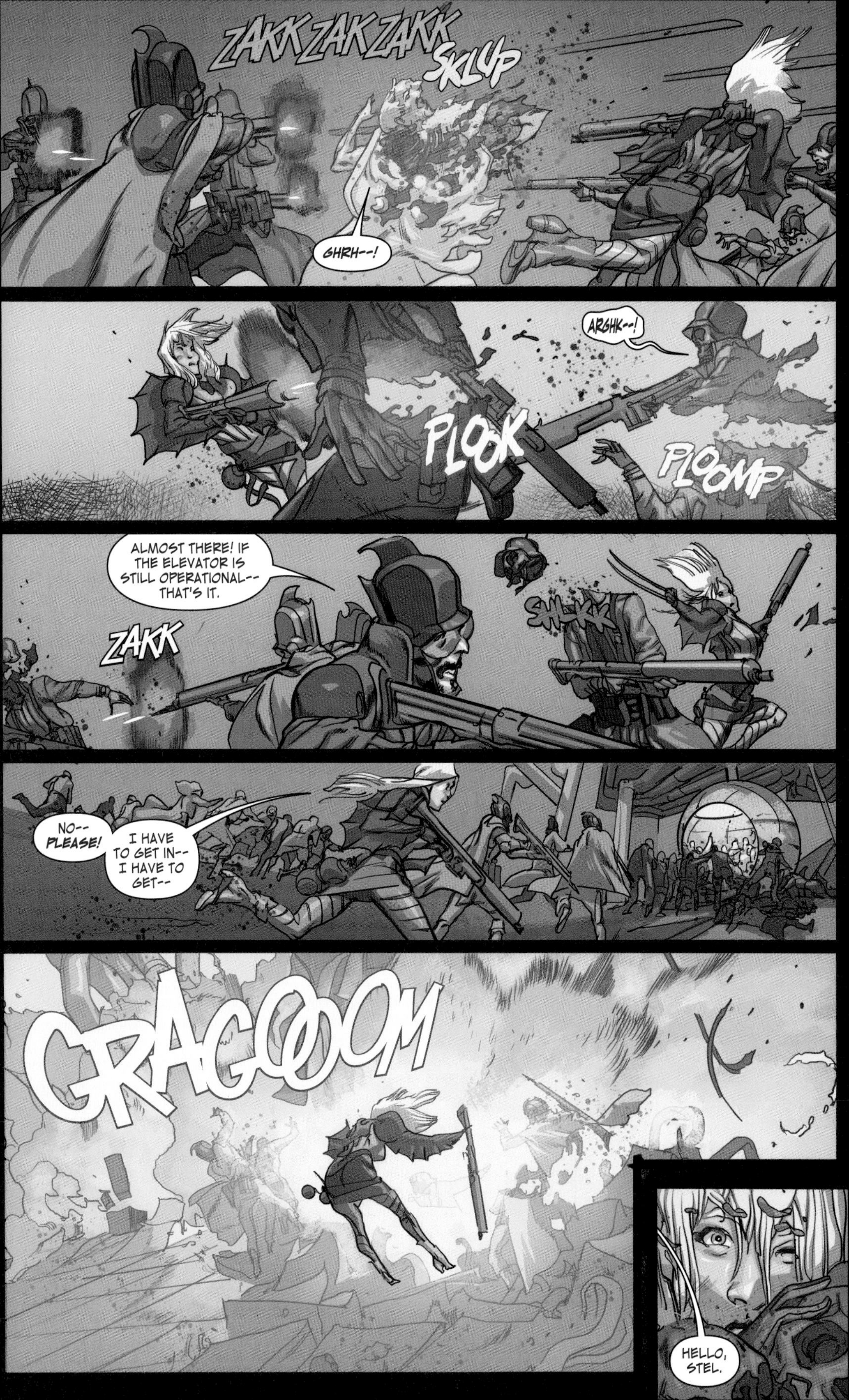
ZAKK ZAK ZAKK
SKLUP
GHRH--!
ARGHK--!
PLOOK
PLOOMP
ALMOST THERE! IF THE ELEVATOR IS STILL OPERATIONAL-- THAT'S IT.
ZAKK
SHLKK
NO-- PLEASE!
I HAVE TO GET IN-- I HAVE TO GET--
GRAGOOOM
HELLO, STEL.

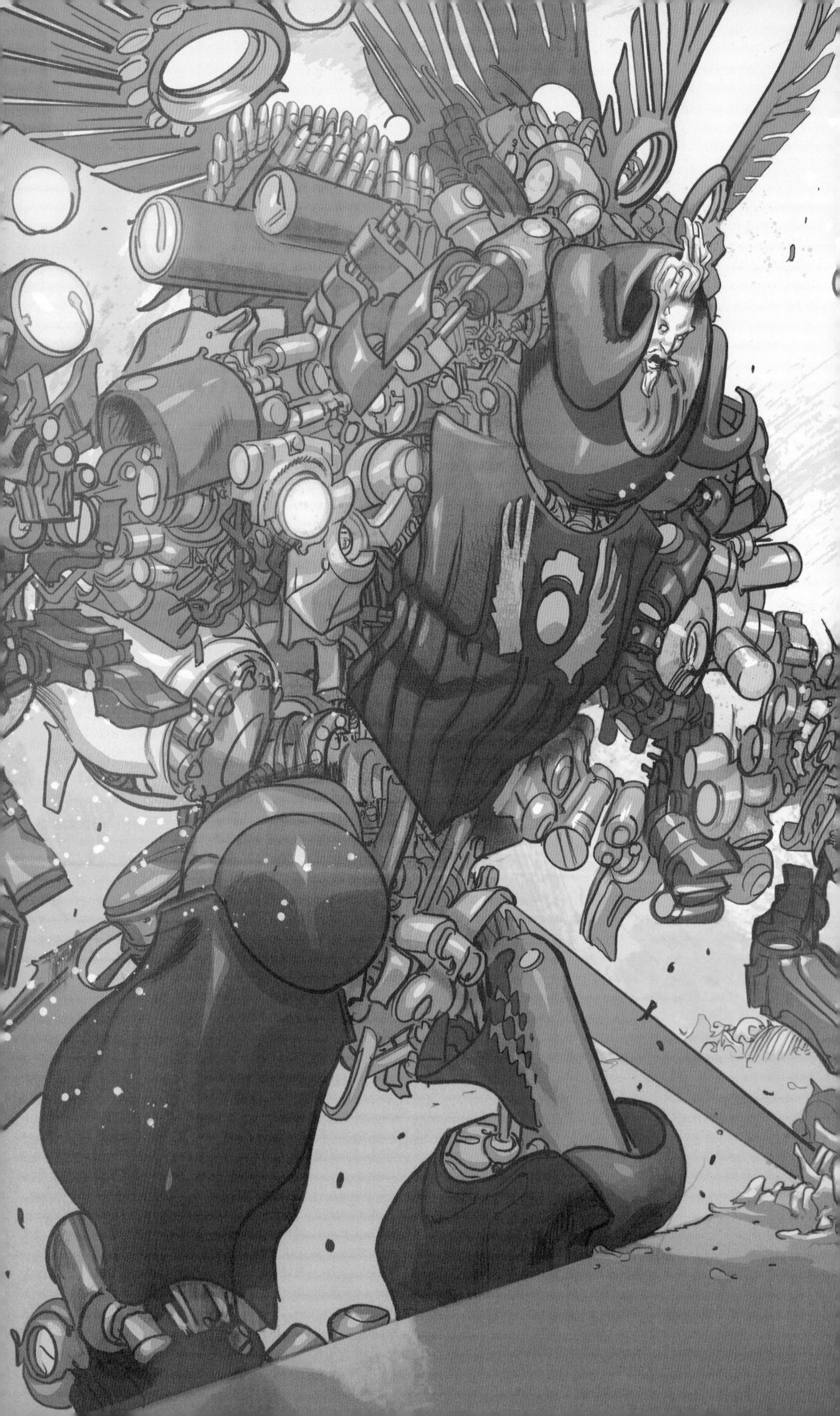

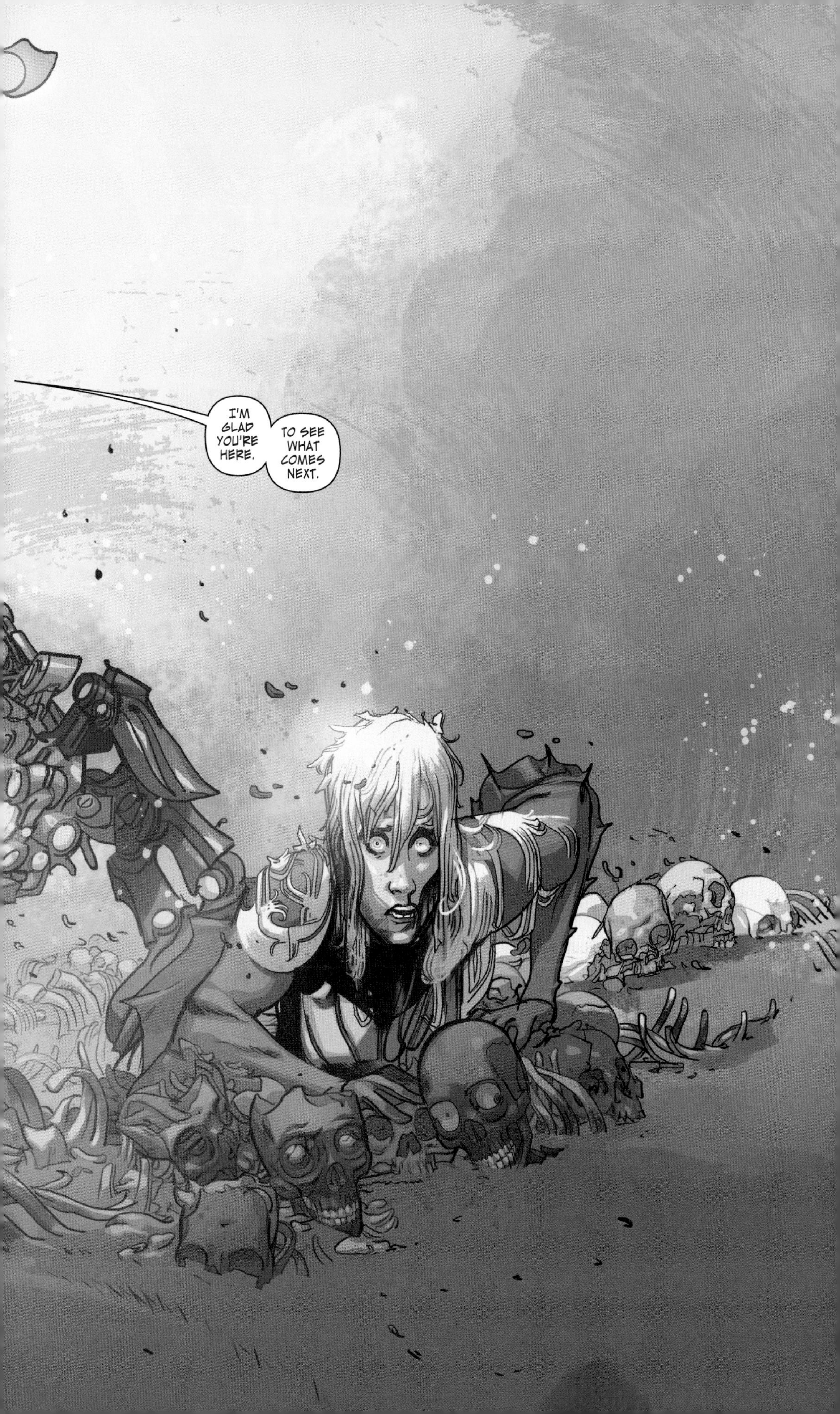
I'M GLAD YOU'RE HERE.
TO SEE WHAT COMES NEXT.

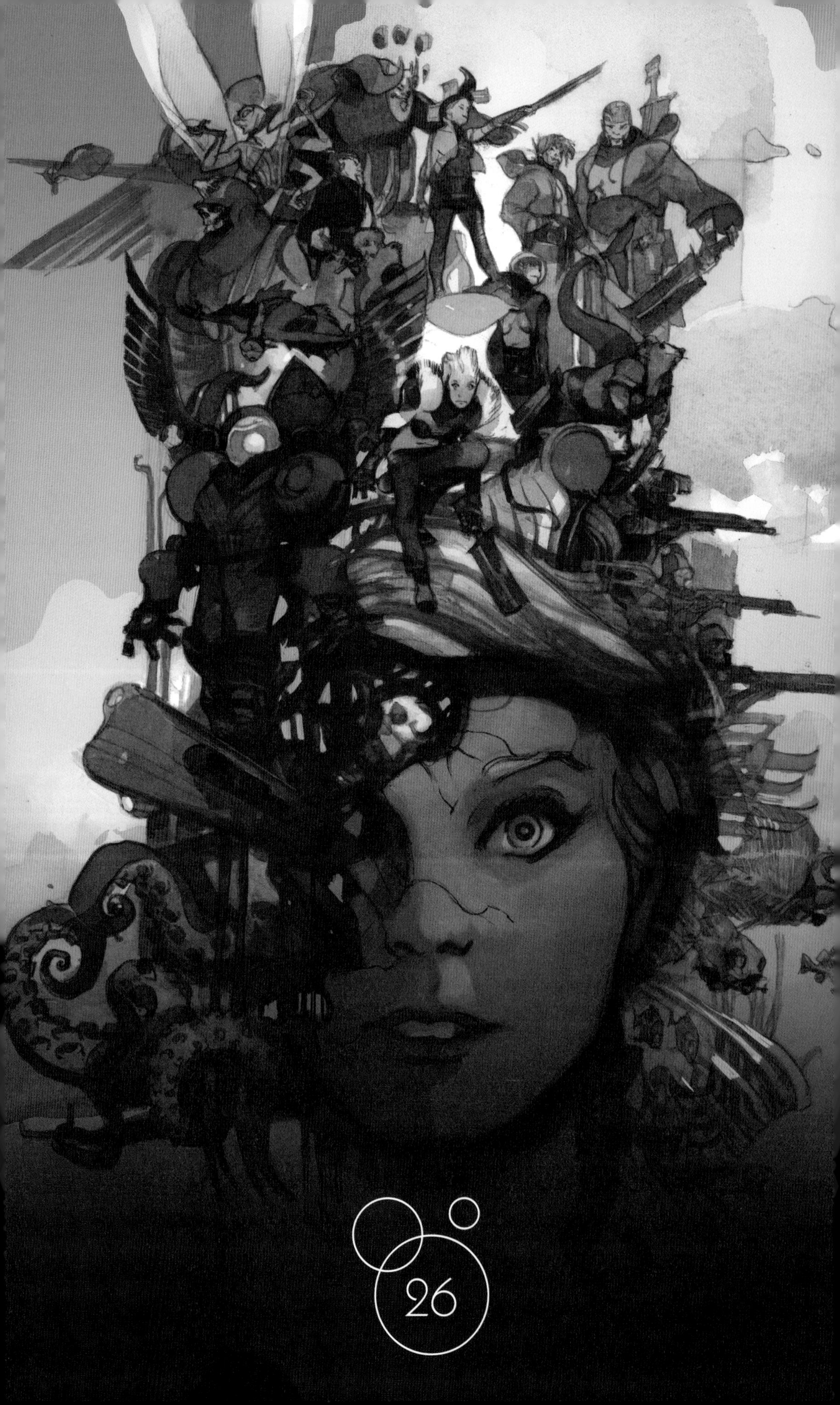

26

IF YOU FELL INTO A BLACK HOLE YOU WOULD
WATCH THE DEATH OF THE ENTIRE UNIVERSE
UNFOLD OVER A MATTER OF SECONDS.

ALL GLIMMERING
STARS WOULD DIM.

ALL CELESTIAL BODIES WOULD
DISAPPEAR, FALLING TO A STATE
OF ZERO THERMODYNAMIC ENERGY.

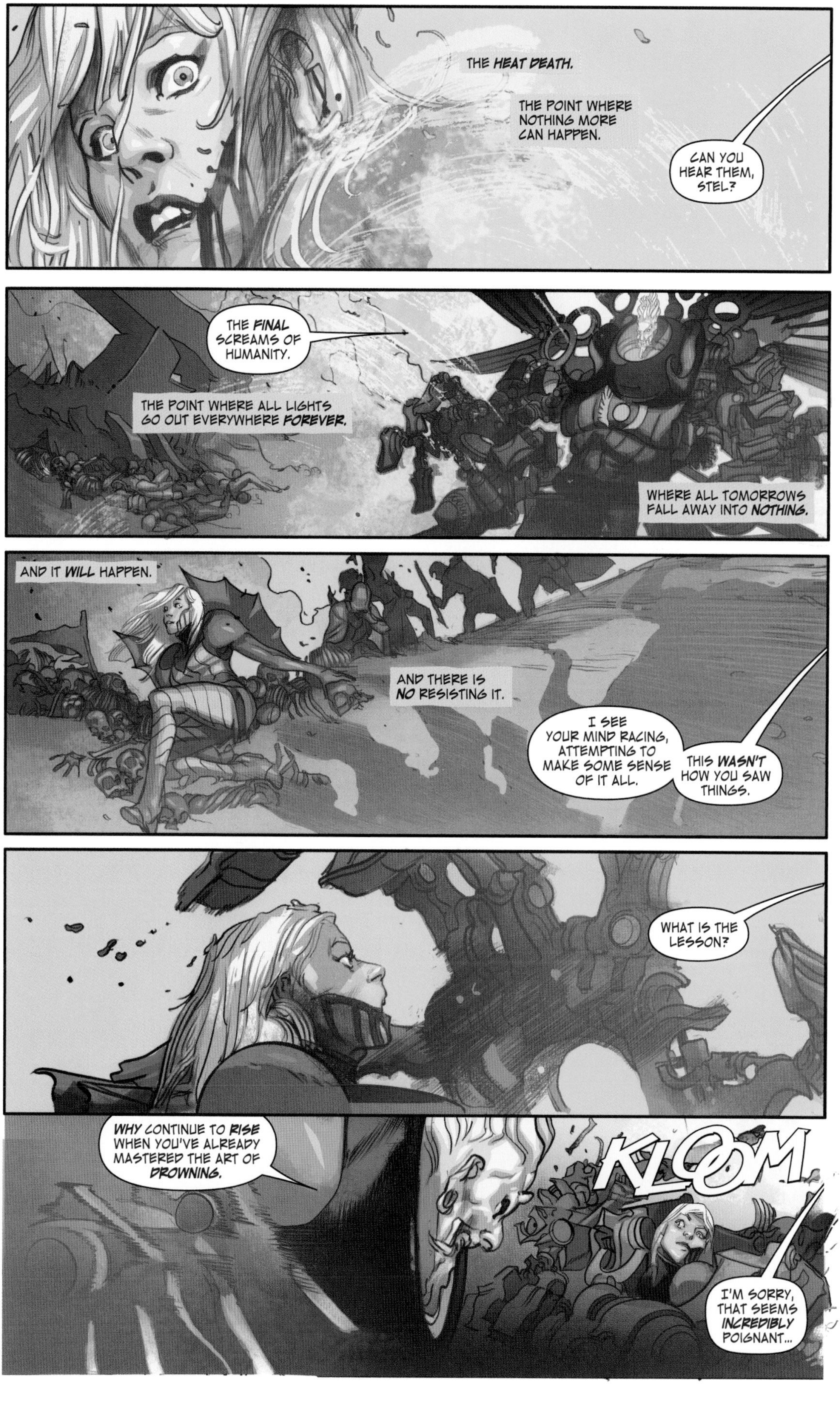
THE HEAT DEATH.
THE POINT WHERE NOTHING MORE CAN HAPPEN.
CAN YOU HEAR THEM, STEL?
THE FINAL SCREAMS OF HUMANITY.
THE POINT WHERE ALL LIGHTS GO OUT EVERYWHERE FOREVER.
WHERE ALL TOMORROWS FALL AWAY INTO NOTHING.
AND IT WILL HAPPEN.
AND THERE IS NO RESISTING IT.
I SEE YOUR MIND RACING, ATTEMPTING TO MAKE SOME SENSE OF IT ALL.
THIS WASN'T HOW YOU SAW THINGS.
WHAT IS THE LESSON?
WHY CONTINUE TO RISE WHEN YOU'VE ALREADY MASTERED THE ART OF DROWNING.
KLOOM
I'M SORRY, THAT SEEMS INCREDIBLY POIGNANT...

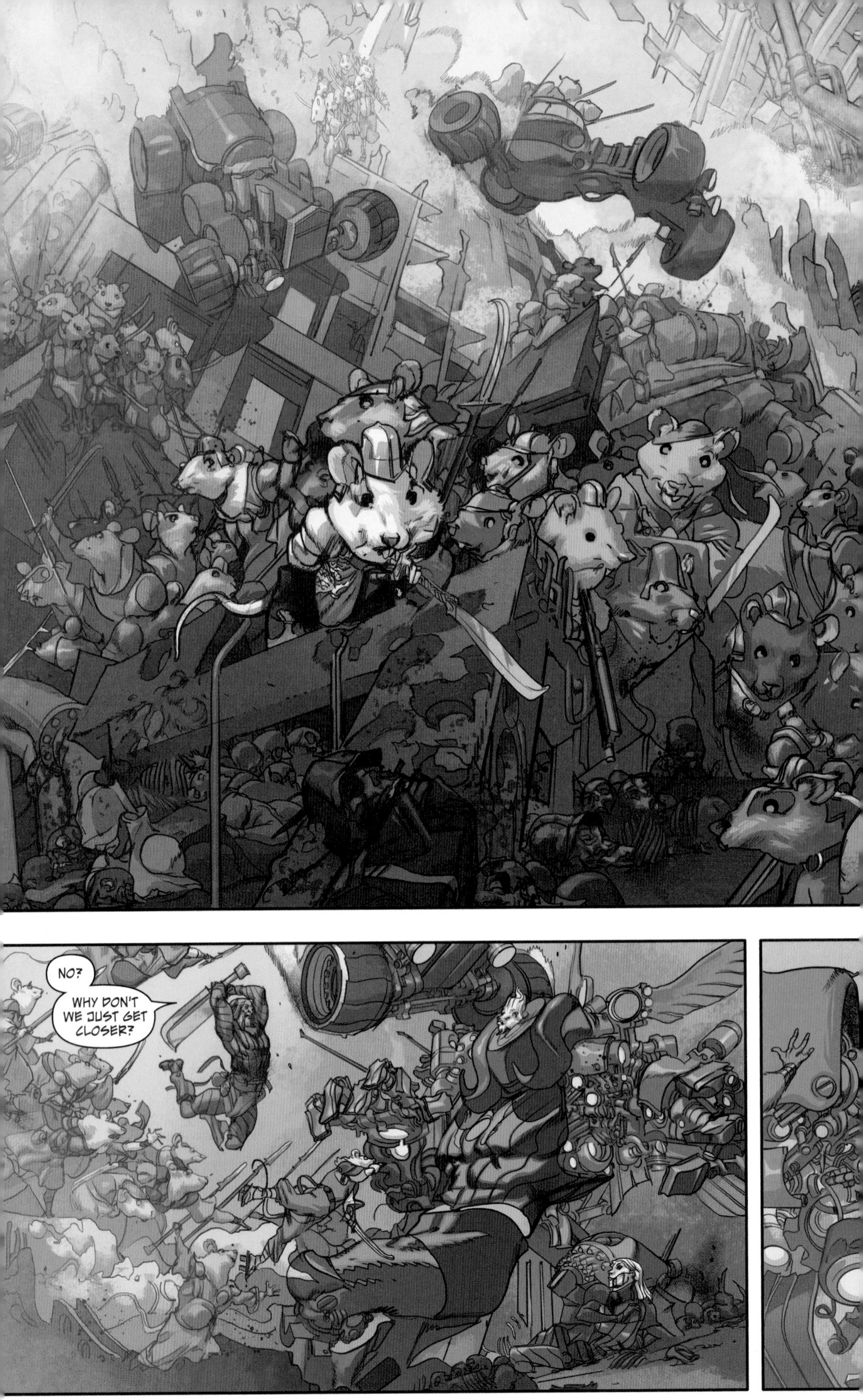
NO?
WHY DON'T WE JUST GET CLOSER?

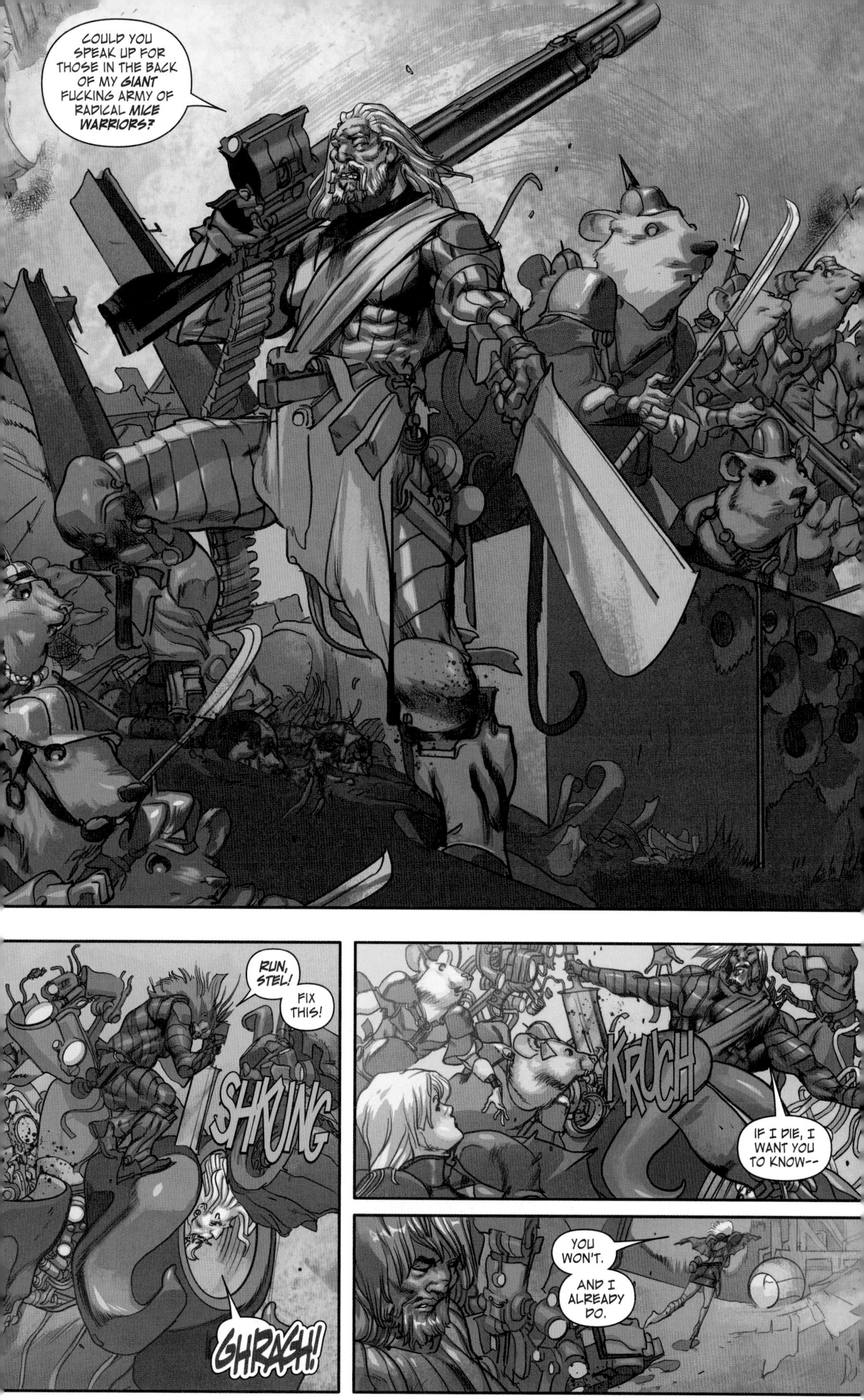
COULD YOU SPEAK UP FOR THOSE IN THE BACK OF MY GIANT FUCKING ARMY OF RADICAL MICE WARRIORS?
RUN, STEL!
FIX THIS!
SHRUNG
GHRASH!
KRUCH
IF I DIE, I WANT YOU TO KNOW--
YOU WON'T.
AND I ALREADY DO.

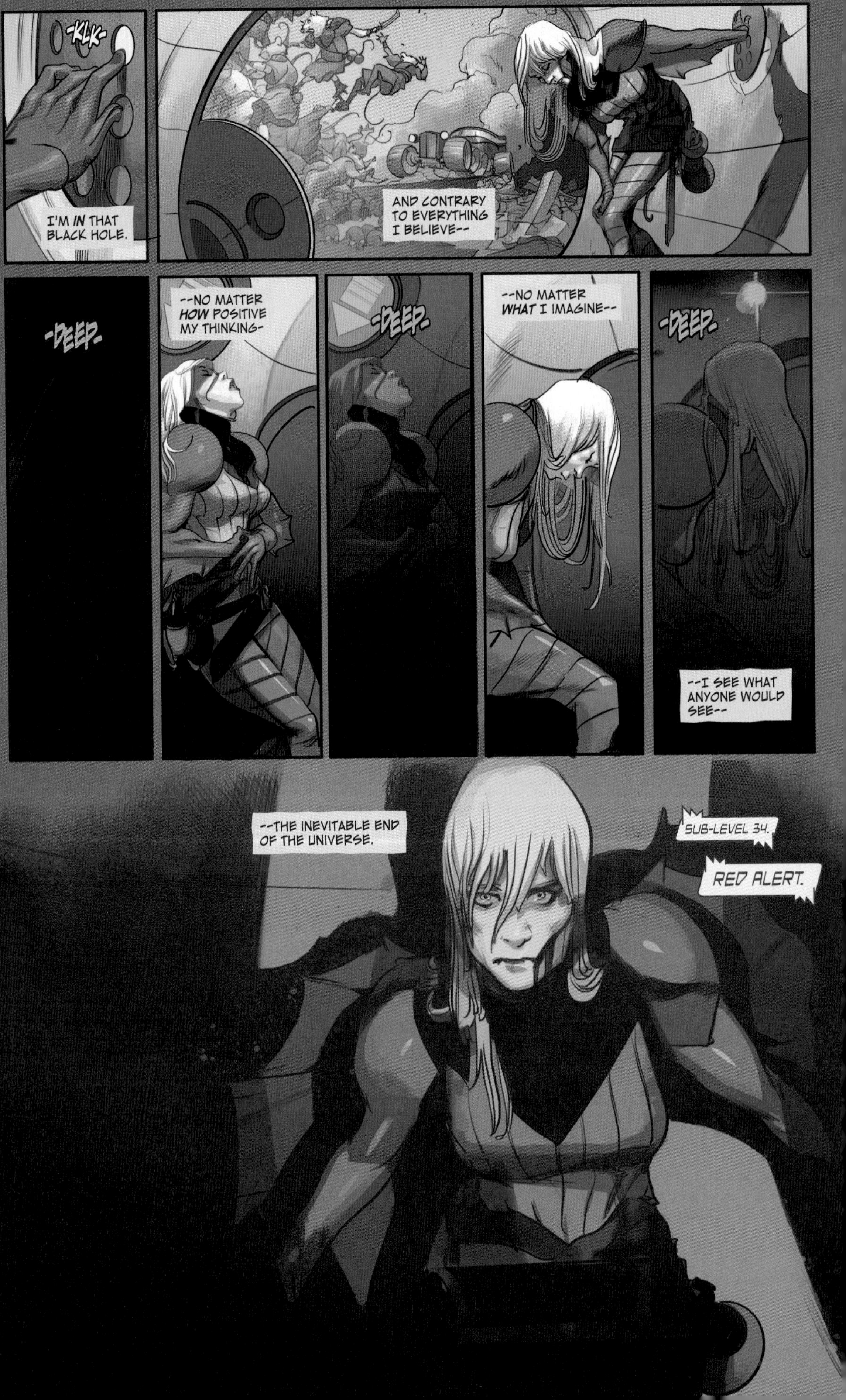
-KLK-
I'M IN THAT BLACK HOLE.
AND CONTRARY TO EVERYTHING I BELIEVE--
-DEEP-
--NO MATTER HOW POSITIVE MY THINKING-
-DEEP-
--NO MATTER WHAT I IMAGINE--
-DEEP-
--I SEE WHAT ANYONE WOULD SEE--
--THE INEVITABLE END OF THE UNIVERSE.
SUB-LEVEL 34.
RED ALERT.

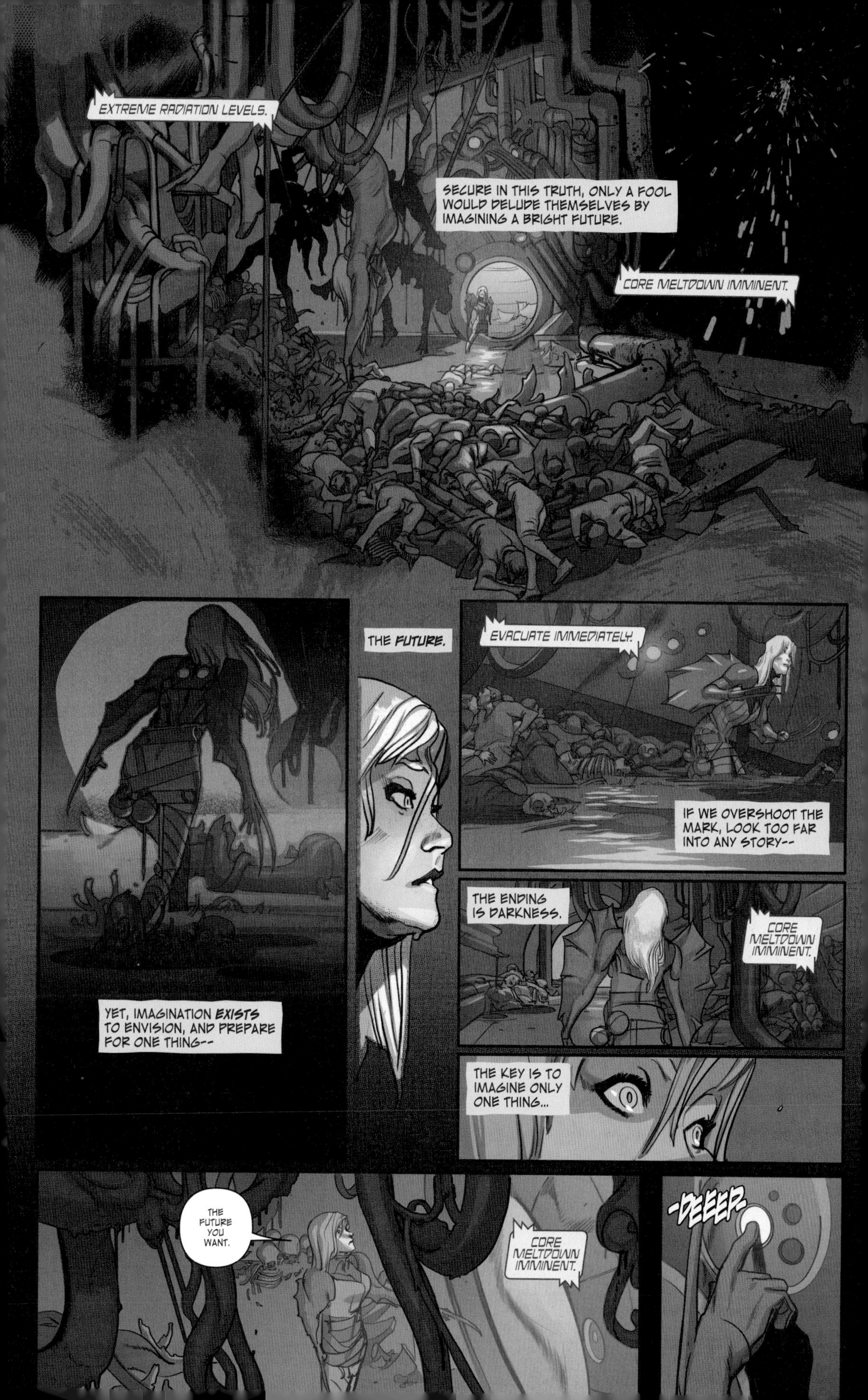

EXTREME RADIATION LEVELS.
SECURE IN THIS TRUTH, ONLY A FOOL WOULD DELUDE THEMSELVES BY IMAGINING A BRIGHT FUTURE.
CORE MELTDOWN IMMINENT.
THE FUTURE.
YET, IMAGINATION EXISTS TO ENVISION, AND PREPARE FOR ONE THING--
EVACUATE IMMEDIATELY.
IF WE OVERSHOOT THE MARK, LOOK TOO FAR INTO ANY STORY--
THE ENDING IS DARKNESS.
CORE MELTDOWN IMMINENT.
THE KEY IS TO IMAGINE ONLY ONE THING...
THE FUTURE YOU WANT.
CORE MELTDOWN IMMINENT.
-BEEEP-

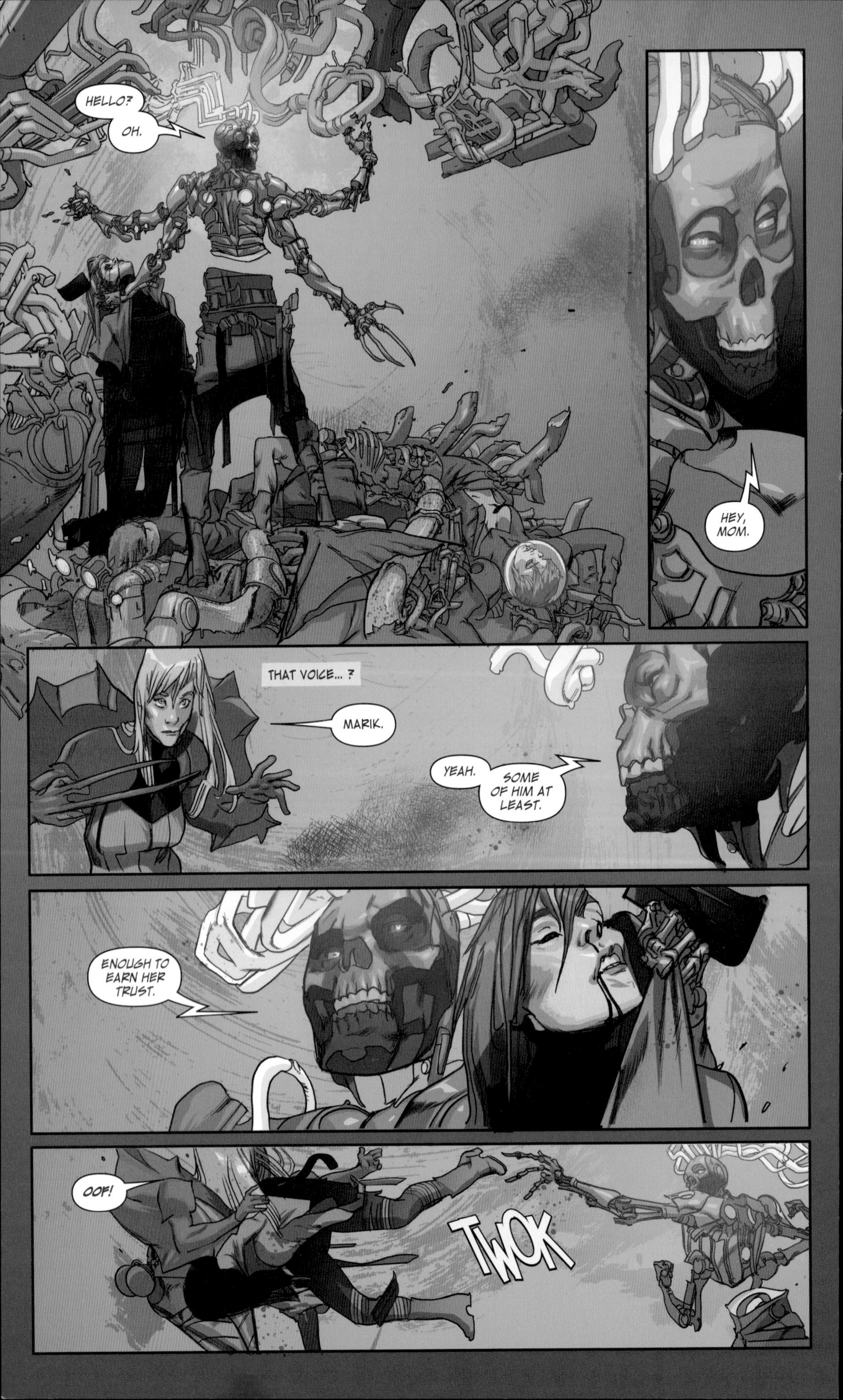
HELLO?
OH.
HEY, MOM.
THAT VOICE... ?
MARIK.
YEAH.
SOME OF HIM AT LEAST.
ENOUGH TO EARN HER TRUST.
OOF!
TWOK

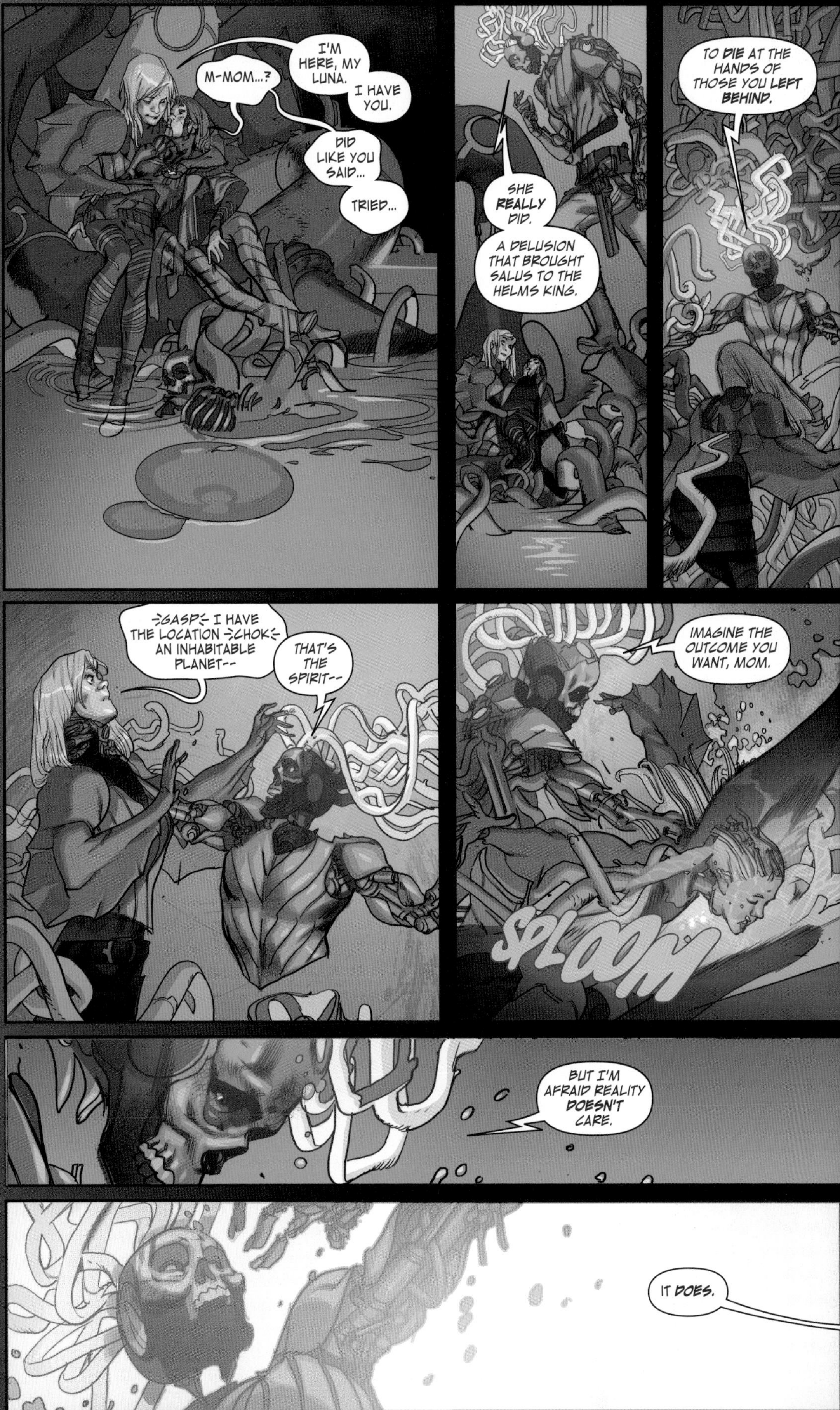
M-MOM...?
I'M HERE, MY LUNA.
I HAVE YOU.
DID LIKE YOU SAID...
TRIED...
SHE REALLY DID.
A DELUSION THAT BROUGHT SALUS TO THE HELMS KING.
TO DIE AT THE HANDS OF THOSE YOU LEFT BEHIND.
-GASP- I HAVE THE LOCATION -CHOK- AN INHABITABLE PLANET--
THAT'S THE SPIRIT--
IMAGINE THE OUTCOME YOU WANT, MOM.
SPLOOM
BUT I'M AFRAID REALITY DOESN'T CARE.
IT DOES.

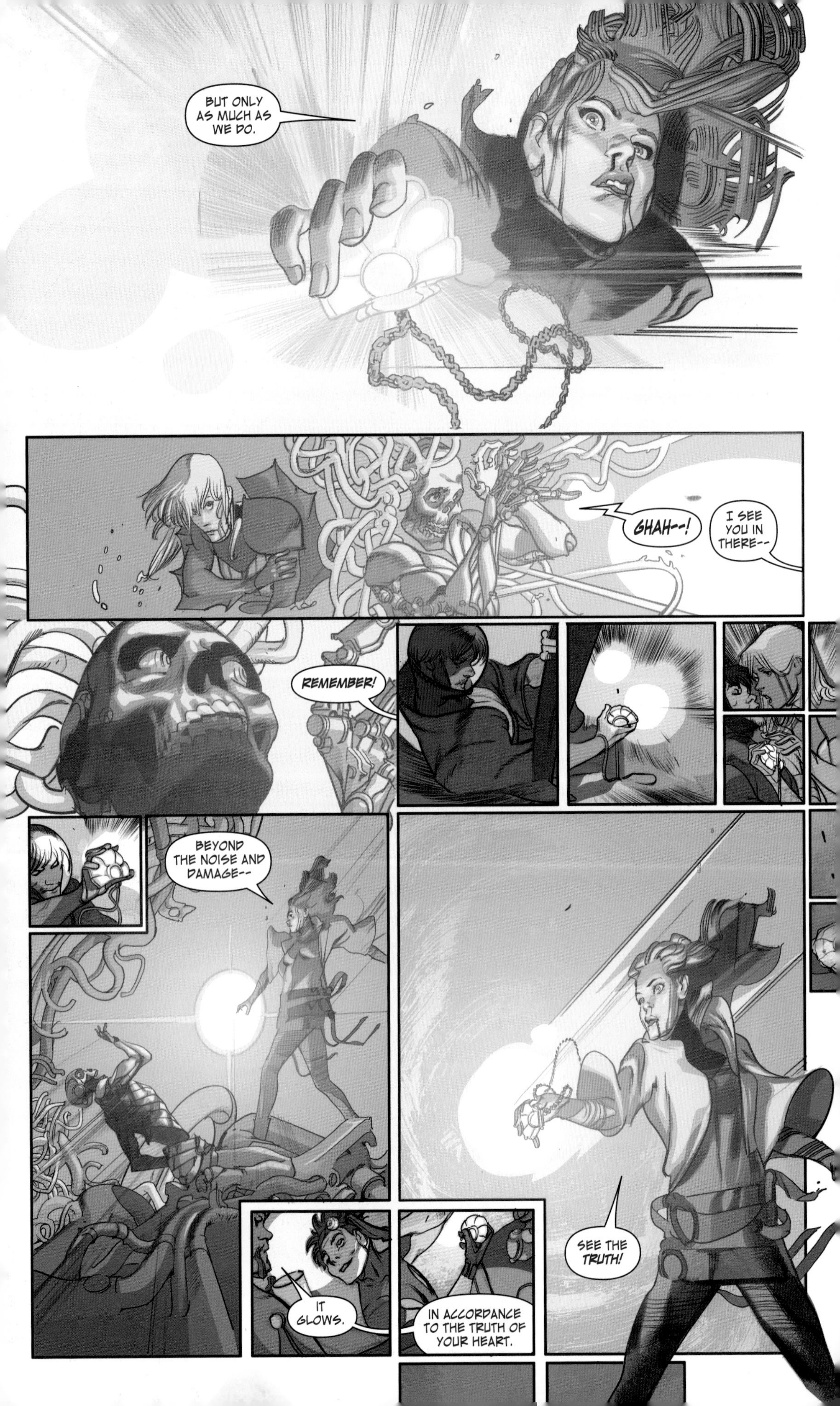
BUT ONLY AS MUCH AS WE DO.
GHAH--!
I SEE YOU IN THERE--
REMEMBER!
BEYOND THE NOISE AND DAMAGE--
SEE THE TRUTH!
IT GLOWS.
IN ACCORDANCE TO THE TRUTH OF YOUR HEART.

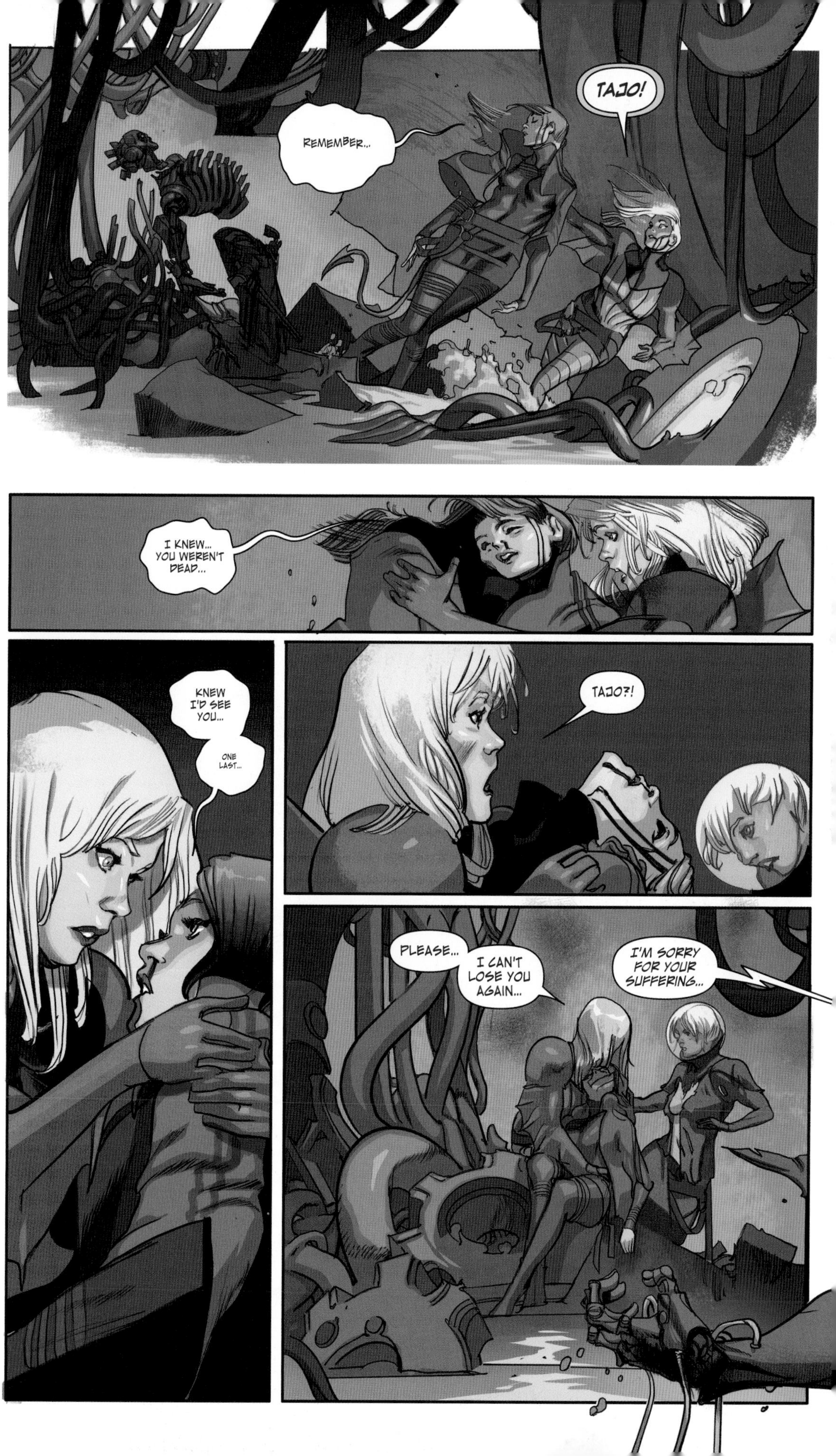
TAJO!
REMEMBER...
I KNEW... YOU WEREN'T DEAD...
KNEW I'D SEE YOU...
ONE LAST...
TAJO?!
PLEASE...
I CAN'T LOSE YOU AGAIN...
I'M SORRY FOR YOUR SUFFERING...

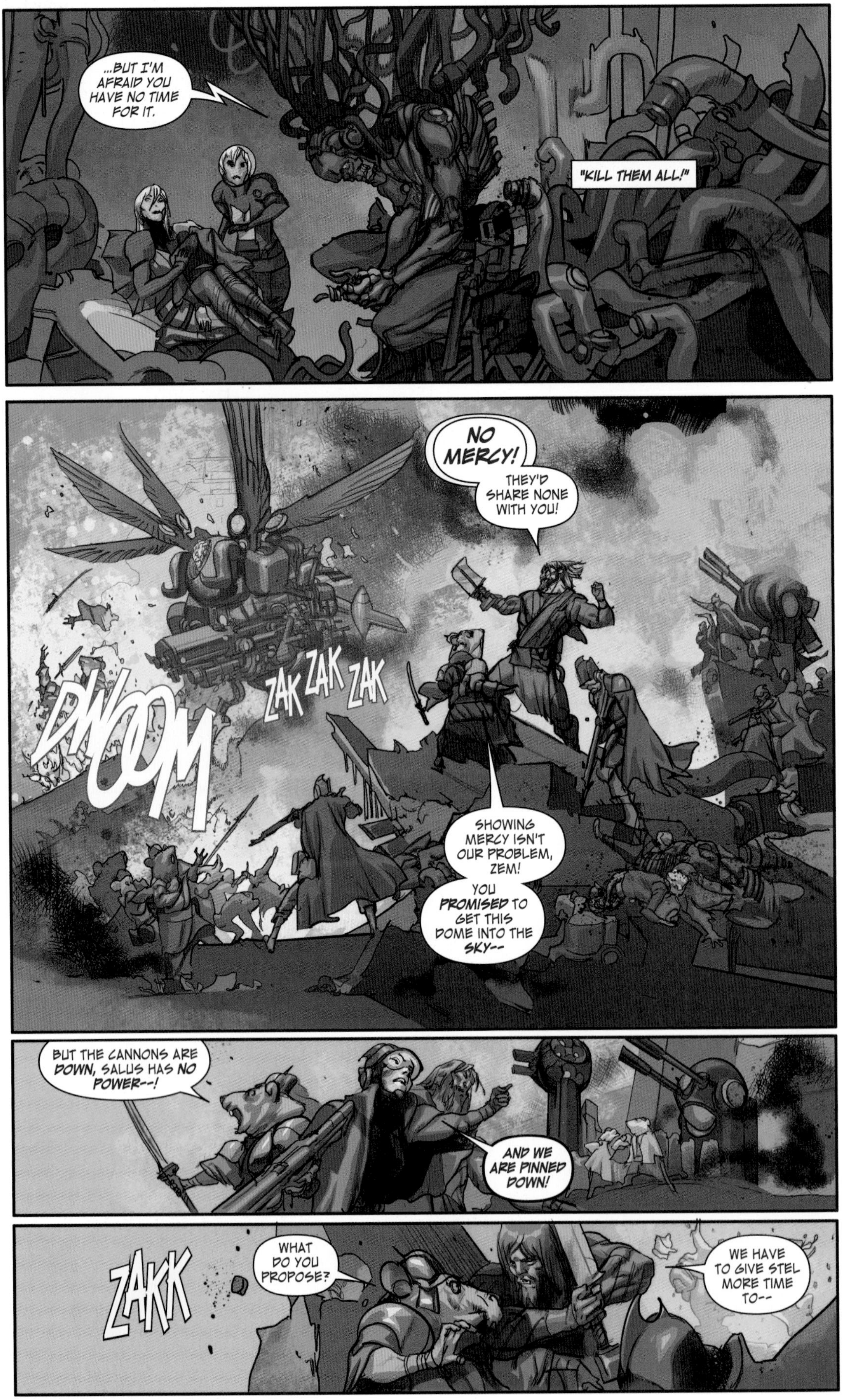
...BUT I'M AFRAID YOU HAVE NO TIME FOR IT.
"KILL THEM ALL!"
NO MERCY!
THEY'D SHARE NONE WITH YOU!
DWOOM
ZAK ZAK ZAK
SHOWING MERCY ISN'T OUR PROBLEM, ZEM!
YOU PROMISED TO GET THIS DOME INTO THE SKY--
BUT THE CANNONS ARE DOWN, SALUS HAS NO POWER--!
AND WE ARE PINNED DOWN!
ZAKK
WHAT DO YOU PROPOSE?
WE HAVE TO GIVE STEL MORE TIME TO--

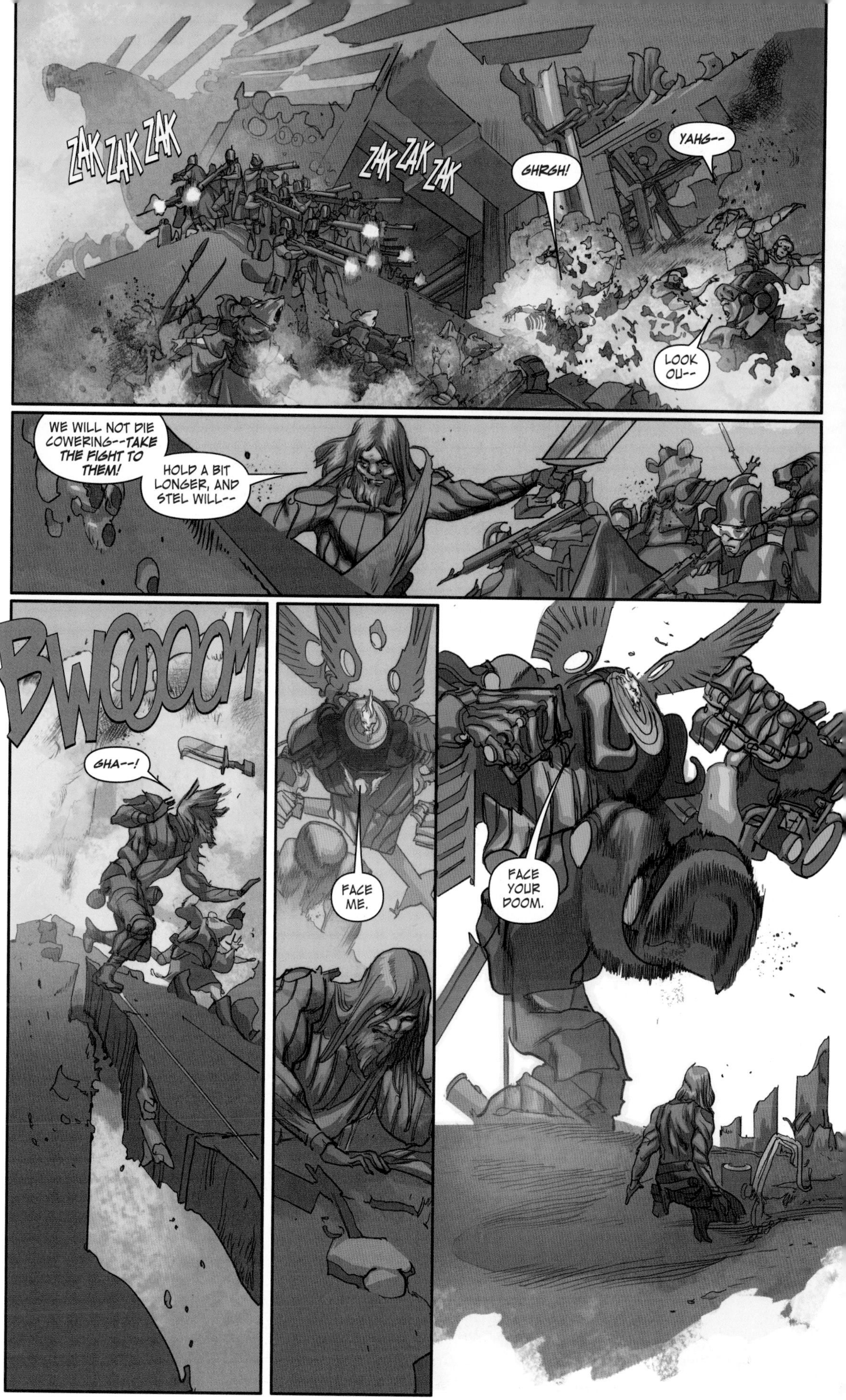
ZAK ZAK ZAK
ZAK ZAK ZAK
GHRGH!
YAHG--
LOOK OU--
WE WILL NOT DIE COWERING--TAKE THE FIGHT TO THEM!
HOLD A BIT LONGER, AND STEL WILL--
BWOOOOM
GHA--!
FACE ME.
FACE YOUR DOOM.

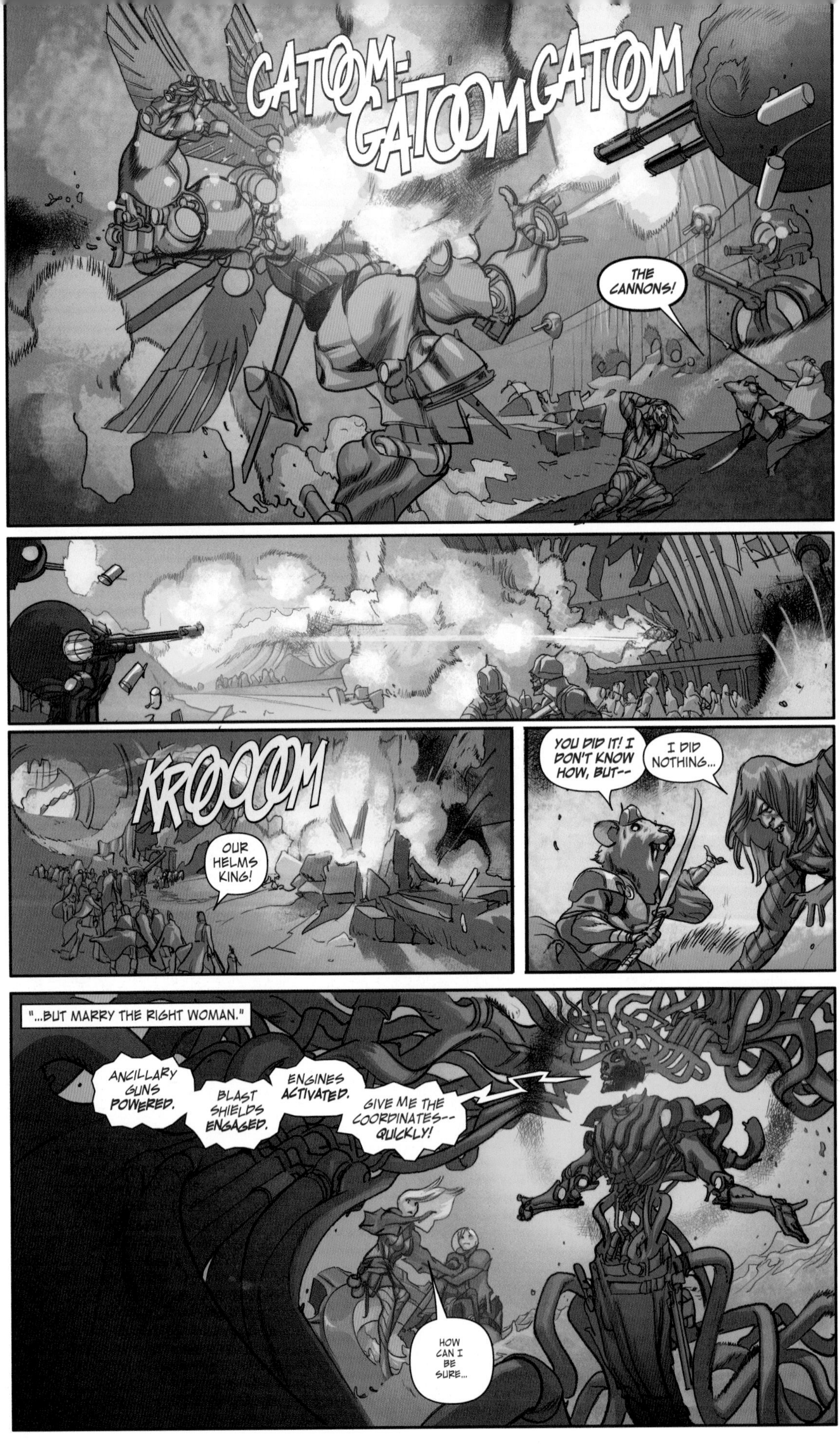
GATOOM-GATOOM-GATOOM
THE CANNONS!
KROOOOM
OUR HELMS KING!
YOU DID IT! I DON'T KNOW HOW, BUT--
I DID NOTHING...
"...BUT MARRY THE RIGHT WOMAN."
ANCILLARY GUNS POWERED.
BLAST SHIELDS ENGAGED.
ENGINES ACTIVATED.
GIVE ME THE COORDINATES-- QUICKLY!
HOW CAN I BE SURE...

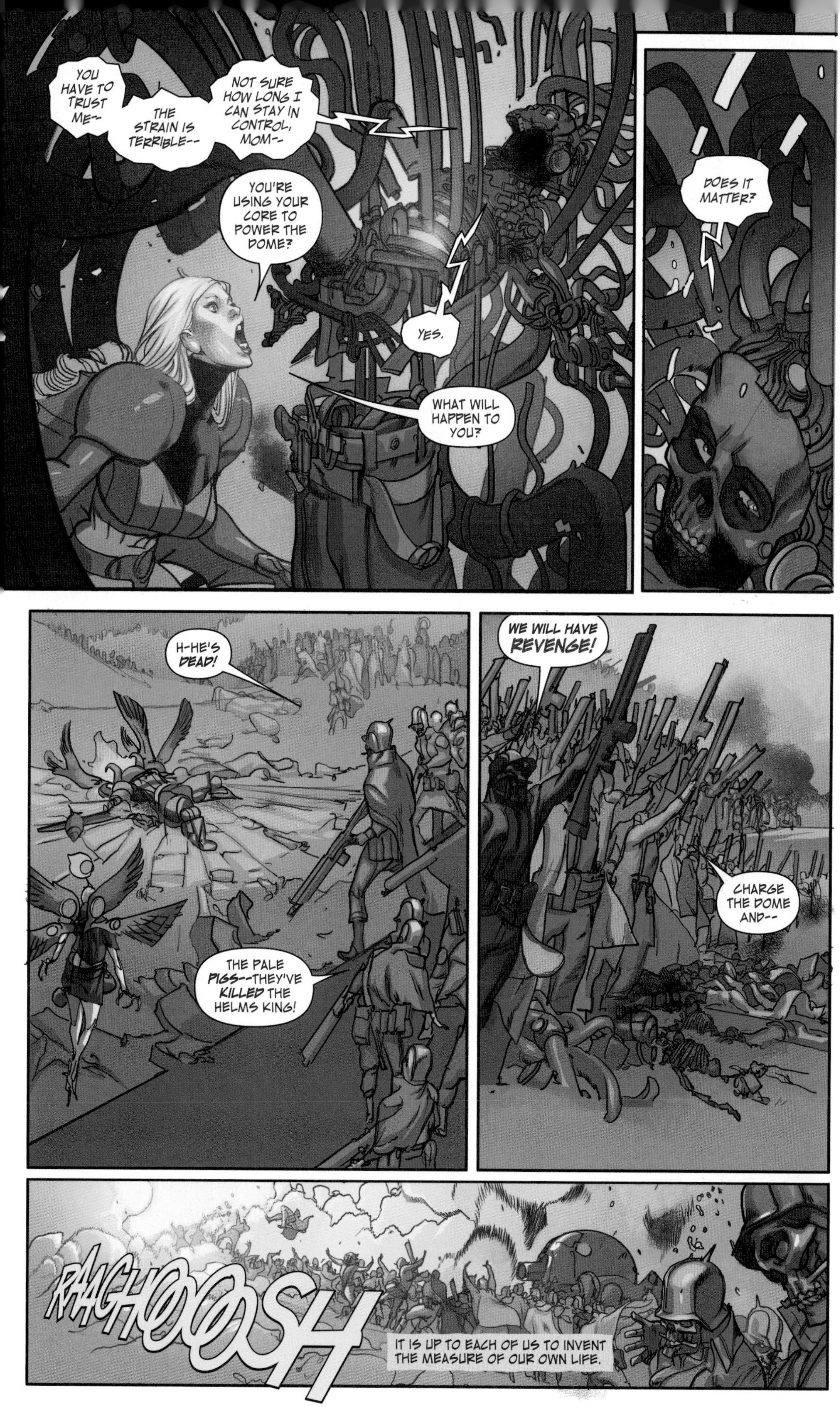

YOU HAVE TO TRUST ME--
THE STRAIN IS TERRIBLE--
NOT SURE HOW LONG I CAN STAY IN CONTROL, MOM--
YOU'RE USING YOUR CORE TO POWER THE DOME?
YES.
WHAT WILL HAPPEN TO YOU?
DOES IT MATTER?
H-HE'S DEAD!
THE PALE PIGS--THEY'VE KILLED THE HELMS KING!
WE WILL HAVE REVENGE!
CHARGE THE DOME AND--
RAAGHOOOSH
IT IS UP TO EACH OF US TO INVENT THE MEASURE OF OUR OWN LIFE.

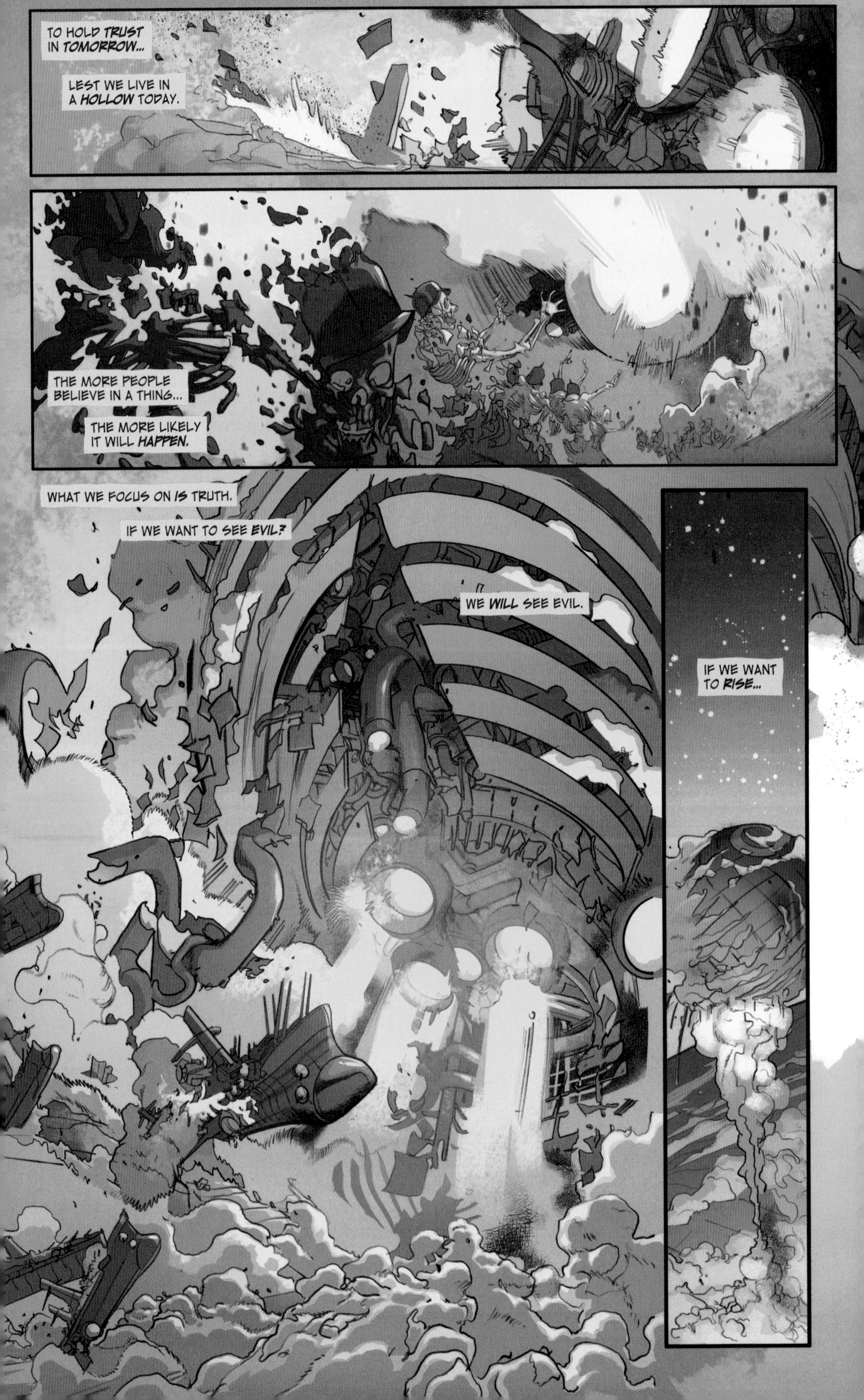

TO HOLD TRUST IN TOMORROW...
LEST WE LIVE IN A HOLLOW TODAY.
THE MORE PEOPLE BELIEVE IN A THING...
THE MORE LIKELY IT WILL HAPPEN.
WHAT WE FOCUS ON IS TRUTH.
IF WE WANT TO SEE EVIL?
WE WILL SEE EVIL.
IF WE WANT TO RISE...

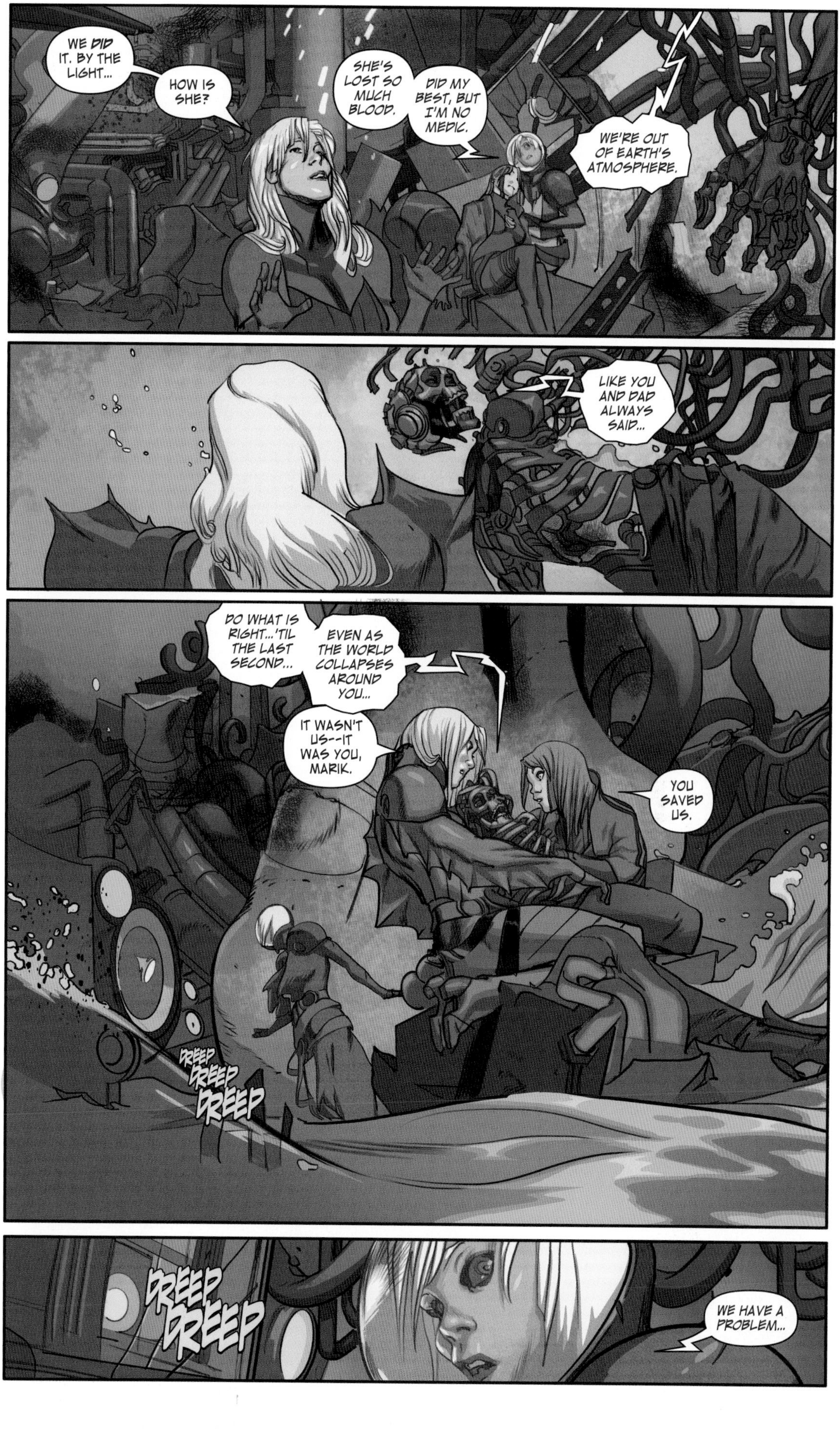
WE DID IT. BY THE LIGHT...
HOW IS SHE?
SHE'S LOST SO MUCH BLOOD.
DID MY BEST, BUT I'M NO MEDIC.
WE'RE OUT OF EARTH'S ATMOSPHERE.
LIKE YOU AND DAD ALWAYS SAID...
DO WHAT IS RIGHT...'TIL THE LAST SECOND...
EVEN AS THE WORLD COLLAPSES AROUND YOU...
IT WASN'T US--IT WAS YOU, MARIK.
YOU SAVED US.
DREEP DREEP DREEP
DREEP DREEP
WE HAVE A PROBLEM...

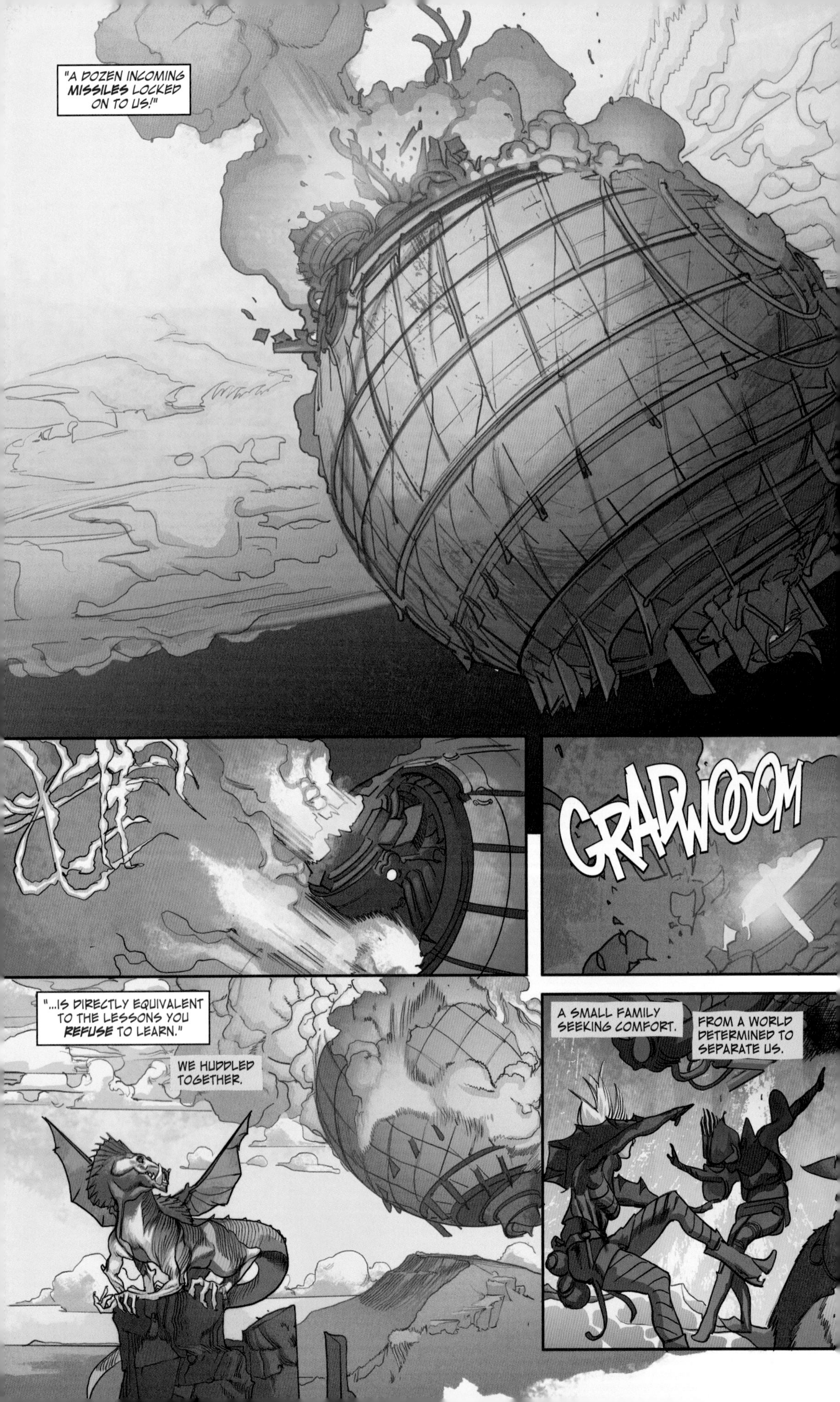
"A DOZEN INCOMING MISSILES LOCKED ON TO US!"
GRADWOOOM
"...IS DIRECTLY EQUIVALENT TO THE LESSONS YOU REFUSE TO LEARN."
WE HUDDLED TOGETHER.
A SMALL FAMILY SEEKING COMFORT.
FROM A WORLD DETERMINED TO SEPARATE US.

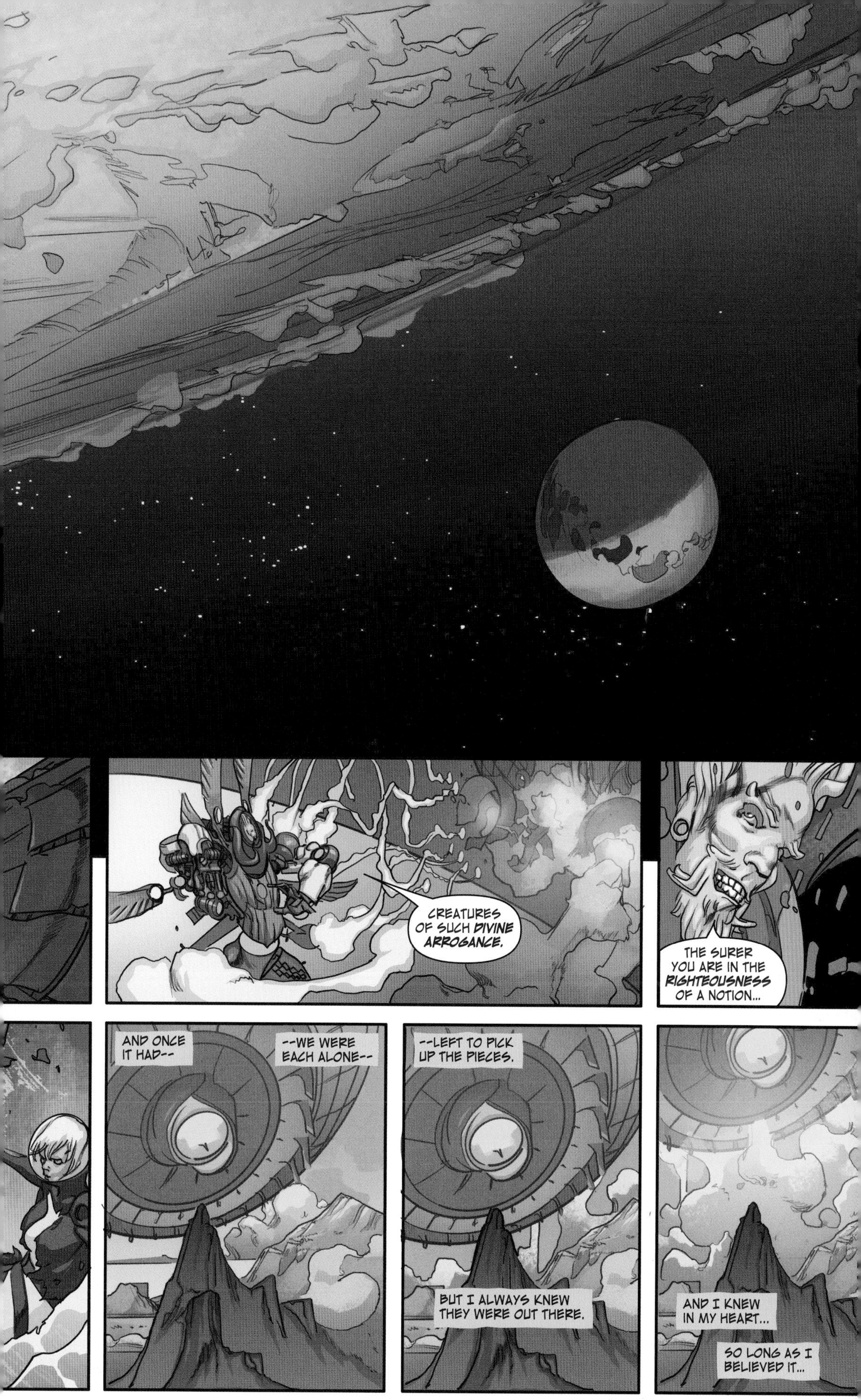

CREATURES OF SUCH DIVINE ARROGANCE.
THE SURER YOU ARE IN THE RIGHTEOUSNESS OF A NOTION...
AND ONCE IT HAD--
--WE WERE EACH ALONE--
--LEFT TO PICK UP THE PIECES.
BUT I ALWAYS KNEW THEY WERE OUT THERE.
AND I KNEW IN MY HEART...
SO LONG AS I BELIEVED IT...

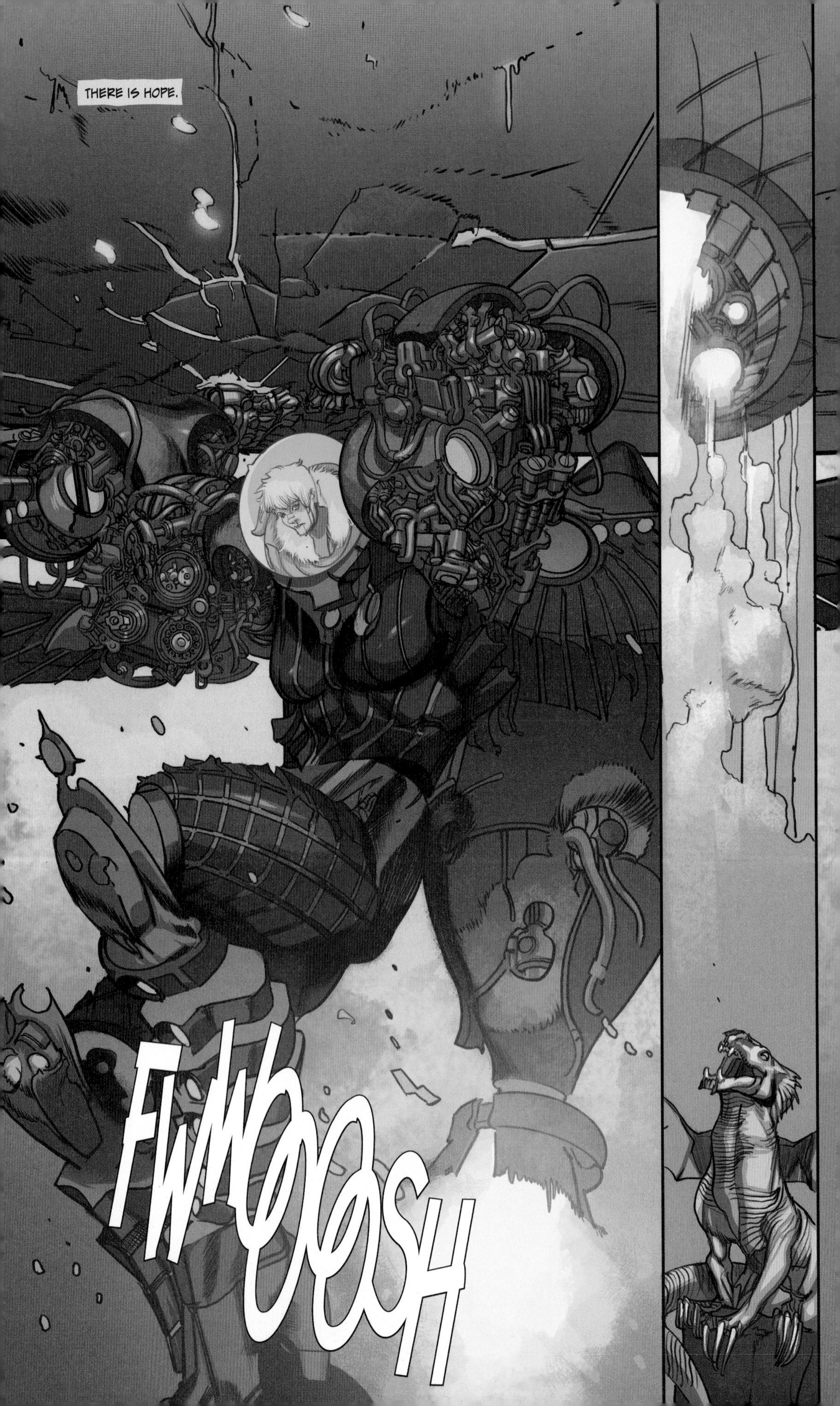
THERE IS HOPE.
FWHOOOSH

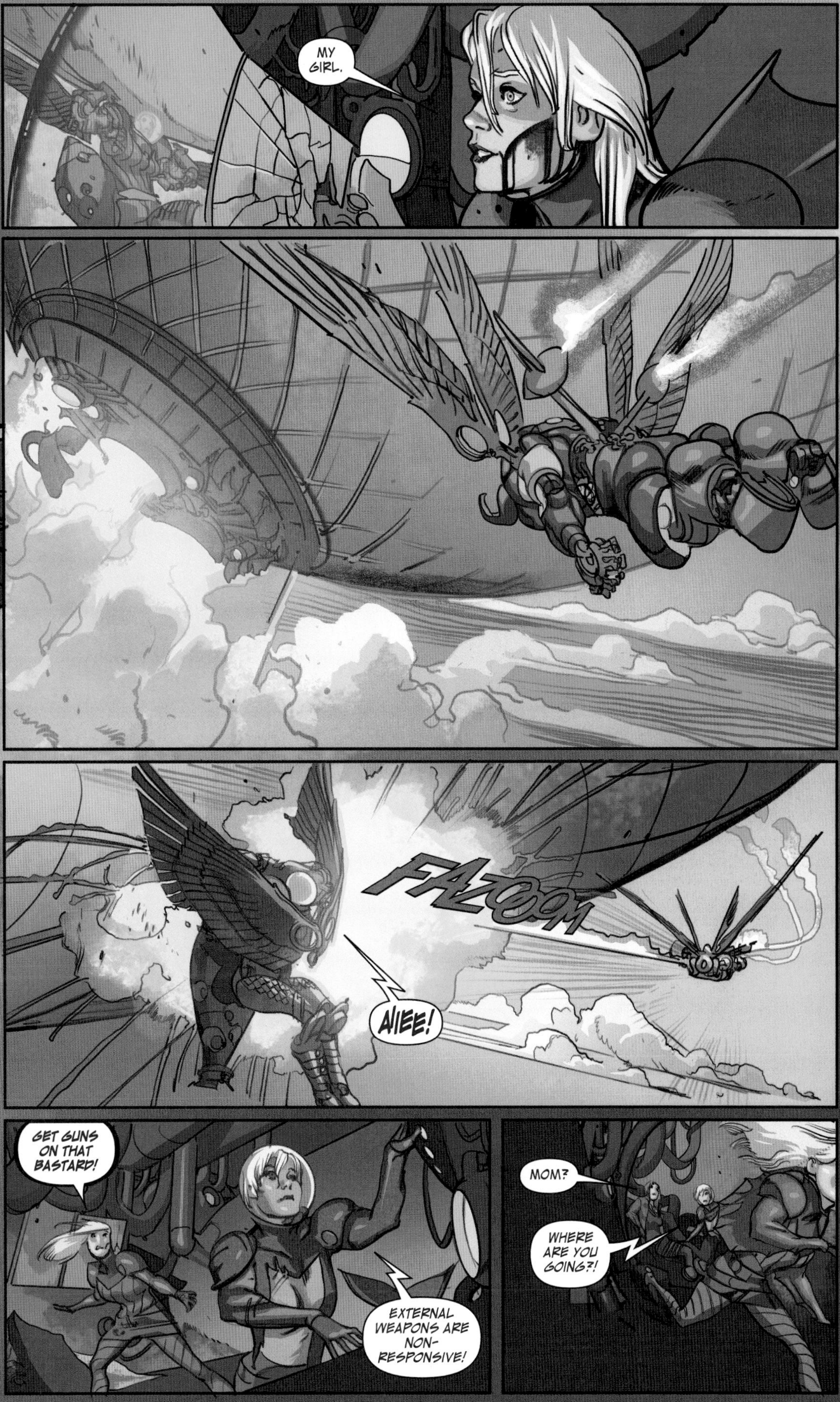
MY GIRL.
FAZOOM
AIIEE!
GET GUNS ON THAT BASTARD!
EXTERNAL WEAPONS ARE NON-RESPONSIVE!
MOM?
WHERE ARE YOU GOING?!

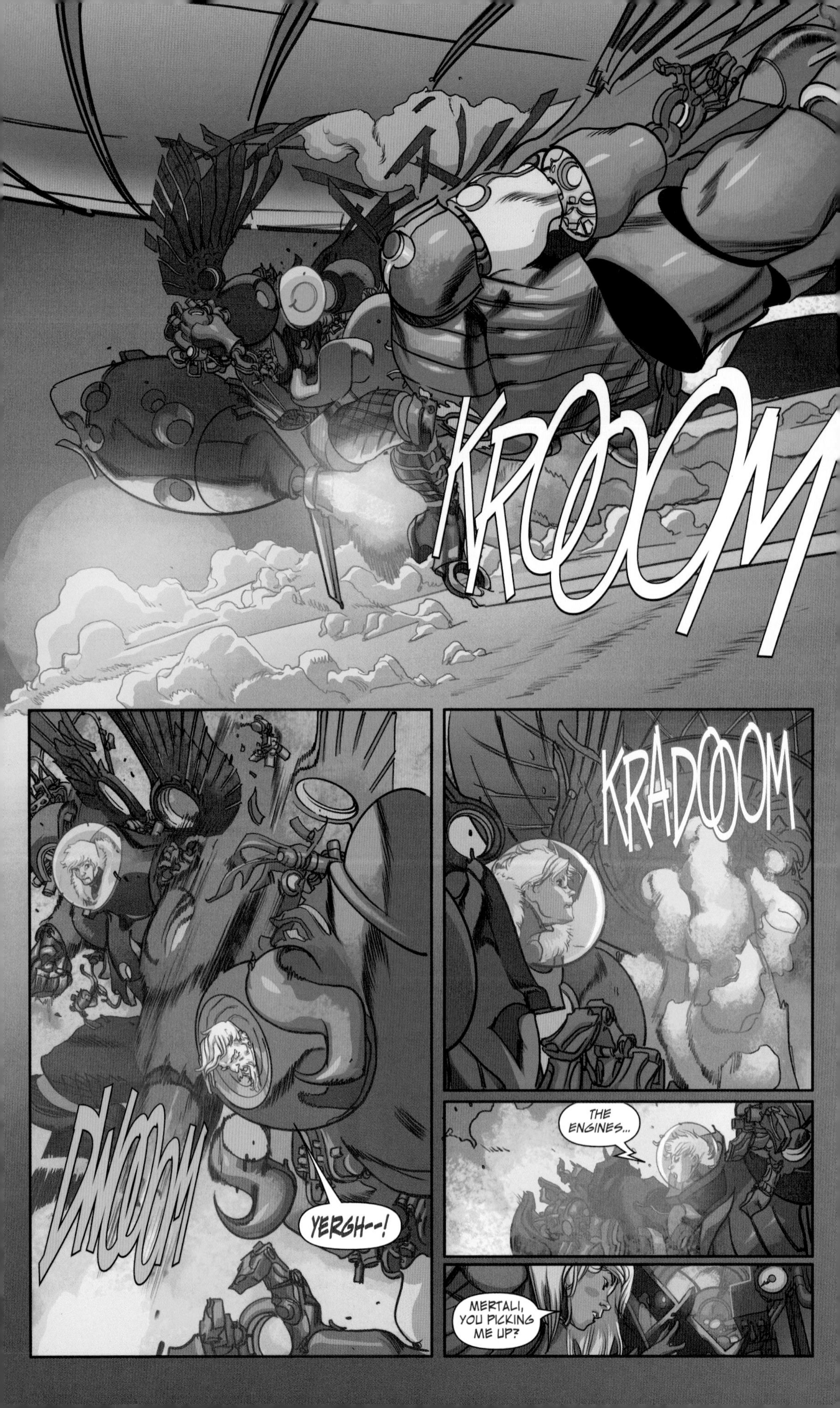
KROOOM
DWOOM
YERGH--!
KRADOOM
THE ENGINES...
MERTALI, YOU PICKING ME UP?

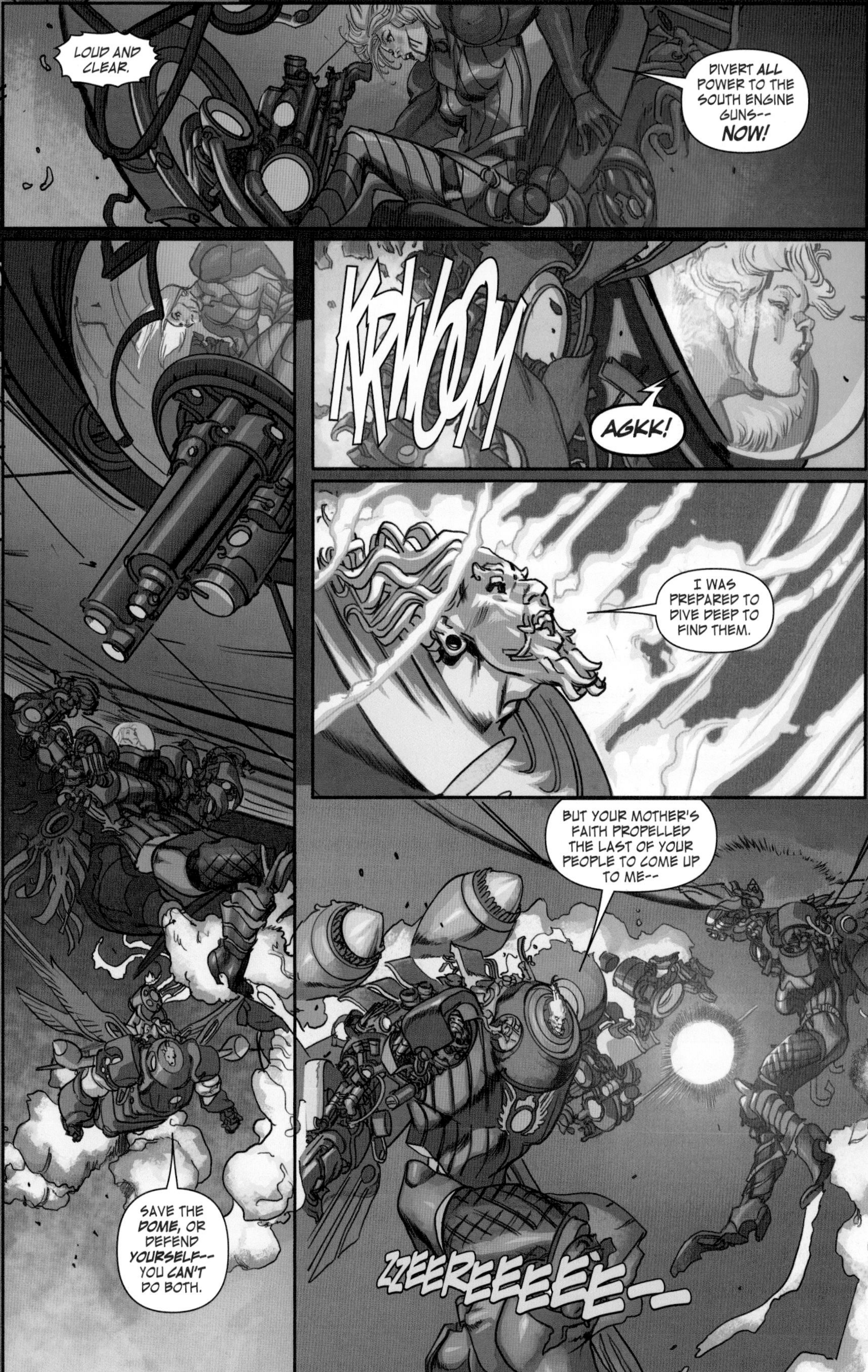

LOUD AND CLEAR.
DIVERT ALL POWER TO THE SOUTH ENGINE GUNS-- NOW!
KRWOOM
AGKK!
I WAS PREPARED TO DIVE DEEP TO FIND THEM.
BUT YOUR MOTHER'S FAITH PROPELLED THE LAST OF YOUR PEOPLE TO COME UP TO ME--
SAVE THE DOME, OR DEFEND YOURSELF-- YOU CAN'T DO BOTH.
ZZEEREEEEEE--

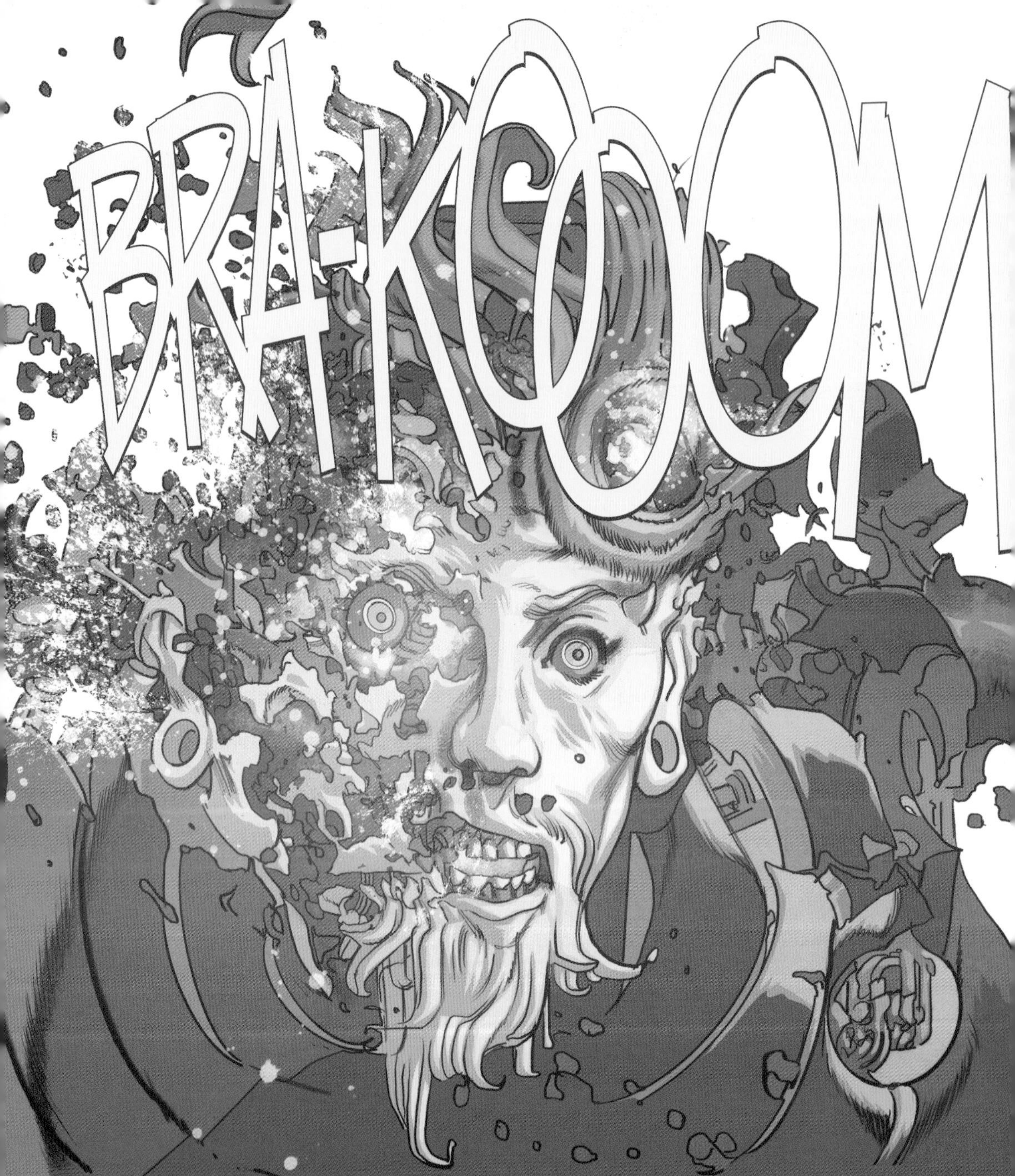
BRA-KOOOM
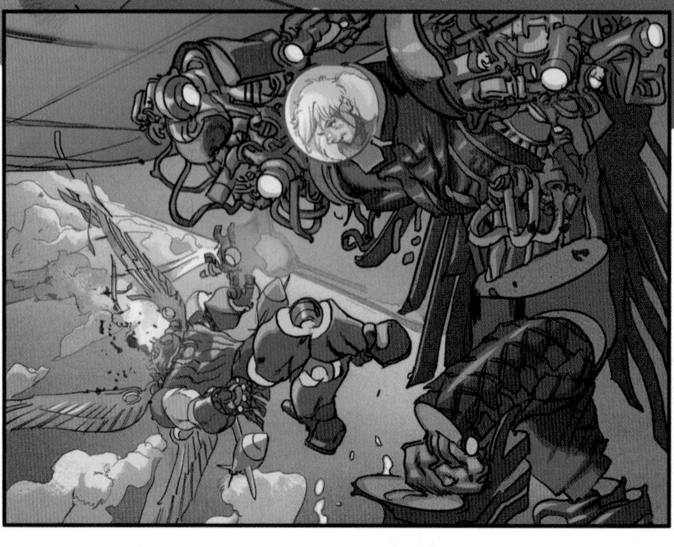
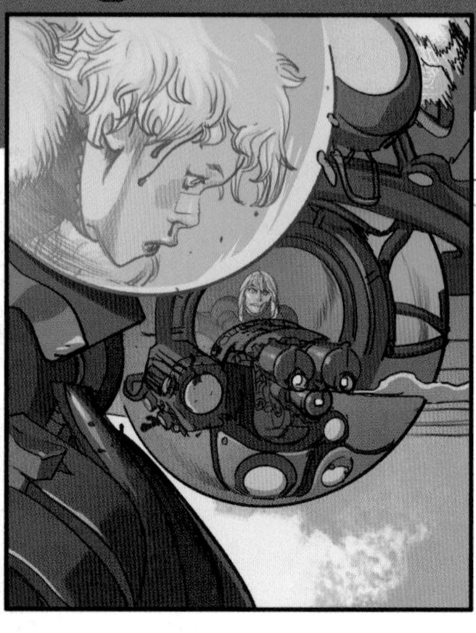

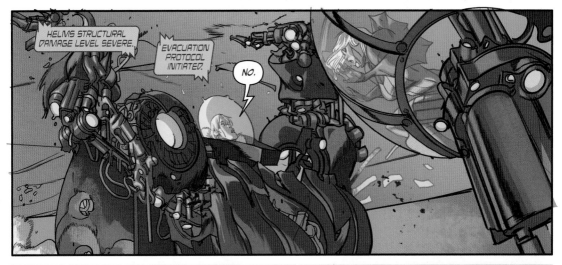

HELMS STRUCTURAL DAMAGE LEVEL SEVERE.

EVACUATION PROTOCOL INITIATED.

NO.

CANCEL THAT.

CORE MELTDOWN UNAVOIDABLE IF--

DIVERT LIFE SUPPORT FUNCTION TO ENGINES.

DELLA...

LIFE SUPPORT FUEL TO ENGINES.

THRWOOOOOOOM

IT'S OKAY, MOM. THERE'S NO OTHER WAY.

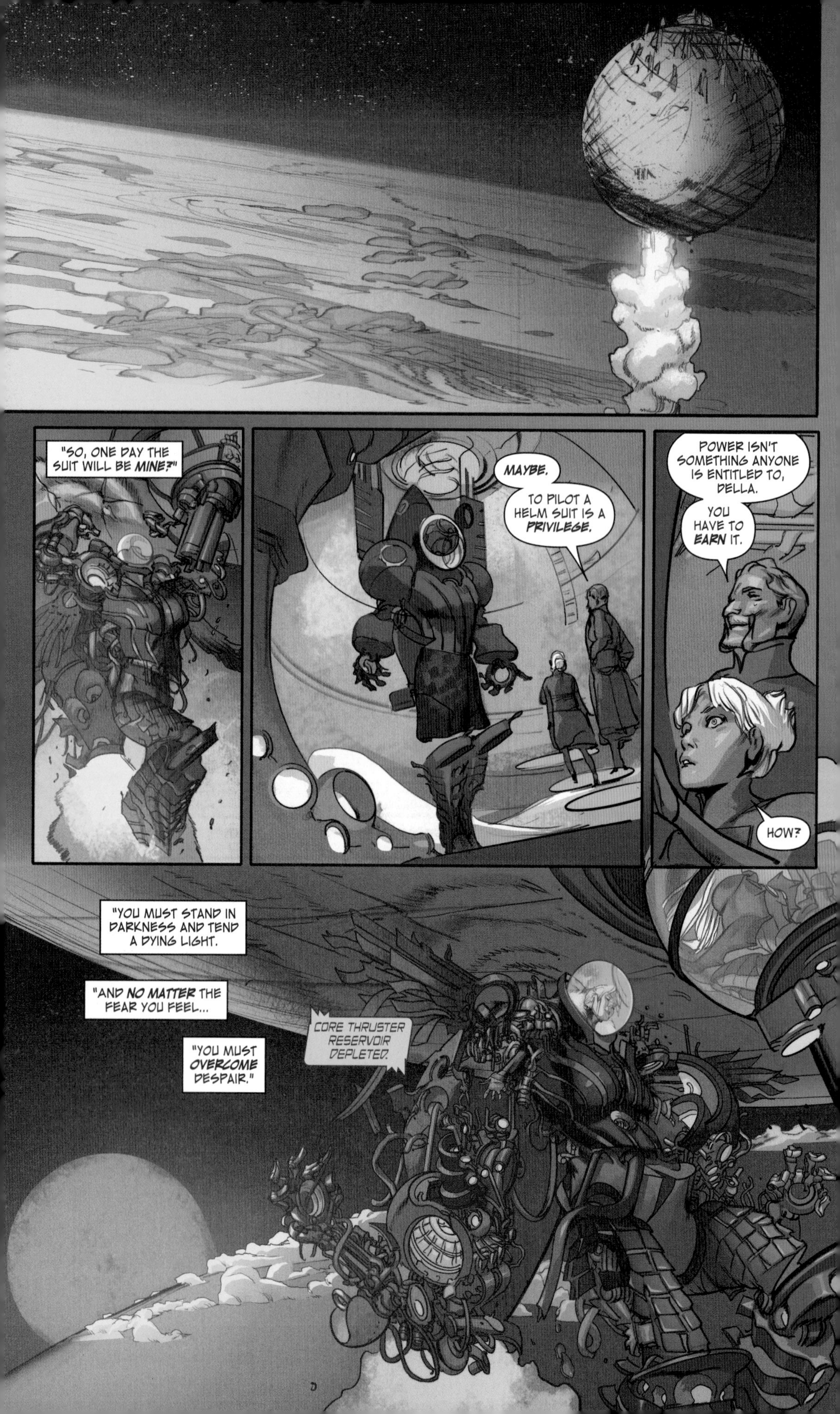
"SO, ONE DAY THE SUIT WILL BE MINE?"
MAYBE.
TO PILOT A HELM SUIT IS A PRIVILEGE.
POWER ISN'T SOMETHING ANYONE IS ENTITLED TO, DELLA.
YOU HAVE TO EARN IT.
HOW?
"YOU MUST STAND IN DARKNESS AND TEND A DYING LIGHT.
"AND NO MATTER THE FEAR YOU FEEL...
CORE THRUSTER RESERVOIR DEPLETED.
"YOU MUST OVERCOME DESPAIR."

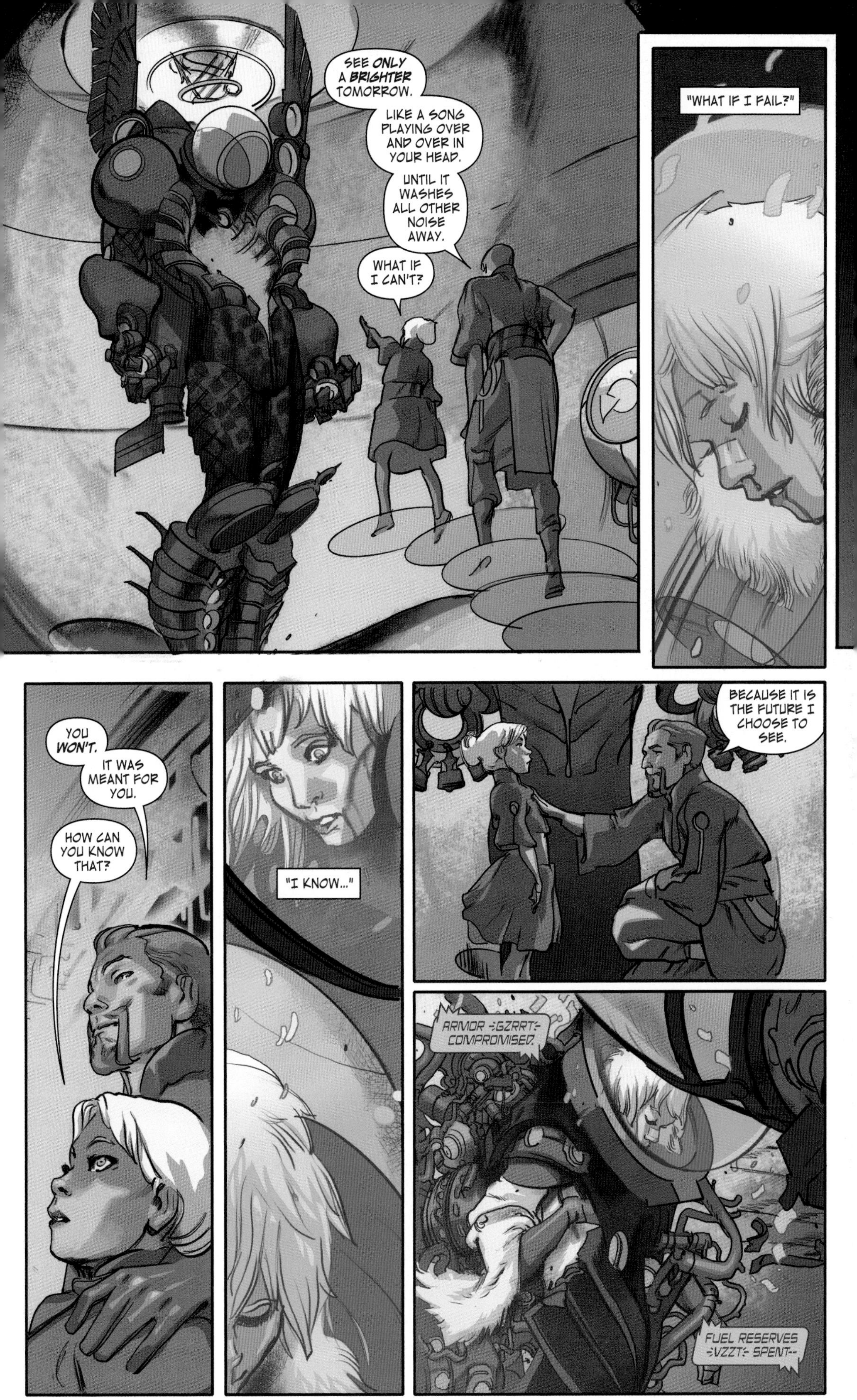
SEE ONLY A BRIGHTER TOMORROW.
LIKE A SONG PLAYING OVER AND OVER IN YOUR HEAD.
UNTIL IT WASHES ALL OTHER NOISE AWAY.
WHAT IF I CAN'T?
"WHAT IF I FAIL?"
YOU WON'T.
IT WAS MEANT FOR YOU.
HOW CAN YOU KNOW THAT?
"I KNOW..."
BECAUSE IT IS THE FUTURE I CHOOSE TO SEE.
ARMOR -GZRRT- COMPROMISED.
FUEL RESERVES -VZZT- SPENT--

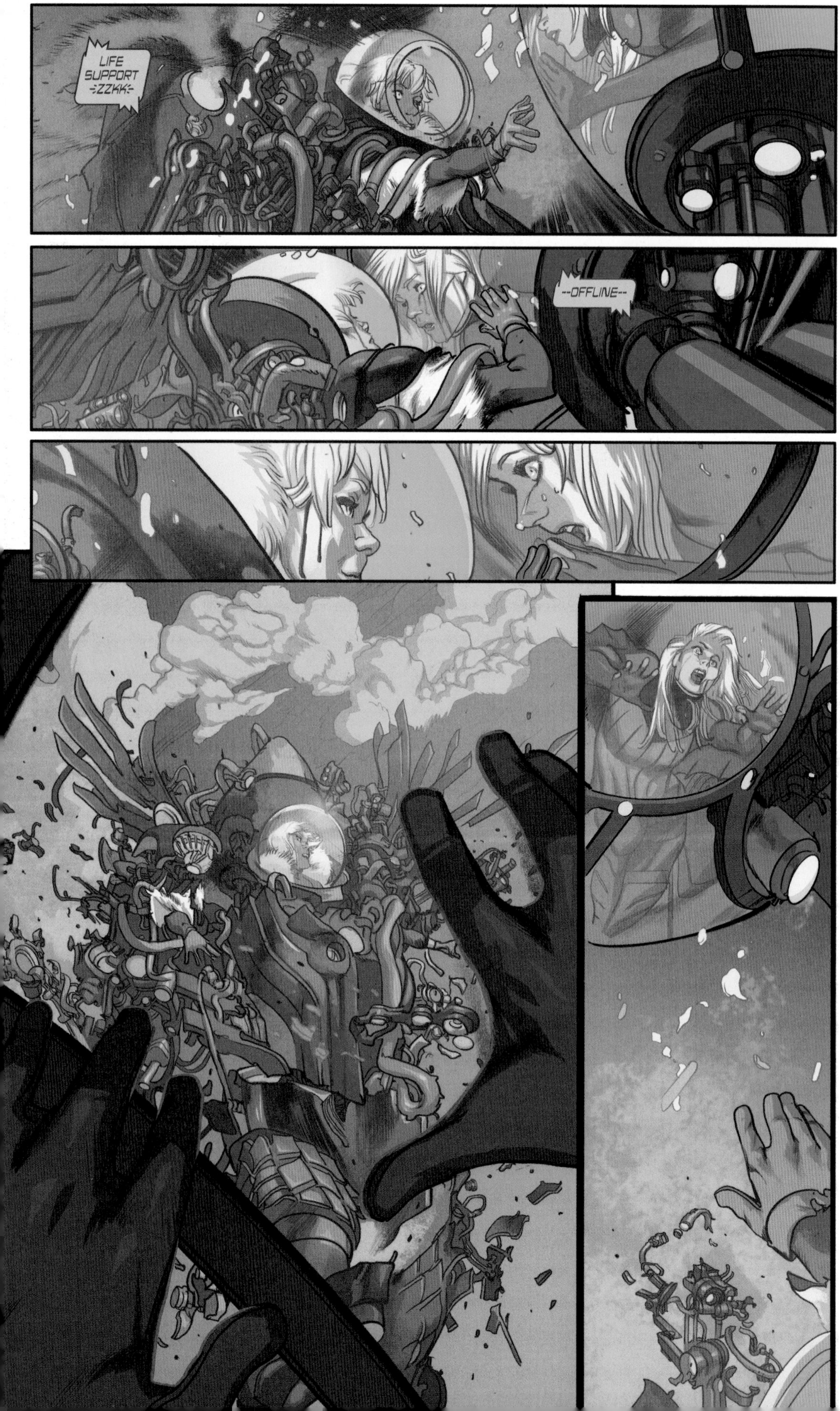
LIFE
SUPPORT
-ZZKK-
--OFFLINE--

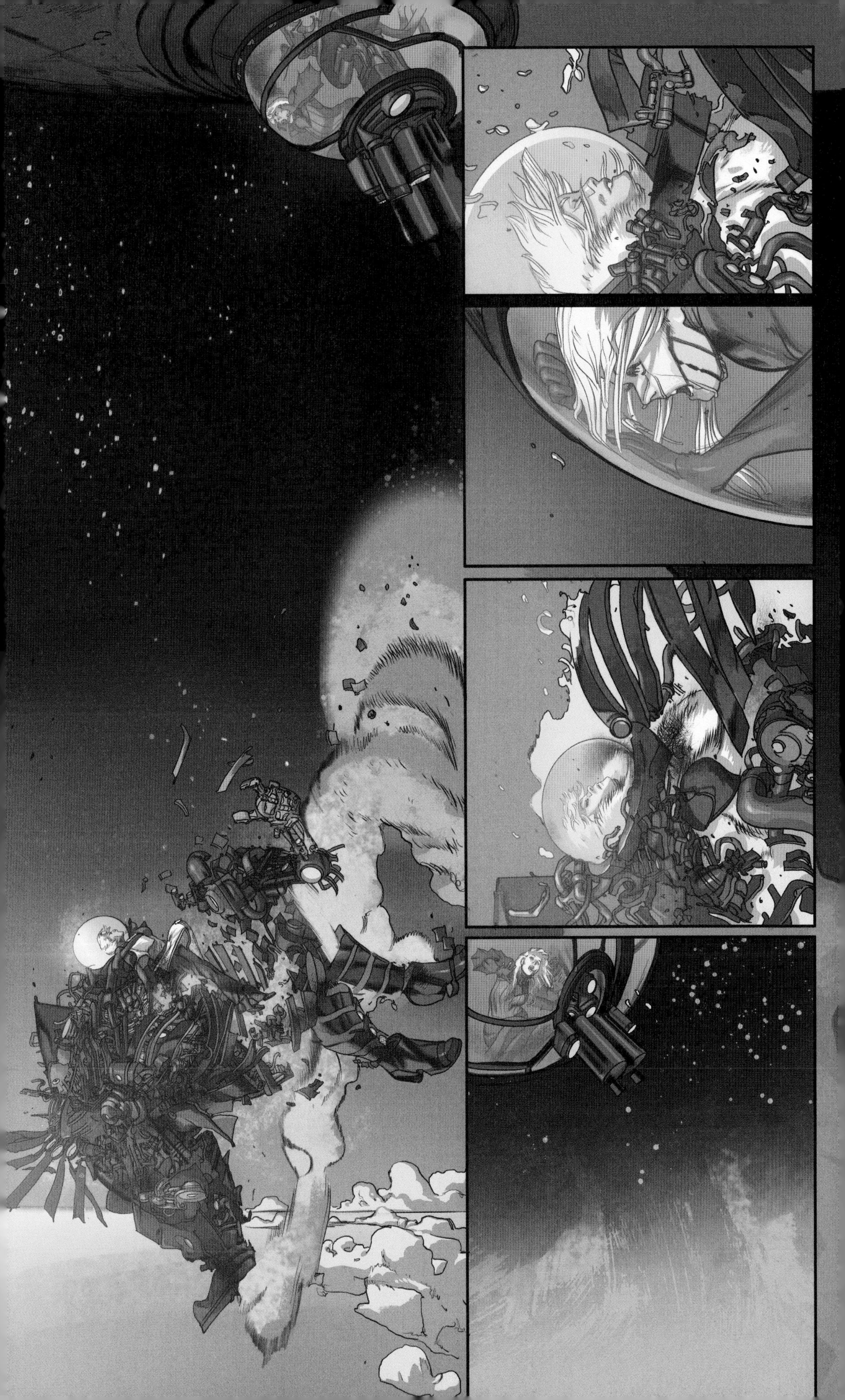

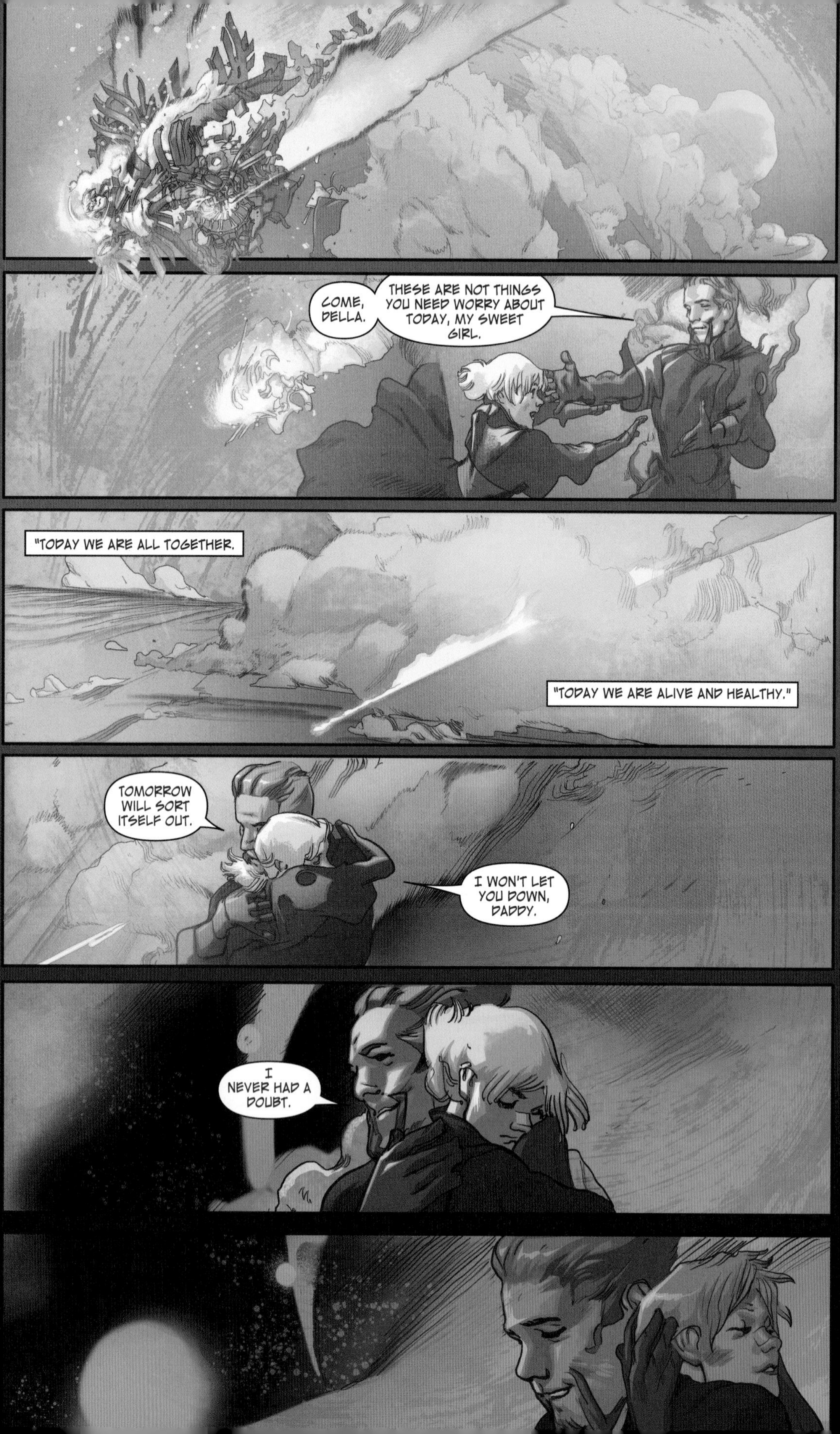
COME, DELLA.
THESE ARE NOT THINGS YOU NEED WORRY ABOUT TODAY, MY SWEET GIRL.
"TODAY WE ARE ALL TOGETHER.
"TODAY WE ARE ALIVE AND HEALTHY."
TOMORROW WILL SORT ITSELF OUT.
I WON'T LET YOU DOWN, DADDY.
I NEVER HAD A DOUBT.

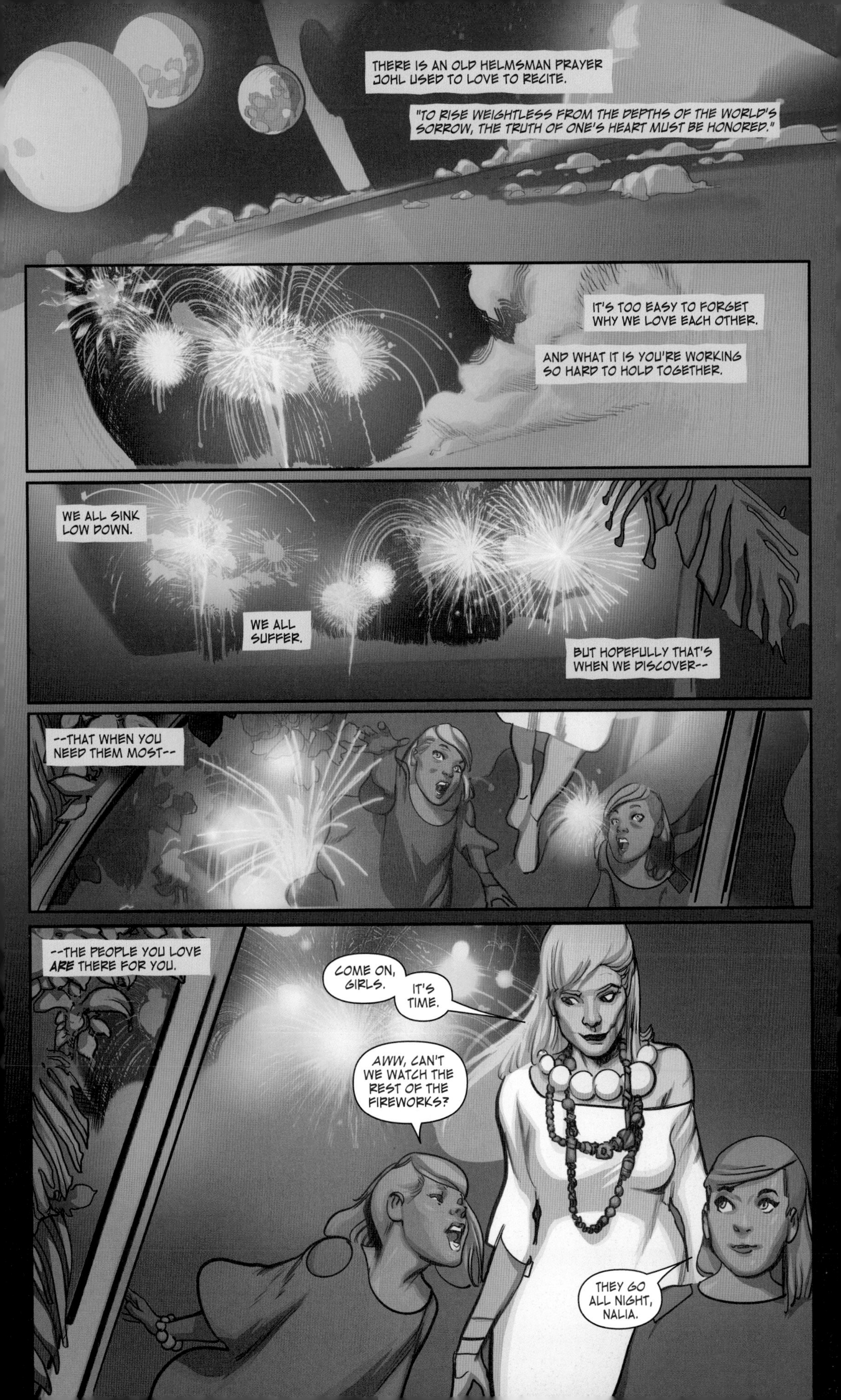

THERE IS AN OLD HELMSMAN PRAYER JOHL USED TO LOVE TO RECITE.
"TO RISE WEIGHTLESS FROM THE DEPTHS OF THE WORLD'S SORROW, THE TRUTH OF ONE'S HEART MUST BE HONORED."
IT'S TOO EASY TO FORGET WHY WE LOVE EACH OTHER.
AND WHAT IT IS YOU'RE WORKING SO HARD TO HOLD TOGETHER.
WE ALL SINK LOW DOWN.
WE ALL SUFFER.
BUT HOPEFULLY THAT'S WHEN WE DISCOVER--
--THAT WHEN YOU NEED THEM MOST--
--THE PEOPLE YOU LOVE ARE THERE FOR YOU.
COME ON, GIRLS.
IT'S TIME.
AWW, CAN'T WE WATCH THE REST OF THE FIREWORKS?
THEY GO ALL NIGHT, NALIA.

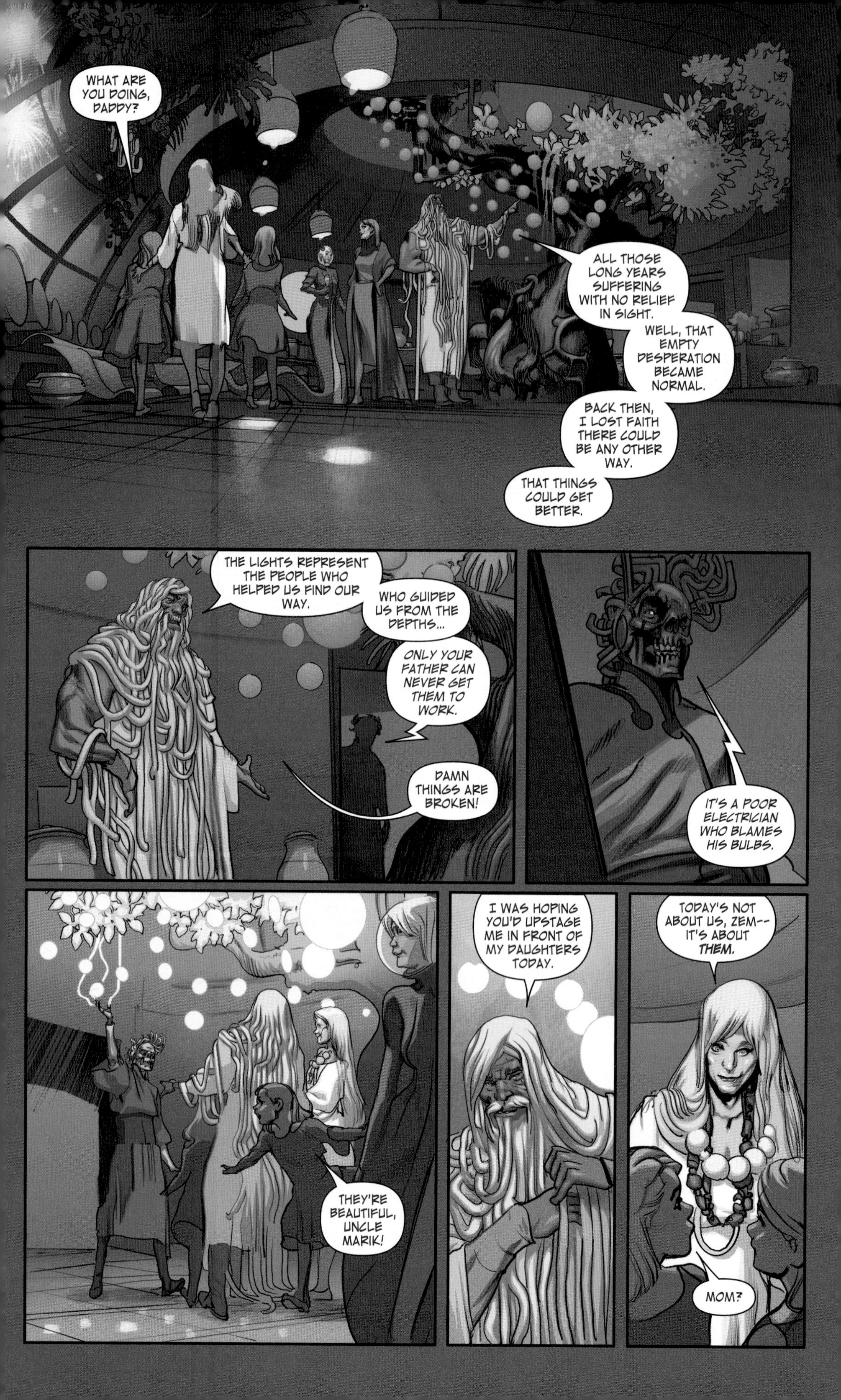
WHAT ARE YOU DOING, DADDY?
ALL THOSE LONG YEARS SUFFERING WITH NO RELIEF IN SIGHT.
WELL, THAT EMPTY DESPERATION BECAME NORMAL.
BACK THEN, I LOST FAITH THERE COULD BE ANY OTHER WAY.
THAT THINGS COULD GET BETTER.
THE LIGHTS REPRESENT THE PEOPLE WHO HELPED US FIND OUR WAY.
WHO GUIDED US FROM THE DEPTHS...
ONLY YOUR FATHER CAN NEVER GET THEM TO WORK.
DAMN THINGS ARE BROKEN!
IT'S A POOR ELECTRICIAN WHO BLAMES HIS BULBS.
THEY'RE BEAUTIFUL, UNCLE MARIK!
I WAS HOPING YOU'D UPSTAGE ME IN FRONT OF MY DAUGHTERS TODAY.
TODAY'S NOT ABOUT US, ZEM-- IT'S ABOUT *THEM.*
MOM?

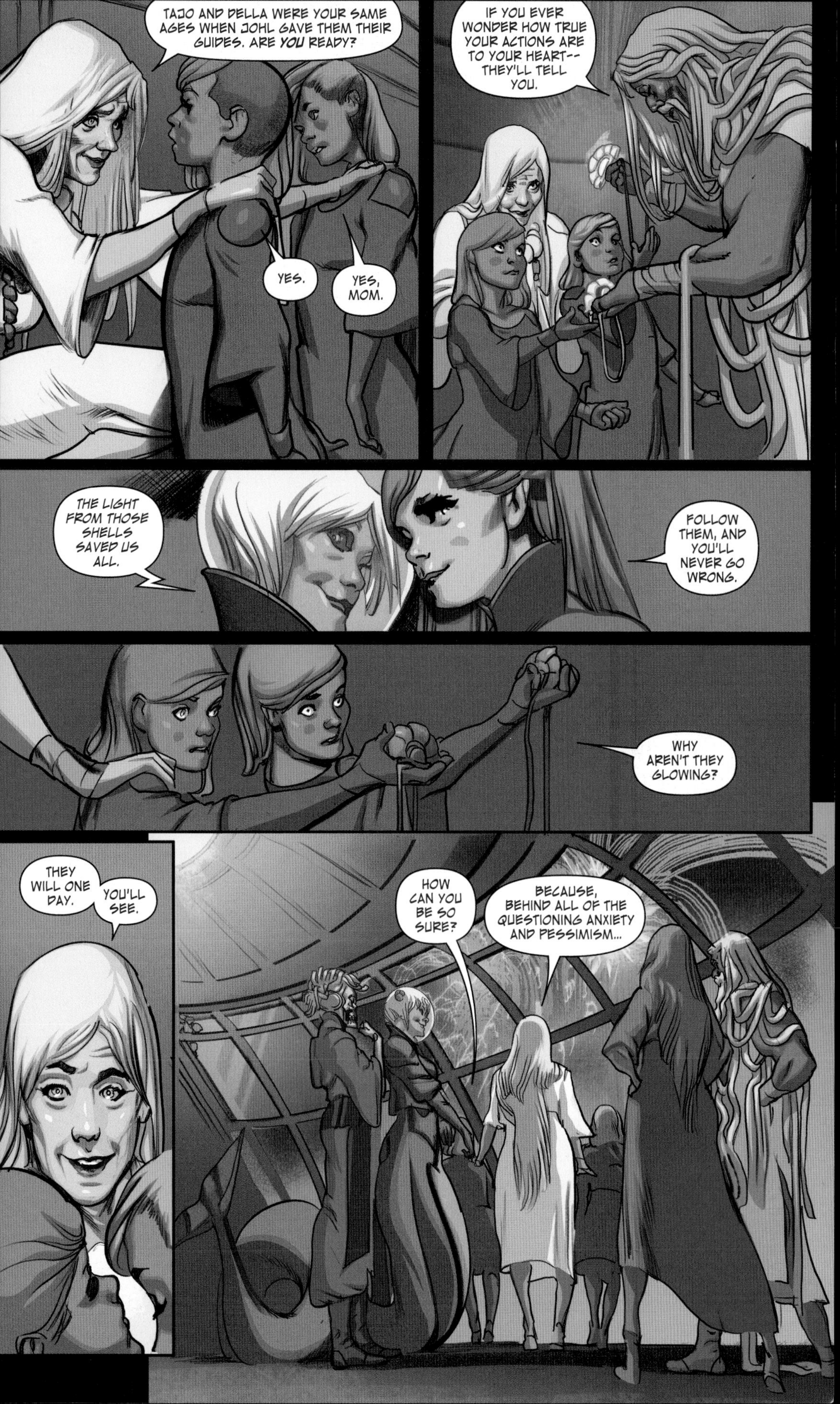
TAJO AND DELLA WERE YOUR SAME AGES WHEN JOHL GAVE THEM THEIR GUIDES. ARE *YOU* READY?
YES.
YES, MOM.
IF YOU EVER WONDER HOW TRUE YOUR ACTIONS ARE TO YOUR HEART-- THEY'LL TELL YOU.
THE LIGHT FROM THOSE SHELLS SAVED US ALL.
FOLLOW THEM, AND YOU'LL NEVER GO WRONG.
WHY AREN'T THEY GLOWING?
THEY WILL ONE DAY.
YOU'LL SEE.
HOW CAN YOU BE SO SURE?
BECAUSE, BEHIND ALL OF THE QUESTIONING ANXIETY AND PESSIMISM...

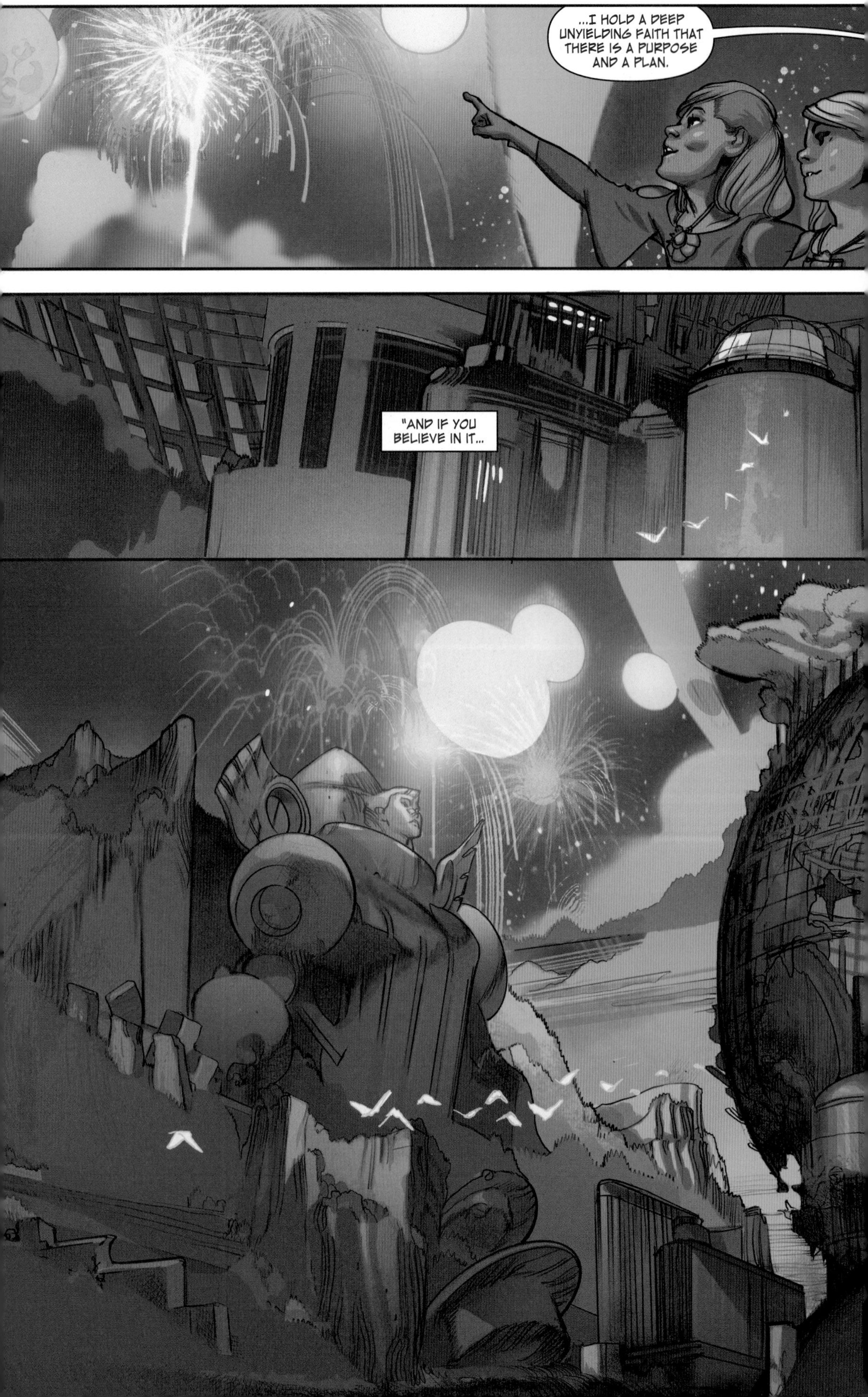

...I HOLD A DEEP UNYIELDING FAITH THAT THERE IS A PURPOSE AND A PLAN.
"AND IF YOU BELIEVE IN IT...

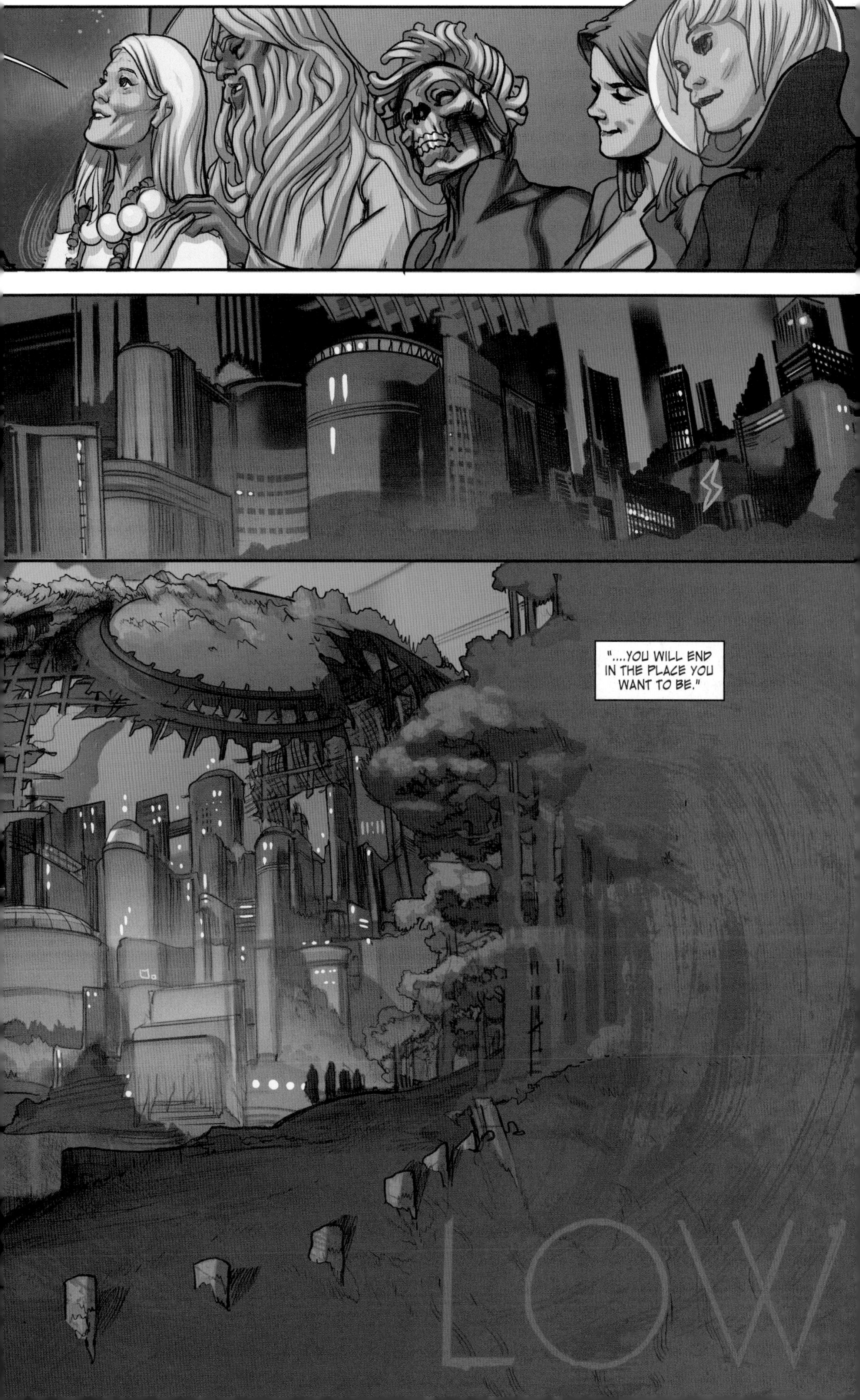
"....YOU WILL END IN THE PLACE YOU WANT TO BE."
LOW

VARIANT COVER
GALLERY

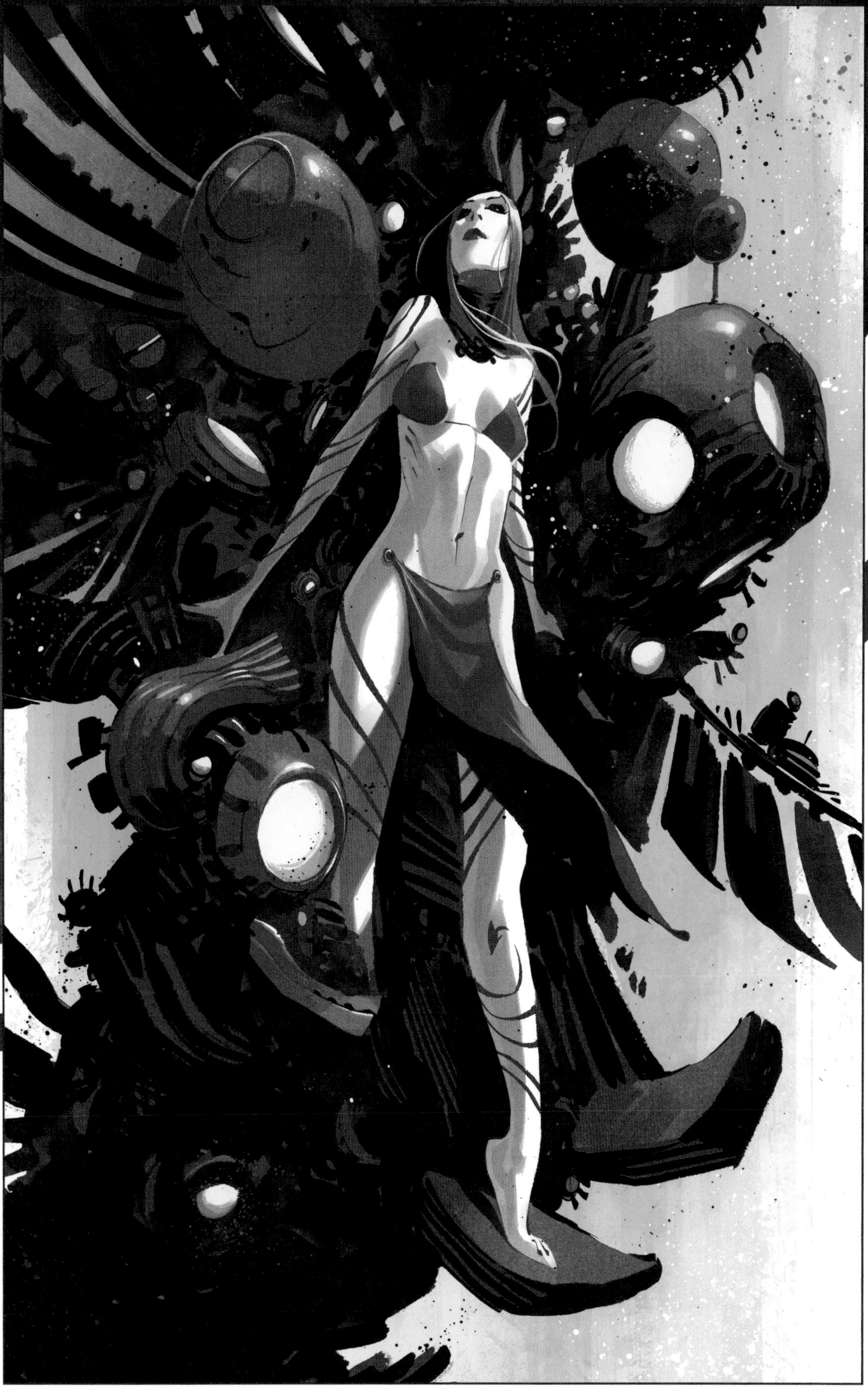

#20 VARIANT BY MATTEO SCALERA & MORENO DINISIO

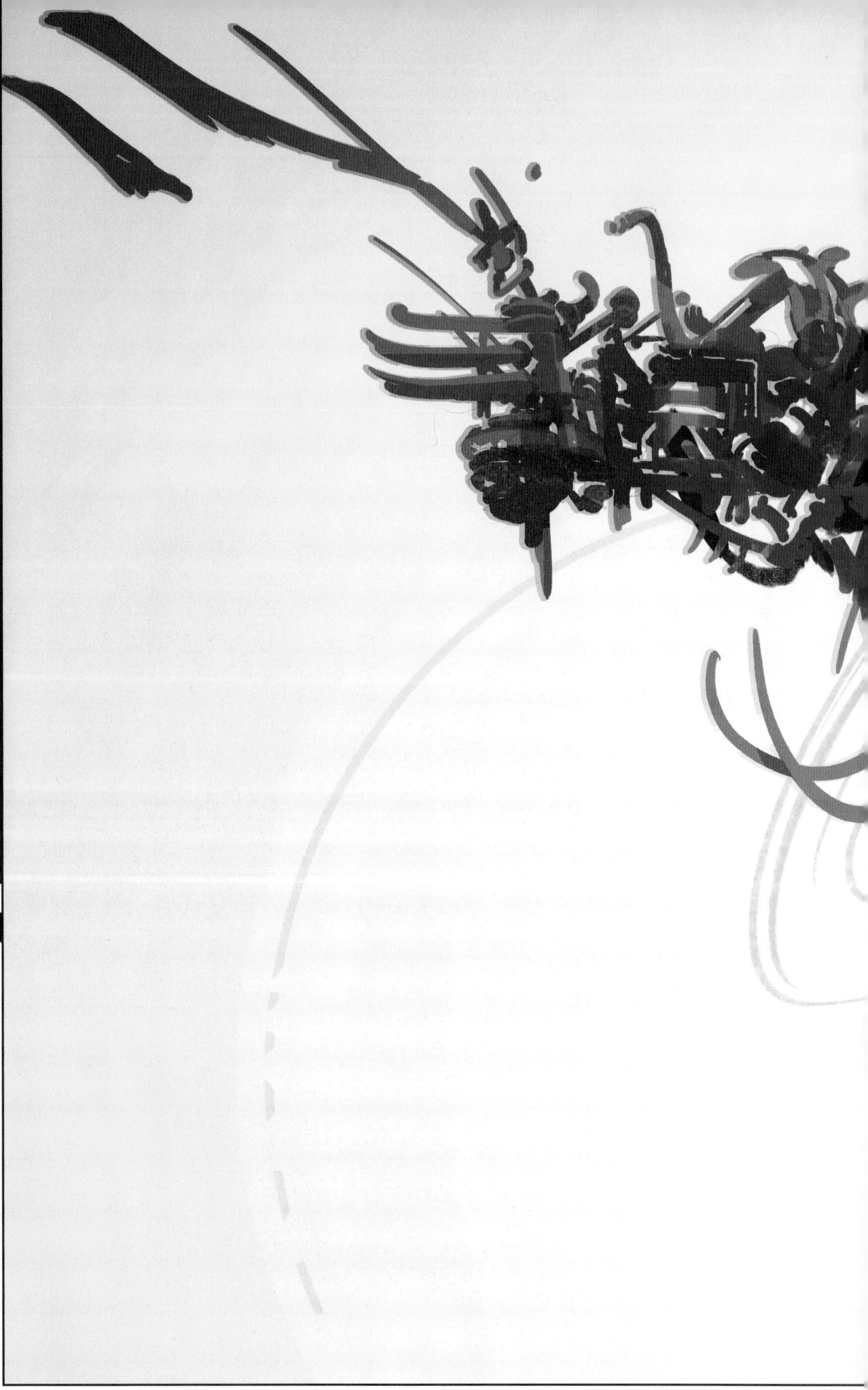

#20 VARIANT BY GREG TOCCHINI

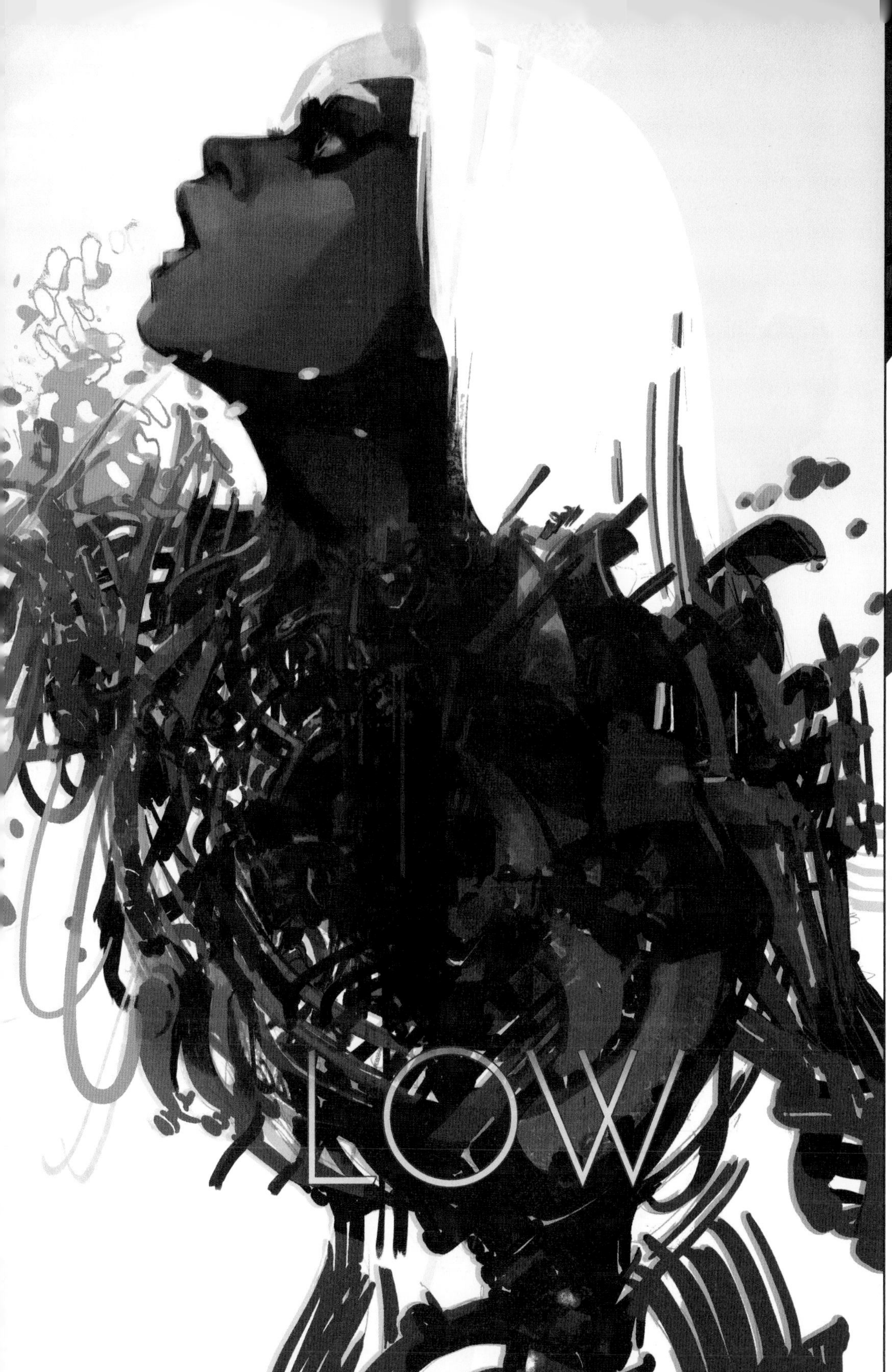
LOW

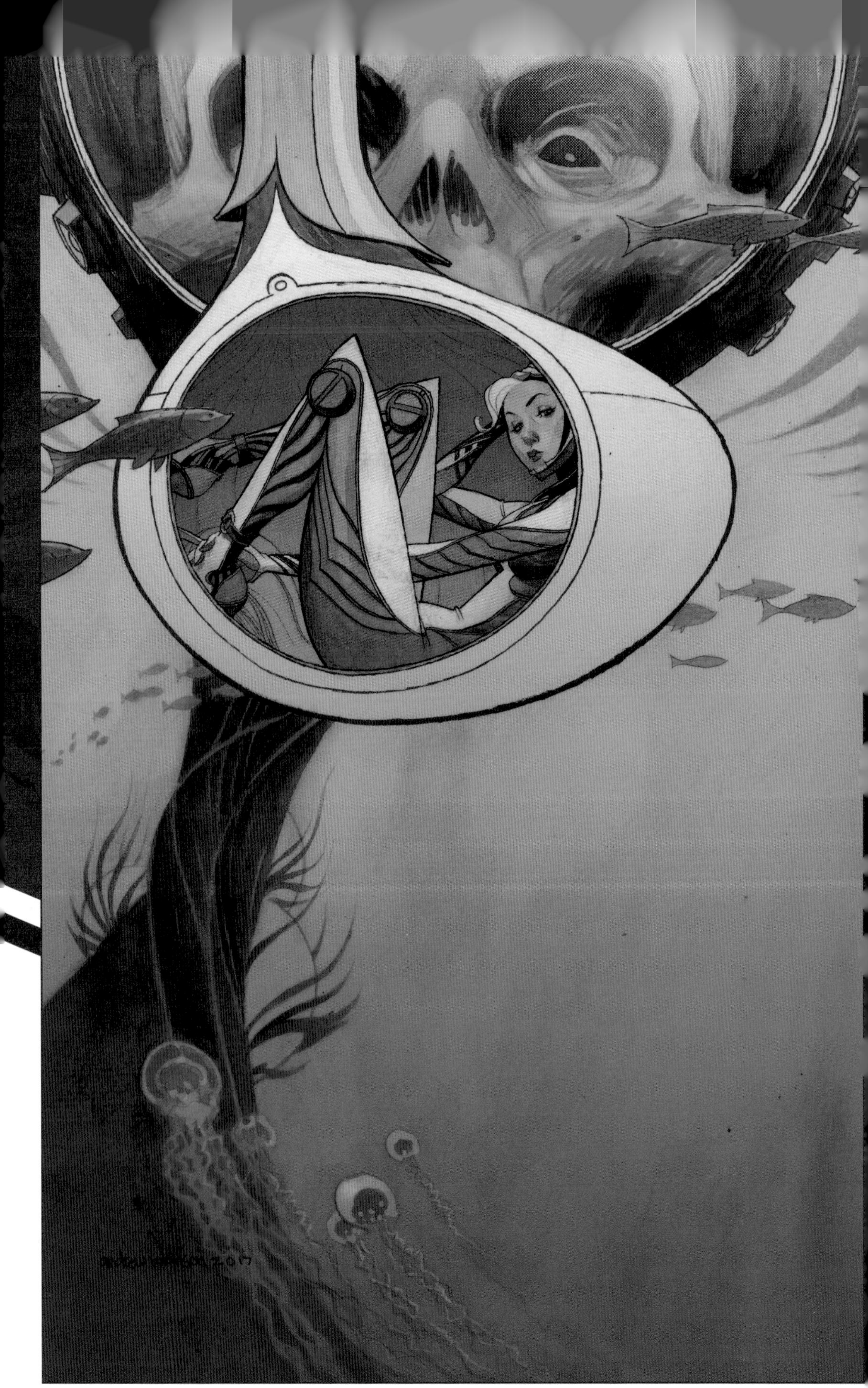

#21 VARIANT BY ANDREW ROBINSON

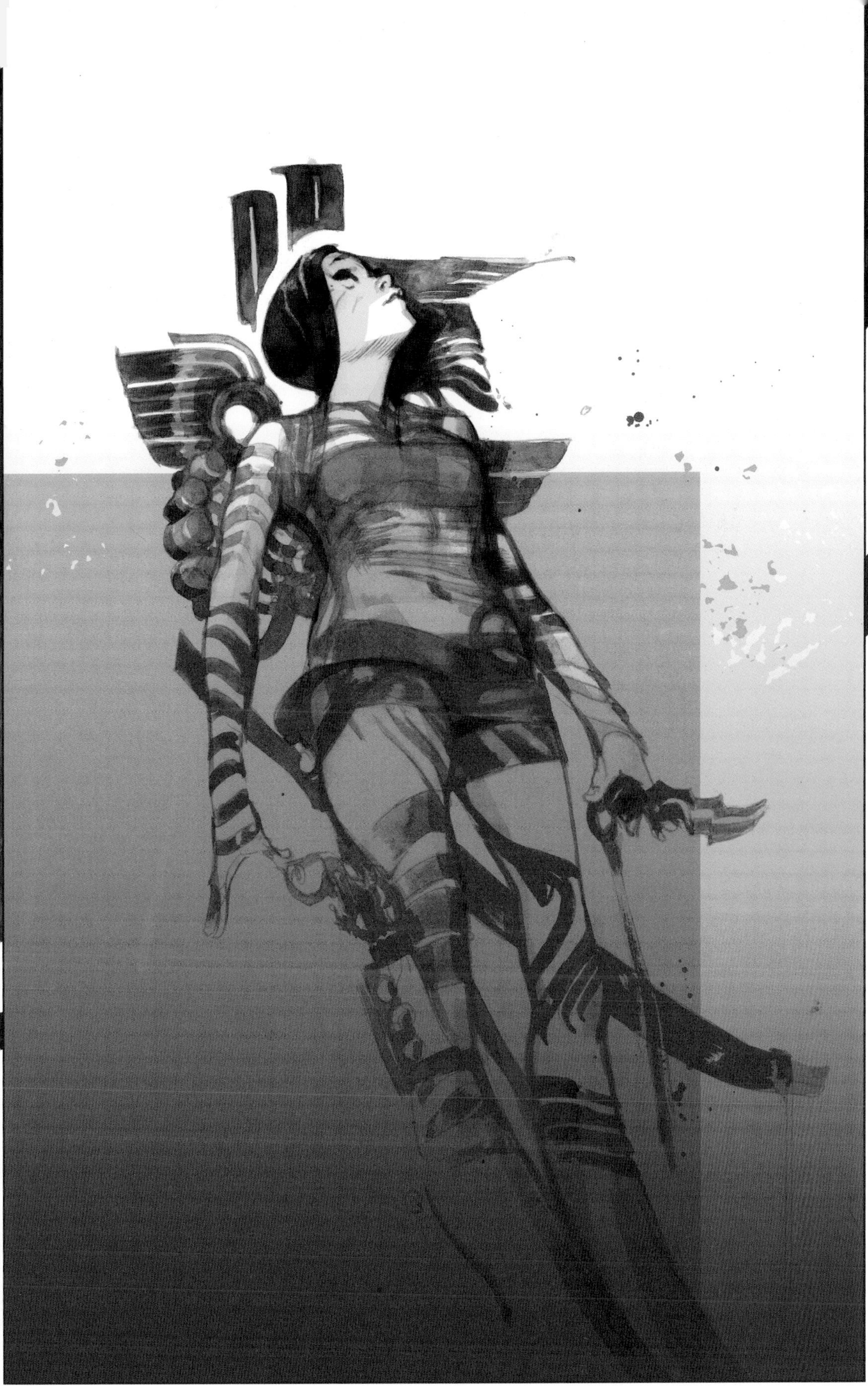

#21 VARIANT BY GREG TOCCHINI

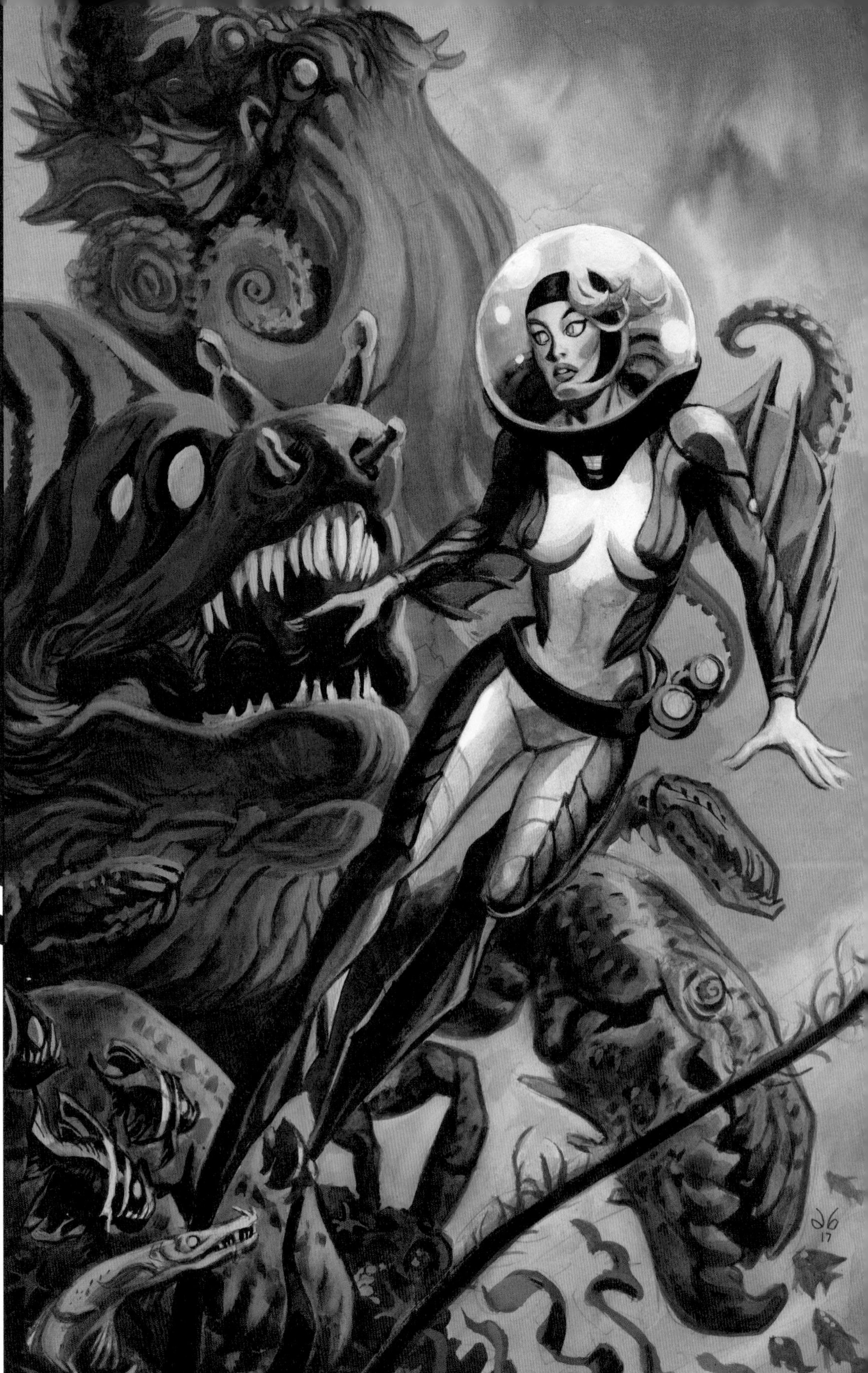

#22 VARIANT BY DAN BRERETON

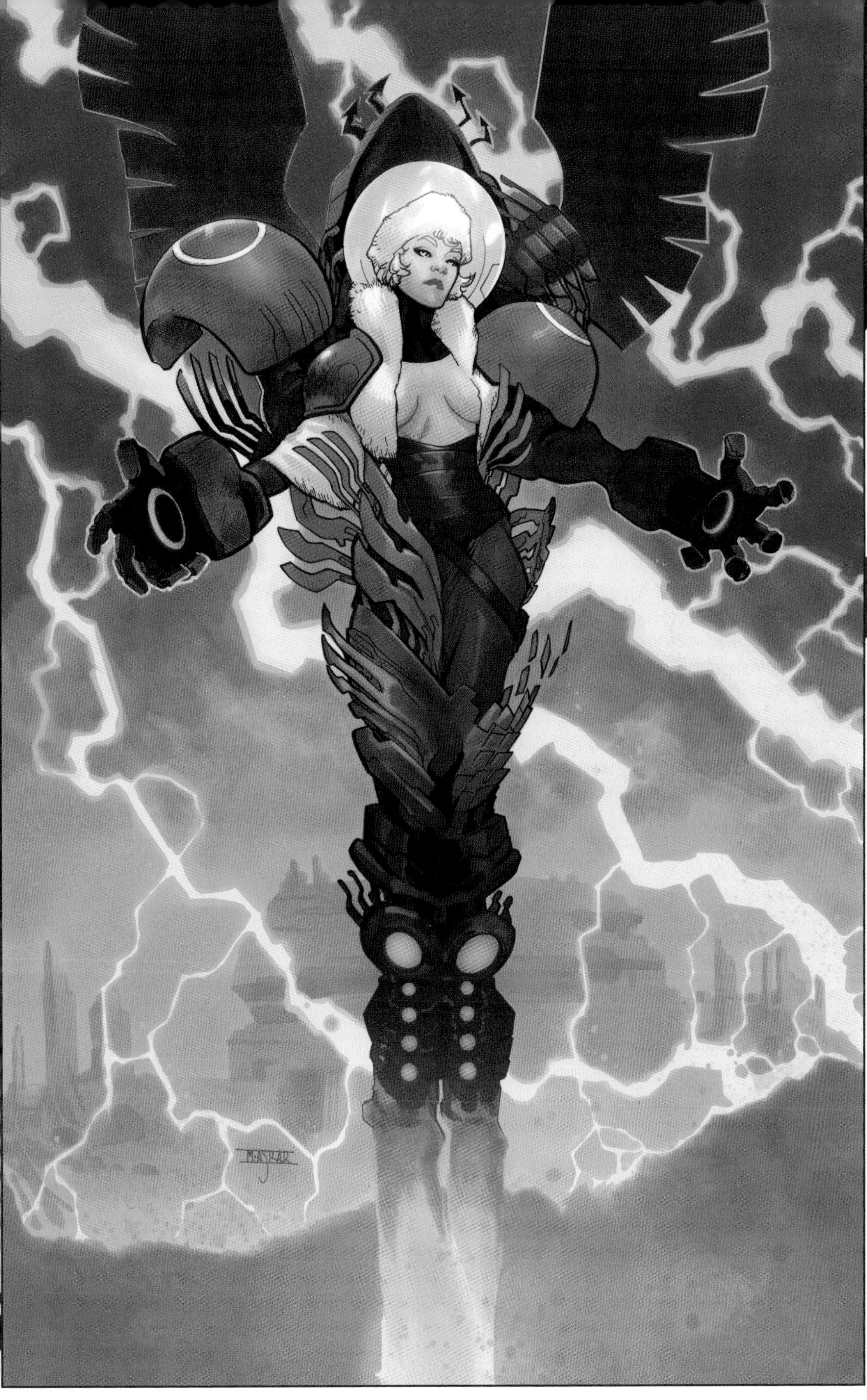
M. ASRAR

#23 VARIANT BY MAHMUD ASRAR & DAVE McCAIG

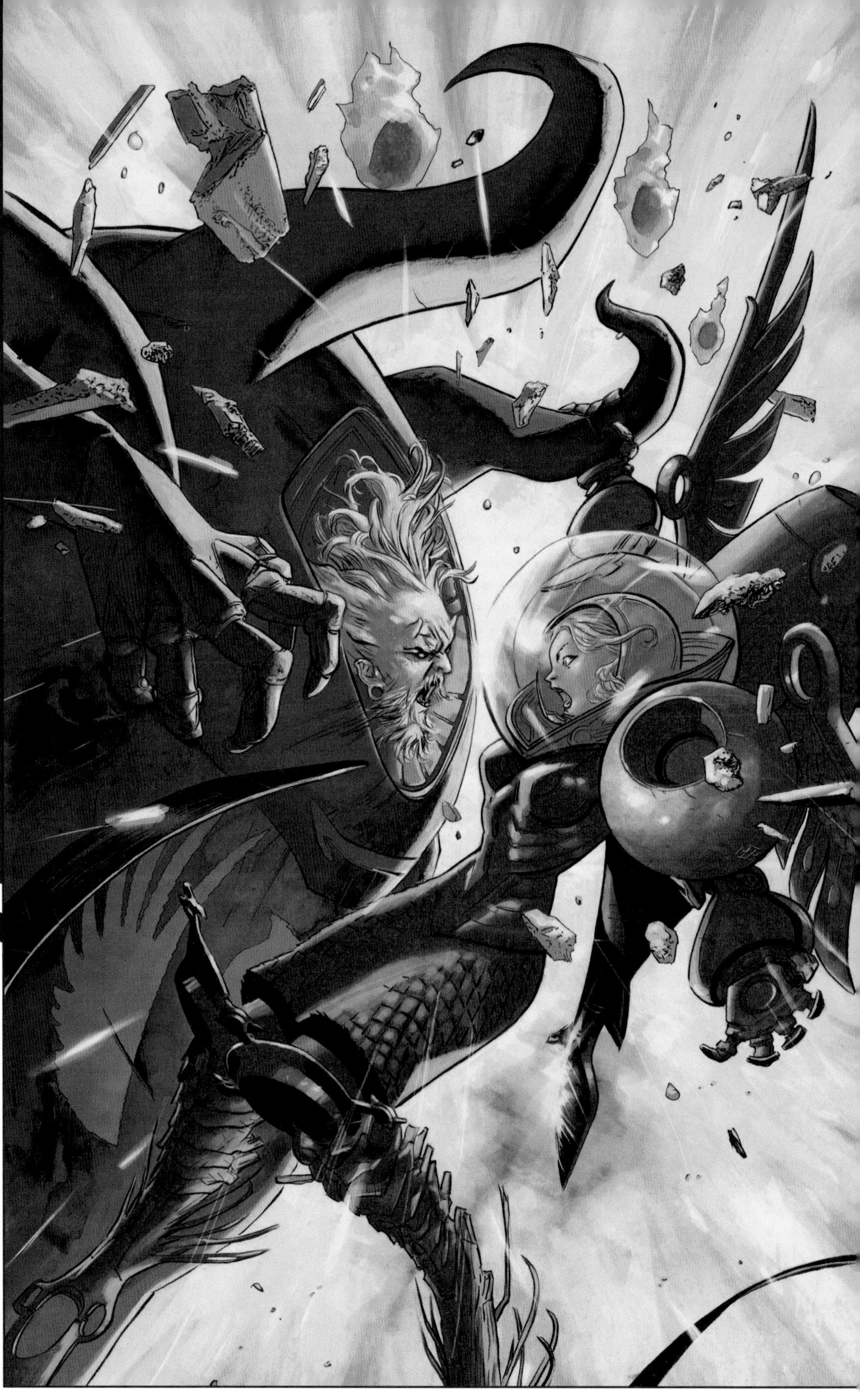

#24 VARIANT BY MAX FIUMARA

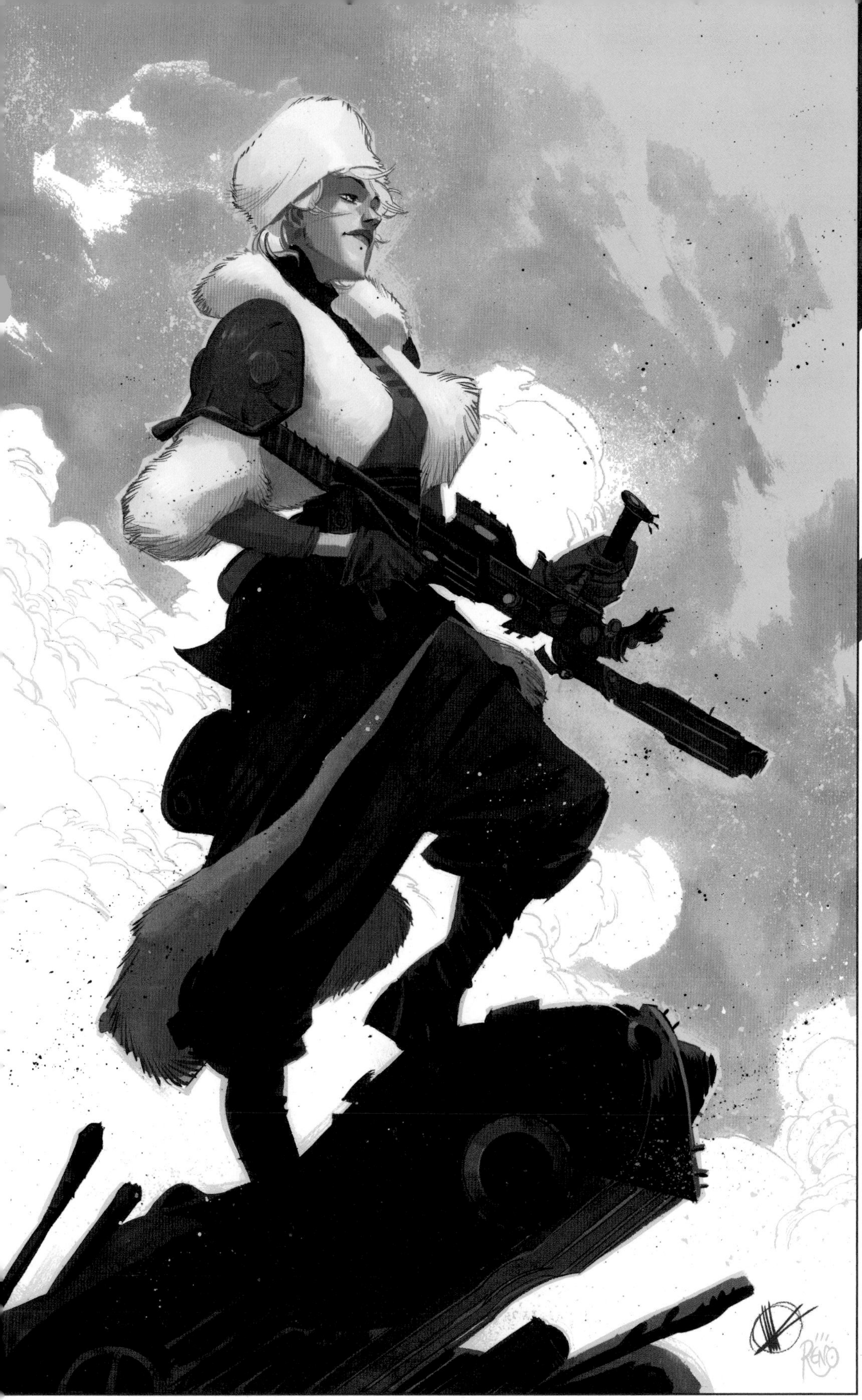
RENO

#25 VARIANT BY MATTEO SCALERA & MORENO DINISIO

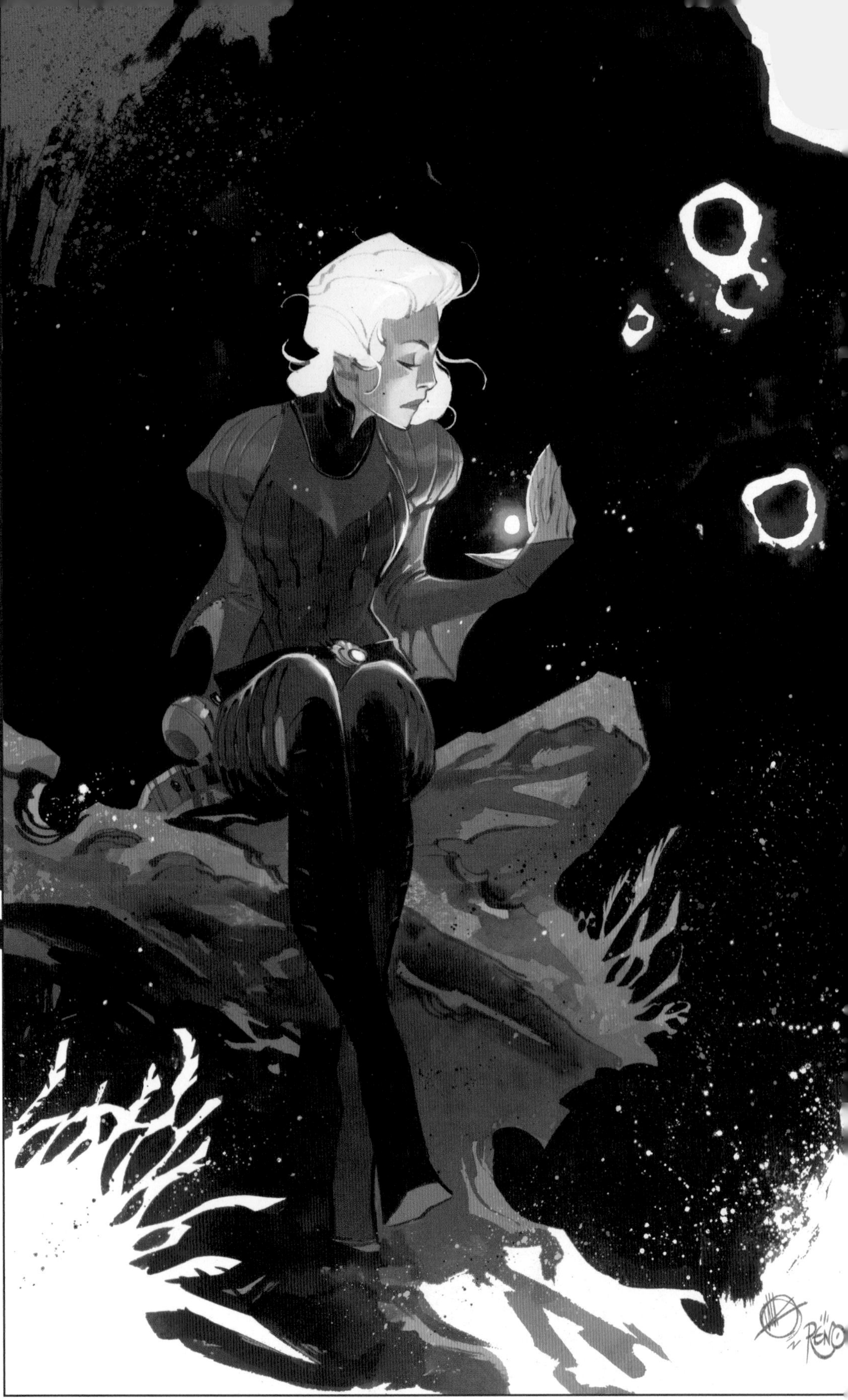

#26 VARIANT BY MATTEO SCALERA & MORENO DINISIO

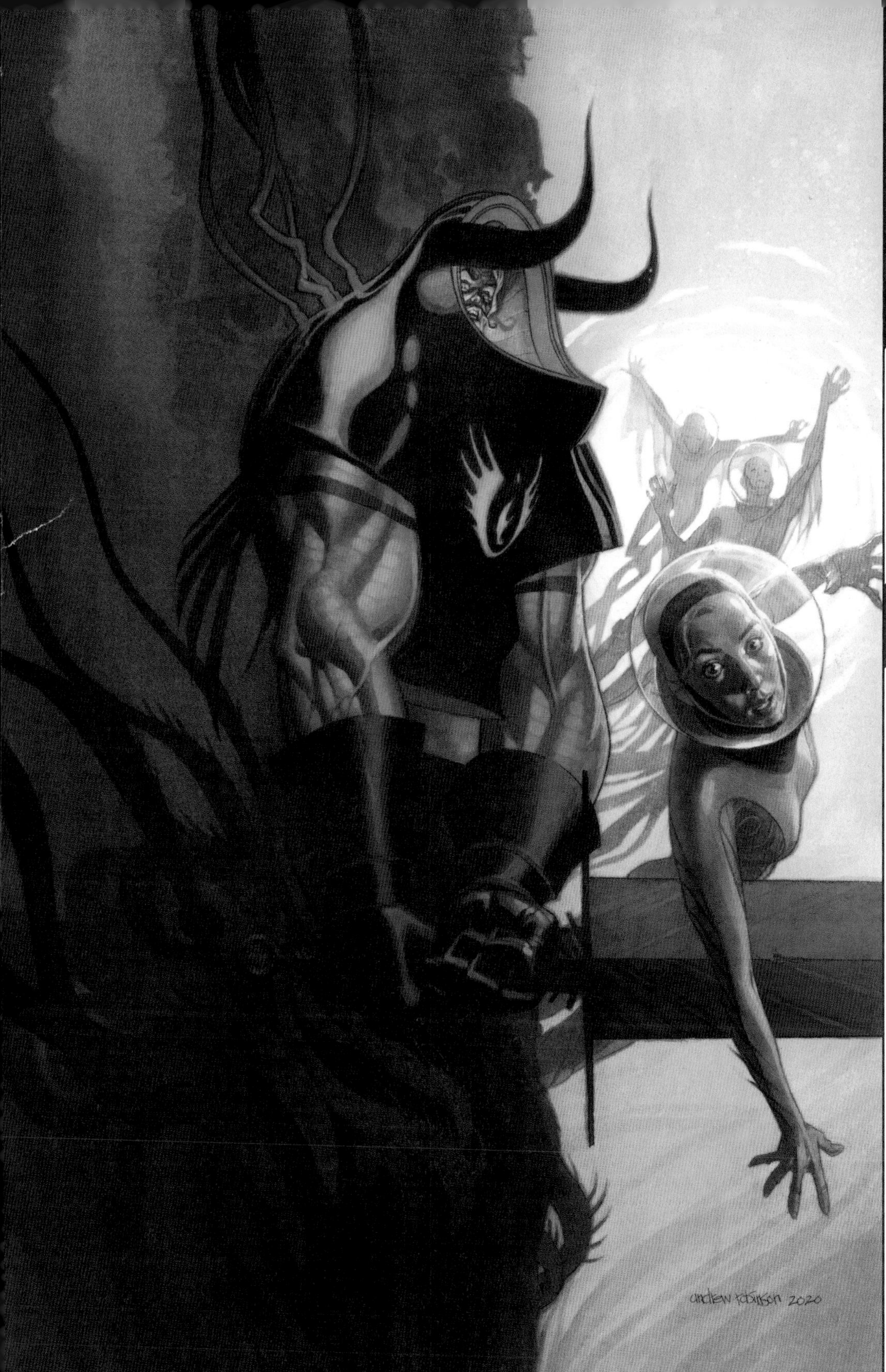

#26 VARIANT BY ANDREW ROBINSON

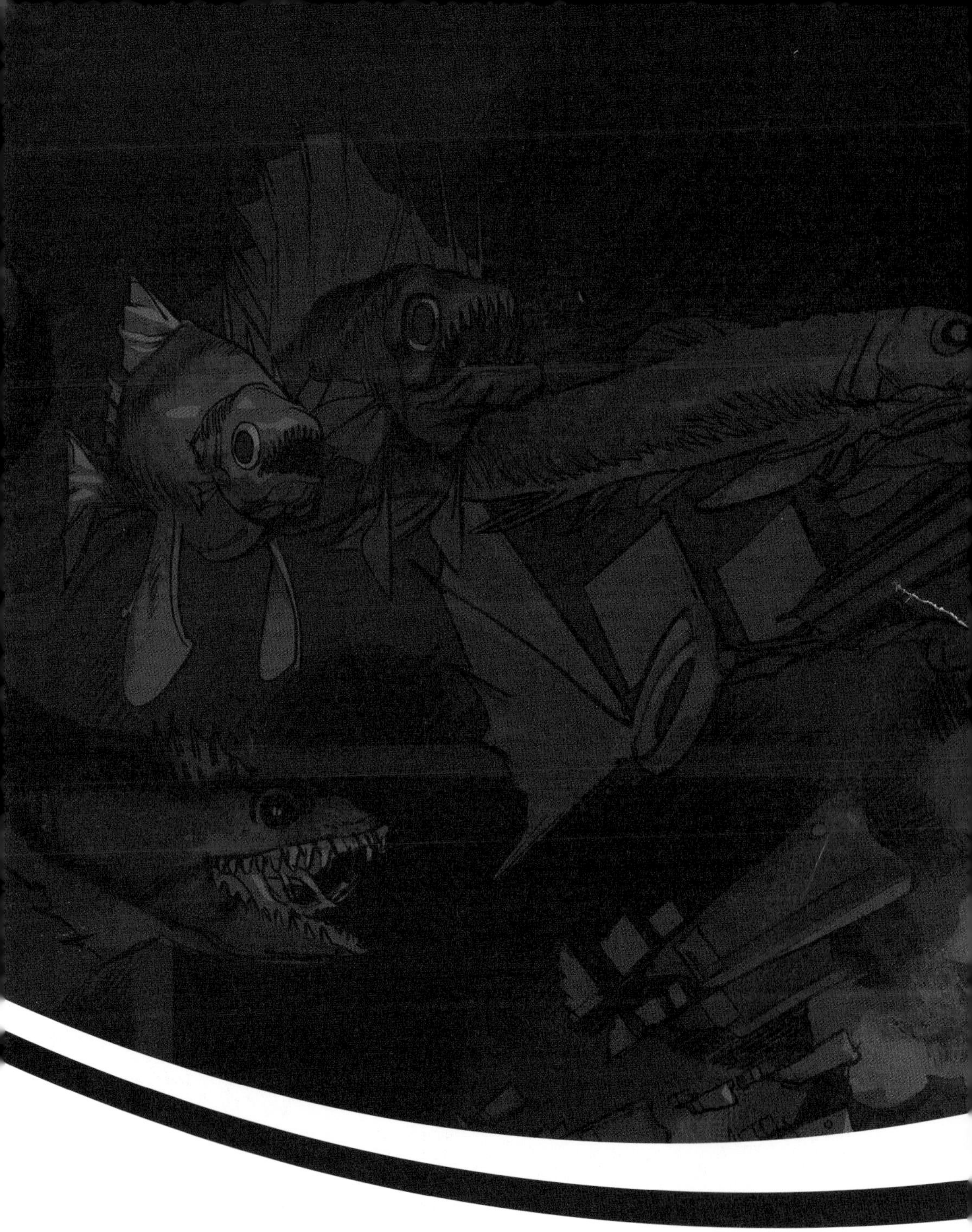

GREG TOCCHINI
SKETCHBOOK

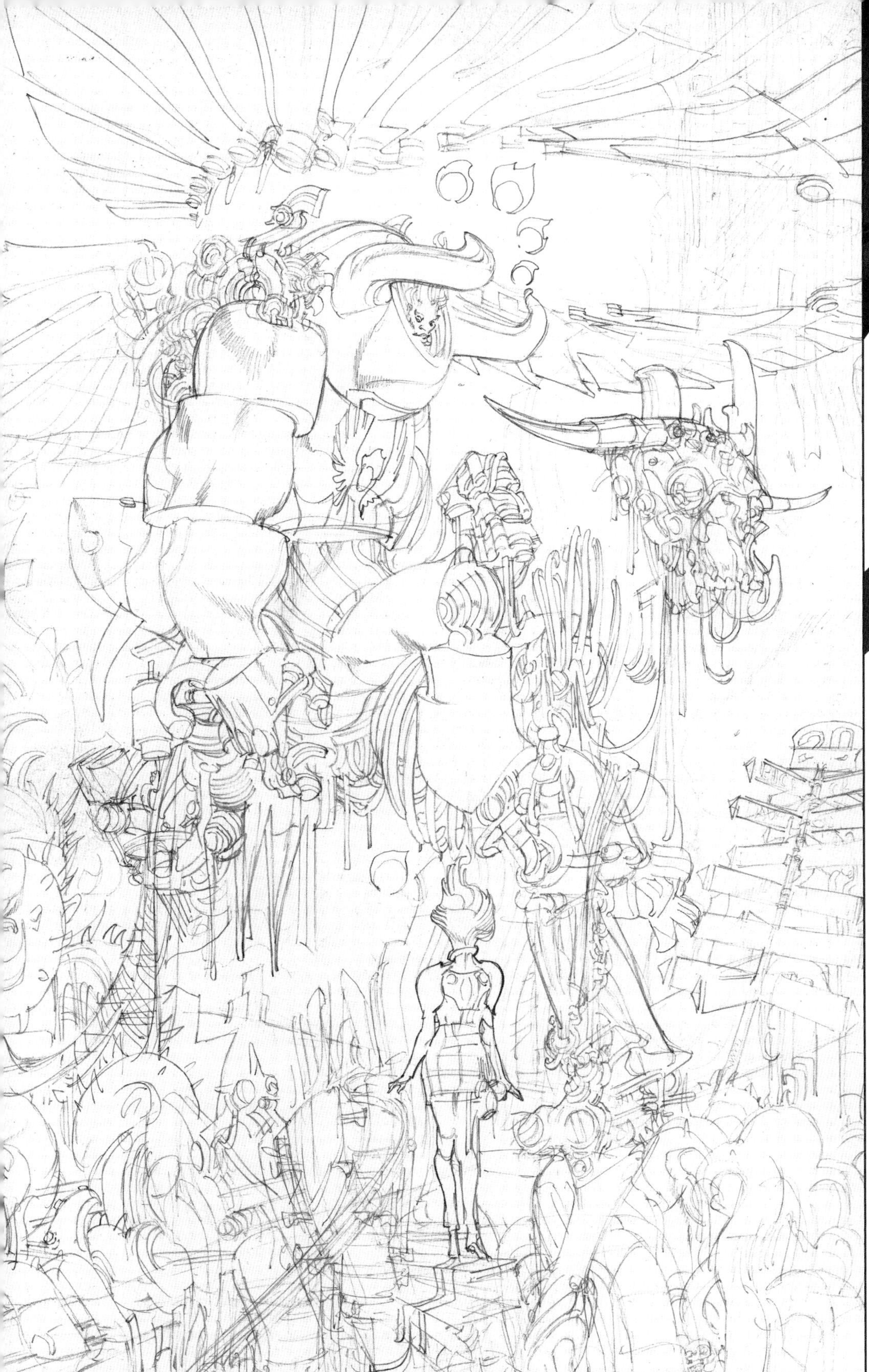

#20 COVER PENCILS

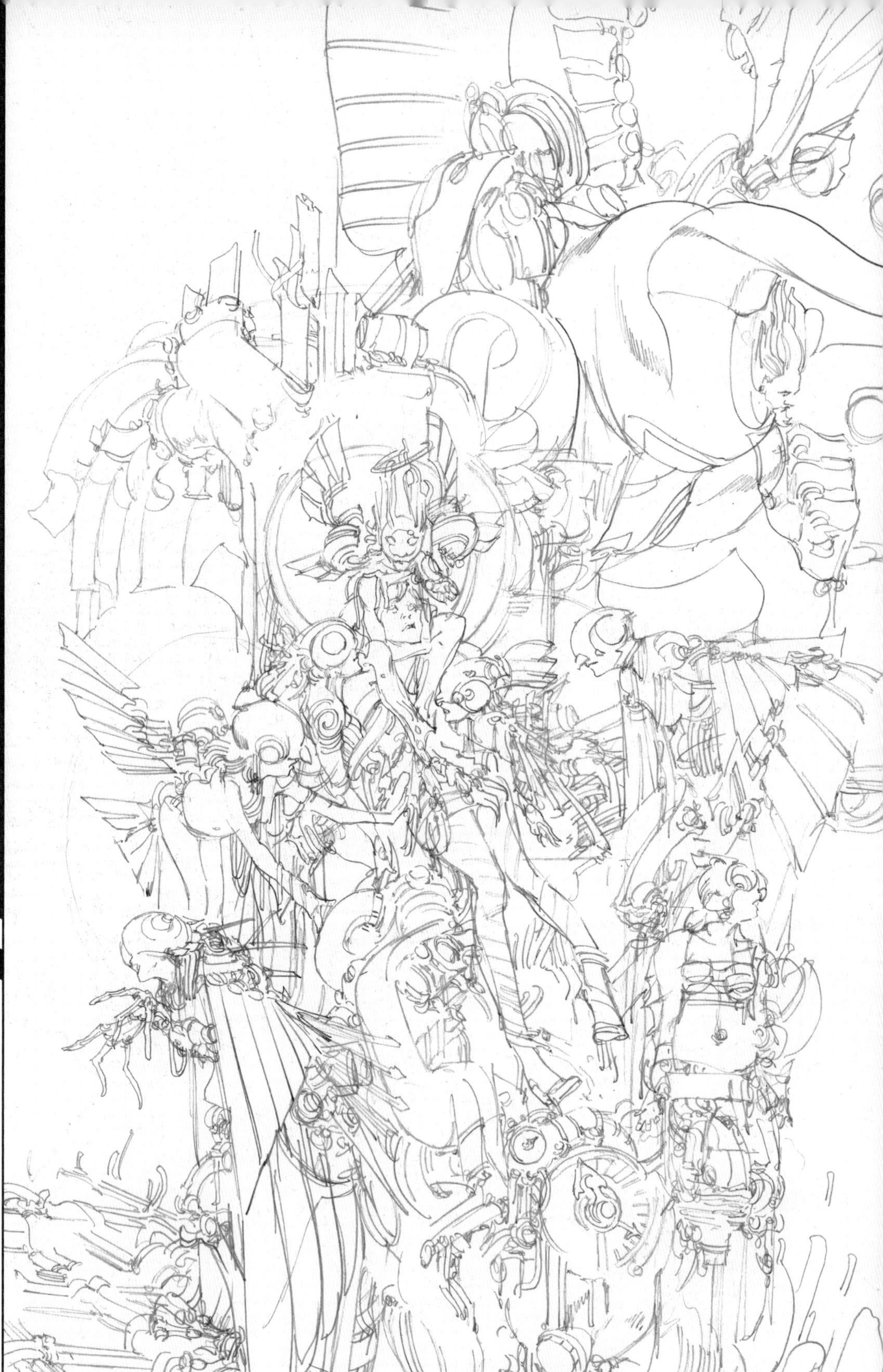

#21 COVER PENCILS

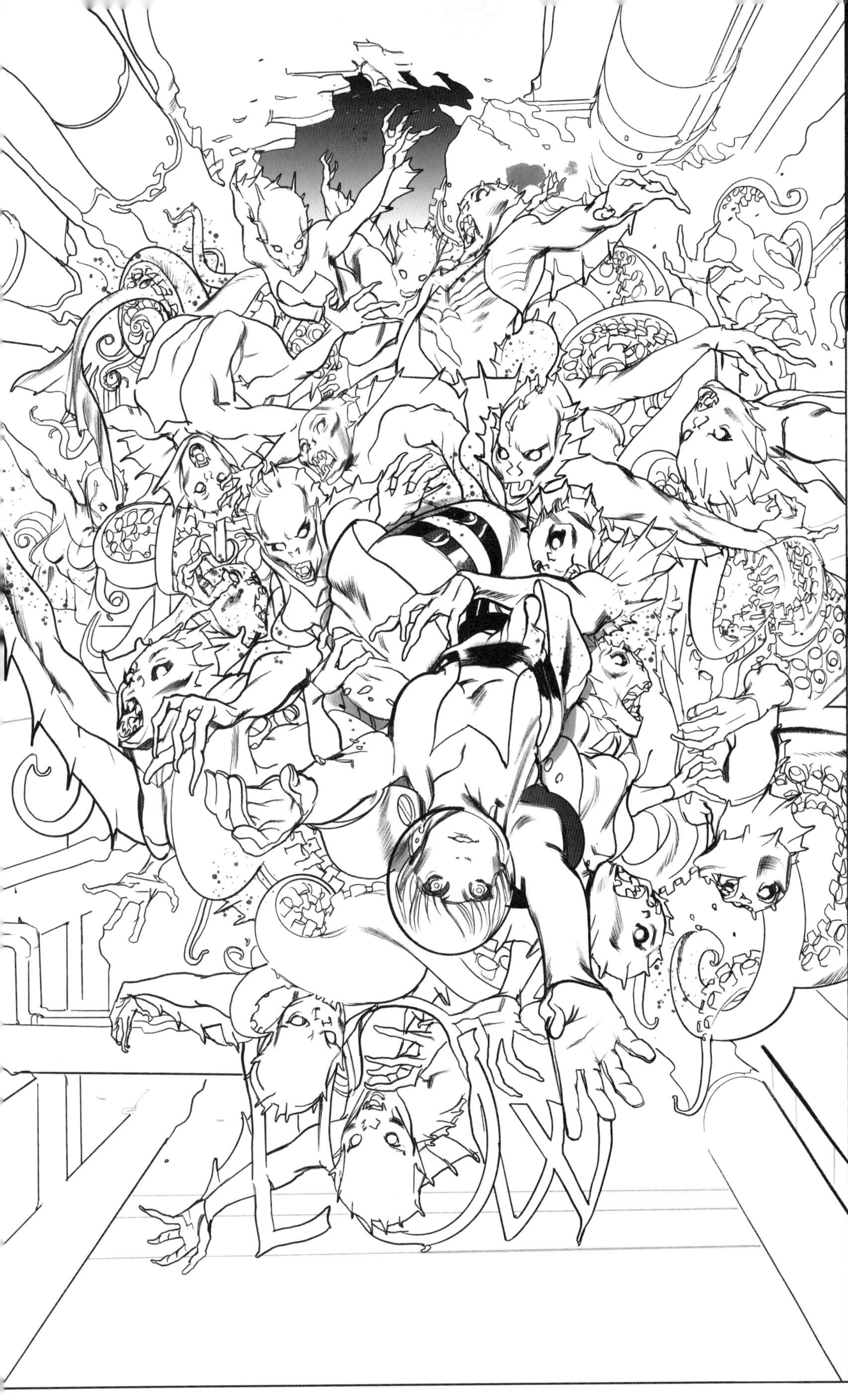

#23 PAGE 20 INKS

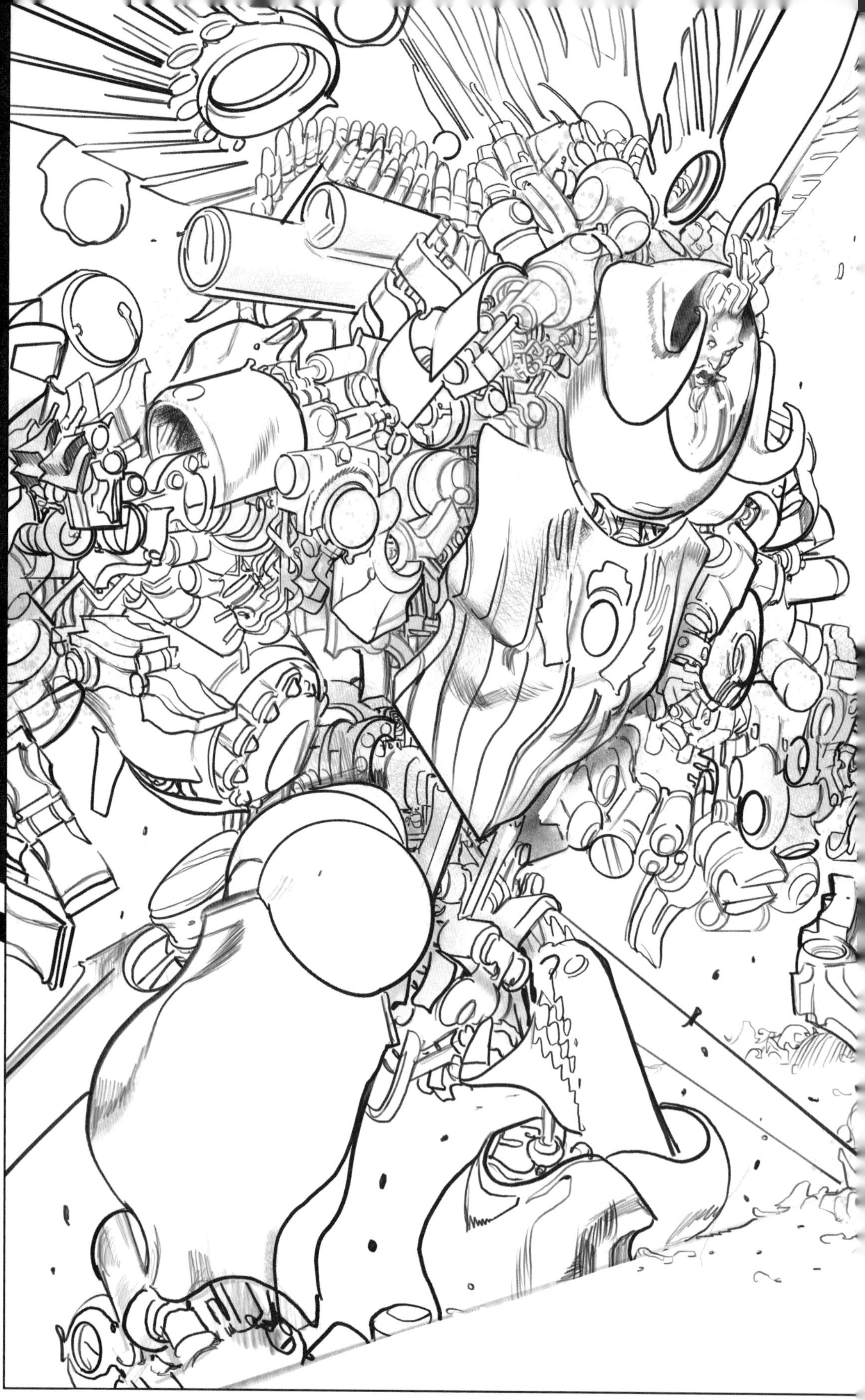

#25 PAGES 22–23 INKS

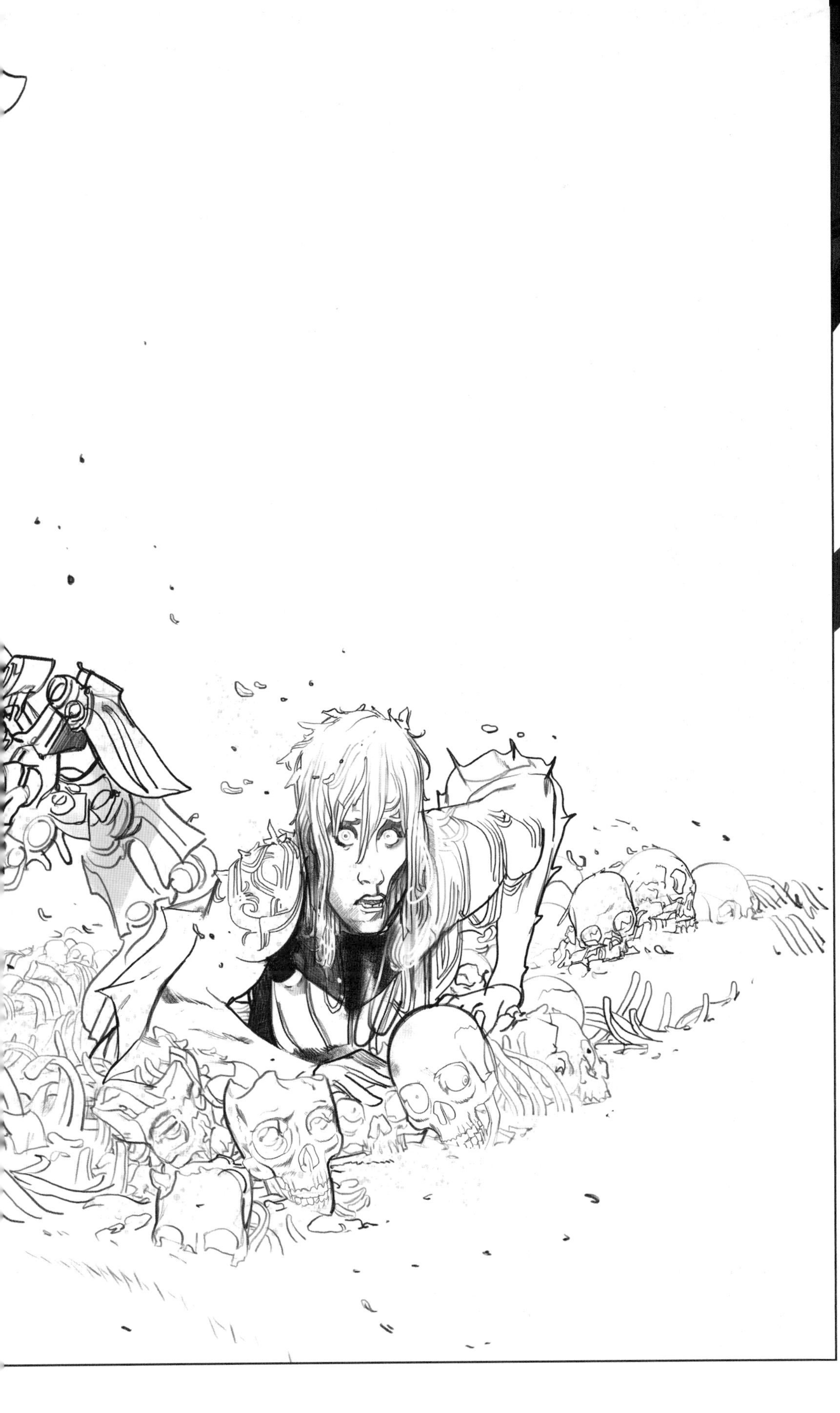

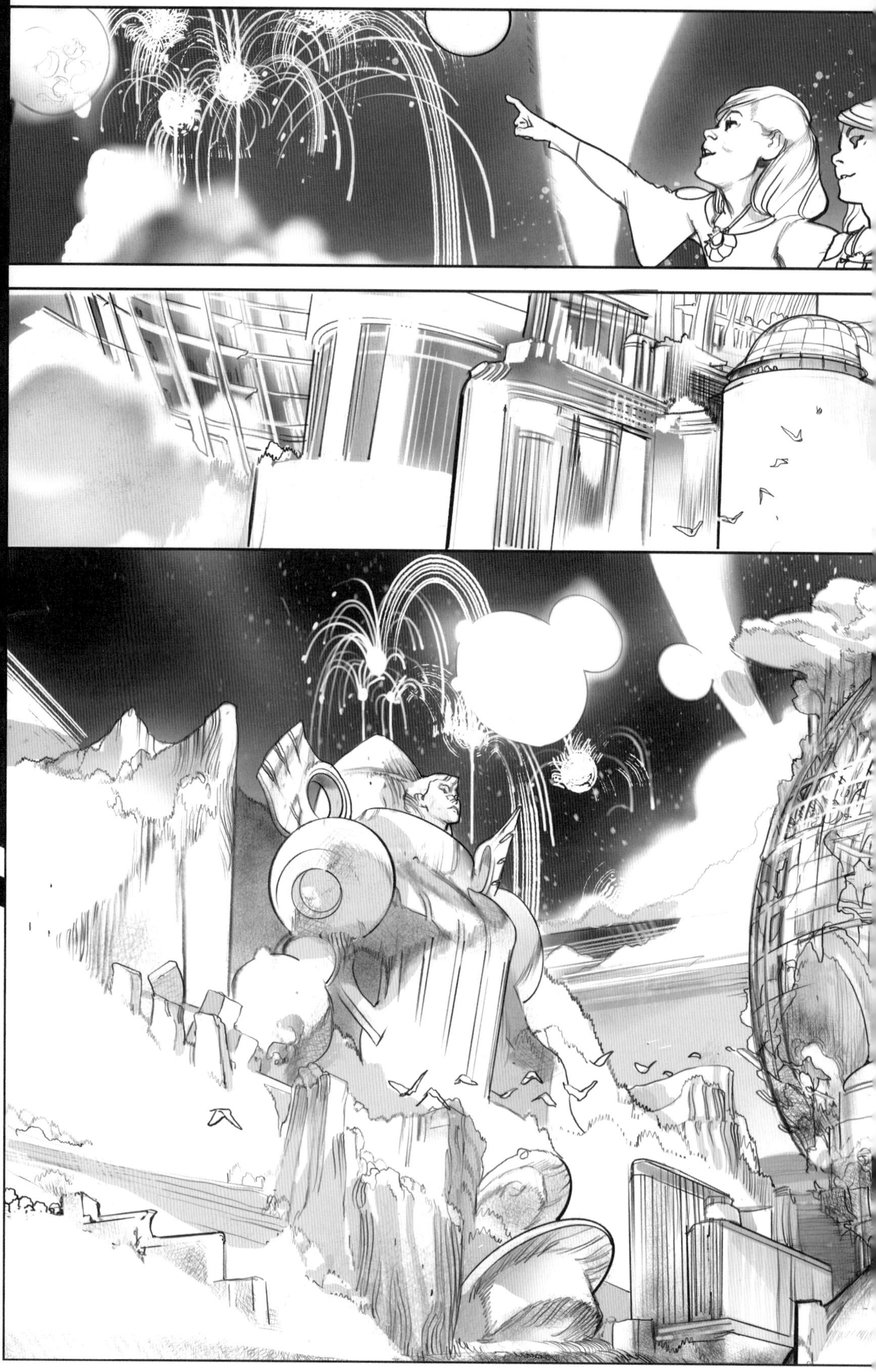

#26 PAGES 32–33 INKS

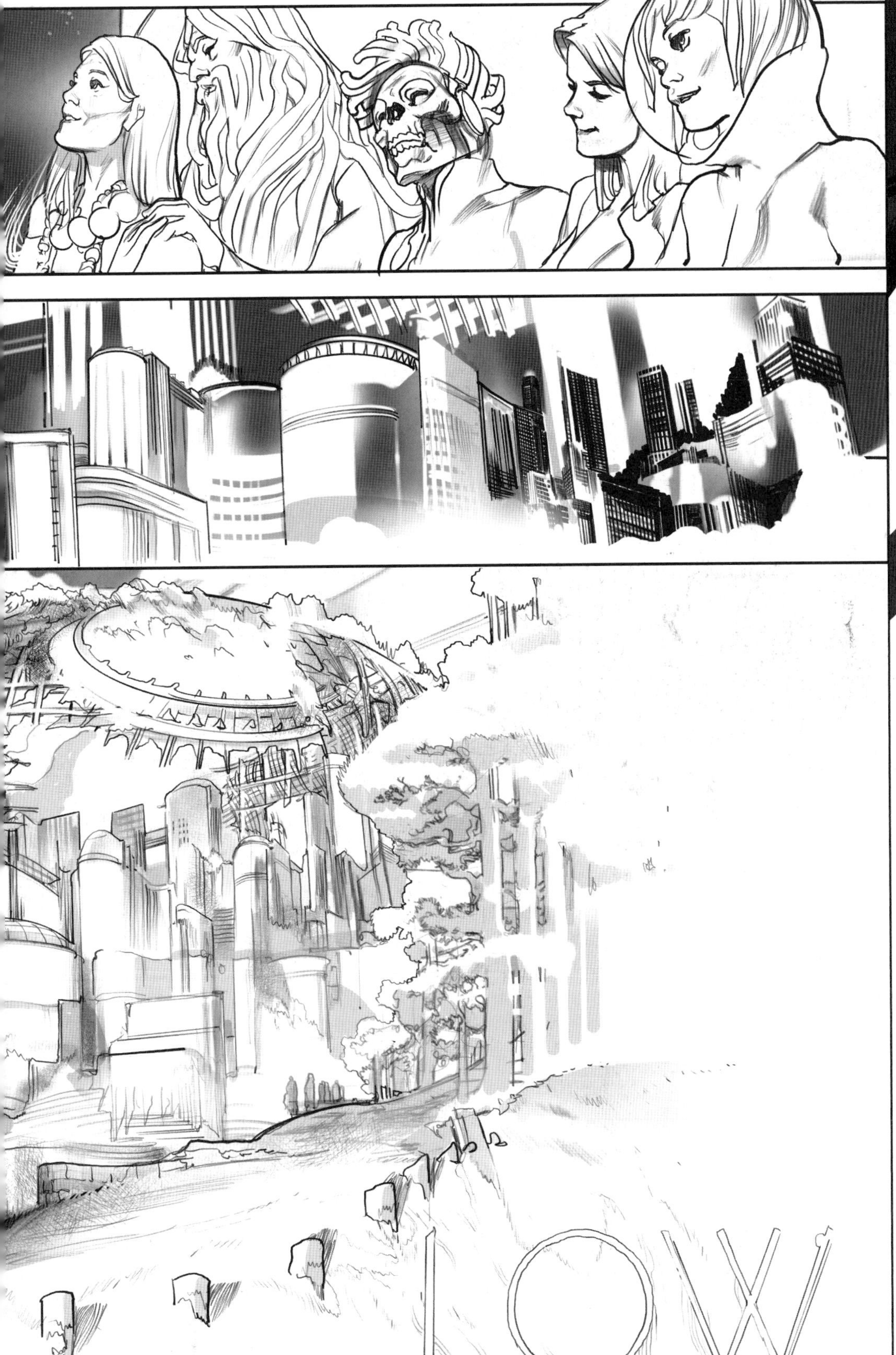
LOW

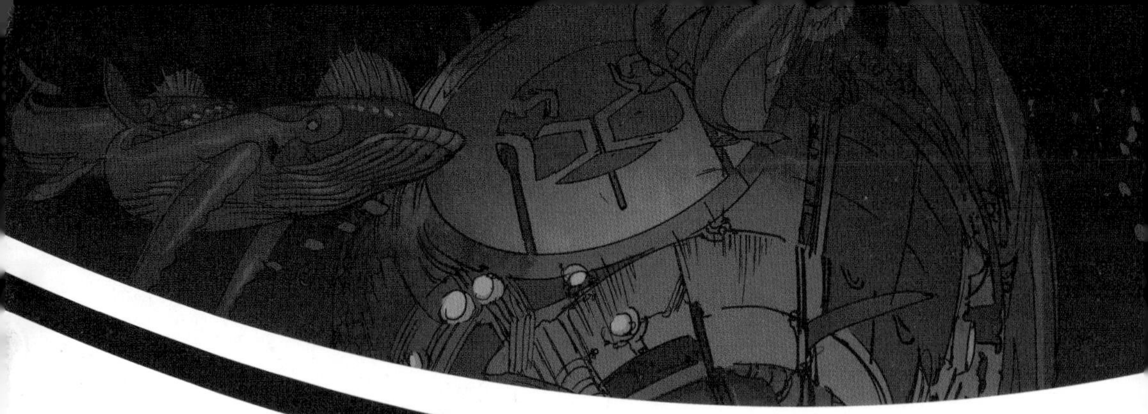

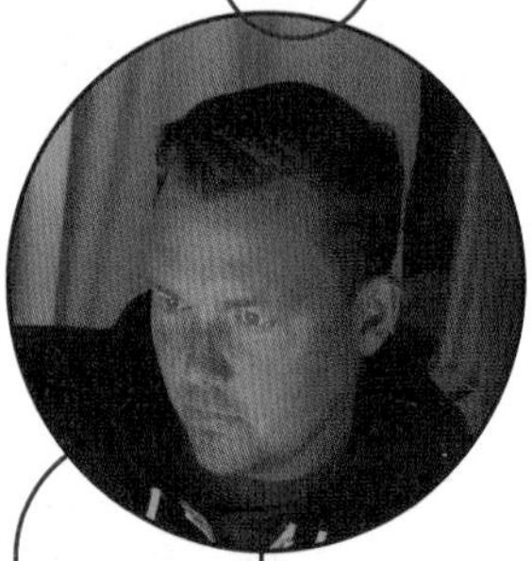

RICK REMENDER is the writer/co-creator of comics such as DEADLY CLASS, FEAR AGENT, SEVEN TO ETERNITY, and BLACK SCIENCE. During his years at Marvel, he wrote *Captain America*, *Uncanny X-Force*, and *Venom* and created The *Uncanny Avengers*. Outside of comics, he served as lead writer on EA's *Bulletstorm* game and the hit game *Dead Space*. Prior to this, he ran a satellite of Wild Brain animation, worked on films such as *The Iron Giant* and *Anastasia*, and taught sequential art and animation at San Francisco's Academy of Art University.

He currently curates his own publishing imprint, Giant Generator, at Image Comics and previously served as lead writer/co-showrunner on SyFy's adaptation of his co-creation DEADLY CLASS.

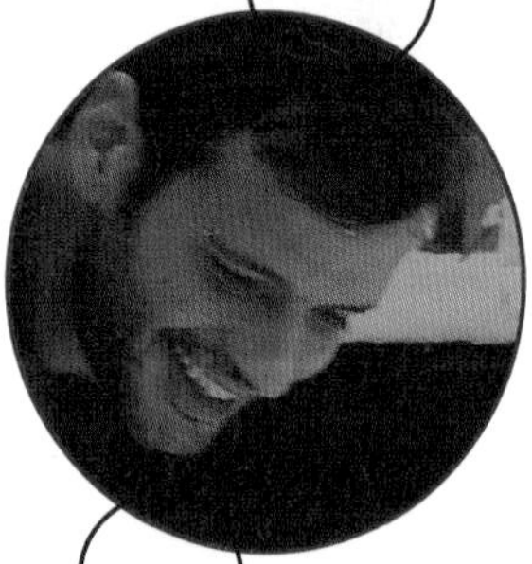

GREG TOCCHINI was born in 1979, in São Paulo, Brazil.

Since 2002 his work has been published internationally by companies such as Marvel and DC Comics (USA) and Le Lombard (France). Some titles include, *The Odyssey*, *Wolverine: Father*, *Fantastic Four*, *Thor: Son of Asgard*, *Captain America*, *Spider-Man*, *1602: A New World*, *ION*, *Batman and Robin*, *Uncanny X-Force*, *Infinity Section*, and many others.

He was the artist on the mini-series THE LAST DAYS OF AMERICAN CRIME written by Rick Remender, with whom he co-created the science fiction series LOW. His independent label Dead Hamster Comics published his graphic novel *Sequence Shot* as well as works by various Brazilian artists.

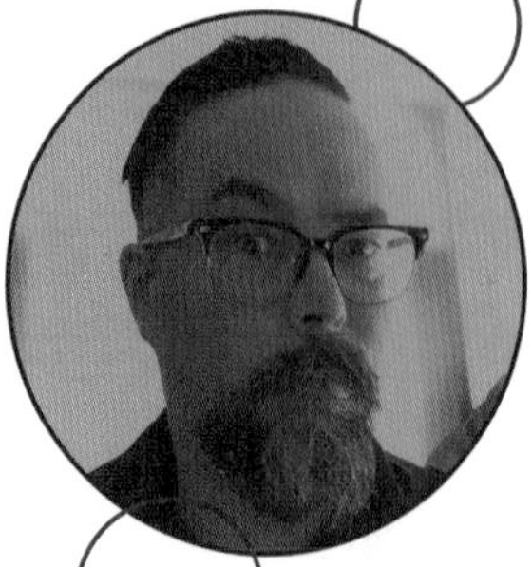

DAVE MCCAIG is an Inkpot and Emmy award-winning colorist for comics and animation. He's known for coloring *Superman: Birthright*, *Nextwave*, *American Vampire*, *Northlanders*, and his work as lead color on *The Batman* animated series. He lives in New York with his two humans and two cats.